THE
INSIDERS

ALSO BY CRAIG HICKMAN

THE INSIDERS

By
New York Times Bestselling Author
CRAIG HICKMAN

Printed by CreateSpace

This book is a work of fiction. Though some names, characters, incidents, and dialogues are based on historical record, the work as a whole is a product of the author's imagination.

Copyright © 2012 by Craig Hickman

Cover art "The Beholder" by April Varner, used by permission.
Author Photo by Steven Seelig, e2Photography, LLC

ISBN :1-4392-1604-5

ISBN-9781439216040

Printed in the United States of America

THE INSIDERS

"This is a government of the people, by the people, and for the people no longer. It is a government of corporations, by corporations, and for corporations."
PRESIDENT RUTHERFORD B. HAYES, 1888

"Behind the ostensible government sits enthroned an invisible government owing no allegiance and acknowledging no responsibility to the people. To destroy this invisible government, to dissolve the unholy alliance between corrupt business and corrupt politics, is the first task of the statesmanship of the day."
PRESIDENT THEODORE ROOSEVELT, 1912

"The real truth of the matter is, as you and I know, that a financial element in the larger centers has owned the government of the U.S. ever since the days of Andrew Jackson."
PRESIDENT FRANKLIN D. ROOSEVELT, 1933

"From time to time we've been tempted to believe that society has become too complex to be managed by self-rule, that government by an elite group is superior to government for, by, and of the people. Well, if no one among us is capable of governing himself, then who among us has the capacity to govern someone else? ... We as Americans have the capacity now, as we've had in the past, to do whatever needs to be done to preserve this last and greatest bastion of freedom."
PRESIDENT RONALD REAGAN, 1981

"Some even believe we are part of a secret cabal working against the best interests of the United States, characterizing my family and me as 'internationalists' and of conspiring with others around the world to build a more integrated global political and economic structure—one world, if you will. If that's the charge, I stand guilty, and I am proud of it."
DAVID ROCKEFELLER, 2002
(Grandson of John D. Rockefeller and Senator Nelson W. Aldrich)

"Let's never forget: Millions of Americans who work hard and play by the rules deserve a government and financial system that do the same. It's time to apply the same rules from top to bottom. No bailouts, no handouts, and no copouts. An America built to last insists on responsibility from everybody."

PRESIDENT BARACK OBAMA, 2012

PROLOGUE

THE NEW YORK TIMES

Wall Street Billionaire Charged with Murder

By CATHERINE ROGERS and GRAHAM NGUYEN

Monday, February 21

SUN VALLEY, ID – Charles Fielder, the billionaire whose consulting firm Fielder & Company is credited with launching more IPOs on Wall Street than any other firm, was found shot in the head in his private ski chalet at a family-owned resort in Sun Valley, ID, on Sunday afternoon. His unconscious body was found lying alongside two unidentified women with fatal gunshot wounds.

The deaths of the two women were confirmed by the Sun Valley Police Department, which said the women were in their late twenties; both had been shot in the head at point-blank range. Mr. Fielder was taken to St. Luke's Wood River Medical Center in Ketchum, ID, where he is still in a coma. Police received an emergency call at 2:18 p.m., Sunday afternoon, from White Horse Resort management, informing them of the gruesome discovery. According to the Sun Valley PD, Mr. Fielder has been charged with murder in what is described as a double murder-suicide attempt.

Daniel Redd, a lawyer for the Fielder family, said that Mr. Fielder was meeting with clients and associates at the White Horse Resort in a company retreat over President's Day weekend. "This is a terrible tragedy, and the family expects Charles to be fully exonerated," Mr. Redd said. "The family will be making no further statement at this time."

Assistant SVPD Chief John Zemke, who is in charge of the case, said that the investigation into the shootings and deaths would remain open for the foreseeable future, a routine course of action in cases where victims remain unidentified. "The Fielder chalet at White Horse has been secured and detectives are currently on the scene," Zemke reported on Sunday evening.

Mr. Fielder is founder and chairman of Fielder & Company, a respected management consulting firm with revenues over $1 billion and just under 1000 employees operating from offices in Boston, Chicago, Dallas, San Francisco, London, and Hong Kong. The company has over 500 active clients worldwide; the company's fees per consulting engagement range from $1 to $10 million. Only McKinsey & Company exceeds Fielder & Company's portfolio of management consulting services targeted toward senior executives of large multinational corporations.

A native of Boston, Mr. Fielder sold his family's business in agriculture and chemicals in 1985 to launch Fielder & Company, following in the footsteps of his father and grandfather, both prominent Boston business innovators who built thriving corporations. Forbes estimates Mr. Fielder's fortune at $10 billion, putting him in the top 100 of the world's richest people.

Like many wealthy families, the Fielders are well known for their business success and philanthropy but tirelessly strive to avoid the limelight. According to friends and clients, Mr. Fielder took great pride in *The Wall Street Journal's* designation of Fielder & Company as "the most secretive consulting firm in America." Mr. Fielder's wife Mary and children Wilson and Rachel were unavailable for comment on Sunday evening.

1

Wilson – Sun Valley, ID

Wilson Fielder powered the SUV through drifting snow to Sun Valley's city hall and police station, determined to confront the officer who'd charged his father with murder. An hour earlier, he had arrived at the airport and headed straight to the hospital, where his father was lying in a coma. After consulting with the neurosurgeon and attempting to comfort his mother and sister, Wilson had called the Sun Valley police, insisting on a meeting with whoever was in charge of his father's case.

Once inside the police station Wilson gave his name to a young female constable stationed behind the reception window. His tall athletic body, deep hazel-green eyes, and thick dark hair were the cause of girlish giggles and whispered comments between the young constable and two other women working behind the counter as he took a seat in the waiting area. He was oblivious.

Within moments, Assistant Police Chief John Zemke leaned over the counter. "Fielder?" he said in a loud, brusque voice.

Wilson's body tensed as he stood up and walked toward the stocky, sunburned detective.

"Come on in," Zemke said, brushing back his thick, wiry gray-white hair. The fifty-something former LAPD homicide captain, turned Sun Valley detective and ski fanatic, wore elk-skin boots, navy-blue ski pants, and a red sweater. Zemke relished what he did for a living, but valued where he did it even more.

Wilson followed Zemke through the western-style swinging doors into an empty office at the rear of the building. He sat down in front of the detective's desk, attempting to control his emotions.

"As far as we're concerned, this case is murder and attempted suicide. We found powder burns on your father's right hand. His fingerprints were on the murder weapon. A dozen witnesses put him and the two women together during the evening. What else do you want to know?"

"Who were the two women?"

"Probably high-end hookers. We get a lot of them this time of year. They look like sisters: same blood type, same physical features, same expensive jewelry. We don't know their names yet. They were carrying phony IDs. But we'll know soon enough."

Wilson decided to ignore the "hookers" comment for the moment. Zemke might be a jaded macho throwback, but he was nobody's fool. Wilson could see that from his eyes. "What kind of gun was it?"

Zemke leaned back in his chair, staring at the ceiling. He didn't care much for Wilson's father, or any of the other wealthy landowners in the area who acted as if Sun Valley was their private playground. "Smith & Wesson Sportsman .22 LR caliber automatic, stainless steel, ten cartridge clip, six-inch barrel, thirty-nine ounces, designed for concealment. Five bullets were discharged. Each woman was shot in the back of the head while sitting in matching chairs in your father's chalet. Both were fully clothed. Blood-soaked. They died instantly. No evidence of a struggle except for a few broken fingernails. These women obviously knew they were going to die. But they didn't have time or were too scared to do anything but grab the arms of their chairs."

"And my father?"

"We found his body lying on the floor next to where the women were executed. Blood from at least one of the women was on his hands and face. Bullet entered his head just below the right ear. Gun was lying next to his right hand. That's about it," Zemke said, anxious to end the interchange.

"What about the other bullets?"

"Embedded in the ceiling beams. Either threatening or torturing shots," he said while turning his attention to a file he'd picked up from his desk.

Wilson didn't say anything. There was a momentary twinge of uncertainty about his father's innocence, but he refused to believe that his father killed anyone. He knew his father. Of course he could never know all the details or secrets of his father's life, but he was well acquainted with his father's character—and it had nothing to do with corruption. His father's life had been devoted to enlightenment and liberation, for himself, his family, his clients, and anyone else he could influence. Wilson had questioned and tested his father's soul for long enough to know.

Zemke looked up from the file, "Unless there's something else, son, I've got work to do."

"A few things you should know, detective," Wilson said with measured delivery as he stood up. "My father abhorred guns and he never used his right hand for anything requiring mechanical precision or applied pressure because of an old injury. He would never have used his right hand to pull the trigger of a gun. As to your explanation of the bullets in the ceiling beams—threatening or torturing shots is how you put it. Strikes me as predisposed, which brings me to my last point." Wilson paused, his emotions rising. "The comment you made about the two women being hookers not only represents gross speculation on your part, but piss-poor police work. Seems the only whore here is you, detective. My father didn't kill anyone."

At first, Zemke was stunned, his eyes blazing, but he held his tongue. He slowly surveyed Wilson with biting anger, then genuine curiosity. He hadn't expected such a tongue-lashing from Charles Fielder's privileged son. The open file on his desk was no longer a distraction.

"I understand your point of view, Mr. Fielder," he said in a calm, almost respectful voice. "We haven't established a motive yet. Until we do, this case will remain open."

"Thank you," Wilson said, feeling slightly better for having vented at least some of his anger. He needed Zemke, and anyone else who might get involved, including reporters, to seriously investigate the possibility that someone other than his father had murdered those women. Otherwise, I'll be doing this on my own, he thought.

"Has your father shown any signs of regaining consciousness?"

"Not yet."

"I'm sorry. Let us know if his condition changes."

"Sure," Wilson said, knowing that Zemke had his own channels of information. At least he's expressing some level of concern, Wilson thought. "One more thing detective, I want access to the family chalet."

"Can't do that. It's a crime scene," Zemke said, his hard-bitten demeanor returning.

Wilson wheeled around. In a deceptively mild tone he asked, "You know what my father's done for this community. Who would you like me to call?"

Zemke's eyes were suddenly on fire again, but he knew Wilson would eventually get what he wanted. Besides, everything had been gone over multiple times. "Fine," he conceded, "but we'll be watching."

Wilson left the detective's office and returned to the hospital and his father's ICU room, where he joined his mother and sister. They looked so much alike—the expressive eyes, elegant noses, and slender frames—it was not uncommon for them to be mistaken for sisters. Seeing the pain on their twin faces made his father's comatose state even more agonizing. *They seem so helpless... we all are... but not for long if I can help it,* Wilson said to himself. He told his mother and sister about his meeting with Detective Zemke. They both seemed relieved that Wilson was taking care of such matters but expressed new concerns about keeping his father in Sun Valley. Wilson had already come to the same conclusion. His father needed better care than the Wood River Medical Center staff could provide.

When the neurosurgeon who'd operated on his father returned to the room, Wilson asked him to step into the corridor for a private word. "I want my father prepared for an immediate airlift to Massachusetts General in Boston."

"The risks of transferring him in his current condition are very high, unless you have medical personnel…"

"That's why I'd like you to go with him. I'll make sure you have a flying ICU by this evening."

"I can't just…"

"You'll have the opportunity to personally turn him over to a group of highly respected neurologists and neurosurgeons at Mass General. I think you know Dr. Joseph Malek. One of your mentors, I believe. He's also a personal friend of my father's. He will be looking forward to reconnecting with you when you arrive. I don't think I need to tell you that every step of how you handle this is going to be scrutinized by the press."

"You're right, I have worked with Dr. Joseph Malek," the neurosurgeon rejoined, his voice rising. "And we both know he would never condone such coercion."

"He would if he thought one of his dearest friends was in harm's way and being framed for murder," Wilson said sternly.

"I can't promise anything until I have arranged for my other patients. What are you going to do about the police?"

"I'll handle them; just get my father ready to fly. I want to leave tonight."

After the neurosurgeon left to make his preparations, Wilson remained in the corridor pacing back and forth while talking on his phone and sending emails to arrange for his father's flight to Boston.

Forty-five minutes later, his father's attorney, Daniel Redd, called to announce that he'd just arrived in Sun Valley. The timing couldn't have been better for what Wilson needed next.

"There's been a change of plans. We're moving my father to Mass General tonight," Wilson said over the phone.

Daniel immediately concurred with the decision, just as Wilson expected he would. He'd known Daniel for several years but had never really dealt with him one-on-one. What Daniel said next both surprised and pleased Wilson: "I'll take care of the legalities," Daniel said. "The Sun Valley Police won't want your father to leave their jurisdiction, but we won't give them a choice. Just make sure his doctor supports your decision and is willing to make the trip with your father."

"Already arranged. Do you anticipate anything we can't overcome?"

"Not if we can demonstrate medical need. I'm licensed to practice law in Idaho and my firm knows a few judges in town. If we run into serious problems, we'll have the FBI claim jurisdiction; they owe us a few favors. But that's a last resort. Don't worry, Wilson. One way or another, I'll make sure your father can leave Idaho. Need any help arranging for a medical airlift?"

"Air Ambulance is a client. The CEO promised me that he'd have one of their jets at the Sun Valley airport by eight tonight," Wilson said.

"I'll have all the legal issues relating to medical transport resolved by five o'clock. Can we find somewhere to meet privately after that? There are a few things I need to discuss with you face-to-face."

Wilson hesitated a moment, wondering why Daniel needed private face time before leaving Sun Valley. Then he dismissed it as nothing more than overly cautious, anal-retentive behavior from a first-rate attorney in difficult circumstances. "I want to spend some time at the chalet before we leave. Why don't we meet there?"

"See you there," Daniel said.

2

Tate – New York City, NY

Wayland Tate simmered with boredom as he listened to his client ramble on about a recent *Business Week* article that had criticized his company's management practices. Clients who'd become overly dependent upon him were the only aspect Tate despised about his chosen place in the world. His pale blue eyes roamed restlessly across the wall of plasma screens at the back of his office, where the news channels showed clips of Charles Fielder every half hour. The pictures make Charles look older than he is, he thought.

Tate stood up, walked to the closet behind his desk, and retrieved a bottle of moisturizing lotion from the top shelf. "I know what you mean, Jim," he said absentmindedly, reassuring his client that he was still listening even though his thoughts were focused on more pressing matters: if Charles regains consciousness, we'll have to extract him from the hospital immediately. But there was nothing to worry about; preparations had already been made. He removed his gold cuff links and carefully rolled up the starched sleeves of his monogrammed shirt. While interjecting an occasional "uh-huh" into his client's soporific litany of woes, Tate rubbed the lotion into his tanned arms and elbows in slow rhythmic motions.

Caring for his physical appearance and personal magnetism had always been a priority for Wayland Tate, making him one of corporate America's more interviewed and photographed executives. GQ magazine had recently included him in its *100 Most Influential People in the World* issue, touting "his gorgeous, gray head of hair ... an intensity behind the eyes that makes you wonder what he's going to do next," and the fact that he was "sporting a six-pack at age fifty-six." But those closest to Tate knew that his high visibility had more to do with shrewd publicity management than with good looks or charisma. Almost half of the firms on *Fortune's* 500 were either current or former clients of Tate Waterhouse, one of the fastest-growing international advertising agencies in the world, and he made sure everyone knew about it. The only criticism his new European and

Asian investors had expressed pertained to his prominent presence in the media. Fortunately, their criticism came at a time when Tate no longer craved attention like he had in his younger days. Promising to tone things down was a fair *quid pro quo* for access to their limitless resources.

Tate's boredom was beginning to burn calories when one of his administrative assistants interrupted with an urgent message that David Quinn, CEO of the J. B. Musselman Company, was on the phone—for the fourth time that day. Excusing himself from his client, Tate disappeared into a narrow corridor that ran along a wall of windows overlooking the East River and the South Street Seaport near Wall Street. He unlocked the door to his private quarters and took his time walking through the luxurious space, which looked more like an exclusive bar than an apartment. Picasso, Pollock, and Kandinsky originals filled the walls. The two de Koonings, one above each fireplace, were Tate's favorites.

He climbed the spiral staircase that led to his silk-walled bedroom and marble bathroom. Pausing in front of the bathroom's gilded mirror between two freestanding water basins, he rolled down his sleeves, and replaced the cuff links. Then he reached for a small tube of eye ointment, squeezing out a miniscule amount and applying it under his eyes and along his eyebrows with his left index finger. Although the anti-wrinkle ointment cost seven hundred dollars an ounce, it was worth every penny—he could easily pass for a man ten to fifteen years his junior.

After sitting down in the bedroom's black leather lounge chair and placing his feet on the matching ottoman, Tate was ready to turn his attention to David Quinn. J. B. Musselman was a twenty-five billion dollar wholesale distribution conglomerate headquartered in Chicago and Tate sat on its board. He picked up the phone.

"David. Sorry I missed your earlier calls."

"I need your help to get Kresge & Company off my back, permanently," Quinn said, noticeably irritated.

"Weren't they your idea in the first place?" Tate's response was glib, deliberately provocative.

"You know the board forced me into this. It was their idea from the beginning. I simply recommended which firm, but that was before the bastards started analyzing ways to break up the company. I need your help to get rid of them before they convince the board."

"I hate to say I told you so, David, but Fielder & Company would have been a smarter choice than Kresge & Company. You would have had more control," Tate kept the smile that played across his features out of his voice.

"It's Fielder's kid who wants to breakup the company into regional businesses to exploit what he calls 'the growing niche-oriented needs of local customers' and give employees more opportunity for ownership," Quinn was seething with anger and defensiveness. "He told MacMillan I was the single biggest obstacle to Musselman's future growth and profitability."

"Well, I don't think you have to worry about Wilson Fielder for a while. He's got his hands full with other things right now."

"Don't get me wrong. I would never wish what happened with his father on anyone, but I'm glad to get that arrogant little prick out of my life. Now, I want him and his firm to stay out."

Tate remained silent and smiling.

"You went to school with his father didn't you?" Quinn asked.

"I did. We were close friends," Tate said, remembering the poetry readings at the SoHo bar where he first met Charles Fielder. He could still hear the message of Charles' revolutionary verse: *generations of concealed corruption enslave us in a system of coerced consent.* He would miss his old friend.

"Do you believe he killed those women?"

"I don't want to believe it, David," Tate said. "But people change."

After a pause, Quinn returned to his original agenda. "How do we make Kresge & Company go away for good?"

"My guess is that Wilson will take a leave of absence, which should slow things down long enough for us to launch the new advertising campaign. Musselman will reposition itself as 'The Next Generation in Mass Merchandising.' Kresge & Company becomes old news. I'm already working with Boggs & Saggett on a presentation for MacMillan and the rest of the board."

"You know I'm not ready to leave this place."

"Stop worrying, David. No one is going to remove you from the helm. The advertising campaign alone will send Musselman stock soaring. The board will think they're in heaven. Trust me."

It had taken Tate three years to get to this point with David Quinn. He'd spent the first year landing the J. B. Musselman account. The next two years were devoted to getting appointed to the company's board of directors, which meant letting go of the advertising relationship, at least on the surface of public disclosure. Four months ago, after a heated board meeting that had resulted in the hiring of Kresge & Company to assist in reorganizing Musselman's operations, Tate asked Quinn for a private meeting. During dinner at Everest, one of Chicago's more private and exclusive restaurants, Tate presented a plan for turning J. B. Musselman into the most visible discount merchandiser in North America, branding his vision as *America's Warehouse*.

Quinn eventually bought the idea, mostly because it gave him another way out of his current difficulties, which was precisely what Tate had anticipated. As Kresge & Company began its analysis of Musselman's operations, Quinn engaged

Boggs & Saggett, an advertising firm with hidden ties to Tate Waterhouse, to develop a marketing campaign for America's Warehouse. Initially, Quinn had hoped the two efforts would prove to be synergistic. But when Kresge & Company expressed doubts about a mass discounting strategy and began pushing for the breakup of Musselman, Quinn decided to bet the company's future on Tate's America's Warehouse strategy.

"There's another thing I want to talk about," Quinn was saying. "I've decided not to use Morgan on our next stock offering. You recommended someone at KaneWeller at our last board meeting."

"Jules Kamin."

"Right. Do you have his contact information?"

"Sure," Tate said, grinning broadly. "What are you doing for the next few days?"

"Warehouse visits in North and South Carolina, Georgia, and then Florida."

"Can someone else handle them?"

"Depends on what you have in mind."

"St. Moritz," Tate said, as he reflected on how much easier it was to manipulate people when they were separated from their familiar surroundings and placed in the lap of luxury with limitless opportunities for pampering, pleasure, and moneymaking. But further manipulation of David Quinn would not be easy, even in St. Moritz, Tate mulled. Quinn was a no-nonsense individualist, a man of principle and integrity who prided himself on being able to come up with a quick solution to any problem 99 percent of the time. It was an acquired malady among CEOs. The trick, as always, would be to discover what Quinn wanted badly enough in order to abandon his usual high road. Getting rid of Kresge & Company would be a good start.

"One of those client retreats you're always raving about?" Quinn asked.

"Jules Kamin will be there."

There was silence on the line as Quinn considered Tate's invitation. He needed Tate's help and he wanted to meet Jules Kamin. A few days in St. Moritz would also give him some long-overdue downtime. "Let me see what I can do," Quinn finally said.

"One of our chartered jets will be leaving Chicago O'Hare at eight tomorrow night."

"I'll let you know if I can't make it," Quinn said. "Otherwise, plan on me."

"See you in St. Moritz. We'll have lunch when you arrive," Tate said.

After hanging up, Tate called his vice president of client relations. She was a beautiful Japanese- American woman blessed with cherubic grace, but it was her flair for orchestrating events and arranging entertainment to the sheer delight of Tate's clients that made her invaluable. "One of the planes needs to pick up Mr. Quinn at O'Hare tomorrow night. Aren't we picking up someone else in Chicago?"

"Yes. Mr. Toffler and Mr. Anderson," she said with characteristic acuity.

"Good. Make sure Quinn receives the full treatment. I don't want to lose him. Let's assign Vargas."

"We'll take care of everything."

"What would I do without you?" Tate said, not expecting a response. "Has there been any change in Charles' condition?" Tate asked.

"No change," she responded. "We now have someone on site monitoring everything."

"Perfect," Tate said before hanging up the phone. Walking back to resume his conversation with the client still waiting in his office, he paused briefly to muse on the colorful chaos of Kandinsky's *Composition VII*, an apocalyptic hurricane of swirling masses and colors. It had been Charles Fielder who taught Tate how to use the world's colorful chaos to exploit his love of manipulation. The rewards had proved to be beyond his wildest imagination. Control, or be controlled, Tate summed up his mantra. Charles taught me well.

3

Wilson – Sun Valley, ID

After passing strict scrutiny from two uniformed police officers and ducking under the yellow crime scene tape, Wilson defiantly trod through the snow to the covered entryway of his family's chalet. Throughout his childhood, Wilson's family had spent half of every summer and three weeks during the ski season at the twenty-room residence. It was one of thirty-two luxury chalets at the White Horse Resort, a complex that also comprised fifty condominiums, a world-class spa, two outdoor swimming pools, three restaurants, and a large conference and entertainment center. Before crossing the threshold to face what lay inside, he took a moment to reminisce about his great-grandfather Harry Wilson Fielder, the resort's founder. It was his great-grandfather who, in the 1930s, had catapulted the Fielder family into the ranks of the super-rich. Construction of the White Horse Resort at the base of Baldy Mountain had begun in 1946 and the Fielder family had been a vital contributor to the cities of Sun Valley and Ketchum ever since.

Wilson opened the front door and entered the large foyer with its huge stone fireplace. His body tensed at the smell of death that lingered in the air. Still struggling with the reality of what had happened here, he walked slowly through the foyer and into the breakfast nook between the kitchen and the family room. White tape marked the floor and the wing chairs, where the bodies had been found. There were bloodstains on the chairs, the Persian rug, and the hardwood floor. Seeing the outline of where his father had been found, he was overwhelmed by memories of the long conversations they'd had here at White Horse—conversations that had shaped his life.

From the time he was a small child, he had experienced profound feelings of guilt for having more than others—very much his father's son on this score. It wasn't that Wilson didn't take great pleasure in the opportunities and advantages his family's wealth provided. Still he despised the clichéd, yet overwhelming, sense of injustice and inequity that came with these privileges. Ridding himself of the nagging contradiction would, he bluntly acknowledged, require more than philanthropy and patronage.

The sound of Daniel coming through the front door brought Wilson back to the present and what had happened in the chalet less than thirty-six hours earlier. Daniel walked into the large family room where Wilson was standing. Physically striking in a manly sort of way, though not particularly attractive, the lawyer's deep-set eyes gave nothing away. Wilson knew only a few things about Daniel: he favored formality, was ten years younger than his father, had a reputation for thoroughness, and acted serious about everything, especially his clients. But if he'd been able to accomplish what he promised, Wilson thought, it would go a long way toward solidifying their relationship. No words were spoken until Daniel was standing next to Wilson and both of them were looking down at the white-taped floor. "What happened here, Daniel?"

Daniel looked directly at Wilson, shaking his head. "I wish I knew, Wilson. How is he?"

"His vital signs have improved, but there are still no signs of consciousness," Wilson said, before asking the obvious. "Are we free to fly?"

"Yes. Whatever you said to the neurosurgeon made him very responsive. The judge signed the medical travel release thirty minutes ago. We didn't have to involve the FBI. But Detective Zemke's not happy. What did you say to him when you met?"

Wilson went over the details of his meeting with Zemke, but Daniel seemed distracted, as if anxious about something Wilson had said. "What is it?" Wilson asked.

"It would be best if the Sun Valley police put their investigation on the back burner. There are better ways to find out what happened here. Your father's estate doesn't need unnecessary scrutiny if it can be avoided, especially with the impending KaneWeller merger."

"What do you mean?" Wilson's eyes had narrowed to slits.

"That's one of reasons we needed to meet. Your father took great precautions to keep the merger talks out of the press, but I thought maybe you knew."

Wilson shook his head but remained silent.

"He struck a final deal to merge Fielder & Company with KaneWeller last week. KaneWeller wants to close by the end of this week. There are papers you'll need to sign."

"Why do I need to sign? It should be my mother's decision."

"There was a change in your father's will, specifying that you become Chairman of the Board of Fielder & Company and assume full control of his shares, in the event of his death or incapacitation."

Wilson closed his eyes, suddenly feeling more burdened. "When did all of this happen?" he asked, beginning to pace.

"A few weeks ago. You and your sister each own fifty percent of his eighty-two percent ownership of Fielder &

Company; however, Rachel's shares are non-voting shares. Your father wanted to respect your sister's disinterest in the company. The remaining eighteen percent is owned by a handful of investors, mostly Fielder & Company executives. He also gave you control of the rest of his investments. Your mother was removed from all rights to ownership. Of course, the will provides for a generous monthly stipend for as long as she lives."

"Does my mother know about all of this?"

"Yes," Daniel said as he set his briefcase on the breakfast table and retrieved an envelope. He handed it to Wilson. "Your father's instructions were very precise. He wanted you to read this if anything happened to him."

Without responding, Wilson looked at the large tan envelope in his hands. Feeling exposed, he muttered, "Give me a few minutes," and walked toward the den off the foyer. Opening the metal clasp on the unsealed envelope and pulling out the hand-written letter, he stepped inside the den, closed the double doors behind him and sat down in his father's favorite overstuffed chair near the fireplace.

Dear Wilson,

If you're reading this without me, it means you're in serious danger. There are people who may try to kill you, especially if they think you know about the full extent of my activities at Fielder & Company. Trust me when I tell you that you're safer not knowing the details. You must convince the people who will be watching that you're not involved and have no desire to be involved. Complete the merger with KaneWeller and then liquidate all my other business assets as quickly as possible. Daniel Redd will help you. If you need additional help, go to Carter Emerson. Trust no one else.

The only explanation I dare give you is that several years ago I embarked upon a path that I believed would make the world a better place. Remember our conversations about humanizing capitalism? Now I'm not so sure that what I did was right. Only time will tell. Sadly, my mistakes have now become your burden and enemy. I know this seems cryptic and enigmatic, but giving you more information will only make you a bigger threat to the people responsible for my demise. That's why you must distance yourself from my business interests as soon as possible. I removed your mother and sister from participation in the business to protect them, but that makes you even more vulnerable.

Eventually, you'll put the pieces of the puzzle together. When you do, I hope you'll understand why I did it and why I didn't tell you everything beforehand. You've been placed in control of the estate because I trust you'll know what to do with its resources, especially if things become more difficult and dangerous than I have anticipated.

Trust your intuition and judgment. You're better than I
ever dreamed of being. Forgive me, if you can.
    All my love,
    Dad

Wilson read and reread the letter, his disbelief and anguish growing more acute with each pass. At one point he found himself speaking his father's words out loud in an effort to understand. Preparing to leave the den and confront Daniel, he rubbed his face to gather his wits. Only then did he notice the tears.

"Did you know what was in this envelope?" Wilson questioned as he strode into family room.

Daniel was listening to voice messages on his BlackBerry. "Yes. Your father's instructions were for me to review the contents of the envelope before giving it to you."

"Would you like to tell me what it means," Wilson said, his head still churning with his own interpretations, replaying conversations from years earlier. His father had told him that Fielder & Company was considering a radical approach to humanizing capitalism, but that he would need a decade or so to see if it actually worked. But that's as far as his father went, even when Wilson had probed for more details.

After a few moments of watching Wilson stare past him toward the chalet's arched windows, Daniel responded. "Are you aware that your father's estate is worth over seventy billion dollars—after taxes?"

"What?" Wilson blurted out. The number astonished him. He knew his father was very wealthy, but he had no idea his financial worth had reached such levels.

His mind raced back to his youth. By the time Wilson graduated from Milton Academy at seventeen, he'd already traveled around the world a dozen times. Then he spent four years at Princeton and two years at Harvard, graduating from both universities with highest honors. All of it should have made him hopelessly full of himself. But surprisingly, his abiding empathy for those who were less advantaged gave him an unusual charm and a curious sort of wise innocence, just like his father. But how, he worried, had my father accumulated this much wealth?

"It's easier to hide wealth than you might think," Daniel said. "Your great-grandfather started by hiding millions during the Great Depression. He was convinced that J. P. Morgan and a group of international bankers had orchestrated the stock market crash of '29 and then severely constricted the money supply in order to buy up depressed assets at a fraction of their value. The result was a massive transfer of wealth to Europe and the megarich, along with the humbling of America. All agendas served the world's money interests. Your father decided to continue his grandfather's wealth concealment practices. The family's seventy billion dollars is distributed across a wide range of stock positions, investment partnerships, and offshore accounts—a result of brilliant money handling for many years. KaneWeller has offered five billion dollars for Fielder & Company. They called me yesterday as soon as they heard the news about your father, wanting to make sure the deal was still on. As I mentioned, they want to close by the end of the week."

Still feeling off-kilter, Wilson gawked at Daniel and then at the white tape on the floor. He motioned for Daniel to follow him to the den. He felt more comfortable there. They both sat down next to the fireplace, Wilson in his father's chair and Daniel on an adjacent sofa.

"What's motivating KaneWeller?"

"Fielder & Company is better at preparing clients for Initial Public Offerings than anyone in the industry. Even in bad markets, the firm stays fully booked with spin-outs, roll-ups, PIPEs …"

Wilson cut him off.

"What I don't understand is what makes Fielder & Company's approach to IPOs, spin-outs, roll-ups or PIPEs worth five billion dollars."

Daniel looked around the den hesitantly, as if seeking Charles' approval to proceed.

"What few people appreciate or understand about Fielder & Company is its ability to structure public offerings so that CEOs maximize their own personal wealth," Daniel said, pausing. "Everything on Wall Street is plagiarized, almost immediately—so Fielder & Company is relentless at keeping secrets and devising new strategies for restructuring businesses without raising red flags with shareholders or the SEC."

"And how do you manage that?"

"Don't misunderstand me, Wilson. Maximizing shareholder wealth has always been a priority at Fielder & Company. We simply accomplish it while maximizing the wealth of the chief executive and select senior executives. It's my job to make sure that everything Fielder & Company does is legally defensible, ethically acceptable, and fiduciarily accountable to shareholders. Fortunately or unfortunately, depending on your point of view, what they say about the rich is true. As long as they stay out of court, their moneymaking activities remain incomprehensible, beyond scrutiny and criticism. Keeping Fielder & Company's clients out of the courtroom, especially their CEOs and CFOs, is what my firm does to earn its fees."

Wilson sat back to contemplate what Daniel had said. When it came to matters of economic logic and business strategy, Wilson was uncommonly astute. But his real reason for becoming a management consultant had been to take on the pompous tyrants who resided at the top of most corporate hierarchies. It was his moxie for standing up to corporate bullies that explained his early business success and charismatic appeal. A mere three years out of Harvard Business School, Wilson had already been identified as a rising star at Kresge & Company. He was a natural at challenging and redressing business leaders who'd become overly dogmatic, in fact he did it better than seasoned partners twice his age. What Daniel said hadn't really surprised him. Some CEOs were magnanimous and empowering, but most were avaricious and domineering.

"Is my father's estate at risk?" he asked.

"Not currently," Daniel said. "However, if an investigation into your father's death uncovers the full scope of his financial dealings, it could tie up assets for a long time. Maybe permanently, if you know what I mean." He shot Wilson a look of caution.

"What *aren't* you telling me?"

"Your father charged me with protecting his estate. It's my first and foremost obligation to him, to you, and to your family. And I will do everything in my power to execute his will. Doing it his way will give you unlimited financial resources," Daniel said, pausing. "When you finally uncover the full story of what happened here, you can do something about it."

Wilson quickly saw the wisdom in Daniel's words, but that didn't keep him from feeling manipulated.

"You told me his methods were legally defensible. Why are you so concerned about an investigation into his business activities?"

"The law is only an interpretation of circumstances, associations, and motives. There are always clients ready to abuse what they learn from Fielder & Company. If such abuses are identified and investigated, they could point to your father as the source. Guilt by association and circumstance. The only motive imputed to him would be greed. We might eventually beat it in the courts, but it could take years, tying up the family estate and crippling Fielder & Company."

Wilson looked suspiciously at Daniel Redd.

"What sort of abuses?"

"Remember Richard Beckstrom?" Daniel asked as he leaned forward again.

"The IPO guru who died in prison?"

Daniel nodded. "He was a client who started inflating earnings before taking companies public to jack up the opening stock price. It took the SEC a few years to nail him, but they finally did."

"Why wasn't Fielder & Company implicated?"

"Fielder & Company terminated its relationship after two years of working with Beckstrom, but he'd already learned enough to become obsessive and dangerous. That's when he began launching his now infamous string of IPOs. There are dozens of examples like Beckstrom, employing all sorts of financial devices -- LBOs, real estate investment trusts, derivatives, credit default swaps, high yield bonds, IPO mutual funds, E-trading schemes, inflated Net stocks, and the list goes on. Your father had enormous influence but avoided the limelight," Daniel said, suddenly looking more intense. "Your father is a financial genius, like his grandfather Harry and J. P. Morgan and John D. Rockefeller, only better. He manipulated capital markets with ease, even though his real desire was to eliminate the possibility of such abuses. He was determined to transform how financial markets worked, for the benefit of everyone, not just the inside elite. Unfortunately, a federal judge might not interpret his intent that way."

Wilson studied Daniel.

"Who were the others, besides Beckstrom?"

"Your father compiled detailed files on the clients he suspected were abusing his methods. I have the files with me. Charles told me to give you access, if you requested it."

"I'm requesting access."

Brow furrowed and eyes penetrating, Daniel removed a stack of files and a thumb drive from his briefcase and handed them to Wilson.

"There are fifty-two files in total. Each one represents a different client."

Wilson nodded as he opened the file on top.

"I'm going to the hospital to make sure the Sun Valley police don't try any last minute stalling tactics," Daniel said as he rose and walked to the double doors. "I'll answer your questions on the flight back to Boston."

Wilson looked up at Daniel. "Call me if there are any issues. Otherwise, I'll be there in a little while," he said before returning to the files.

4

Inflight – Air Ambulance MD-90

A few minutes past eight o'clock, the Air Ambulance MD-90 jet lifted off from the Sun Valley airport. The neurosurgeon, two nurses, and three medical technicians hovered around Charles Fielder in his in-flight ICU while Wilson, his mother, sister, Daniel Redd, and a few staff sat in the passenger cabin, where the seat configuration looked like a typical first class cabin.

Wilson and Daniel sat next to each other at the back of the cabin, an empty row separating them from the others so they could discuss the client files without being overheard. It hadn't taken Wilson long to discover that each file was

a history of seemingly legitimate management practices—
senior executive hirings and firings, company reorganizations,
high profile strategy consulting engagements, new product
introductions, competitor intelligence reports, IPOs,
divestitures, acquisitions, marketing campaigns, internal
crises, product failures, press releases, and leaked corporate
memos—all carefully designed and executed to manipulate
the company's stock price. However, the main focus of the
summary briefs was on the abuses each client had resorted to
when legitimate activities failed to produce the desired effect
on company stock prices.

In one case, a pharmaceutical company, unable to create
the desired volatility in the market, purposely tainted its own
leading cold decongestant with mild bacteria before ordering
a massive recall to send its stock price plummeting. The press
was quick to herald the action as one of taking responsibility,
while the company arranged to purchase millions of shares of
its own stock at rock bottom prices behind a veil of affiliate
companies. Within six months, the company's stock price
was soaring well above previous highs, making the CEO a
billionaire.

In another case, a major software developer fabricated
and then leaked a highly negative and false report about a
competitor's new product to stimulate its own sagging sales.
Within thirty days, sales shot upward and the stock price
doubled. Then, there was the CEO of a retailing giant who

secretly owned several Asian sweatshops. He surreptitiously manufactured merchandise for his competitors. Whenever he wanted to control a supplier or burn a competitor to enhance his own company's position and stock price, he'd blow the whistle on one of his own operations.

"Your father's methods were always legally defensible," Daniel said, his eyes fixed on Wilson. "He showed clients how to establish patterns of volatility through carefully planned and timed management actions—completely legitimate business practice. Believe me, he knew exactly how to avoid attracting undue attention from the SEC. He also stayed off the radar screens of aggressive plaintiff's lawyers eager to file shareholder lawsuits."

"If it worked so well, why were there abuses?"

"Clients like Michael Garvey, Chairman and CEO of AikoChem. You read the file. He didn't have the patience to keep the cycle going through legitimate business practices ..."

Wilson interrupted, "So he resorted to leaking insider information shortly after his brokers and trading buddies had already acted on it."

"That's the way it is with all of these clients. They pushed things a little too far. Even with Fielder & Company's thorough screening methods, your father couldn't stop them."

Before he could ask about Fielder & Company's screening methods, Wilson noticed his mother and Rachel getting up from their seats.

"I'll be right back," he said to Daniel, who was sitting in the window seat. Wilson stood up, joining his mother and Rachel as they walked through two sets of doors into the ICU cabin.

By the time Wilson returned to his seat after having checked on his father, the lights along the southern shore of Lake Ontario were becoming more visible. The MD-90 was an hour and a half out of Boston. Wilson picked up where he and Daniel had left off.

"What were my father's methods for screening out potential abusers?"

"Extensive background checks, comprehensive interviews, occasional surveillance, the usual. Except for a handful of abusers, his system worked for many years. It was only recently that more clients began crossing the line."

"Why?"

"The appetites and hubris of some clients became excessive over time. That's usually when they started crossing the line. Of course, Fielder & Company had already shown them how to skirt the system by managing market regulators, preempting lawsuits or getting cases dismissed, and a few other tricks of the securities and exchange trade," Daniel said, dryly.

"How do you manipulate market regulators or preempt lawsuits?"

"You hire the best white-collar criminal defense attorneys in the country—most of whom are former directors or branch chiefs from the Enforcement Division of the Securities and Exchange Commission. They know how to get an investigation sidetracked and killed. Preempting lawsuits can be accomplished in a number of ways, but the simplest way is to pay a plaintiff's lawyer to file early, become lead counsel, and then drop the case. Problems arise when clients begin using such measures as a rule, not an exception."

"Let's go back to Garvey," Wilson said, opening one of the files. "What was his excuse for crossing the line?"

"Expensive art, lavish estates, a four-hundred-foot yacht, and beautiful women depleted his wealth. After Fielder & Company terminated its relationship with him, he began implementing a combination of bribes, price-fixing, and a new version of stock pooling to keep a ninety-day cycle of volatility going. He was successful for more than eighteen months. Like clockwork, AikoChem's stock climbed to over twenty dollars and then slowly dropped to below ten dollars every ninety days or so. Trading volume stayed at over two million shares per day for more than a year. But rumors began to circulate that AikoChem's pattern of volatility was being illegally induced. The institutional investors and professional traders who'd been playing the cycle pulled out. AikoChem's stock plummeted to four dollars a share and trading volume dropped below 25,000 shares a day. By that time, Garvey had already cashed out and was humbly acknowledging to the business press that it was time for him to step down as CEO."

"So he got away with it?"

"That's right. Great lawyering, savvy lobbying, and lots of institutional investors capitalizing on AikoChem's cycle convinced the SEC to drop its investigation. Garvey pulled off the perfect charade. And of course, all of your father's clients were watching."

"Any one of these clients could have shot my father, just to keep him quiet," Wilson said.

"The White Horse retreat was planned for them. Your father wanted to halt all illegal practices among current and former clients. He threatened to expose anyone who would not conform. I warned him against having the retreat, but he insisted. He believed the abuses were his fault and he was determined to stop the escalation. 'Never be afraid to correct a mistake, no matter how big,' was all he said. It was a favorite quote from his grandfather," Daniel said. In an uncharacteristic show of emotion, he muttered, "I should have done more to dissuade him from holding the retreat."

Wilson leaned forward frowning at Daniel. "What do you expect to accomplish by feeding me bit by bit?"

"Your father gave me strict instructions to share this information only if you requested or needed it. That's what I'm doing, Wilson."

Wilson closed his eyes, taking a moment to evaluate what he was about to say. He wasn't exactly sure why he was choosing to trust Daniel and his firm—maybe it was his father's trust, or Daniel's adeptness in handling the Sun Valley police, or the sincerity Wilson sensed in him. Daniel's loyalty was now a life preserver in a sea of doubt. He hoped he wouldn't regret his decision.

"I want to distance myself and the family from my father's business affairs as quickly as possible, starting with signing off on the merger with KaneWeller," Wilson said.

"Good," Daniel exhaled a sigh of relief. Guiding Wilson to make the right moves was what he'd promised Charles and he always delivered on his promises. It was the least he could do for Charles Fielder—the best client he'd ever known. "I'm meeting with KaneWeller's attorneys in the morning. Can you come to a closing tomorrow afternoon?"

"Yes," Wilson said. "I want you to liquidate my father's holdings as quickly and discreetly as you can. And I want you to continue using his wealth concealment practices."

"Trust me, I will."

"I *am* trusting you, Daniel. Let me know if there are any surprises. Otherwise, I'm empowering you to get us out of his investments posthaste. I want anyone who's watching to assume that we're cashing out and moving on."

Daniel leaned over to remove his briefcase from under the seat in front of him. He took out a manila folder marked Fielder Estate. "I need you to sign these power-of-attorney documents," he said as he handed the papers to Wilson and pointed to the removable green arrows indicating where to sign.

Wilson pulled down his tray table and began signing the documents.

"Your father told me you were a rare combination of wisdom and will."

"Save your bets, Daniel."

"You should probably spend some time with Carter Emerson when we get back. He knew your father better than anyone," Daniel said.

"I've known Carter Emerson all my life, and not only as my father's closest friend. He was a mentor to me at Princeton when he taught there as a visiting professor from Harvard. He's definitely on my list," Wilson said, wistfully. When he finished signing the papers, they both switched off their reading lights and reclined their seats. As Wilson closed his eyes, he recalled how often his father and Carter Emerson had spent hours in private conversation at the family home in Cambridge.

5

Quinn – O'Hare Airport, Chicago, IL

Comfortably ensconced in the executive lounge at Chicago's O'Hare Airport, Quinn read the latest issue of *Discount News* while waiting for Wayland Tate's envoy, Andrea Vargas. She arrived a few minutes after six o'clock looking as if she'd just walked off a runway of another sort.

"Mr. Quinn?" Vargas said, approaching him gracefully on long, shapely legs.

"That's me," Quinn said, pushing himself up from his chair.

"I'm Andrea Vargas," she introduced herself, her large brown eyes glistening with charm. She extended her hand. "I'll be your personal assistant during the retreat."

Quinn shook her hand while considering the possible implications of her greeting. *In what ways has she been asked to assist me?* He chided himself for abandoning his latest attempt to lose thirty pounds, his usual response when faced with beautiful people.

"Someone will be here to get your luggage in just a moment," she said, looking out the door toward the tarmac. "Is this your first visit to St. Moritz, Mr. Quinn?"

"No, but it's been a few years. And please, call me David," he said.

In heels, she was only slightly taller than Quinn's six feet, but everything else clashed like Waterford crystal goblets and Melmac dinnerware—his roundness, her sleekness; his balding head of mousy brown hair, her tumble of loose, shoulder-length, auburn blonde waves; his bunchy gray rain coat over a stressed navy wool suit, her stylish black trench atop a short, powder blue jersey wrap dress.

After arranging for Quinn's luggage to be loaded, Vargas escorted him across the tarmac toward the Boeing 767. Two other executives and their personal assistants were boarding ahead of them. The airplane looked like any other Boeing 767, except for the small gold letters on the fuselage near the tail wing. Executive Class was in the business of leasing aircraft and selling fractional ownership on larger jets to corporations. They were also one of Wayland Tate's clients. Quinn followed Vargas up the stairs at the rear of the aircraft to a lavishly designed interior, reminiscent of an exclusive European hotel. She showed him to a cozy private cabin where his luggage had already been secured at the foot of a queen size bed. A seating area across from the bed comprised a round mahogany table flanked by matching leather lounge chairs. Beyond the lounge chairs was a short hallway lined with shelves holding magazines and books that led to a private bathroom with steam and shower.

Having assured herself that everything was in order, Vargas relieved Quinn of his overcoat and suit jacket, hanging them both in the mahogany closet. "We'll be serving dinner after takeoff. If you need anything, just press 'seven' on your stylus," she said while lifting an armrest, removing the cordless stylus, and handing it to Quinn. She explained how to access the onboard library of films, music, and financial market information, and then promised to return after takeoff.

As Quinn made himself comfortable in one of the lounge chairs, he found a leather folder with his name on it stuffed in a pocket below the window. It contained a personalized letter from Wayland Tate, welcoming him to the St. Moritz retreat. Accompanying the letter was a small brochure detailing the activities scheduled for the next three days. Quinn read with curiosity. Each morning from eight to eleven o'clock, well-known management and financial gurus were available for small group discussions and personal coaching on various issues and dilemmas facing today's CEOs. Dinner would be served every night at eight o'clock. Between the morning sessions and evening dinner, leisure time had been scheduled for active or passive pleasures such as downhill or cross-country skiing, indoor and outdoor ice skating, winter golf on the frozen lake, international horse racing, steam and geothermal health baths, body massages, mud packs, or sightseeing in St. Moritz and the surrounding area.

Quinn was still perusing the lineup of activities when the plane reached its cruising altitude. Vargas returned with a dinner menu and handed it to Quinn. "I recommend the scallops. The veal reduction sauce is lovely."

"When you have a minute, I have a few questions," Quinn said.

Moving with effortless grace, Vargas lowered herself into the lounge chair across from him. "What's on your mind, David?"

His eyes roamed over her as she crossed her legs and smoothed out her dress. She was easily one of the most beautiful women Quinn had ever seen.

Men were so pathetically predictable, Vargas thought. They were so easy to fuck with, especially for a woman who looked like Andrea Vargas.

Quinn chided himself for admiring her, restricting his attention to her eyes. "Can you tell me who else will be at St. Moritz this weekend?" he asked.

"Of course," she said without hesitation. For the next few minutes she thoroughly reviewed the list of attendees by name, position, and company. There were twenty CEOs from major corporations, eight of whom were on the same flight with Quinn. Staff members, private bankers, various special guests, and personal assistants would be working behind the scenes to ensure that the St. Moritz retreat unfolded stress-free with as much enrichment and enjoyment as possible.

Quinn asked a few more questions about accommodations, departure schedule, Internet access, and dress code, all of which Vargas answered. When he finished, he took a few moments to look over the menu. "I'll take your advice and have the scallops. You can choose the rest."

During the next hour of their flight to St. Moritz, Vargas presented Quinn with plate after plate of gourmet fare⊠Kobe Beef Carpaccio, a mixed salad with Gorgonzola cheese, lobster bisque with chanterelles, North Atlantic sea scallops with veal reduction sauce and risotto, wine pairings from Napa and Sonoma, and Grand Marnier soufflé for dessert. Although he thoroughly enjoyed the dinner, while listening to Mozart and watching a brief travelogue on St. Moritz, Quinn could never completely let go.

After dinner, he caught up on his latest pile of reading material from the office, interrupted only by Vargas' occasional check-ins to make sure he was in need of nothing. With four hours left in the eight-hour flight, he told Vargas he was going to get some sleep.

"Can I get you something to help you relax? Ambien? Chamomile tea?" she asked.

Quinn knew he needed something to relieve the tension that had been building ever since he received news earlier in the day about next week's board meeting. Kresge & Company had been invited to attend the board meeting, presumably to unveil its strategy for breaking up J. B. Musselman. "Sure," he said, nodding. "Chamomile tea would be great."

As Quinn changed into pajamas and a silk robe, he considered Wayland Tate and next week's board meeting. Although Tate's aggressiveness and manipulative style often made him anxious, Quinn was glad to have him on the board, especially now that control of the company's future was in jeopardy. For David Quinn, J. B. Musselman was much more than a hodgepodge of distribution warehouses in the U.S., Canada, and Mexico, distributing everything from bulk packages of Fruit Loops to Adirondack furniture. It was the embodiment of everything he'd chosen to become. It was his seed, his immortality. And no board of directors or outside consulting firm was going to stop him from preserving what he'd built.

When Vargas arrived five minutes later, she placed a pot of Chamomile tea on the small coffee table and poured two cups. "Mind if I join you?" she asked.

"Not at all." Quinn settled into one of the lounge chairs.

"You seem stressed," Vargas said as she sat down across from him.

"It's a troublesome time for my company," Quinn said.

"So what worries you most when you lie down to sleep?" Vargas asked with disarming sincerity.

"Musselman's stock price," Quinn said, matter-of-factly. "Ultimately, market value is what every CEO frets about, and right now we're not doing very well."

"Based on what I've heard about you," Vargas said with admiration in her voice, "you won't have much trouble turning things around."

Quinn was tempted to ask her exactly what she'd heard about him, but he didn't. "That's assuming I can keep my company from being dismantled," he said. "Your boss is a member of our board and he has a crucial role to play over the next couple of weeks."

"A man in your position could do anything he wanted at this stage in his life. Why do you still keep your nose to the grindstone?" she asked, anxious to get beneath Quinn's thick exterior. She already knew his net worth exceeded a billion dollars and that his annual compensation with stock options ranged from five to over a hundred million dollars, depending on performance, but she wanted to know what was driving him at a deeper level.

"I suppose it's the only thing that makes me feel alive," Quinn said, realizing that she'd made him think beyond the platitudes of his life.

"Hmmm," she said, smiling while crossing her legs.

"Okay, Andrea. I have a question for you," Quinn said, suddenly feeling vulnerable. "What exactly does Wayland Tate expect you to do for his clients?"

"He expects me to take care of them," she said, taking pleasure in the fact that she'd aroused him. Time to increase the sexual tension, she thought to herself. "What I do on my own time is my business."

"Don't tell me you're here sipping tea on your own time," he said sarcastically.

"Of course I am," she said with conviction. And she wasn't lying. Everything Vargas did was on her own time. She was an independent contractor, with enough accumulated wealth to live comfortably for the rest of her life. Contracting her services to Tate Waterhouse was something she did because she loved it—and she was good at it.

"Let's be honest here. I'm overweight, I can't remember the last time I worked out, and I haven't had a full head of hair since you were in diapers. So tell me what Tate really wants you to do for me."

"He told me to make sure you were comfortable and that you enjoyed yourself. Nothing more," she said, nonchalantly. "Any attraction I have to you has nothing to do with Wayland Tate."

"Give me a break. A woman like you is rarely attracted to a man like me unless…"

She finished the sentence for him, "…unless she's paid to be? Is that what you think? Sorry, David. I have no such arrangement with Wayland Tate." She stood up and began walking away. Before reaching the door, she looked back at him. "Sometimes, women like me are only attracted to men like you."

"Why?" Quinn said. He was certain she was lying, but still curious about how she might respond.

"Because you're fascinating," Vargas said, taking a step toward him and then another. "You're a man who can have anything he wants. You could walk away from Musselman today and enjoy a life of indulgence and pleasure, but you won't because the challenge of taking your company to new heights makes you feel alive. Men like you are not common, David. Besides, young and handsome is overrated and much too predictable."

"You're almost believable," Quinn said, smiling at her. "And you're right, I won't throw away my life for a passing indulgence."

"I don't want you to throw anything away, David," she said, taking another step toward him. "I know what kind of reputation you've spent your life creating. I'd just like to get to know you better."

"Sorry, Andrea, I'm not your man."

She raised her eyebrows with a charming coyness. "See you in the morning, David. Our relationship will remain strictly professional." She opened the door to the cabin and exited without looking back. Seducing David Quinn may prove tougher than originally planned, she mused, but the challenge excited her.

After Vargas left, Quinn took off his robe and got into bed. He'd allowed himself to be enchanted by Vargas' stunning beauty and disarming openness, but it wasn't the first time something like this had happened to him. Vargas was right. A man's power and wealth attracted some women far more than all the other male attributes combined. But he'd decided long ago that one woman in his life was enough, and although Vargas had aroused him, his years of resolve had taught him how to quickly overcome such temptations. Within minutes he was enjoying the comfort of his principles while falling asleep. No second thoughts.

6

Vargas – Boeing 767, Inflight

Andrea Vargas' international call from onboard the Executive Class charter came through to Wayland Tate's suite at Suvretta House a few minutes before six o'clock in the morning, St. Moritz time. Tate had just finished showering and was primping in front of the mirror, when he lifted the cordless phone to his ear. "Yes?" he said, walking to the beige chenille sofa in boxers and an unbuttoned shirt.

"Sensual desire does not seem to be David's weakness, although he's tempted," Vargas said, getting straight to the point. She relished her interactions with Wayland Tate because she loved the challenge of manipulating powerful men almost as much as he did.

"I'm not surprised. What else?" Tate asked as he sat down on the sofa, eager to obtain Vargas' initial assessment of David Quinn.

"Musselman's depressed stock price is causing him a lot of anxiety. It seems that the only reason he accepted your invitation to St. Moritz was to meet with you and Jules Kamin. He sees you playing a key role in holding his company together."

"Why do you think he's so obsessed with staying at the helm of Musselman?" Tate asked, standing up and stepping to the balcony windows that overlooked the frozen lake. He knew from past experience with Vargas that when it came to quickly diagnosing a client's peculiar mix of hidden motivations and obsessions, her intuition and judgment were usually spot-on.

"Based on what's in his file and reading between the lines of our brief conversations," Vargas said, pausing a moment to confirm the words she was about to speak. "I'd say he's obsessively conscious of his place in the world. Breaking up Musselman, especially during this time of difficulty, is completely unacceptable to him because it would undo what he's already done."

"In other words, he's willing to betray his precious principles to avoid getting ousted by the board."

"Musselman is David Quinn. The company's future is his offspring. He'll do whatever is takes to guarantee survival."

"Perfect," Tate said, mentally reviewing his history with David Quinn. Like most people with substantial wealth and power, Quinn would justify unprincipled behavior to preserve his institution. They all did it, because they could get away with it. Whoever has the money makes the rules.

"I don't need to tell you that Quinn is nobody's fool, even if he may look and act a little frumpy," Vargas said.

"Getting attached?"

"I wouldn't have a problem staying with David for awhile," she said, feeling more and more energized by the challenge. She admired Quinn's obsession and fantasized about having it directed at her. Of course there was also the money. Tate's compensation program was extremely generous, as long as he got what he wanted.

"Really? Well, let's make sure he doesn't get away. Nice work, Andrea. I'll see you in a few hours. Get some sleep," Tate said, smiling to himself as he said good-bye and put down the phone. Vargas could make any man want her, Tate imagined. Thanks to Morita, she'd become an invaluable contributor to Tate Waterhouse and its clients.

7

Weintraub, Drake, Heinke & Redd's law offices were unmistakably designed for discreet client handling, Wilson thought as he introduced himself to one of the three receptionists sitting behind a large circular desk. She was an Asian woman, with severe looking black glasses, who quickly ushered him into one of several small conference rooms encircling the foyer. As she closed the door behind her, she informed him that Mr. Redd would be with him momentarily.

Within seconds, Daniel Redd walked through a door at the opposite end of the elegantly sparse conference room.

He was dressed in uniform—dark expensive suit with white monogrammed shirt. Only their ties were different: Daniel's was yellow, Wilson's purple. "How's your father?" Daniel asked.

"Stable. They're still doing tests, but Malek's team seems optimistic about him regaining consciousness. Injury to his medulla seems less likely than the doctors in Sun Valley originally diagnosed, which means brain damage is no longer as much of a concern."

"We may need to increase security around him," Daniel said.

"Two men from your firm are outside his ICU along with two uniformed policemen. Detective Zemke alerted Boston's police chief, who happens to be a close friend of his. The uniforms have been there around the clock. If you think we need more than that, then there's something you're not telling me," Wilson said, suddenly anxious about Daniel's comment.

"Maybe I'm being paranoid," Daniel said. "Let's get this closing over with; then we can talk."

Wilson's anxiety lingered as Daniel led him into the mahogany filled boardroom. KaneWeller's Chairman and CEO Marshall Winthorpe, COO Jules Kamin, and their team of executives were already assembled at one end of the forty-foot conference table, ready for the signing. Bill Heinke, managing partner of Weintraub, Drake, Heinke & Redd, along with Daniel's team of lawyers entered the boardroom next. After Daniel made the formal introductions, Wilson shook hands with the eight KaneWeller executives, Bill Henke, and Daniel's team of six lawyers. When everyone had shaken hands, they sat down in the burgundy leather chairs and turned their attention to the task at hand. Wilson and Marshall sat next to each other under the ornate crystal chandelier at the center of the room.

Marshall began by giving a brief speech summarizing how Fielder & Company would become KaneWeller's flagship for entering the management consulting business. Thanks to changes by the Federal Reserve concerning investment banks along with green lights from the SEC and Justice Department, management consulting businesses and investment banks could now be comingled under the same ownership and management. Historically, investment houses such as KaneWeller had been prevented from owning or operating traditional management consulting businesses, even though they'd been offering management advice to their corporate clients for years. Marshall Winthorpe seemed particularly pleased that the business press was heralding the acquisition as a predatory coup for KaneWeller and a major step toward strengthening the nation's commercial and investment banking institutions. "The long line of Fielder financial giants should be very proud of this merger," Winthorpe said in conclusion, looking at Wilson.

"I'm sure they are," Wilson said before graciously expressing his satisfaction in being able to execute his father's desire to merge Fielder & Company with KaneWeller. After Wilson's brief remarks, he and Marshall turned to the four piles of papers in front of them on the conference table. Daniel directed the order of the signings from a seat he had taken on the other side of the table. Jules Kamin, President and COO of KaneWeller, who Wilson remembered as a business associate of his father's, stood behind Wilson and Marshall. The others sat watching and quietly conversing. At one point during the signing, Wilson turned to look at Kamin. As their eyes locked, they smiled at each other, but the sardonic look on Kamin's face left Wilson with a strange uneasiness that lingered throughout the signing.

KaneWeller's lawyers had spent several days reviewing the company's client files and discussing them at length with Fielder executives. How much have Kamin and Marshall missed or ignored in their due-diligence evaluation of my father's business practices? Wilson wondered. What about Kamin? He's been an associate of my father's for years. How much does he know? What about the others? Daniel had assured Wilson that neither he nor his family would suffer any liability, regardless of what might come to light after the transaction was completed. Everyone in the room seemed satisfied, except maybe Cheryl O'Grady. She was one of KaneWeller's attorneys, who kept staring at Wilson like a schoolteacher suspecting a student of cheating during an exam, which only served to amplify Wilson's anxiety and wariness.

When all the documents were signed and properly distributed, Marshall Winthorpe handed Daniel a wire transfer order for $3.2 billion and stock certificates worth $1.8 billion to be deposited in an escrow account at UBS, where they would remain for the next thirty days. To speed up the negotiations, Daniel had proposed a thirty-day grace period during which KaneWeller could back out of the deal with sufficient cause, namely the discovery of any material misrepresentation of the facts by Fielder & Company. Daniel didn't expect any problems since KaneWeller wasn't looking for a way out. Wilson hoped he was right.

Less than forty-five minutes after they'd sat down at the boardroom table, Marshal Winthorpe and Wilson Fielder stood, shook hands, and congratulated each other. KaneWeller's acquisition of his father's eighty-two percent ownership of Fielder & Company had been consummated, at least provisionally. As the hand shaking and congratulations extended to the others in the boardroom, staffers from Daniel's law firm brought in the traditional cigars and whiskey—Bolivar Corona Gigantes and Chivas Regal Royal Salute. An hour later, only Daniel and Wilson were left in the boardroom.

"I'm glad that's completed," Daniel said.

"You're worried, aren't you?"

Daniel gazed at Wilson for a prolonged moment. "Just glad there were no last minute surprises. Now we can accelerate the rest of the liquidation."

"What else?"

"We have about seventy percent of your father's stock positions and investment partnerships left to monetize."

"No. I mean what else is bothering you? You said we'd talk about it after the signing," Wilson said.

"Nothing that time won't resolve," Daniel said as he began picking up the documents from the conference table.

Wilson's frustration was rising. He placed his hand on Daniel's arm to stop his busywork. "I need to know what else is going on, Daniel."

Daniel glared at Wilson before responding. "I'm concerned about the mounting surveillance," he said abruptly and then returned to picking up papers.

This time Wilson grabbed Daniel's arm. The jolt sent some of the papers sliding across the table and onto the floor. "Goddammit. What aren't you telling me?" Wilson demanded.

"We didn't expect this level of surveillance," Daniel said, his eyes like pinwheels. "The number of people, the equipment, it's more than we…"

"Where are they?"

"One of their locations is across the street from your family's home on Brattle Street, on the top floor…"

"The Broadhead place? They wouldn't…"

"The Broadheads don't know about it. They're in the Bahamas for four more weeks. Looks like the graduate student taking care of the house in their absence couldn't resist the opportunity to make some extra cash. He's temporarily moved into a bedroom in the basement."

"How many people?"

"More than a dozen—four at the Broadhead house."

"What kind of equipment?"

"Everything. Remote listening devices, motion-sensitive cameras, scanners that identify phone numbers and email addresses, car tracking satellite systems . . . you name it, they've got it."

"Our security service hasn't reported anything unusual," Wilson said.

"They're looking for burglars and intruders, not highly trained surveillance professionals."

Wilson studied Daniel. The mix of puzzlement and fear in his eyes remained. Daniel's in over his head, Wilson thought. "Can they hear everything we say in the house?"

"Probably."

"What about here?"

"No. We're jamming any surveillance."

"Who else are they watching?"

"Carter Emerson and your girlfriend Emily Klein."

"I haven't seen her in months," Wilson said, his anxiety spiking again. "Why the sudden escalation?"

"I can only assume they're worried about what we know and what we intend to do about it," Daniel said and then lowered his voice. "The completion of this deal should ease their concerns. It shows you're separating yourself from your father's business activities and moving on with your life."

"What if it heightens them?" Wilson said.

"What do you mean?"

"KaneWeller could uncover the abuses."

"We've taken care of that. KaneWeller has agreed that it's in their best interest to refrain from working with certain former and current clients. The background files on our fifty-two problem clients will remain in our possession. It was the only way to control access. My firm's management committee isn't all that excited about it, but under the circumstances, we had no choice. Like I said, today's transaction should improve things."

"Are you trying to convince me, or yourself?" Wilson asked.

"We have to assume that the people watching us already know that we're keeping the files. Preventing the information in those files from getting to the press, the SEC, the FBI, and anyone else is also in our best interest. They have to know that," Daniel said and then paused. "How much longer are you going to need the copies I gave you?"

"Why?"

"Whoever tried to kill your father will strike again if they perceive any risk."

Wilson studied Daniel again. "The same people who had Richard Beckstrom killed in prison?"

"Possibly."

"You're holding out on me again."

"No, I'm not. The increased surveillance simply suggests a more serious investment in finding out what we know and what we plan to do about it. In my opinion, it's the work of a well organized group of people."

"How much do they know?"

"We have to assume they know everything, which means they know you have copies of the fifty-two file summaries."

"I'll have them to you tomorrow," Wilson abruptly put an end to their conversation, saying good-bye to Daniel and leaving the boardroom. He found his own way to the elevator. Daniel's in over his head, Wilson thought again, and his firm can no longer be trusted to protect my loved ones.

What little Wilson knew about surveillance and counter-surveillance he'd learned from Hap Greene, a former head of covert operations for the CIA. Hap ran Greene Mursin International (GMI), a highly discreet private investigation firm that Kresge & Company employed to ferret out hidden background information on clients, acquisition candidates, and prospective hires. Wilson met Hap several years earlier during a high profile Kresge project. They had quickly developed a close relationship, mostly because they shared each other's irreverent attitudes toward society and the world in general. Hap was part of a growing trend among government and military trained spies, who were leaving the ranks of government service for the more lucrative and private world of corporate espionage. Corporate spying had become a hot growth business in recent years and no one was better at it than Hap Greene.

Before leaving Daniel's offices, Wilson stepped into one of the small conference rooms encircling the foyer and called information for GMI's New York office. When the call was connected, a GMI receptionist answered. Wilson introduced himself and asked for Hap.

"What firm are you with Mr. Fielder?"

"Kresge & Company. Hap and I have worked together on a few projects."

"Do you have a number where he can reach you?" she asked.

"It's urgent. I need to speak to him as soon as possible. Is there any way you can connect me with him now? I only need a couple of minutes," Wilson said, his voice straining.

"I'm sorry, Mr. Fielder. He will not be available for contact until tomorrow afternoon. Can I have someone else help you?"

"No, thank you. Tell him I'll call him tomorrow afternoon," Wilson said before hanging up. He needed a crash course on counter-surveillance, and he needed it now.

8

Tate – St. Moritz, Switzerland

As soon as David Quinn appeared in front of the maître d' of the Grand Restaurant at Suvretta House a few minutes after noon, he was escorted to Wayland Tate's table near the windows. When Tate saw him, he stood to shake hands and welcome Quinn to St. Moritz. After the obligatory chitchat about Quinn's flight and hotel accommodations, they ordered an assortment of sausages, salads, cheeses, and a bottle of Chasselas wine. During lunch, their conversation was light, mostly about the next three days of activities and events.

After lunch they traveled by horse-drawn sleigh to the north end of the lake, where Vargas had arranged reserved seating for St. Moritz's renowned international horse races. The White Turf races had been rescheduled from their usual mid-February date because of an unusually severe winter in Switzerland. But today the weather was a balmy five degrees Celsius, no wind, and nothing but blue skies—proclaiming why St. Moritz was the world's oldest and most famous ski resort. Thoroughbreds and jockeys from Europe's premier racing stables were ready to compete in the hundred-year-old contest. The magnificent mountains, twenty-five thousand spectators, a royal betting frenzy, and extraordinary Swiss catering made this one of the most celebrated winter events on the continent.

To Tate's relief and delight, Quinn took great pleasure in the spectacle of specially shod horses churning up the freshly packed snow on the frozen lake. The passion and excitement of the international horseracing crowd was electrifying. Each new heat of thundering hooves and spraying snow seemed to loosen Quinn a little more, especially after he started betting.

With the races and betting over, they retired to the Kurhaus Spa—a classic Walser timber chalet at the edge of the forest—for more serious conversation. It was there, alone together in the steam room inhaling eucalyptus vapors, that Tate began the process of identifying Quinn's deepest, most exploitable weaknesses.

"Is Andrea taking care of all your needs?" Tate asked.

"She's delightful, but I couldn't do that to Margaret," Quinn said.

"I'm talking about logistics, David," Tate said with a wry smile. "What are you talking about?"

"Is that what you call plausible deniability?"

"We pay our personal assistants to provide professional pampering to our clients. That's it. Anything beyond that is between consenting adults."

"You really expect me to believe that?" Quinn said, indignantly. He flinched as he leaned back against the hot tiles. "That's like unbridling a horse on a grassy meadow and expecting it not to graze."

Tate looked over his shoulder at Quinn, assuming an expression of concern. "If Andrea has made you feel uncomfortable in any way, I'll have someone else assigned immediately."

"No. She's fine. A little too assertive maybe, but fine."

"We can easily make a change, David," Tate repeated, sitting back—every inch the relaxed host, whose only concern is his guest's comfort.

Quinn rubbed his hands over his face to remove the excess moisture. "She knows where I stand. She'll be fine."

After a moment of silence, Tate decided to push the issue to see how Quinn would respond. "This is the first time anyone has called Andrea too assertive. Most clients think she's the consummate professional. You must have made an impression on her," Tate said as he leaned forward, resting his elbows on his knees and looking back at Quinn. "I'd say she likes you."

Quinn's only response was to sneer.

"I'm serious," Tate said, in response to Quinn's obvious skepticism. "Everything Andrea does and says is deliberate and well-reasoned. She has a Masters degree in social anthropology from Swarthmore and is one of our best associates. In the three years she's been with us, I've never had a single complaint."

"I'm not complaining, Wayland. Like I said, she's delightful. Let's leave it at that."

Tate finally let it drop, but not without noting that Vargas had already gotten under Quinn's skin. He stood up and walked over to the oversized showerhead, positioning himself directly beneath it before pushing the button that drenched him in ice-cold water. As he stood there, tightening every muscle in his body to keep from shaking, he looked at his client. Quinn was a talented, accomplished CEO, hungry for even greater success and power. And Tate was just about ready to bet that Quinn would risk everything he had to get what he didn't have. Still tingling from the ice water, he sat down again on his towel next to Quinn. This time, however, he waited for Quinn to initiate conversation.

After a few moments of silence, Quinn bent his head down over his knees and stretched his arms to the tiles beneath his feet. On his way back up, he said, "Let's talk about Kresge & Company. Slowing down the project isn't going to be enough."

"America's Warehouse launches in a few weeks. After that it will be a non issue," Tate returned.

"Doesn't matter. The project needs to be terminated now."

"That won't be easy, given the board's commitment to it," Tate cautioned.

"I'm aware of that, but I can't let it continue any longer. MacMillan scheduled Kresge & Company to present its recommendation for breaking up the company to the board next week, complete with a detailed implementation plan. Wilson Fielder already signed off on it. The managing director of the Chicago office is going to make the presentation. I found out about it just before I got on the plane to come here," Quinn said before standing up and wrapping the towel he'd been sitting on around his waist. He paced back and forth for a few moments before he said, "I won't let it happen, Wayland."

"What did you have in mind?" Tate asked as he tried to hide his glee: their conversation was unfolding exactly as he'd hoped.

Just then, a large man opened the glass door to the steam room and stepped inside. Tall, blonde, and imposing, he looked German or Scandinavian. Unwilling to continue their conversation in another's presence, Tate and Quinn took turns drenching themselves in cold water, waiting for the intruder to leave. During the quiet, Tate continued his assessment. David Quinn wanted what every other person on Forbes' list wanted—power, glory, and dominion by controlling as much capital, land, and labor as possible for the endless benefit of themselves and their posterity. By virtue of his wealth, Quinn already had plenty of power, but keeping J. B. Musselman intact and under his control was his only chance for both continued dominion and lasting glory. Fortunately, the America's Warehouse advertising campaign would give Quinn the status and a promise of the legacy he craved. Not permanently, but just long enough to allow Tate and his partners to pocket several billion.

When they were alone once again, Quinn picked up the thread of their conversation: "I want to use Wilson Fielder's family problems to raise questions about his competence."

"He's on a leave of absence, isn't he?" Tate asked, even though he already knew the answer. "Why not tell the board that Wilson's sudden leave of absence raises serious questions about the project's continuity. Then, all we have to do is postpone Kresge & Company's presentation."

"Too risky," Quinn said, getting up again and wrapping his towel around his waist. "Kresge's already trying to convince the board that Fielder's absence is not a factor. We need to put his competence in question. But it can't appear as if I'm pulling the strings."

"How do you expect to place his competence in question?" Tate asked, egging him on.

"I'll need your help," Quinn replied without prevarication, "Yours and Kamin's."

Perfect, Tate thought, he's exactly where I want him to be. He leaned over his knees, remaining silent for several moments. Then he looked up at Quinn. "What do you want me to do?"

"If you were to raise certain questions about the Fielder family, suggesting that Charles may have suffered a mental breakdown and that the entire family had been in turmoil for some time, it would raise doubts about Wilson's judgment on the Musselman project."

"How would that play when I was the one who recommended his father's firm instead of Kresge & Company in the first place?" Tate said, pretending to be reluctant.

"You simply tell them that you had no idea about Charles' condition until you received certain information from one of his closest associates. Here's where you'll need to take some creative license. You could say that a confidential source told you that Charles Fielder has had mental stability issues for years. In recent months, his son Wilson had become increasingly troubled, even obsessed, over his father's condition, displaying evidence of the same mental instability. It runs in the family. Bringing down the CEO of a large corporation and then dismantling his company are merely manifestations of Wilson's self-destructive behavior and a deep-seated rebelliousness toward authority. He's seeing a psychologist, which is true, by the way. His girlfriend is a psychologist. He'd become suicidal himself. His judgment on the Kresge project has to be questioned. Turn up the heat on Wilson Fielder," Quinn said as he sat down again.

Tate sat in quiet admiration, his back pressed against the tiles. Very impressive, he thought to himself. Quinn had definitely done his homework on Wilson Fielder. Heart-felt motivation was such a beautiful thing. He was more than happy to let Quinn do the talking.

"Jules Kamin could add to the concerns about Wilson Fielder's competence," Quinn said. "If he could show how a breakup of Musselman will decrease rather than increase shareholder value, over the next five years, it would cast even more doubt on the project."

Tate stood up and walked over to the ice-cold drench one more time, putting Quinn on a different kind of ice. As he stood there, his thoughts turned to Vargas. She had accurately assessed Quinn's core obsession and now he'd confirmed it. There were no more lingering doubts about his ability to manipulate David Quinn. Tate walked back to the tile bench and sat down. It was time to see just how far Quinn would go.

"We may have to create some additional evidence to support our claims of incompetence," Tate said.

"As far as I'm concerned, Wilson Fielder mismanaged this project from the beginning. Whatever we have to do to convince the board of his incompetence is fine with me."

"What if Wilson comes back to defend himself?"

"Then, we'll play hardball."

"What are you thinking?" Tate asked, making Quinn specify exactly what he was willing to do.

"We'll sue Kresge & Company for gross mismanagement of the project and demand damages of ten times their two million dollars in fees," Quinn said with anger.

Tate pushed further, "What if Wilson decides to play hardball?"

"Then, maybe his family will have to suffer again," Quinn said, standing up once more and turning around to face Tate. "Nothing physical you understand, just some ugly gossip. A few damaging rumors with enough manufactured evidence to make the family seem out of control."

Tate raised his eyebrows, feigning surprise. "You'd actually go that far?"

"It's not something I'd enjoy doing. But if I had to, I would. This arrogant little prick tried to destroy me and everything I built at Musselman," Quinn said, his eyes like beacons. "The gloves came off after Fielder told MacMillan that I should step down. The brass knuckles went on when he recommended the company's breakup."

The room turned dead silent except for the sound of hissing steam.

Tate couldn't help chuckling to himself. The dual threat of being ousted by the board and having his company broken into pieces was enough to make Quinn vulnerable to a melody of manipulations. Maybe David Quinn wasn't yet ready to cheat on his wife or trade on insider information, but he was willing to defame Wilson Fielder in order to keep Kresge & Company from forcing a breakup of Musselman. It was time to set the hook.

"Okay, David. We'll take care of it," Tate finally said. "I'll track down MacMillan and express my concerns about Wilson Fielder. You can count on Kamin and me replacing Kresge & Company at next week's board meeting. One way or another, we'll make it happen."

"Thank you, Wayland. You've just taken a big load off my mind," Quinn said.

"Oh, we'll do more than that, David. Just wait until the launch of America's Warehouse. By the way, Kamin is anxious to meet with you about Musselman's next stock offering. He arrives tomorrow morning. Let's plan on having a private dinner tomorrow night."

"Marvelous," Quinn said. His reason for coming to St. Moritz was well on its way to being realized. All he had to do now was let Wayland Tate perform his magic.

"Have you set your schedule for tonight and tomorrow?" Tate asked.

"I think I'm going to retire early tonight. Catch up on some sleep. Andrea has me scheduled to hit the slopes first thing in the morning."

"Perfect," Tate said with his infectious smile. "Jules and I will be ready for you tomorrow night."

9

Tate – St. Moritz, Switzerland

After spending the evening with clients, Tate returned to his room to make a few international calls. He started with Jules Kamin. It was midnight in St. Moritz, six o'clock in Boston.

The secure cell phone buzzed in Kamin's pocket as he walked to the small conference room that had become his office at KaneWeller's Boston offices. At age fifty-five, Kamin looked like a young and trim Henry Kissinger, which Tate attributed less to heredity and more to the rigorous regime he'd convinced Kamin to adopt several years earlier. Kamin's face, however, looked more weary and aged than his years when he answered Tate's call. He'd just returned from the Fielder & Company closing.

"How did things go?" Tate inquired as soon as the ringing stopped and he heard Kamin's voice.

"The closing went as planned, but we may have a problem," Kamin said resignedly.

"Fielder?" Tate said annoyed.

"No. Our attorneys want to conduct a second round of inquiries into some of Fielder & Company's client relationships."

"This could scuttle the entire deal, Jules," Tate said, beginning to pace back and forth in the sitting area of his suite. "Who's behind it?"

"Cheryl O'Grady has been working Winthorpe behind the scenes, trying to convince him that Fielder & Company's consulting practices may have involved conspiring to manipulate company stock prices."

"Every company conspires to manipulate its stock price. That's what free enterprise is all about," Tate said, feeling his blood pressure rising. "What's motivating O'Grady?"

"She doesn't like me. Never has. She knows this is my deal. I think she would jump at any chance to keep me from taking over when Winthorpe retires next year," Kamin said. He, too, began to pace back and forth in the conference room.

"You should have fired her when you had the chance," Tate said, turning off the lights in his suite to look at the moonlit mountains surrounding the resort.

"You know why I didn't. There were too many rumors that I was out to get her. Letting her stay was the only way to stop the rumor mill," Kamin said.

"Okay. Okay. It's water under the bridge. How do we deal with her?"

"Something's given her new hope."

"Or someone. Who?" Tate asked, becoming more agitated by the second.

"I don't know. Maybe Redd," Kamin said.

"Not likely."

"He hasn't been the same since Charles was shot."

"No one has!" Tate said emphatically.

"I'm not suggesting Redd did anything intentionally. An offhanded comment or a hint of uncertainty might have been the only excuse O'Grady needed to intensify her probing."

"You think she baited him?" Tate asked.

"Redd's too smart for that. But she may have convinced him …"

Tate interrupted, "… to tell her what's really going on? Forget it."

"No," Kamin said, his voice rising. "She may have convinced him to admit his own growing uncertainties."

Tate fell silent. He slid open the balcony door and walked out into the cold, hoping it might help drop his blood pressure.

"Redd's vulnerable, Wayland," Kamin continued. "Has been since White Horse. And if he is, we are."

Bristling at the comment, Tate watched a red fox chase a snow rabbit across the blanket of white into the dark pines. The more unpredictable the fox, the more rabbits it snares. He smiled and walked back into his suite. "Maybe it's time to kill the KaneWeller deal."

"We can't …"

"Easy, Jules," Tate said. "I know you've been waiting a long time to assume the helm at KaneWeller, but Musselman will give us the resources to acquire Morgan. Anything you want to do at KaneWeller you can do at Morgan or another investment house, and that includes acquiring Fielder & Company. You may be right about Redd, and O'Grady is clearly a threat. It's time to move the game to a new playing field," Tate said, knowing it would be brutal for Kamin to leave KaneWeller after so many years of patiently positioning himself for the top spot. But there was no other alternative, Tate mulled. Not if we expect to preserve the partnership. O'Grady had always been a free spirit. She should have been removed from the equation when Kamin had the chance. Now, it was too late. Control had been lost. And Kamin knew it. If there was any lesson Tate had learned from history, it was that control belonged to the ruthless. Whenever it was lost, it had to be retaken immediately, no matter the cost.

"How do we kill it?" Kamin asked wearily.

"Leave that to me. Contingency plans are already in place," Tate said. "Right now we need to focus on Musselman. It's time to start buying as much stock as we can."

"You've confirmed Quinn?"

"Yes."

"I'll put things in motion before I get on the plane. Buying can start first thing Monday morning," Kamin said with a deepening resignation in his voice. He'd learned a long time ago that it never paid to disagree with Wayland Tate—not once he'd made a decision.

"How many entities do we need?" Tate asked.

"At least thirty," Kamin said.

"I'll let Swatling know. If you have any reservations about Quinn tomorrow night, you can call it off," Tate said, attempting to appease Kamin.

"The stock was selling at ten percent below book value at today's closing," Kamin said, just having pulled up Musselman's stock report on his screen.

"Perfect. If Quinn is as hungry as he seems, we'll be able to generate several billion on Musselman."

"I look forward to meeting him," Kamin said, a slight glint returning to his eyes.

"Needless to say, he's very anxious to meet you. The depressed stock price is driving him crazy. We're scheduled for dinner tomorrow night at eight."

"Have you talked to our new investors?" Kamin asked.

"Not yet, but I will. Opportunities like this don't come along everyday," Tate said, feeling invincible. Things were coming together on Musselman just as he'd planned. The advertising campaign alone could double the company's stock price within thirty days of its launch. Even if the America's Warehouse strategy turned out to have no long-term sustainability—as Wilson Fielder and his Kresge team were predicting—Musselman's stock price was projected to quadruple by the end of summer. Tate and his partners were not only poised to harvest a financial windfall from J. B. Musselman, they were insulated against all downsides. Any implementation failures would be laid at the feet of David Quinn and his management team. It was exactly the sort of scenario Tate relished.

When Tate said good-bye to Kamin, he walked to the closet and retrieved another cell phone—one of the encryption phones he would use and discard. He punched in the number and waited for his personal assassin. Within seconds the call was received in Boston by a similar phone. "This is Marco."

"It's Wayland. I want you to go ahead as planned. Tonight."

"Done," Marco said, before ending the call and dismantling the phone. He dropped the pieces into a frog pond in Boston Common.

10

Daniel – Boston, MA

Cheryl O'Grady was waiting when Daniel Redd arrived at the bar of the Exelsior, a swank New American-style restaurant overlooking Boston Public Garden. The maître d' escorted them to a table in one of the restaurant's secluded alcoves. Cheryl had called Daniel after the merger closing and asked for a private meeting. He'd quickly decided that a public meeting would raise fewer questions than a private encounter. When they sat down in the Queen Anne wing chairs, Daniel casually placed a small surveillance-nullifying device in the middle of their table.

"Is that what I think it is?" she asked.

"Depends on whether you're thinking like KaneWeller or Fielder & Company."

"Both, and I'd say it's a counter-surveillance device, not a recorder."

"Correct."

"You know what I want to talk about, don't you?"

"I think so."

"Can I see them?"

"We agreed they would remain in our custody," Daniel said. "It was all spelled out in the documents we signed a few hours ago. Remember?"

"Let me make this simple, Daniel. Either I get access to those files or I scuttle the merger."

Daniel searched her eyes. They looked no more sympathetic than an attacking Doberman's. She was not about to back down. "I'll let you see the files under my supervision—in our offices—on one condition."

"What's the condition?"

"You can only use the information as background. None of it can be copied or shared with your colleagues. And none of it can be used in any way to justify your scuttling of the merger."

"Agreed. My only interest is to understand exactly what we're walking into—so we know what to avoid going forward."

"Let's have a drink," Daniel said. "Then I'll take you back to our office."

After sharing a bottle of Shiraz and a platter of imported goat and sheep cheeses along with professional small talk, Daniel and Cheryl exited the restaurant onto Boylston Street. They walked to the intersection of Arlington and Boylston across from the Boston Public Garden and waited for the light to change.

Daniel hoped he wouldn't regret bringing Cheryl to the office to examine the fifty-two files. But all things considered, he had little choice. As Deputy General Counsel for KaneWeller, Cheryl certainly had the power and influence to scuttle the deal if she were so inclined. Allowing her to review the files with an opportunity to explain their true purpose, he told himself, might well be the only way to save the merger and distance Wilson from Fielder & Company. Hopefully, it would also avert any negative press that might compromise liquidation of Charles' other assets.

When the traffic light changed, Daniel and Cheryl began crossing Boylston Street. They walked past the center island, commenting on the beautiful budding elms and maples that lined the edge of the Public Garden.

Suddenly, without warning, a car swerved out from behind a lane of stopped traffic, crashed through a street construction fence, and headed directly for them at high speed. As soon as the two attorneys grasped the horrifying reality that the car was targeting them, they changed directions and began to run, but it was too late. The car struck them in the crosswalk before crashing into the back of a parked delivery van and exploding into flames. Their bodies were crushed instantly, hurled from hood to windshield and into the air. Cheryl's body hit the asphalt like a ragdoll, twisting and rolling for fifty feet until it came to a stop beneath a parked car. Daniel's was thrown against the back of a parked SUV, shattering the vehicle's windows before dropping lifelessly to the street. Both of them had died instantly.

Later that evening, *The Boston Globe* posted a preliminary online report of a fatal Back Bay accident:

Boston Globe City & Region Desk

By Susan Kite.

A car racing at high speed hit two pedestrians in Boston's Back Bay earlier this evening. The car swerved from behind a lane of stopped traffic and struck attorneys Daniel Redd of Boston and Cheryl O'Grady of New York City, who were walking in the crosswalk at Boylston and Arlington. Both were killed instantly. The car continued through the intersection and crashed into a parked delivery truck before exploding into flames. Remains of the driver have not yet been identified.

Even though the publicly reported details were sketchy, it was sufficient confirmation for Marco. No one had seen or heard anything unusual. It was a clean remote hit. The remains of the driver would soon be identified as a drunken street bum who'd gotten behind the wheel of a stolen car. The remote control equipment inside the car had exploded into a million indiscernible pieces, a method he'd employed for a dozen other hits. Marco's two million dollar fee, with another million for no loose ends, would be wired to his Nevis account within twenty-four hours, as promised. Doing business with Tate was truly a pleasure.

11

Wilson – Cambridge, MA

Wilson lay sprawled across the overstuffed chair and ottoman in the belfry library of the Fielder family home in Cambridge, Massachusetts. The two-story library had always been Wilson's lair. His father turned the circular belfry into a cozy library lined with maple bookshelves when Wilson was eight. The large oculus window provided a lookout to the outside world and a beautiful view of Cambridge Common and Harvard Square. Growing up, he and his friends had used the library and its large round window as an imaginary battle station with a strategic lookout. That's when he started calling the Fielder family home Brattle House. When he'd gotten older, the library became another place to have long intimate conversations with his father.

Last night, after spending several hours researching the latest surveillance and counter-surveillance practices online, Wilson had fallen asleep in his favorite overstuffed chair. His sister Rachel woke him with a violent shake. "Wilson. Wilson. Wake up. Daniel Redd was killed last night."

Wilson cracked opened his eyes gummed up from sleep, struggling to bring them into focus. Rachel's face was distorted. She looked horrified. "What?" he said, as her words began to sink in.

"Last night, just before eleven o'clock, Daniel and another attorney were hit by a drunk driver on Boylston."

"Where's the driver?"

"Dead. The car struck a truck and exploded."

Still dumbstruck, Wilson grabbed the morning edition of *The Boston Globe* from Rachel's hands.

Daniel Redd of Boston and Cheryl O'Grady of New York City were killed yesterday evening when a car racing at high speed swerved from behind a lane of stopped traffic and struck the two attorneys who were walking in the crosswalk at Boylston and Arlington Streets. The car continued through the intersection and exploded when it crashed into a delivery van. Remains of the driver have been identified as Thomas Wilkins of Boston.

Wilkins, who had been living on the streets of Boston for the past year, was driving a stolen vehicle at the time of the accident. Daniel Redd, age 47, was a partner with the Boston-based law firm of Weintraub, Drake, Heinke & Redd. He is survived by a son, William, age 24. Cheryl O'Grady, age 42, was Deputy General Counsel for the New York investment banking company KaneWeller. She is survived by her husband, Connor. The two attorneys had been working on KaneWeller's recent acquisition of Fielder & Company, a Boston-based financial consulting firm. Chairman and founder, Charles Fielder, is still in a coma at Mass General suffering from a gunshot wound he sustained just last week in Sun Valley, Idaho. While the police have not officially drawn any connection between the two tragic events, they have not ruled out the possibility.

Wilson read the report two more times, still unable to fathom that Daniel was suddenly gone. Killed in a crosswalk because of Fielder & Company's secrets. Why now? The fifty-two files? Sharing them with me? Meeting with Cheryl O'Grady? Had Daniel shared the files with her? Or was there something else Daniel failed to tell me?

"They did it. I know they did it," Wilson said under his breath.

Rachel looked as pale as death, staring at Wilson in disbelief. "What's happening to us?" she whispered.

An hour later Wilson was sitting in Bill Heinke's office at Weintraub, Drake, Heinke & Redd, listening to Heinke's account of Daniel's tragic death.

"We're all in shock around here," Heinke said, placing his hand over his forehead and sighing. "However, I assure you that nothing with respect to your family's assets or concerns has been jeopardized. Twenty-four hour security protection for your father, increased surveillance and counter-surveillance, liquidation of assets—everything will continue as planned." Heinke paused a moment, his face distorted, before adding, "I can't believe he's gone."

Wilson waited for a few moments out of respect for Daniel, but his sorrow had already turned into rage. There was no question in his mind that the people who had tried to murder his father had now killed Daniel Redd. "Why were Daniel and Cheryl meeting?" Wilson asked.

"Wrapping up loose ends on the merger, before Cheryl returned to New York for meetings today."

"What loose ends?"

"She wanted additional information about some of Fielder & Company's clients. Daniel had been working non-stop, hoping to finish everything by this morning."

"Which clients?" Wilson asked, feeling uneasy as he shifted in the leather wing chair across the desk from Heinke. He already knew the answer.

"We're not sure. There was nothing found at the scene of the accident. We're going through his files this morning. Daniel was very particular about his client files. He kept some in his office, some in the firm's vault, and others in safety-deposit boxes. Give us the rest of the day," Heinke said, sighing again as he folded his short, plump arms over his swollen stomach. Sweat had formed along his furrowed brow below a crop of receding gray-brown hair slicked back with gel. He looked like a heart attack waiting to happen. He continued, "We'll have everything accounted for by this afternoon. As for your father's estate, we have more than a dozen attorneys working on it as we speak. Daniel trained an exceptional group of attorneys. I'm personally assuming a supervisory role. Everything is proceeding as planned. Your father's assets should be fully monetized within thirty days. KaneWeller is also anxious about the files, the late-night meeting between Daniel and Cheryl, and, of course, the expected negative publicity. They've been checking in every half hour for updates."

"Please keep me informed," Wilson said as he got up.

"Of course. By the way, do you happen to have copies of any of Daniel's files?"

"No, I returned everything I had," Wilson said, disguising his lie with abruptness. *There's no way I'm turning over my copies of the fifty-two files. Not now that Daniel's gone. Fuck the bastards. I'll be ready for them when they come after me.*

Heinke grimaced slightly as he stood up. Things were obviously worse than Heinke was letting on. Hopefully, his body would be able to handle the added burden. The KaneWeller merger, the Fielder estate, and the reputations of all three firms were at stake, but none of that was Wilson's primary concern at the moment.

Before leaving the building, he called his former mentor and family friend, Carter Emerson. Carter said he'd been expecting Wilson's call. They arranged to meet in thirty minutes at John Harvard's Brew House in Harvard Square, where the thick stone walls and heavy music of the subterranean pub would be enough to prevent anyone from eavesdropping. Walking to his car, he repeated the words of his father's letter:

Complete the merger with KaneWeller and then liquidate all my other business assets as quickly as possible. Daniel Redd will help you. If you need additional help, go to Carter Emerson. Trust no one else.

Now, there was no one else. As he drove his father's car from Back Bay to Harvard Square, his thoughts turned to

Emily Klein and the first day they met in Carter Emerson's history class. It was his sophomore year at Princeton.

Emily was late for Emerson's course on interpreting history. As she rushed through the door, anticipating the distinguished professor's glare, something entirely unexpected happened. The first person she looked at when she entered the amphitheater-style classroom was Wilson. Their eyes locked for several seconds. He had no idea who she was, but he watched her every move. Emily told him later that she could feel him watching her. Even though she was used to having men ogle her striking features, thick shoulder-length blonde hair, and well-defined, five-foot-seven body, this felt different for both of them. She quickly took an empty seat across the aisle from Wilson in the third row of the amphitheater. He continued to glance at her throughout the class until she opened her mouth to ask a question. After that his glances turned into near constant staring.

Professor Emerson had just finished reviewing the objectives for his course, "Patterns of American Thought and Their Influence on the Interpretation of History," when he asked the class if there were any questions. A flood of mundane and predictable queries about books, reading requirements, tests, and papers spewed forth. After twenty minutes of these unbearably boring questions, Emily raised her hand and said, "Professor Emerson, based on the past twenty minutes, how would you evaluate our interpretation of the patterns of learning in American higher education?"

The class burst into laughter.

When things quieted down, Professor Emerson responded, "In answer to your question, I think we have a few misinterpretations to correct in the coming weeks."

Another round of laughter rippled through the seventy or so students in the room.

Smiling at Emily, Professor Emerson dismissed the class a few minutes early. Afterwards, Professor Emerson approached Emily to thank her for the question. As they bantered sarcastically about the hidden barriers to getting a superior college education, Wilson joined them. Emily was noticeably impressed that he and Professor Emerson had known each other for years. Wilson introduced himself to Emily and the three of them talked and laughed about a variety of topics, until Professor Emerson had to leave. While walking out of the amphitheater together, Professor Emerson invited both of them to dinner at his home on Sunday.

After that, it didn't take long for Emily and Wilson to become close friends. Carter had recognized the unusual chemistry between them from the beginning. They were seniors at Princeton when they started living together and began discussing a longer-term relationship, but neither of them had been ready to commit to anything other than their own career goals.

When Wilson turned into the parking garage across from John Harvard's Brew House, his reminiscences shifted to Sun Valley, where a day earlier he'd driven past the Sun Valley Lodge. The Old World elegance, surrounded by rustic pine timbers and natural stone, made the famed lodge and its Duchin Lounge one of Wilson's favorite spots for socializing after a day of skiing. It was there that he'd proposed to Emily a year ago last Christmas. He'd gotten down on one knee as the Duchin's live jazz-blues band played "At Last," and presented Emily with a four-carat diamond ring.

Six months later, they were still fighting over where to live and how to resolve their insane work schedules. He lived in Chicago; she lived in New York City. She was finishing a manuscript and treating patients; he was fast-tracking his career and traveling incessantly. When they finally decided to postpone the wedding until their career obstacles and obsessions subsided, Emily returned the ring and their relationship foundered.

It had been almost a year, and he still hadn't gotten over her. Now the sobering effect of his father's coma and Daniel's death was forcing him to take stock of his life in ways he never had—especially his relationships. It was time to admit, even celebrate, that he'd always loved Emily and always would. Time to correct a big mistake and protect the woman he loved.

12

Carter – Cambridge, MA

When Wilson arrived at John Harvard's Brew House, Carter Emerson was standing at the polished-brass and dark-wood bar with an Irish stout in his hand. He looked more like an adventurer than a famed History of American Civilization professor at Harvard University. His rugged features and thick brown hair, not to mention the robust athletic body, belied his status as one of the world's most respected public intellectuals. They embraced as old friends. "It's good to see you," Carter said, his bright blue eyes uncharacteristically gentle.

Having known him in his Princeton days, Wilson appreciated that expressions of empathy were a rare commodity with Carter Emerson. "Thank you for your messages of sympathy and support to the family," Wilson said.

"I visited your father this morning," Carter said slowly. "Dr. Malek seems genuinely optimistic, which is marvelous. But if Charles regains consciousness, he could become a target again. Malek's an old friend of your father's and mine. He told me you asked him about moving your father to a more secure location. I think it's a good idea."

Wilson nodded as the host escorted them—at Wilson's request—to a thick stone-lined corner of the pub. When they were seated, Wilson dispensed with the normal social niceties. "Daniel Redd's death wasn't an accident."

Carter concurred solemnly, without saying a word.

Wilson leaned over the table. It was time for plain talk. But before he began, Wilson reminded himself to be calm. His relationship with Carter had been nothing but stimulating and inspiring. If he couldn't trust Carter Emerson, he couldn't trust anyone. With measured delivery and a voice reserved for discreet conversation, he said, "Why has it taken my father lying on his death bed to find out what he was really doing at Fielder & Company? And I'm sure I don't know the half of it. Daniel was feeding me bits and pieces, but only in answer to specific questions. Now he's dead. Probably murdered by the same people who tried to kill my father. Who's next? You? Me? We're all under mounting surveillance, but we can't go to the authorities because their involvement could jeopardize the liquidation of my father's assets, which unknown to me until a couple of days ago, total more than seventy billion dollars. I need answers, and according to my father, you're the only one left who I can trust."

"I learned a long time ago that certain conversations must remain absolutely private," Carter said in a dry voice as he looked down at the briefcase resting on the floor next to his foot. "The technology in that briefcase radiates digital noise interference, essentially turning our conversation into white noise. It also immobilizes and nullifies listening devices such as wireless microphones and GPS tracking devices. There are two telephone scramblers inside as well. You can take the briefcase with you when you leave. Operating instructions are inside."

Wilson sat back, contemplating the mystery that was Carter—so like his father. "Tell me everything you know," he said firmly.

"Your father came to me a week ago, expressing grave concern about clients who were misusing his methods of wealth creation. His plan was to blow the whistle on them, regardless of the consequences to Fielder & Company. He asked for my assistance in documenting the abuses, including historical context and economic impact, to prepare stories for *The New York Times* and *The Wall Street Journal*. I immediately began clearing my calendar to concentrate on the files he promised to deliver upon his return from White Horse," Carter said, his eyes heavy.

What Carter said made sense and even sounded like something his father would do, Wilson thought, but was it true? Wilson's cynicism was growing. How much does Carter really know?

"Are you still willing to do what my father asked?"

"Now more than ever," Carter didn't hesitate.

"I have the files with me," Wilson said, looking down at the briefcase sitting next to his side of the table. "Daniel reviewed the files with me on the flight back from Sun Valley."

For the next forty-five minutes, while they ate a lunch of sandwiches and fruit, Wilson summarized the major areas of abuse by Fielder & Company's clients. He cited several examples from the fifty-two files and answered Carter's probing questions. When there were no more questions, Wilson looked deep into Carter's eyes. "I don't know how many people have already died, or how many may yet die to keep this information hidden, but I want to be ready to give this story to the press as soon as my father's assets have been liquidated and all of us are under the best protection I can find."

Carter nodded admiringly. "I am in full accord and eager to commence."

"I can arrange to give you access to all of the company's files. My father's administrative assistant Anne Cartwright will be your contact. I'll tell her you're compiling a corporate history of Fielder & Company as a way of offsetting some of the unfavorable press surrounding my father," Wilson said as he finished his meal.

They paid the check, left the underground pub, and walked out onto Dunster Street, carrying each other's briefcases.

"Did Daniel identify any major suspects from among the fifty-two?" Carter asked as they walked toward Harvard Yard.

"No," Wilson said sharply. If Carter knows more than he's telling me, he'll be able to boil the list down to prime suspects much faster than I can. "I was hoping you would..."

"That's the first thing I'll do," Carter said, interrupting. "Do you anticipate carrying out the KaneWeller merger, or have the deaths of Daniel Redd and Cheryl O'Grady changed things?"

"I don't know yet," Wilson said, struck by Carter's decisiveness and his sudden return to analytical detachment. He must know more than he's telling me. "If Daniel's law firm fails to produce and/or adequately explain the requested files, KaneWeller may have legitimate cause to back out of the deal. On the other hand, if the law firm hands over the files, KaneWeller may choke on the information. Either way, there's a good chance they'll back out."

"What then?" Carter asked as the two of them entered Harvard Yard through Johnston Gate.

"Fielder & Company becomes a stand-alone entity again," Wilson said.

"Who would assume control of the operation?"

"I would," Wilson said, anxious to see how Carter would respond.

"After what happened to your father? That's foolhardy."

"Who else is going to stop the carnage?" Wilson said goadingly. "If KaneWeller backs out, no other firm will consider acquiring Fielder & Company for at least a year."

"Whoever disposed of Daniel will do the same to you," Carter said with surprising intensity. "You must assume that the people watching us have sufficient means to get away with anything. And I do mean *anything*."

Wilson stopped in front of the Widener Library to search Carter's eyes. What Carter had said was true. So why isn't he telling me everything? For protection? There's only one way to find out. "Then I'll have to convince them to trust me."

"You expect to reason with these people?"

"Why not? What better way to expose them?"

"The journey could damage you more than you can imagine."

Wilson's eyes narrowed as he responded, "If the deal with KaneWeller goes sour, I don't see an alternative. I didn't ask for this mess, but I can do something about it."

"Take perspective, Wilson," Carter said, as they faced each other in the quad between the Widener Library and Memorial Church. All of a sudden there were students everywhere. "Do you honestly believe that saving the world from one more corrupt conspiracy will make a difference?"

"Of course I do, and so do you."

"Don't be so sure."

"Then why work so hard to keep your students from succumbing to the misinterpretations of one more historian? Why write so prolifically about what we haven't learned from history's bitter ironies? Why help me document the abuses at Fielder & Company? I'll tell you why. To be free from lies. Your whole life has been about saving the world from one more corruption—one more lie. I was your student for two years, remember?"

Carter contemplated Wilson for several moments as passing students stared. "You are your father, Wilson," he said warmly. "You have his gift for distinguishing the core of things. I saw traces of it in you at Princeton, but you have travelled well beyond those days. Your father would be proud."

Wilson appreciated the comment but winced at "would". He remained silent.

"You may be right about my longing to save humanity, but I assure you, it is not necessarily a godly trait," Carter said with a solemn face.

Wilson smiled at the conundrum.

"If you decide to proceed with this," Carter continued, "you may not be able to protect the people you love."

"I'm working on that," Wilson said as they resumed walking.

When they walked past Memorial Church, Carter slowed and turned to Wilson. "Leaping into the abyss rarely offers an attractive reward-to-risk ratio," Carter said.

Wilson attempted to hold his gaze, but Carter had already picked up the pace again.

"Who do you trust at Fielder & Company?" Carter asked as they continued walking toward Robinson Hall.

"No one."

"Keep it that way."

Wilson nodded. Reconfirm the obvious.

"You know your every move will be scrutinized," Carter said.

"I won't be able to stomach the charade for long, I know that. Days, maybe weeks, definitely not months," Wilson said when they arrived at the entrance to Robinson Hall, where Carter was scheduled to give a lecture in five minutes. He invited Wilson to listen in, but Wilson declined. He still had to find a solution to everyone's safety.

"Tedious and treacherous, requiring immense patience and resolve. The stress on you and everyone around you will become unbearable. And the surveillance will only get worse," Carter said, looking every bit the adventurer ready to embark on a new crusade.

Wilson nodded again, resigning himself to the reality that Carter, like his father, would never divulge anything before he was completely ready to do so. And right now, Carter was primarily preoccupied with Wilson's safety, which left Wilson only one option—choose a course of action that would make Carter encourage him or stop him.

"Let's hope we make it," Wilson said.

They shook hands and arranged to meet again once Carter had been able to study the files. Walking away from Robinson Hall, Wilson felt like an overloaded pack mule. The looming prospect of taking over the helm at Fielder & Company unnerved him, but it seemed there was no other way to correct his father's mistakes.

13

Tate – St. Moritz, Switzerland

Wayland Tate entered his suite at Suvretta House and deposited his gloves and parka on the entryway settee. He'd received Marco's confirmation call a few hours earlier when he was on the slopes with clients. Everything had gone as planned. No loose ends. The promised funds had already been wired. Although extreme measures weren't Tate's first choice, he never hesitated to use them when necessary.

Tate opened the door to the adjoining suite where he found Diane Morita waiting for him at a marble table near the arched window. She looked dazzling in her red Japanese silk robe, but they had work to do. As he sat down at the table, Morita commented that the sun had accentuated the lines around his eyes, giving him a sexy weathered look. His only response was to retrieve a tube of eye cream from the bathroom.

"Where are the next two retreats?" Tate asked when he returned to his seat at the table and began gently applying the cream to the area around his eyes.

Morita smiled at his vanity. Turning her attention to the calendar spread out in front of her, she said, "Banff and Capri."

"What do you think David Quinn would prefer? Snow lodge or Roman Villa?" Tate asked.

"Vargas says he's totally relaxed and skiing his brains out. Seems he also has a thing for Banff."

"Okay. It's a little sooner than I'd like, but we can be ready. I'll invite him tonight. Make sure Kamin's available for Banff."

Morita nodded and then gave her long black hair a flip over her shoulder as she looked directly at Tate. "I think it's time to expand Vargas' role."

Tate sat back in his chair to observe her. Diane Morita had fastidiously handled Tate Waterhouse's diverse array of client entertainment needs for the past seven years, including all the arrangements for Tate's three-dozen client extravaganzas each year. Her MBA from Stanford and fifteen years of human resources experience at the Walt Disney Company had prepared her well, but it was a personal tragedy and an intimate relationship with Tate that had ultimately honed her unique client-handling techniques.

Ten years earlier, shortly after joining Tate Waterhouse as vice president of human resources, Morita had gone through an ugly divorce followed by a romantic fling with Tate, who'd just separated from his wife. When Tate ended the affair a few months later because he felt she was getting too attached, Morita tried to kill herself with an overdose of prescription drugs. It was Tate who rescued her and then nursed her back to health. Now, in addition to being business associates, they were friends with benefits. The bond that had developed between them during her recovery, however, went much deeper than sexual intimacy. What they'd discovered was a mutual lust for the emotional highs that came from exploiting the concealed flaws and obsessions of the world's powerful elite. Like mythical gods toying with mere mortals, they shared a common vision of eternal glory—whoever manipulates most and best is the one and only true god. Their united lust for manipulation had become Tate Waterhouse's most distinctive competence, something Tate playfully referred to as an unfair competitive advantage. And they made sure that each of the firm's personal assistants possessed a natural affinity for it. Tate smiled appreciatively at Morita. "What did you have in mind for Vargas?"

"Client coordinator on the America's Warehouse campaign," Morita said, smiling back.

Tate raised his eyebrows slightly as he watched Morita. "She'll be in daily meetings with him."

"Exactly," Morita said, looking as sly and cunning as a minx.

"You still believe she can penetrate Quinn's armor of tradition and habit?" Tate asked, continuing to feel somewhat skeptical about Vargas' ability to get Quinn into bed with her. If she could, it would make Quinn's continued compliance that much smoother. But experience told him that piercing the veil of marital fidelity wouldn't be easy with a legacy-driven moralist like Quinn. Unless, that is, recent pressures had opened more cracks than Tate realized.

"Unquestionably," Morita returned, her eyes like steel.

"He may be warming up to her, but I don't see him going that far, at least not in the near term. Our best bet is to stay focused on his zeal to create a legacy," Tate said.

"I don't have a problem with our strategy. Quinn wants the corporate hall of fame; we'll give it to him. But there's a hidden recklessness in the man, beneath his corporate exterior. It's not just posthumous glory he wants."

"Based on what?" Tate asked, growing more curious.

"Asking you to manipulate the board. His willingness to sue Kresge & Company. And the comment about Wilson Fielder."

"He hasn't sued Kresge yet," Tate said, before pausing a moment, then he added, "What comment are you talking about?"

"He told Vargas that he wouldn't hesitate resorting to dirty tricks to get Wilson off his back."

"That's just talk," Tate said, downplaying the comment to see how Morita would respond. "He said the same thing to me at the Kurhaus."

"My first impression as well. Then Vargas told me about his skiing. He takes risks. Reckless chances. Vargas grew up on skis; her parents were ski patrol at Aspen for years. I think her father still is. Trust me, she's good. Quinn scared her today, doing figure eights on a near vertical slope with a cliff halfway down. She almost lost it."

Tate leaned back in his chair again, this time crossing his legs and folding his arms with a sardonic smile forming on his lips. "Maybe he's more frustrated than I realized."

"Suppressed desires," Morita said. "He's lapping up her praises like a schoolboy and she believes he's vulnerable. Getting her more involved will allow us to monitor him more closely, just in case he begins to mourn any of his lost integrity."

"You think Vargas can pull it off?"

"When we give Quinn what he wants, his euphoria will have to go somewhere. Just like it did today. In that sort of situation, Vargas could make anyone vulnerable."

"Are we vulnerable?" Tate asked.

"Vargas' net worth passed the ten million mark last week. She's elated and she likes Quinn. Give her a few weeks, and she'll have him buying her diamonds."

"That's not what I mean. Are we vulnerable if we let Vargas get closer to us?"

"Absolutely not. I know this girl. She's like you and me. She loves what she does."

"Remind me, what's our contingency with her?" Tate asked, knowing full well what the contingency protocol was for Andrea Vargas, in case she ever decided to blow the whistle on Tate Waterhouse or any of its clients. There were contingency protocols for each of the personal assistants who worked with Tate Waterhouse's most preferred clients. To earn the seven figure incomes that went along with escorting such clients, each personal assistant had to designate a member of her family or a close personal friend for ongoing surveillance. The unspoken implication was that, if she ever divulged sensitive information about the internal workings of Tate Waterhouse and its clients, someone close to her would suffer. Tate wanted to make sure Morita had been thinking about Vargas' contingency protocol and was satisfied with it.

"Her parents," Morita said. "She knows the game and the stakes. And she loves playing it."

"I'll talk to Boggs & Saggett about the new assignment when we get back. Then I'll talk to Vargas. In the meantime, let's figure out how to deepen her commitment to us. Maybe a special bonus of Musselman stock if she breaks him," Tate said as he stood up.

"I'm going to take a shower before dinner."

"Would you like some company?"

"Will your offer stand for a few hours?" he asked with a charming smile. "Right now I'm in desperate need of some down time before the mingling resumes—and a chance to visualize Quinn's wilder side."

"The offer expires at midnight," Morita said temptingly.

During a luxurious dinner buffet at Rotisserie des Chevaliers, Wayland Tate and Jules Kamin enthusiastically informed David Quinn that Musselman's Chairman of the Board, James MacMillan, had made it official: instead of breaking up the company, Tate and Kamin would be discussing Wilson Fielder's mismanagement of the Kresge consulting project at next week's board meeting.

"What did MacMillan say?" Quinn asked anxiously. James MacMillan had mentored Quinn earlier in his career. Quinn returned the favor by asking MacMillan to be Musselman's chairman. At age seventy-eight, MacMillan was healthier than most forty- year-olds. He'd been the perfect chairman, giving Quinn free reign as CEO, until profits started declining a couple of years ago. That's when things had changed, much to Quinn's dismay. MacMillan's deep sense of fiduciary responsibility to Musselman's shareholders had caused him to get increasingly involved in company issues. Now Quinn wanted his former mentor off his back.

"He asked a lot of questions about Wilson's father, mostly out of curiosity, I think," Tate said. "Then he asked about Fielder & Company. He was especially interested in why *The Wall Street Journal* had dubbed it the most secretive consulting firm in America. When we finally got around to discussing Wilson, I told him that I'd done some probing and discovered that Wilson exhibited the same tendencies of mental instability as his father. I also said that he had serious problems with authority figures, in general, just as we discussed. I informed him that Wilson was seeing a psychologist about his extreme behavior and growing irrationality."

"He believed you?" Quinn's eyes grew wide.

"Let's just say it's impossible to disprove a negative," Tate said, enjoying the drama. "One threatening cloud can convince anyone of an impending storm."

"You're sure he's convinced?"

"Kresge & Company's presentation has been postponed indefinitely," Tate said with a wily smile. "Jules and I will make some summary comments next week, but I think the project is going to be permanently buried. MacMillan seemed particularly concerned when I informed him that Wilson had been seeing a clinical psychologist. Of course, I didn't mention that the psychologist was his girlfriend or that they broke up several months ago. By the time I was finished, he began discussing avenues of redress against Kresge & Company."

"Beautiful! Absolutely beautiful," Quinn said, reaching over and squeezing Tate's shoulder. The three of them burst into mercenary laughter, tinged with relief in Quinn's case.

When their laughter died down, Quinn became serious again, wanting more assurances.

"Did he seem at all suspicious or reluctant?"

"Not at all," Tate said. "He thanked me for doing my homework. You were right. The fact that I had recommended Fielder & Company instead of Kresge & Company a few months ago made me even more credible."

For the next hour, the three of them strategized about the timing of Musselman's next public stock offering and how to put J. B. Musselman on Fortune's top ten list of most admired companies. To Tate's pure delight, Quinn was spinning into executive bliss.

After dinner, Tate invited Quinn to the Banff retreat.

"My most memorable day of skiing was at Banff fifteen years ago," Quinn said before pausing a moment, "Until today, that is."

"I heard about your figure eights in the powder above the Diavolezza Bowl," Tate said with raised eyebrows. "Here's an opportunity to do it all again next week. We can finalize everything, America's Warehouse grand opening and the Musselman stock offering."

Quinn was silent for a few moments before he grinned broadly and said, "I'll be there."

There was another round of toasts to skiing and lavish corporate retreats before they decided to call it quits for the evening. Tate excused himself from Quinn and Kamin who were sharing a few last minute thoughts on how to reduce Musselman's ballooning debt in the next stock offering. As soon as Tate had left the dining room, he called Vargas to inform her that their dinner had concluded and that Quinn was feeling rather euphoric. Then he dialed Morita's cell. "It's 11:40 and I'm on my way."

"I'll be ready and waiting," Morita said seductively.

Fiery melodies and exotic rhythms from a Spanish guitarist and his band wafted beguilingly through the hotel lobby, as Quinn returned to his room. Still on cloud nine, he decided to stop at the Club Bar and enjoy the music. The crowd was abuzz as he slowly made his way to the bar and ordered a scotch. While surveying the scene around him, he spotted Vargas alone at the end of the bar.

She looked up in feigned surprise when he sat down next to her. Quinn's suspicions about Vargas' true intentions were gone. And despite his occasional discomfort with Tate's aggressiveness and unpredictability, he knew that Tate was the only member of Musselman's board who could have accomplished what he did today. For that, Quinn was deeply grateful to Tate and his entire organization.

Quinn and Vargas enjoyed the romantic music, the drinks, and each other until the band stopped playing around two. As they said goodnight in the foyer, Vargas leaned in to kiss Quinn on the cheek, the way friends do when saying hello or good-bye. At the last second, Quinn turned slightly and kissed Vargas on the lips.

She responded with a soft and sensual "hmmm." Then she stroked his neck lightly with her fingers before leaving for her room. They agreed to meet in the lobby at eleven to share a limo to the airport.

14

Wilson – Cambridge, MA

It took three calls for Wilson to track down the former head of covert ops for the CIA and founder of Greene Mursin International. After an exchange of pleasantries and a heads-up from Wilson about the telephone scrambler he was using, Hap Greene assured him that his end of the conversation was also protected. Wilson gave Hap a ten-minute summary of everything that had happened during the past few days. Then he asked, "How long will it take you to clear the decks?"

"Give me a week. I'll meet you at the Bostonian Club next Thursday for lunch," Hap said. "But I need to warn you, this could get expensive."

"Not an issue. I'll see you Thursday. In the meantime …"

Hap cut him off. "An advance team will arrive tomorrow to perform an initial assessment and begin surveillance. I'm also going to send you a package of surveillance busters. You'll have them in the morning. And don't move your father. My guys will keep him protected. I want to assess the entire situation first. Moving your father will send a message that you're preparing for battle. We need to be ready before we send that message."

"Just make sure nothing happens to him."

"My guys will be there by morning. Don't do anything rash. I can hear the anxiety in your voice. Focus on deciding what you're going to do with Fielder & Company. Let me worry about protecting you and your family. If you need to reach me, call this number. Otherwise, my people will be in contact with you as soon as they arrive."

When they hung up, Wilson left Brattle House to join his mother and sister who were already at the hospital. There still had been no change in his father's condition. Dr. Malek was slightly more optimistic after the latest round of tests, but with a disturbing caveat: his father might remain in his present condition for years.

A reclining chair next to his father became Wilson's bed, after his mother and sister left at midnight. Two police officers and two security guards from Weintraub, Drake, Heinke & Redd remained on duty all night, monitoring every medical interaction and procedure. This had greatly reduced Wilson's lingering concern about not moving his father. At seven o'clock in the morning, as he watched his father breathe, Wilson began a one-sided conversation, expressing a flood of concerns and questions.

"Why didn't you tell me about what you were doing at Fielder & Company? Thanks to your strict instructions, Daniel only gave me bits and pieces. And now, Carter's doing the same thing. Everyone's going to be dead before I figure it out. How can I correct your mistakes if I don't understand them?" Wilson asked, frustrated at the impossibility of a response.

Suddenly, there was movement in his father's left hand. Wilson squeezed his hand and cried, "Dad, it's me." But there was no more movement. He called for Dr. Malek, who'd just arrived at the hospital. He came within minutes. A battery of pupillary reflex tests was performed to determine any changes in his condition. The room quickly filled with nurses, policemen, and hired security personnel. But there was nothing. Only the almost imperceptible rise and fall of his father's chest, his perilously shallow breathing. Wilson asked Dr. Malek to call him immediately if there was any further sign of movement or consciousness.

"We'll keep him under close observation for the rest of the day," Malek said. "This is a good sign though. I think he likes having you here. Did you say anything especially stimulating? Something he would definitely want to address?"

"I had an entire conversation with him about things he needs to address," Wilson said nervously.

"He may have heard everything. But the slight movement in his hand was all he could do to communicate," Dr. Malek said.

Wilson stared at the doctor, wondering whether his father had tried to encourage or restrain him.

An hour later, the door to his father's room opened. One of the security guards informed Wilson that two men were there to see him. Wilson ran his fingers through his unkempt hair and tucked in his shirt as he got up from the chair. He met the two men in the corridor outside his father's room. Both men stood over six feet and looked extremely fit, with eyes that seemed to take in everything. One was Caucasian, the other African American. These have to be Hap's men, Wilson thought.

They introduced themselves as Driggs and Savoy, confirming that they worked for Hap Greene. Four other team members were already establishing a base of operations near the hospital. Hap had briefed them last night, but they wanted Wilson to give them some additional background.

Thirty minutes later, Wilson and Savoy left the hospital for Brattle House, where three packages of electronic surveillance-busting equipment were waiting for them. For the next two hours, Wilson and Savoy searched the house for electronic bugging devices using a handheld state-of-the-art surveillance buster, with enough detection power to ferret out any electronic bug within thirty feet of its sensory nodes. They found eight bugs distributed throughout Brattle House.

With Savoy's concurrence, Wilson decided to leave each of the bugs in place, allowing the surveillance crowd to believe the devices had not yet been discovered. The only bug they removed was the one in the belfry library, carefully transferring it to the family room. The library would become the one secure room in the house, and just to make sure, they unpacked the most sophisticated piece of equipment that Hap Greene had sent. It was a hi-tech nullifying device that looked like a Sharper Image sound machine, five inches in diameter and five inches tall, with a nine-inch cube recharging base—much smaller than the one Carter Emerson had given Wilson the day before. According to Savoy, the nullifier could eliminate all possibility of voice detection or recording for a radius of fifty feet around the device. There were two nullifiers in the package. The last package contained four small telephone scramblers designed to prevent electronic surveillance on one or both sides of a telephone conversation.

When his mother and Rachel arrived at the house, having picked up Rachel's husband Darrin at the airport, Wilson gave them hand-written notes. The notes advised them of the listening devices and directed them to the belfry library. The looks of anxiety on their faces were sobering. I have to protect them, Wilson said to himself. Anita, the house manager, took four-year-old Mary, Rachel and Darrin's only child, to the playroom.

Once everyone was in the library with the nullifier on, Wilson introduced Savoy, informed them about the expanded surveillance, and described the equipment Hap Greene had sent. After angrily speculating about how, when, and by whom the bugs had been planted, they agreed that it must have happened when they were in Sun Valley. Wilson then told them about his conversation with Carter and what had happened earlier with his father at the hospital. His mother's eyes widened as he spoke, but she said nothing.

Rachel broke the stillness that had descended on the room.

"How long are we going to leave the bugs in place?"

"At some point, they'll expect us to find and remove them. But for the next week or so, we need to use their bugs to let them know that we're worried enough about our safety to back off and leave them alone."

Nodding his agreement, Savoy said, "You're dealing with what seem to be very unpredictable and dangerous people. We need time to assess the threat and prepare an adequate defense. If they think their listening devices are working, they won't be as likely to employ more sophisticated equipment such as thermal imaging, wall-penetrating cameras, and de-nullifiers."

Just then Anita opened the door to the library. She and little Mary entered. "Sorry for the interruption," Anita said. "There's a Detective Zemke from Sun Valley, who wants to talk to Mr. Fielder. I asked him to wait in the study."

"Thank you, Anita. I'll take care of it," Wilson said, surprised by Zemke's presence in Boston, but even more surprised by the unannounced visit. Looking at Savoy in frustration, he said, "Guess we can't use the nullifier, can we?"

"Not if you expect them to believe you," Savoy said.

Seconds later, Wilson strode into his father's Victorian-style study, furnished with cherry wood shelves and heavy drapes. "Detective Zemke," he said as he closed the double doors behind him.

"Didn't want to bother you, but figured you'd appreciate the latest update on our investigation. I know I would, if it were my father in a coma," Zemke said as he shook Wilson's hand.

"Thank you, detective. Can I get you something to drink?" Wilson asked.

"Oh no, I won't be long," he said as he gazed around the two-story study with its book-lined walls. Then he looked more closely at some of the titles. "Impressive collection," Zemke said.

"My father has been collecting first editions of early American literature ever since I can remember."

"Must be worth a fortune," Zemke returned with a slightly sarcastic edge.

Wilson remained quiet, standing in front of one of the study's brown leather sofas, waiting for Zemke to join him. The detective's congenial curiosity contrasted sharply with the gruff disinterest Wilson had experienced in Sun Valley.

"Smart guy, your father. Guess he could buy anything he wanted."

Wilson's heart beat faster. He didn't respond.

Zemke continued to look around the study for a few moments before he sat down on a matching brown leather sofa across from Wilson. He looked more official this time— light gray slacks and a golf shirt, the same color as his wiry hair, paired with a navy blue blazer. But the same cynical insolence radiated from his penetrating eyes, despite the outward pleasantness.

"We've uncovered a piece of new information since we last talked. The two executed women were daughters of one of your father's business associates," Zemke said, watching closely for Wilson's reaction.

"From Fielder & Company?" Wilson blurted, shocked by the news.

"No. One of your father's clients. Davis Zollinger, Chairman and CEO of Dutton Industries. Know him?"

"No," Wilson said, his head was spinning. "Was he at White Horse?"

"No chance of that. Died six months ago. Apparent suicide. Boston PD's looking into it again."

Reeling with new questions about Zollinger and his daughters and what they had to do with his father, Wilson waited in anguish for Zemke to tell him more.

"Zollinger allegedly shot himself in the head with a .22 LR caliber pistol. Same type of gun used at White Horse. They found him the next day in his office on the twenty-ninth floor of the Dutton Industries Building, downtown Boston."

"You're assuming his death is related to the murder attempt on my father?" Wilson said, leaning forward.

"Won't know that for a while," Zemke said, maintaining his relaxed, authoritative position on the couch, but his bright blue eyes were actively probing Wilson. "There's more here than I thought, especially after your father's attorney was killed. We're stepping up our investigation."

"Good," Wilson managed to say, but without much conviction.

"Boston PD is getting ready to close its investigation into the accident that killed Mr. Redd and Ms. O'Grady. With nothing at the scene of the accident and no charges from Fielder & Company or KaneWeller, there's little reason to keep the case open. If we find a connection to what happened in Sun Valley, they promised to reopen the case," Zemke's sharp eyes were still trained on Wilson, watchful for any reaction.

Wilson's grief and anger over Daniel and his cold-blooded murder, while in the service of Fielder & Company, returned with a vengeance, making him feel guilty and— irrationally—complicit in some way. But Wilson wasn't yet ready to tell the police or any other law enforcement agency about Fielder & Company's dark side. Daniel's words rang in his head: *There are better ways to find out what happened here.* Ironically, following Daniel's advice meant treating his death like an accident—at least until he could prove otherwise. Shaking his head in disgust, Wilson said, "I still can't believe he's gone—and in such a senseless accident."

Zemke studied Wilson for several moments. "By the way," he finally said, raising his chin and looking down his nose at Wilson. "I meant to thank you for the tip you gave me about your father hating guns and favoring his left hand—doesn't make sense that he'd shoot those two women and himself with his right hand. We're considering the possibility that someone tried to make it look like a murder-suicide."

"I continue to believe he's innocent, detective," Wilson said as Daniel's words reverberated in his head. At times like these, Wilson regretted his penchant for bully busting. The way he'd handled Zemke in Sun Valley had not only empowered the detective, but the Boston PD as well. It would only be a matter of time before they began investigating his father's financial and business activities, he thought. "Do you have any other leads?" Wilson asked.

"Nothing right now, but something'll break. Always does."

"Thank you, detective," Wilson said, standing up and waiting to escort Zemke to the front door.

Ignoring Wilson's attempt to conclude the conversation, Zemke dug deeper. "Apparently, Davis Zollinger was a longtime associate of your father's."

"I wouldn't know," Wilson said, annoyed by Zemke's persistence. "I haven't been involved in my father's business. I only know a handful of his clients and associates."

"Your father's firm helped Dutton Industries sell off some of its divisions. I don't understand all those financial manipulations, but I'd wager that you *do*," Zemke said, making no attempt to veil the accusation.

Wilson cringed at the detective's tone and his choice of words. "I'm a management consultant, detective, not an investment banker," Wilson retorted, feeling more vulnerable by the second.

"Has anyone ever tried to blackmail your father?" Zemke asked.

"Not that I know of, why?" Wilson said, sitting down again while keeping his eyes fixed on Zemke.

"Zollinger's daughters tried to get the FBI to investigate their father's death. Claimed their father was a member of some sort of secret society that was blackmailing him into siphoning money out of Dutton Industries. When their father decided to go to the authorities, he was killed."

"What did the FBI find?"

"Not a thing. Pretty much closed the investigation after a couple of months. Lack of evidence. Considered it to be one more unsubstantiated conspiracy theory. According to friends of the family, the daughters went into hiding out of fear for their lives. Said they'd received a bunch of threatening phone calls."

"That explains the phony IDs."

"Sounds pretty farfetched, huh?" Zemke said, beginning to believe that Wilson indeed knew very little about his father's business activities.

Wilson didn't respond to Zemke's probe.

"We need access to Fielder & Company's files. Any problems with that?"

"Not at all," Wilson pretended. "Contact Weintraub, Drake, Heinke & Redd. They're the company's legal counsel," Wilson said, nervously questioning whether Bill Heinke would be able to restrict the scope of access to Fielder & Company's files afforded to Zemke, the Boston PD, or the FBI. He wanted to prevent a full-blown, asset-freezing investigation into his father's life and business practices. He needed to go through his father's files at Fielder & Company before they did, cleansing them if necessary. Not because he wanted to obstruct justice, he just needed to slow things down until the estate was liquidated and his loved ones were protected.

"We'll be in touch." Zemke stood up abruptly. As the detective was about to leave the house, he turned to Wilson. "Before Boston PD closes the Daniel Redd case, do you have any reason to believe that his death was something other than an accident?"

"No," Wilson said. Then, with feigned surprise, he asked, "Do you?"

Zemke trained his eyes on him like a hawk ready to snatch its prey, but Wilson didn't flinch.

"Be careful, Mr. Fielder. Seems your family has chosen a dangerous business," he said as he turned and walked away.

Wilson watched Zemke stroll to his car, troubled by what an intensified investigation might bring. When he went back inside the house, his mother was in tears. Rachel, Darrin, and Savoy were standing next to her in the foyer hallway. "What's wrong," he cried.

"She just received a threatening phone call," Rachel said, her voice trembling with fear and anger.

"Do we have any idea who it was?" Wilson asked, putting his arms around his mother while looking at Savoy.

His mother shook her head. "No. Just a man's voice."

"My team initiated a trace, but the signal was bouncing. These guys are professionals and very serious," Savoy said.

"What did he say?" Wilson asked.

"He said you were putting the family in danger. They want you to stop asking questions and stop helping the police. He said if you ignore his warning, our family will pay the consequences," his mother said before bursting into tears.

Wilson could see the terror in her eyes. He wrapped her in his arms again, attempting to console her. But inside his anger was raging, as fifty-two avenues of retaliation flew through his head.

"I think we should call the police right now," Rachel said, feeling powerless.

"No," her mother said, emphatically. "Let Wilson do what he's planned."

Wilson continued comforting his mother for several minutes before excusing himself. He went to the library. Emily needed to come to Boston as soon as possible. He picked up the phone. The scrambler was attached but not turned on.

After two rings, Emily answered, "Wilson?"

"Yeah, it's me."

"Finally. I've been worried sick. How's your father?"

Wilson gave her a brief description of his father's condition. Then, after telling her to hang on a minute, he turned on the scrambler and said, "Don't say a word. The phones are bugged. I just turned on a scrambler at my end so they can hear you but not me."

For the next three minutes he told her about the surveillance, Daniel Redd, Hap Greene, and everything that had happened in the past few days, including the threat to his mother. He also told her about his plan to make the surveillance crowd think they were afraid and distancing themselves from his father's business affairs. When he finished, he turned the scrambler off again.

"I'm back. Sorry. My mother's not in very good shape. She received a threatening phone call a few minutes ago from the people who shot my father. They think I'm a threat, which is ridiculous. All I want to do is sell Fielder & Company and give my father the best medical care we can find. You and I have a lot to talk about. How soon can you come to Boston? I'd come to you, but there's too much going on here for me to leave right now."

Emily remained silent in utter disbelief, but she immediately understood Wilson's dilemma. She wanted nothing more than to be with him.

"I've been so foolish, Em."

"Oh God, Wilson. We've both been foolish."

"I miss you. More than you know. "

"You have no idea," she said before promising to be on an airplane the day after tomorrow, once she'd turned her patients over to colleagues and wrapped up a few other loose ends.

As they hung up, he vowed to never again cause their separation.

15

Wilson – Boston, MA

Wilson stepped into the newly renovated lobby of the Harry Wilson Fielder Building, located on the Charles River in Boston's Back Bay near Copley Square. His great-grandfather had built the ten-story edifice in 1921. Two security guards approached—not the usual uniformed types, more like undercover agents—quickly recognizing Wilson and escorting him to the elevators. One of them pushed the button to the executive offices on the top floor, while asking Wilson about his father. Wilson responded with a brief update.

Once inside the elevator riding up to his father's office, he felt strange knowing that the office would be empty. When Wilson got off on the tenth floor he was greeted by another security officer, who seemed to expect him. The guard asked if he needed help finding anything.

"No, thank you," Wilson answered, heading toward his father's office. The most secretive consulting firm in America, Wilson said to himself, repeating words from a recent edition of *The Wall Street Journal*. The article stated that his father was considered by many to be one of the most brilliant business minds in America, having turned Fielder & Company into a highly influential corporate priesthood, with offices in Boston, Chicago, Dallas, San Francisco, London, and Hong Kong. But now there were only clouds of doubt and suspicion hovering over his father's firm and legacy.

He walked through a maze of corridors lined with contemporary art to his father's office and was surprised to see so many staffers and consultants working at their desks after hours. Luckily, Anne Cartwright, his father's senior administrative assistant, was sitting at her desk outside his father's office. She stood up to greet him.

"I'm glad you're here, Anne," Wilson said.

"It's nice to see you, Mr. Fielder," she said, looking surprised. Then, softly, she asked, "How's your mother doing? I talked to her this morning about your father, she seemed so worried."

"She's doing fine, all things considered," Wilson said, feeling uncomfortable. He didn't like the idea of putting his mother through more pain, but they had to talk, either tonight or tomorrow morning. He couldn't wait any longer. "Thanks for asking."

"Is there something I can do for you, Mr. Fielder?"

"Please, call me Wilson," he said, looking around to see if anyone else could hear him. The nearest desk was empty. "I'd like to look through some of my father's files."

"Mr. Emerson was here today. I gave him access to all the files, just as you requested."

"Thank you, Anne. Hopefully, his history of the company will help us dispel some of the rumors."

Anne nodded hesitantly. "Let me show you where things are and you can help yourself."

She obviously wasn't used to giving such free reign to anyone other than his father. Anne was a tall, professional-looking woman in her late fifties with an expression of sadness in her eyes. Wilson let her unlock the office door, even though he had his father's key. "How many people have keys to this office?" he asked.

"Just myself, the security company, and, of course, your father had his key."

Wilson nodded as he followed Anne into the office. He could almost feel his father's presence in the room. The wall of glass overlooking the Charles River, the elaborate

Italian renaissance ceiling, the exposed columns of stone, the collection of unusual books and curious artifacts from around the world, it all reflected his father's eclectic tastes.

At the far end of the sizeable office was his father's workstation, which covered an entire wall. A variety of electronic devices and gadgetry were spread across the built-in black walnut desk. Two fax machines, a paper shredder, three computer screens, two printers, a scanner, three flat-screen TVs, stereo equipment, and four telephones. There were also a number of family pictures from their travels around the world, which brought a new wave of emotions. Wilson looked away to stay focused. A few feet in front of the workstation was a gray stone conference table, oblong and irregular in shape, surrounded by seven black leather wing chairs.

Emotions returned as Wilson remembered a time, eight months earlier, when he'd come to talk about his career at Kresge & Company. Secretly, Wilson had wanted his father to say, Why don't you come to work for me? Even though he probably never would have accepted, he still wanted the invitation. But his father had never asked. He remembered wondering whether his father was waiting for him to make the overture, asking outright: I'd like to join you at Fielder & Company. Now, he wished he had. Maybe both of them had been too proud or too fearful of rejection. Or was my father simply trying to protect me? Mental images of his father in the hospital brought him back to the present, as Anne opened the twelve file cabinets on each side of his father's workstation.

"How long do you need me to stay?" Anne asked.

"You can go home when you like, Anne. I'll be here for a few hours. I've got my father's keys, so I can lock up," Wilson said, taking the keys from his pocket. "Do I have everything I need?"

She examined the keys closely before showing him which ones were file keys, office keys, and building keys. Then, she held up an oddly shaped gold key. "This one opens the vault in the clothes closet," she said, pointing to the bookshelves at the other end of the office, past the matching French sofas and large wrought iron and glass coffee table in the sitting area. "You also need to key in the password HWF1952. I haven't given Mr. Emerson or anyone else access to the vault."

They both walked toward the wall of bookshelves. Wilson opened the shelf-faced door leading to a private bath, shower-steam room, and large walk-in closet. His father's wardrobe filled the racks and drawers of the closet. Over the years, he'd occasionally borrowed his father's clothes, having worn the same-sized pants and jackets since he'd turned twenty.

"It's on your right, behind the suit coats. Only your father had this key," Anne said before handing the keys back to Wilson. Then she excused herself.

After inserting the key and entering the password, he opened the concealed vault. Inside he found a solitary folder containing a computer disk and a paper printout of all the corporations, general and limited partnerships, limited liability companies, investment trusts, stocks, bonds, and other money instruments in which his father held partial or controlling interests. He'd seen a similar list in Daniel's office. Many of the entities had Nevada and Wyoming addresses, others had Nevis and Cayman Island addresses, and still others had Swiss addresses. His father had obviously gone to great lengths to protect his privacy and conceal his assets. Under Nevada and Wyoming state law, only one name and signature was required to register a business entity, making it easy to keep owners and officers anonymous. Wilson could appreciate the appeal of Nevada and Wyoming, the most secretive states in the union. And Nevis, a tiny island country in the Caribbean, had even more favorable and flexible offshore banking laws than the Cayman Islands or Switzerland.

According to the latest update of the files a month earlier, his father owned or controlled one hundred and ninety-eight different entities or instruments, each of which held ownership positions in a wide variety of publicly and privately held corporations. After reexamining the long list of additional investments, Wilson breathed a sigh of relief, having found no indication that his father owned shares in

Zollinger's Dutton Industries, Zebra Technology, or any of the companies identified in Daniel Redd's fifty-two files.

However, there was more in the concealed vault—an old book, *Capitalism's Flaw* by William Tate Boyles, and a stack of loose papers and press clippings. He opened the cloth-covered book. It was a publisher's bound proof. The pages were worn with age and brown at the edges. There was an inscription from his great-grandfather to his grandfather in blotchy blue ink, faded but still legible.

Dear Son,   *December 25, 1935*
I tried to dissuade William from writing this book because it has placed his life in grave danger. Nonetheless, it is a vitally important work and you should be aware of its contents. It explains the real forces behind this nation's debilitating depression. Lord Montagu Norman of the Bank of England is one of the vilest practitioners of the evil gift in our times. But he is only one of a corrupt society. Benjamin Strong of the New York Federal Reserve Bank, Hjalmar Schacht of the German Reichsbank, and the entire House of Morgan are also nefarious practitioners. Whether the Hoover Administration and Lord John Maynard Keynes were active participants or mindless facilitators is, at present, uncertain.

These are indeed desperate times, not merely because of the human suffering brought on by our economic woes,

but also because of the mystification and manipulation
wrought by hidden tyrants in high places. They are the
authors of our needless woes and suffering, but now is not
the time to expose them. We have neither the resources
nor the mandate. The best we can do is protect ourselves
and those around us from the corruption.

I hope you can enjoy some peace during the holidays.
Merry Christmas,
Father

After pondering the inscription, Wilson read the book's introduction. It was a compelling summary of how a handful of men brought about the stock market crash of 1929 and the Great Depression of the 1930s, simply because they wanted to slow middle-class wealth creation in America and shift economic power back to Europe. According to the book, the flaw in capitalism was that it allowed elite private corporations with captive customers and government protection—such as the Federal Reserve, international banks, stock exchanges, and insurance companies—to preserve their power and wealth at the expense of the masses. Capitalism's first movers had used their early success to structure the system to their advantage and entrench their control.

Wilson reflected on the many conversations with his father about corrupt authority and exploitation. They were conversations that had fueled his deep-seated distrust of authority. He quickly scanned the rest of the book, but he was preoccupied with reflections on what sort of men his great-grandfather and grandfather had been.

He turned his attention to the stack of loose papers. The press clipping on top of the stack was a *New York Times* article about the death of Congressman Louis T. McFadden in 1936. Wilson sat down on the floor and began to read. Congressman McFadden was a Republican from Pennsylvania. He served as chairman of the Banking and Currency Committee of the United States House of Representatives from 1920 to 1931. According to hand-written notes on some of the press clippings and documents, McFadden had also been a close personal friend and associate of Wilson's great-grandfather, Harry Wilson Fielder.

On May 23, 1933, Congressman McFadden brought formal charges against the Board of Governors of the Federal Reserve System, the Comptroller of the Currency, and the Secretary of the United States Treasury for numerous criminal acts, including, but not limited to, conspiracy, fraud, unlawful conversion, and treason. From the floor of the House of Representatives, Congressman McFadden accused international bankers of orchestrating the stock market crash of 1929 and creating the nation's Great Depression. He called the bankers a "dark crew of financial pirates who would cut a man's throat to get a dollar out of his pocket... They prey upon the people of these United States."

Congressman McFadden and Wilson's great-grandfather had worked together with author William Tate Boyles to expose the hidden tyranny of the Federal Reserve and international bankers who controlled the world's credit and money supply, until lives were threatened. Boyles' New York publisher was threatened with the death of his family if he printed *Capitalism's Flaw* and McFadden barely escaped an assassination attempt near the Capitol Building. Wilson's great-grandfather argued vehemently against further attempts to expose the corruption and severely reprimanded McFadden for his increasingly anti-Semitic views. Boyles agreed, but McFadden disregarded the warnings and continued fighting until his untimely death in 1936.

Wilson scanned the news clippings from *The New York Times*, *The Wall Street Journal*, and other major newspapers about Congressman McFadden's speeches between 1932 and 1934. Congressman McFadden accused the Federal Reserve Board and the Federal Reserve Banks of being "the most corrupt institutions in the world." He claimed they had impoverished and ruined the people of the United States and almost bankrupted the government. On the floor of the House of Representatives in 1933, Congressman McFadden called the Federal Reserve and its power-over-money supply the greatest conspiracy of modern times. Wilson was captivated by the speech:

Some people think that the Federal Reserve Banks are United States Government institutions. They are private monopolies that prey upon the people of these United States for the benefit of themselves and their foreign customers; foreign and domestic speculators and swindlers; and rich and predatory moneylenders... These twelve private credit monopolies were deceitfully and disloyally foisted upon this country by the bankers who came here from Europe, and repaid us our hospitality by undermining our American institutions. Those bankers took money out of this country to finance Japan in a war against Russia. They created a reign of terror in Russia with our money, in order to help that war along. They instigated the separate peace between Germany and Russia, and thus drove a wedge between the allies... In 1912, the National Monetary Association, under the chairmanship of the late Senator Nelson W. Aldrich, made a report and presented a vicious bill called the National Reserve Association Bill. This bill is usually spoken of as the Aldrich Bill. Senator Aldrich did not write the Aldrich Bill. He was the tool, if not the accomplice, of the European bankers who for nearly twenty years had been scheming to set up a central bank in this country and who in 1912 had spent and were continuing to spend vast sums of money to accomplish their purpose... We were opposed to the Aldrich plan for a central bank. The men who rule the Democratic Party then promised the people that if they were returned to power there would be no central bank established here while they held the reigns of government. Thirteen months later that promise was broken and the Wilson administration, under the tutelage of those sinister Wall Street figures who stood behind Colonel House, established here in our free country the worm-eaten monarchical institution of the "King's Bank" to control us from the top downward, and from the cradle to the grave. It fastened down upon the country the very tyranny from which the framers of the Constitution sought to save us... These men and those who replaced them are still in power and control every aspect of your life. They will not give up a slave just because the slave no longer wishes to be a slave.

After Wilson had finished reading McFadden's other speeches, he found more firsthand accounts and press reports on the assassination attempts against the congressman. In early 1934, two ambush shots were fired at the congressman as he was getting out of a taxi near the Capitol Building. A few months later he became violently ill after dining at a political banquet in Washington D.C. and would have died if not for his friend and physician who was on site to administer an emergency stomach pump. Finally, on October 3, 1936 at age sixty, McFadden died of sudden heart failure after an usual bout with intestinal flu. His associates were convinced he'd been poisoned, but investigations into his death were squelched. Wilson's great-grandfather and William Boyles continued to distance themselves even further from their earlier quest. They vowed to live within the system without being destroyed or corrupted by it, until 1952, when both Boyles and his great-grandfather died.

What Wilson read next from an obscure collection of copied journal pages grabbed him by the throat like a hangman's noose. He literally could not breathe. Just as he was beginning to lose consciousness, he gasped for air. With his heart racing, he read the words again:

> *Harry Wilson Fielder was killed on November 11, 1952, one week after Dwight D. Eisenhower was elected president, in a hit-and-run accident outside his Back Bay office. William Tate Boyles was poisoned two days later and died of a heart attack after being rushed to the hospital. Both men were murdered in order to keep them quiet.*

Wilson's body was still shaking as he read the words again in utter disbelief. He now knew why his father had never told him the truth about his great-grandfather's death. It would have magnified his natural rebellion a hundredfold. He never would have made it to age thirty-one. Now I might not see thirty-two.

As Wilson regained his composure, his shock turning to sadness, he continued to read everything he could find on his great-grandfather. According to a set of journal pages written by Harry's son, Wilson's grandfather, both Harry Wilson Fielder and William Tate Boyles had long feared for their lives. As they grew older, they had been secretly preparing to simultaneously publish their memoirs as witnesses to a hidden tyranny. Extensive notes from Harry's son confirmed that they had indeed been murdered. Investigations into their deaths were taken over by federal authorities and then shelved. Wilson's grandfather never pursued the matter out of fear for his family and in heed to his father's warning.

When Wilson finished reading the journal notes, he sat in the corner of the closet and cried—mourning the death of a murdered great-grandfather he'd never known, but who had shaped his life. It all made such tragic sense. His father had been preparing him all along, without telling him the ugly details. It was like finally uncovering the cause of an ancestral curse—or blessing. Only time would determine which was the case.

He finally left Fielder & Company a little after midnight, resolved to confront his mother first thing in the morning. A new mantra had taken hold of him: revenge and redress are now mine to pursue.

16

Tate – New York City, NY

Looking out at the East River and Governor's Island from his downtown Manhattan office, Wayland Tate mulled over the Musselman stock-manipulation plan he'd received from Jules Kamin. After convincing Musselman's Board of Directors that Wilson Fielder was unstable and incompetent, the twelve directors agreed that the Kresge consulting project had been mismanaged from the beginning. A unanimous vote terminated the project. Now the stage was set to begin manipulating Musselman's stock, but the plan needed tweaking.

Jules Kamin, and John Malouf from Fielder & Company, who'd also worked on the plan, were recommending six successive events designed to maximize the peaks and valleys in Musselman's stock price over the next several weeks. The first event called for a leak to the business press that Kresge & Company had been fired because it concluded that the J. B. Musselman Company had no viable future as presently constituted. The second event to follow two weeks later would come in the form of an announcement that Musselman was hiring the number two man at Costco or Sam's Club to launch a new discount retailing strategy. Four weeks after that, a third event would create a scathing criticism of the America's Warehouse campaign, quickly followed by a spectacular fourth event launching the advertising campaign and grand opening for America's Warehouse. The fifth event called for another leak, six weeks later, this time about merger talks with Wal-Mart executives. At that point, the partnership would cash out its shares of Musselman stock and exit the picture, unless a profitable merger could be executed as a sixth event.

During the three months it would take to execute these six events, Musselman's stock price was expected to fluctuate between an estimated low of twelve dollars and a potential high of ninety, giving the partnership multiple opportunities to sell short and buy long. Prior to the events designed to drive the stock price down, the partnership would short the stock, meaning that it would borrow stock from a brokerage firm and sell it before buying the stock back at a lower price to replace the borrowed shares. Prior to events intended to push the stock price up, the partnership would simply buy long, meaning that they would buy low and sell high. The plan projected that the partnership would net over ten billion dollars in profit without ever letting Musselman's stock price drop more than thirty percent in value during a single week of trading. No red flags would be raised at the SEC or with plaintiff lawyers looking for their next shareholder lawsuit. It would be the most money the partnership had ever plucked from a single client company in a three-month period.

But Tate was concerned that the plan was too tame, and he didn't like the sequence of events or the timing. He attributed the error in judgment to John Malouf, who would never know David Quinn the way Tate did. Conceptually, Malouf was every bit as strong as Charles Fielder, but his perspective favored the inanimate—systems, structures, and strategies. He lacked Tate's sensitivity to human frailty and Kamin's political savvy. Tate asked one of his administrative assistants to get Malouf on his secure line.

When Malouf came on the line, Tate picked his words carefully, "I have some concerns about the stock-manipulation plan."

Malouf was a tall imposing man with a habit of using his words sparingly, especially when it made the other person feel uncomfortable. Like his mentor Charles Fielder, he relished the aura of enigma that surrounded him and he rarely explained himself to anyone. But Malouf had proven his loyalty to Tate on more than one occasion.

"I'm listening," Malouf said now.

"David Quinn needs to be pushed to the brink. I don't think this plan will do it," Tate replied, getting straight to the point.

"He's your client, Wayland. I defer to your judgment."

"Can I run a few suggestions by you?"

"Go ahead," Malouf said.

Gazing at the Brooklyn docks across the river, Tate slowly and precisely communicated his suggestions to Malouf.

"David Quinn will suffer through the first event of Kresge's recommendations getting leaked to the press. It will force him to tell more lies, which is good because it will help deepen his resolve. However, I don't think event two should be designed for an upswing. And if the event is used later, the new head of merchandizing for America's Warehouse must come from inside Musselman, one of Quinn's protégés, who can then hire the rising stars he needs from Costco or Sam's Club. Events three and four should pose no problem as long as the sequencing and timing are modified. Event five has to change. There can be no merger talks, only acquisition talks. Musselman must do the acquiring, keeping Quinn in control. Possible acquisition candidates might include Star

Warehouses or Hardware City, but I'll leave those details to you and Kamin. Event six will pose no problem, as long as it occurs as an acquisition."

"I have no issues with your suggestions. In fact, I told Jules that events two and three were questionable. Rest assured, we'll make the necessary changes," Malouf said.

"Thank you, John," Tate said, suddenly concerned about Kamin. Was he still obsessing about the scuttled merger? "Keep me in the loop."

"Absolutely."

"I assume you'll be ready to execute the first event during the Banff retreat?" Tate asked.

"Yes. Just as you specified," Malouf said.

"Perfect," Tate said. "I'll give you any additional thoughts I have on events two and three by tonight." There was still something else missing from the plan, but for the moment he remained uncertain as to what it was. It would come to him. It always did.

Several hours later, after dealing with a dozen needy clients, Tate breathed deeply as he returned to pondering the Musselman stock-manipulation plan and David Quinn's psyche. Even if the strategy to make America's Warehouse a new leader among mass discounters didn't work, he thought, the marketing campaign alone would drive the stock price up to ninety dollars in less than three months. After that, the business press could assert that Kresge had been right about breaking up Musselman into smaller more manageable pieces, but it wouldn't matter. The partnership would be cashed out, and Boggs & Saggett would continue to be praised for a brilliant advertising campaign. Only Quinn would be blamed for failing to deliver.

On the other hand, if the strategy did work, and Tate still believed it would, there would be much more than ten billion dollars to be made from David Quinn and the J. B. Musselman Company. And that's why the stock-manipulation plan needed something else to lock Quinn into the partnership long term, Tate concluded.

After the plan's first event, when the stock had dropped because of a press leak, Quinn would feel distraught and vulnerable. That would be the time to add another event. An imminent hostile takeover of Musselman by Hardware City would push Quinn from feeling distraught and vulnerable to the brink of utter despair. Musselman didn't have a poison pill to ward off a hostile takeover, and it would never be able to borrow enough money to buy back its own shares because the company already had too much debt. A public stock offering would not only take too long, it would merely exacerbate the problem. And of course selling the company to a friendly suitor would never be acceptable to Quinn, because he'd lose too much control. Quinn's only option to remain at the helm of Musselman, Tate mused with a smile, would be to accept an offer that he and the partnership would devise—an offer that would force Quinn to do something illegal.

Tate picked up the phone and ran the idea past Bob Swatling. Swatling assured Tate that such a maneuver could be successfully orchestrated. It was a manipulation scheme that Charles Fielder would never have allowed, but things were different now. Tate grinned as he stroked his slightly jutting chin, satisfied that this plan would take Quinn to the brink and provide enough leverage to keep him loyal to the partnership for years to come.

Tate called Malouf to tell him about his final modification. Malouf had no objections, assuring Tate that it fit perfectly with their own modifications. He promised to prepare a final draft of the plan and distribute it by encrypted hush mail within the hour. Sixty minutes later, Tate called Kamin to review the final plan. "Do you anticipate any problems with orchestrating the hostile takeover?" Tate asked.

"Not with Hardware City involved; they owe us big time," Kamin said.

They both laughed.

"The only concern I have is David Quinn. Are we pushing him too hard, too fast?" Kamin said.

"I know Quinn. He won't like this, but he'll do it," Tate said.

"What does Swatling think?"

"He's on board," Tate said, put off by Kamin's questions. First he let the KaneWeller situation get out of control, then he ignored Malouf's input on the plan, and now he's questioning my judgment. Is Jules getting soft? Time will tell. Tate shifted gears. "What's happening with the Fielder & Company acquisition?"

"It hasn't died yet, but it will soon," Kamin said.

"It's better this way."

"I'm there, Wayland," Kamin said.

"Good."

After disconnecting, Tate called Swatling to arrange a meeting with Lester Pickering, CEO of Hardware City Stores. Kamin was right. Pickering would jump at the opportunity to make a quick killing in the market, but, more importantly, he would jump at Tate's request, because of past favors. Leverage was such sweet currency.

17

Emily – New York City, NY

Manhattan's Upper West Side was bustling with activity when the taxi dropped Emily Klein at her apartment a little before ten o'clock in the evening. The endless comings and goings had always been one of the main reasons she felt safe living alone in the city. As Emily entered the lobby of her apartment building, she noticed at once that the night security guard was not at his usual post behind the reception desk. Before she had time to become concerned, someone slipped through the door behind her. When Emily turned around, she let out a scream, dropping her shopping bags to the floor. She backed up slowly.

A man with a gun stood in front of her. He was wearing a black leather jacket, a tan T-shirt, and blue jeans. His expressionless eyes and close-cropped hair were dark brown. In a low gruff voice with a British accent he said, "I'm only here to deliver a message, Ms. Klein. Tell your boyfriend to stay out of any investigation into Daniel Redd's death or what happened to his father in Sun Valley. Both of you will live longer that way."

Emily took another step backward until she felt leaves from a planter brushing against her back. She stood motionless.

The intruder stepped toward her until he was literally breathing down her neck. He raised his gun to her left ear and then slowly ran the barrel along her chin to her right ear.

"Convince him not to do anything stupid."

Although Emily started shaking like a leaf, every fiber of her being strained to prevent him from seeing it. With his eyes glued on Emily, the intruder stepped backward toward the entrance door.

"Goodnight, Ms. Klein. Please forgive the intrusion." And then he was gone.

Emily didn't move for several seconds as her body uncoiled. There was still no sign of the security guard. Composing herself, she gathered her shopping bags and took the elevator to her sixth floor apartment where she threw her bags against the wall in utter frustration. She immediately called Wilson's cell phone, but there was no answer. After leaving a message for him to call as soon as possible, she poured a glass of Shiraz to calm her nerves.

When she called the security guard who'd returned to his station in the foyer, she discovered he'd been called to the eighteenth floor on what turned out to be a false alarm. He apologized and asked if she'd encountered any difficulties during his absence. Reluctantly, she said no, deciding to wait until she talked to Wilson. She tried Wilson again. There was still no answer, so she called Brattle House and got Anita, the live-in house manager. She left a message for Wilson to call when he arrived, no matter how late.

For the next hour while waiting for Wilson to return her call, Emily sat in her living room with the bottle of Shiraz, deconstructing her day and its disturbing end. The first thing she'd done was drop off her completed manuscript, *The Psychology of Illusion: Perception, Bias, and Assumed Truths*, at Random House a week earlier than planned. Then she did some last minute shopping on Fifth Avenue. After grabbing a bite to eat at Café Europa on Fifty-Seventh Street, she took a cab to her office at Columbia University where she packed up her remaining personal items, saw a few long-standing clients, and said good-bye to colleagues. In between these preparations to leave for Boston, she reminisced and obsessed about Wilson. No matter what happened in their lives or how many other people they dated, it seemed they kept coming back to each other. Their physical chemistry had been apparent from the first day they met, but it was a deep emotional and spiritual connection that bonded them, despite their very strong-willed natures. They were both fiercely independent people who didn't want anyone telling them what to do. The consequence, not surprisingly, had been an on-again, off-again relationship with some rather painful arguments. While packing items from her office, she began recounting their last big argument eight months earlier, the one that had led to postponing their wedding.

Wilson had flown to New York City for the weekend. During dinner at a trendy Upper West Side restaurant, they began commiserating about how little time they spent together. Several minutes later, after having fully vented their relationship woes, Wilson had asked his dispiriting question.

"Should we consider postponing the wedding until our schedules get lighter?"

Emily became emotional, launching them into a dialogue neither one of them would soon forget.

"I can't believe you'd consider putting us through this again," she said.

"Through what?" he said.

"Through another breakup," she said, throwing her hands into the air.

"This is not a breakup," he said, reaching for her hand, but she withdrew it.

"Seems like one to me."

"Why always assume the worst?"

"Experience!" she said, loud enough for the waiter to come to the table and ask if everything was okay.

"Look," he said in a soft voice, leaning across the table. "As long as I'm in Chicago traveling around the world for Kresge and you're in New York writing books and counseling patients, getting married is only going to make us more frustrated."

"So you want me to give up my practice and move to Chicago?"

"No! I'm just asking whether it makes sense to postpone the wedding until I can move to New York."

"Interesting word, postpone. What does it mean? Defer? Delay? Hold back? What are you holding back, Wilson?"

"I'm not holding anything back. I'm trying to avoid something that could make us feel guiltier than we already do about putting our professional lives first."

"And what's that? Commitment?"

He frowned at her. "Don't do this, Emily."

"I'm not doing anything. You're doing it."

"I just asked a question. What I wanted was a conversation, not an argument."

"You're right. Cancel the wedding. We're not ready for this," she said, standing up. She took off her engagement ring and placed it in the middle of the table. Then she walked out the door and hailed a taxi. Wilson got a hotel room in the Upper West Side for the night.

Early the next morning, door chimes yanked Emily from her sleep. She came to the door a little groggy, still struggling to tie her robe. It was Wilson with a peace offering. Coffee and hot croissants from the Silver Moon Bakery. He put his arms around her, telling her he was sorry and that he wanted to get married as soon as possible. She said she was sorry, too, and that he was right. They should wait until their lives were less out of control before they discussed marriage again.

After a day immersed in their passions, they became more rational and grounded, deciding to postpone the wedding indefinitely. It had all seemed so logical at the time. For the next eight months they both pursued their careers with a vengeance. The last time they'd been together was one hundred and six days ago.

Emily looked at the clock. It had been an hour since she left messages for Wilson. As she took another swallow of wine, her cell phone rang right on cue. It was Wilson's ID. Thank God.

"Emily, you okay?" Wilson said, concerned by the tone of voice in her message. But he didn't turn the scrambler on. He was in no mood for games. Besides, Emily knew the phones were monitored.

"It's so good to hear your voice," Emily said, her voice cracking slightly.

"You sound frazzled. I know I'm asking a lot to have you drop everything and come to…"

She interrupted, "It's not that, Wilson. There's no place I'd rather be right now."

"What is it, Em?"

"A man with a gun followed me into the foyer of my apartment building tonight."

"Oh God! Did he hurt you?"

"No. I'm an emotional wreck, but he didn't hurt me. He gave me a message for you."

"What did he say?" Wilson said, his stomach twisting.

"He said: tell your boyfriend to stay out of any investigation into Daniel Redd's death or what happened to his father in Sun Valley. Both of you will live longer that way."

"That was it?"

Emily hesitated a moment. "Then he said: goodnight, Ms. Klein. Please forgive the intrusion. After that he left," she said, deciding to tell him about the gun barrel along her chin when they were together. She was well acquainted with Wilson's dragon-slayer side. The last thing she wanted was for him to do something irrational, based solely on impulsive emotion—something that could turn out to be stupid.

"God, I'm so sorry, Em. The same message was given to my mother yesterday over the phone. I didn't mention it when we talked because I didn't want to worry you. Things are obviously getting more serious…"

"Whatever it is, we'll deal with it together," Emily said, interrupting again. "I'm fine now. I just needed to hear your voice."

"You're not fine," Wilson said, his voiced raised. "You were just threatened at gunpoint."

"Wilson. I promise you, I'm fine. I'll finish packing in the morning. My plane gets in at two—United 1011."

"I hate bringing you into this nightmare."

"I want to be with you."

"I love you, Em. More than words…"

"I'll be there in less than fourteen hours, then you can show me," she said playfully. "I adore you, Wilson. Please be careful."

How could I have been so stupid to risk losing her? he asked himself. "I'll be there waiting."

After saying good-bye, Emily felt relieved, though the fear that had gripped her in the lobby continued to linger. Nothing mattered more than her relationship with Wilson, no matter how difficult or dangerous his circumstances had become.

18

Wilson – Cambridge, MA

Wilson found his mother in the backyard with the gardener, preparing for spring planting. It was an unusually warm and sunny morning for late March in Boston. He watched her from the verandah. The sun highlighted the copper undertones in her short brown hair, making her seem more youthful than usual. From her outfit—sandals, Capri jeans, and a bright pink jacket over a floral top—she seemed eager for the newness of spring. Wilson was glad to see her up and active.

He reminisced a moment about her motherly tenderness. She had always been there for him, attending to his every need. Regrettably, he'd grown up like most children, more or less oblivious to her personal aspirations and dreams outside of being a wife and mother. In the years after Wilson left home for college, she'd become more introspective. But he'd made no serious effort to find out why. Now he wondered whether it had something to do with his father's business activities. Wilson needed to find out, and she was the only one who could tell him. He walked out into the spacious yard, still unnoticed.

"Good morning," he called out as he got closer.

"Hi, dear, did you get some rest? You got in so late," she said, looking at him with warm but strained eyes. "Anita said Emily called. Is everything okay?"

There could be no more holding back, he thought. "I talked to her last night when I got home," he said before hesitantly proceeding. "She was threatened at gunpoint in the lobby of her apartment building. She received the same message you did."

"Oh no!" she said, horrified. "Did he do anything to her?"

"No, he didn't touch her. But the emotional trauma that both of you have suffered is unforgiveable."

"She needs to be here with you, Wilson."

"I'm picking her up at the airport this afternoon."

"Thank God," she said, her voice breaking. Tears began filling her eyes; she turned toward the verandah. "I can't believe all this is happening. When is it going to end?"

Wilson took her arm and they walked to the house. He loathed the idea of subjecting her to an inquisition of kinds, but he had no choice. "I'm sorry Mother, but I need to ask you some questions."

As their eyes fused he could see her grief. There was a prolonged silence before she finally said, "About your father?"

"Yes."

"I may not have the answers you want," she said, removing the gloves from her hands and setting them on the slate stone verandah. "Let's go upstairs," she whispered.

Once inside the belfry library with the door closed and the nullifier on, they sat down at the round table. Wilson began, "Why did he change his will?"

"He called it a prudent update of our legal affairs, since I had no interest in being involved in any business decisions. I knew he was trying to protect me, but that wasn't the only reason."

Wilson sat back studying his mother. "Mom, I need to know everything. No more secrets."

Tears welled up in her eyes again and began to trickle down her cheeks. She reached for his hand. "Just give me a minute, I'll be fine."

Wilson took her hand in his. Dressing down CEOs was child's play compared to this.

She wiped her eyes and nose with a handkerchief from her jacket pocket. "Okay," she said.

Wilson took a deep breath. "Did you know that his net worth is over seventy billion dollars?"

"Yes," she said evenly, without a hint of surprise.

Wilson wrestled with whether to show her the letter his father had left him. He decided against it for now. He reached into his pocket, removing the folded copies he'd made of the press clippings on Congressman McFadden and the pages about his great-grandfather's death. He handed them to her.

His mother took a few moments to study the copies before leaning back in her chair and closing her eyes. She sighed before opening her eyes again, then in a monotone voice she said, "Before your grandfather died, he regretted sharing this with your father."

"Why?" Wilson asked, remembering little about his grandfather, who'd died when he was six years old. All he could recall was that he had been kind and gentle and went by the name of Wilson.

"Your father was determined to become a writer when he was younger, but his father insisted that he begin presiding over the family's assets and businesses," she said calmly, but her eyes were intense and roaming. She held up the copies of press clippings and journal pages he'd given her. "He used this to convince your father. When he learned that his grandfather had been murdered by the same people who killed McFadden and Boyles, he vowed to change everything. He made drastic changes in the family business, growing it exponentially. He was a natural, as if born to it…" Her voice trailed off.

Wilson remained silent, waiting for his mother to resume her story.

"When your grandfather was near death, suffering from leukemia, he forced a public stock offering of Fielder Industries, which controlled the family's major businesses. He'd hoped your father would sell his shares and return to a literary life. He asked me more than once to forgive him for taking your father away from a more tranquil existence. He was afraid your father would waste his entire life pursuing wealth and seeking revenge," she said, her words becoming more emotion-filled. "I shared the same fear, but by then it was too late. After quadrupling the profits of Fielder Industries in less than two years, your father realized that his business savvy offered him a better way to change the world. When his father died, Charles did sell his shares in Fielder Industries, but he didn't return to a literary life. He started Fielder & Company."

"Why didn't we talk about this when I was growing up?" Wilson asked, leaning forward perplexed.

"Because of his experience with his own father," she said, her eyes were gentle, sympathetic. "He was a lot like you growing up—rebellious and easily upset over any form of injustice or inequity. He swore he'd never coerce you the way his father had coerced him. The irony is that you still chose business as a career, driven by his same desires to cleanse a corrupt system."

"I can't believe we never talked about this..."

"We did. All the time. Especially you and your father, only without the family history," she said, looking away wistfully. "He didn't want you to become burdened like he was."

"Burdened because of Harry's murder?" Wilson asked, burying his hurt over being shut out of family secrets.

His mother shifted her gaze to the ocular window overlooking Cambridge Common. "When your father began assuming the reins at Fielder Industries and started attending business school, his resentment and bitterness changed him. The passion he once had for writing evolved into an obsession for creating wealth. It was all he talked about. He felt more and more responsible for correcting the inequities in society—just like you."

"So he didn't tell me about my great-grandfather to keep me from making the same vow?" Wilson said sarcastically.

"Your father gave his life to this obsession. Neither one of us wanted the same thing happening to you."

"Well, so much for that fucking plan..."

"Wilson, don't. We made mistakes. We were only trying to do what we thought was best for you and Rachel. I'm so sorry," she said. She began crying again.

Wilson's anger softened. "It's not your fault. I grew up with the same damn burden, despite your efforts to shield me. I know you and Dad worried about my anger. And you were right, if I'd known about my great-grandfather when I was younger, it would have made me that much angrier," Wilson said, pausing to reflect. "Where are Harry's memoirs now?"

"Only your father knows," she said. "His father charged him with keeping them safe until they could be put to good use."

Wilson shook his head in disbelief.

"Now you know what's been driving your father for so many years" she said, gently touching his arm. "His grandfather's story had an enormous influence on him. You know that he taught American literature and philosophy at Harvard before starting Fielder Industries. What you don't know is how he speculated on stocks and futures prior to the crash of 1929 and then acquired troubled business assets during the depression. He considered the windfall profits to be both a blessing and a curse. He promised to preserve the blessing for posterity and avoid the curse by giving back to society, trying to make amends for his enormous gains. The company he started in the early 1930s grew so rapidly he never went back to full-time teaching, although he lectured regularly at Harvard and MIT until he died. I only knew him through your father, and your father only knew him through his father and the memoirs. He died when your father was only three." She paused, caught in reflection. "Your father and I used to talk about him a lot. We stopped when you were still young."

"Why? Because of me?"

"No, not entirely," she said, tears filling her eyes again. "I love your father very much, but I couldn't live with his obsession. We found great joy in you and Rachel, but we've lived in different worlds for most of our lives. I'm ashamed to say that I don't really know what's happened at Fielder & Company in the past several years."

"You don't need to..."

"It's okay, Wilson," she said softly. "I was afraid of becoming consumed by his burden so I withdrew to a safe distance. He wanted me to be involved the way I was with his writing, but it wasn't the same," she said, dabbing at her eyes with her handkerchief. "I should have never distanced myself. I could have been stronger."

"Listen to me, Mother," Wilson said, reaching across the table for her hand, which she took and squeezed for a moment. "When I met with him in his office last summer to talk about Kresge & Company, we also talked about marriage. Emily and I had just postponed the wedding. He told me how much he adored you and was looking forward to spending more time with you...living more simply. He actually talked about retirement and writing books. There was a weariness about him. I noticed it, but I didn't say anything. I should have probed further. Both of us should have been stronger."

By this time his mother was sobbing. Wilson felt like a heel for making her cry so much, but it didn't stop him. When she regained composure, he continued, albeit reluctantly.

"Did you know Davis Zollinger, the CEO of Dutton Industries?"

"Yes. He was one of your father's clients."

"Did you know he was found dead in his office six months ago?"

"Yes," she said, nodding her head and dabbing her nose. "Your father said he'd crossed the line, but I wasn't sure what he meant. I decided a long time ago not to ask too many questions. Whenever I did, your father would tell me more than I wanted to know. I don't know what to tell you, Wilson," she said, her voice breaking again.

"Mom, don't. You're not to blame."

"Okay, Wilson. No blame." She nodded, firmly clutching his hand. "Your father called Davis Zollinger a narrow-minded, greedy man who had turned from friend to foe."

"Did you know the two women at White Horse were his daughters?"

"No!" she gasped, placing a hand over her mouth. He could see the pain and suffering in her eyes. She dropped her hands to her lap and closed her eyes for several moments.

When she opened them again, Wilson hated himself for continuing, but he did. She had to know.

"Detective Zemke said the two daughters claimed their father was being blackmailed."

"By who? Your father?" she said in a voice of alarm.

"No," he said quickly to allay her concern. "He thinks Dad might have been blackmailed too."

"Was he?" she asked, leaning forward and closer to him.

Wilson agonized over the fear on her face. She had told him everything she knew. "I don't know, but I'm going to find out."

"These people are deadly, Wilson," she exclaimed.

Wilson nodded. "I'm fully aware of that."

"A few months ago your father told me that one of his partners was being wined and dined by the heirs of those who'd killed his grandfather. I tried to put it out of my mind because the fear consumed me. Now look where we are," she said with more tears.

"Was that all he said?"

She nodded.

"Which partner?"

"He didn't say and I didn't ask. Have you asked Carter Emerson?"

"No, but I will when he comes for dinner on Sunday."

"Anita and I have made all the arrangements."

"Great," he said, realizing that his mother had already retreated back to a safe distance. "Thanks, Mom. I know this hasn't been easy. And I promise not to do anything before all of us are adequately protected." He leaned over and put his arms around her.

She lingered in the library for a few more minutes chatting casually, until Wilson had to leave for the airport to pick up Emily. His mother had indeed told him everything she could.

19

Emily – Logan Airport, Boston, MA

Emily landed at Boston's Logan Airport sixteen minutes late, unable to reach Wilson fast enough. She exited the security section of the airport searching for Wilson. When she found him, their eyes locked just as they had on that first day in Professor Emerson's class. Deep down, she felt as if they'd always belonged to each other. She couldn't wait to feel his arms around her. Rushing to each other, they embraced and kissed, oblivious to the crowd of people watching.

She looked stunning in her designer jeans, high-heel boots, teal top, and brown silk jacket. And Wilson immediately told her so. They were a strikingly handsome couple. Once they had retrieved Emily's luggage, they drove to Brattle House. On the way, Wilson asked her how she was handling what had happened the night before.

She hesitated momentarily and then decided to tell him.

"I didn't tell you this last night because I didn't want you to worry or overreact."

"What?" he said suddenly swerving out of his lane. When he was in control again, he repeated his question. "What didn't you tell me?"

"I think we should pull over," she said.

"Oh God," he said, considering a series of horrible possibilities. He swung over to the Copley Square off ramp and stopped on Newbury Street behind a car miraculously leaving its parking spot. He quickly pulled into the empty space and jammed the gear shift into park. "Okay, what happened?"

"It's not as bad as you're thinking. He placed the barrel of his gun under my ear and then ran it along my chin to my other ear. That's when he said, convince your boyfriend not to do anything stupid."

"Goddamn bastards. I'm going to rip…"

"Wilson, I'm fine. This is exactly why I didn't tell you over the phone. I was afraid of you'd overreact."

"How can you expect me not to overreact?"

"Because I'm fine and I'm here next to you," she said, leaning over and kissing him.

Wilson inhaled deeply. "You're right," he said, putting his arms around her. " I'll try not to overreact, but you have to trust me."

"I trust you, Wilson, but I don't want to lose you."

After embracing and kissing again, Wilson started the car and pulled out onto Newbury. When they reached Brattle House, Wilson's mother, Rachel, Darrin, and little Mary were delighted to see Emily. They socialized in the living room under full surveillance for over an hour. Then they migrated to the kitchen for a light dinner buffet and more conversation on the verandah. The threats to Emily and Wilson's mother were discussed only briefly. To leave the incidents unaddressed would have been a mistake, but no one liked rehashing the frightening experiences. Wilson made it abundantly clear that he had no intention whatsoever of putting his family and loved ones in jeopardy.

A little before eight o'clock, Wilson and Emily went to the belfry library where he sent an email to the managing partner of Kresge & Company's Chicago office. He inquired about his current projects. Making the surveillance crowd think that he was going back to work might help diminish their obvious paranoia. Emily began reading the few pages Wilson had copied from the material in his father's secret vault. They traded longing looks at each other every few seconds, impatient to spend the night together.

Thirty minutes later, they retreated to the guest room to unpack Emily's bags. Emily brushed against Wilson as she walked into the room.

He inhaled her scent, watching as she walked to the bed where her bags had been placed by the house staff.

As Emily opened a suitcase, she suddenly realized how awkward and nervous she felt. Wilson came up behind her. When she felt his breath on the back of her neck, she froze.

He slid his hands up her arms and turned her to face him. He began kissing her slowly and tenderly, hoping to convey his love and regret for all that had separated them.

She returned his kisses. But there was no need for prolonged tenderness. She loved Wilson unconditionally. Her passion for him was full—heart, mind, and body. She could feel the heightened blood flow coursing through her veins. Her only desire was to be with him. She pressed her mouth deeper into his kiss, her fingers knotting in his hair.

Wilson pulled back in surprise. But he'd seen that look on her face before. They laughed at the mutual understanding, trying to kiss each other while quickly removing their clothes. But it was taking too much time. They wanted desperately to feel each other's warm naked flesh. They separated only enough to watch every piece of clothing drop to the floor.

The sight of Wilson's obvious arousal made Emily feel powerful and secure in her ability to draw him fully into a world that was only theirs.

He pulled her to him roughly and in a rush of tongue and teeth and searching fingers, they dropped to the beautiful Persian rug. Later, they would take time to explore and savor. But now, Wilson wanted nothing but to be inside her.

Emily curled her hips to meet him.

20

Tate – Banff, Canada

The legendary Banff Springs Hotel ,built in 1888 by the Canadian Pacific Railroad, rose majestically from the pines atop a confluence of spiritual mountain crossings. Wayland Tate's fondness for the Scottish baronial hotel and its mystical environs brought him to the resort at least twice a year. On this trip, he'd wanted to accompany the group of clients he was sending off on a two-day helicopter skiing trip to remote slopes in British Columbia. These were undoubtedly some of the most beautiful mountains on the face of the planet, but even greater pleasures awaited him today. David Quinn's manipulation was about to reach new heights.

Outside the hotel's elegant lobby in the large roundabout, Tate's clients finished loading their gear and entering the vans that would take them to the helipad. He half-warned, half-bantered with them about sudden avalanches and sheer cliffs while, out of the corner of one eye, he watched David Quinn and Jules Kamin arrive in the lobby. As planned, Vargas had convinced Quinn to ski with her later in the morning instead of going on the heli-skiing trip. Now it was just a matter of minutes before Tate would be determining Quinn's future.

Once the vans were on their way, Tate joined Kamin and Quinn in a secluded part of the lobby next to an immense fireplace. Quinn was venting his frustration to Kamin.

"Somebody at Kresge & Company spilled the beans," Kamin said, clueing Tate in on what Quinn was saying. However, both Kamin and Tate knew perfectly well what had happened, since they were the ones who'd set things in motion. The first event in the Musselman stock-manipulation plan had been implemented.

"They'll pay for their arrogance," Quinn said, still fuming. "They promised both me and MacMillan that they wouldn't talk to the press. That was the only reason we let them keep the fees we'd already paid them. You watch me sue their asses for defamation, mismanagement, and fraud."

This was the moment Tate had anticipated. Everything had come together as planned.

"What happened exactly?" Tate asked, his characteristic smoothness and feigned concern oozing from every pore.

Quinn looked like death as he told Tate about the call he'd just received from his administrative assistant.

"A reporter at *The Wall Street Journal* says he has confirmed information that Kresge & Company was fired because it questioned Musselman's future viability. He knows all the details about Kresge's recommendation to break up the company."

"Are you sure he's got confirmed sources?" Tate asked, for effect.

"He says the story's going to run Monday morning, with or without confirmation from Musselman," Quinn said.

"What was MacMillan's reaction?" Tate asked.

"I haven't talked to him or any other members of the board. You're the first," Quinn said, rubbing his hands over his balding head.

"Word of the story must be spreading by blogs," Tate said, letting a look of anguish fall over his features.

"This is exactly what I was afraid of. And it only gets worse," Quinn said, shaking his head and closing his eyes. "Hardware City has been buying our shares for the past several days. They've already acquired close to fifteen percent of the company and we don't have a poison pill because I don't believe in them. Our shareholders are salivating over the imminent tender offer. God, I'm such a fool."

There was a prolonged moment of silence as Tate stared out the large windows at the snow-speckled pines near Bow Falls. He could barely contain himself. Having placed Quinn in this predicament gave him a rush of pure psychic energy. This is what Tate lived for—the artful, unfair, and always deceptive manipulation of a rich and powerful CEO. In fact, he could no longer live without it.

"Maybe there's another way to look at this, David," Tate finally said to break the silence.

"If you can find a silver lining in this, I'll write you a blank check for your services."

"That won't be necessary, David. There's always opportunity in crisis."

"Of course there is for Hardware City's management. They've been dying to get their hands on my warehouses for years."

"No. For you, David. For us. For our friends."

"What are you talking about?"

"We've seen this scenario before," Tate said. "Bad news gets leaked just before the weekend, the stock price begins dropping, and everyone in the trading community knows the details before the market reopens. The Monday morning sell-off, combined with the bad press, drives the stock price to new lows. Bottom line? One investor's nightmare becomes another investor's dream. When the stock bottoms on Tuesday, we buy more than we can afford." Tate paused and placed his hand on Quinn's shoulder. "And, that's exactly what we're going to do."

"Who's we?"

"You and I, Jules, and a group of clients committed to helping each other make a lot of money."

"That's not going to stop Hardware City, and you know as well as I do we don't have the debt capacity to buy back our stock."

"No need for that," Kamin said, having remained quiet since Tate arrived, just as rehearsed earlier. "Our way is better. A consortium of clients purchases twenty-six percent of Musselman's stock before closing on Tuesday. A second suitor, friendly, of course, buys another fifteen percent at the same time. You purchase another ten percent and we're completely insulated from any takeover, without raising suspicion. We'll do it all simultaneously. While Hardware City is busily acquiring shares to establish a minimum ownership position, which will probably be something around forty percent, we'll shut them out."

"You know I can't do it. In the first place I don't have a billion dollars lying around to invest. In the second place, it's illegal. Not only do we release quarterly earnings next week, we're about to launch America's Warehouse. I'm in a blackout period, you know that. The SEC would crucify me."

"We can take care of the legalities," Kamin said, stepping closer. "The first thing we'll do is collateralize your Musselman stock options through a foreign lender into a blind Nevada corporation owned by a Nevis Trust. Everything will be completely untraceable. The Nevis Trust will then use the proceeds from the collateralization to obtain a line of credit. That line of credit will be used to buy ninety-five million shares of Musselman stock on margin. Only twenty-five percent of the value of the stock will be required for deposit. The rest can be borrowed from the broker. The stock price doubles before margin call, and the Nevis Trust cashes out over a three-day period. You make a killing and prevent a takeover."

"Why can't your partnership of clients or this new suitor you're going to arrange buy the remaining ten percent?"

Tate came back into the conversation, "Because they'll want to know you're in this with them, David."

Quinn looked scared and trapped. He was in over his head. In less than forty-eight hours when the New York Stock Exchange reopened for trading, Musselman's stock price would continue dropping and Hardware City would give shareholders a way out, by buying their shares at a premium. Life as Quinn knew it would be over by Wednesday, unless he accepted Tate's offer. He should have done more to prepare for the possibility of a takeover, as remote as it may have seemed weeks ago. And he might have, had he not been so involved preparing for America's Warehouse. Now, he had to choose. Either accept Tate's offer and be beholden to Tate for the rest of his life or reject it and lose everything. There were no other options, at least none that could be developed in time to stop a Hardware City takeover, and Quinn knew it.

Tate didn't expect it would take long for Quinn's moral dilemma to give way to his obsession for preserving control of the J. B. Musselman Company.

Quinn rubbed his fingers across his large forehead and peered at Kamin.

"You've done this before?"

"Yes," Kamin said.

"How many times?"

"Dozens."

Quinn's face froze in astonishment.

"No, David, we didn't create this situation," Tate said. "Actually, it happens more often than you might think. We just know how to turn it to our advantage."

Small beads of sweat began forming across Quinn's forehead. He took a deep breath. "You're certain there's no way to trace my involvement?"

"Absolutely no way," Tate said with his characteristic arrogance.

"And if you're wrong?"

"We're not," Tate said. "You once told me you wanted to buy a ski resort in Idaho."

"I've considered it, but what does that have to do with…"

Tate interrupted, "The Nevada Corporation will be set up as a resort development company. The investment coming from your collateralized stock options will be made to look like foreign investment, to be used as working capital for the selection, acquisition, and development of ski resort properties. The cash will remain in the Nevada corporation at all times, and will only be used by the Nevis Trust as collateral for obtaining a line of credit to purchase the ninety-five million shares of Musselman stock on margin."

Quinn folded his arms across his chest and glared at Tate. "Is this what you wanted, Wayland, to own me lock, stock, and barrel?"

"Don't be silly, David," Tate said, putting his hand on Quinn's shoulder. "This is what friends do for each other. Don't forget, we all have a lot riding on the success of America's Warehouse. A takeover by Hardware City could jeopardize everything." Tate paused a moment to let his words register. "Your interest is our interest. We can have all of this worked out by Monday morning. It's what we do for clients in crisis. In the meantime, enjoy your day of skiing with Andrea. They say it snowed all night at Sunshine Village, two feet of fresh powder."

Quinn's face was flushed. He said nothing.

"If you're not comfortable, we won't go through with it. It's your call, David." Tate could see Quinn's anger, but the trap had already caught its prey. That was life. It was time for Tate to cash in on his investment in David Quinn.

Quinn walked over to the huge window and stared at the snow-covered pines. A couple of minutes later, he returned to where Tate and Kamin were standing. The look on Quinn's face had changed from anger to resignation.

"Okay," he said. "Tell me exactly how we go about borrowing the money against my stock options."

That was it. Quinn was now theirs for as long as they wanted to manipulate him. He savored the moment as Kamin answered Quinn's question in precise detail, assuring him that the funds could be made available immediately, through a European investment fund created for just this sort of emergency. After that, Kamin suggested they meet before dinner to sign all the necessary papers.

Looking stoic yet relieved, Quinn agreed to the meeting and then shook hands with Tate and Kamin before leaving for his room.

As Quinn walked away, Tate leaned over to Kamin and whispered, "I think events one and two of our plan can be considered a success."

They exchanged roguish smiles.

Several hours later, alone in the private smoking lounge of the Banff Springs Hotel, with its dark cherrywood walls, plush Persian rugs, and soft leather sofas, Wayland Tate and Jules Kamin lit nine-inch Havanas and raised their Dirty Martinis to the initial success of their stock-manipulation plan. After a beautiful day of skiing with Andrea Vargas, Quinn had quietly acquiesced, signing all of the necessary paperwork to collateralize his Musselman stock options. The dinner that followed had been extremely pleasant, and Vargas later reported that she and Quinn shared several goodnight kisses before bedtime. Everything was going as planned. David Quinn had now been locked into the secret partnership until he died.

As the buzz from their martini's and cigars grew, Kamin turned to Tate with a question. "Are you anticipating any last minute reversals from Quinn?"

"No," Tate said. "We just need to make sure there are no hitches in the ongoing execution."

"He's feeling trapped and he doesn't like it," Kamin persisted.

"Of course he doesn't like it. He's addicted to running his own show. But what choice does he have?"

"Like I said before, we don't want another Zollinger on our hands."

"Where's all this worry coming from? You keep asking me the same damn question," Tate said without hiding his annoyance. Then he sucked on his cigar while considering Kamin's enduring fear. Kamin had to be obsessing over more than the failed acquisition of Fielder & Company, Tate thought. Was it the neutralization of Charles Fielder? Whatever it was, Tate didn't like it.

"I don't know, Wayland," Kamin said, exposing his feelings of uncertainty and vulnerability. "Maybe it's the rising body count."

"There's huge risk in what we've decided to do, Jules," Tate said. "Charles' disclosure plan used to be our immunity blanket, but now it's gone. This is a whole new ball game with higher stakes and even greater rewards, which means whenever things go bad, our damage control must be swift and merciless. Call it our new competitive advantage."

Kamin smiled as Tate sucked heavily on his cigar and then blew perfect smoke rings into the air. They both laughed.

"You really think we're moving too fast with Quinn?" Tate asked after a few seconds of silence.

"I'd feel more comfortable if he were sleeping with Vargas," Jules said.

Tate sat back, his arms stretched out along the back of the sofa. With the confident air of a pimp fully in control, he said, "I didn't believe I would ever say this, but it's just a matter of time. When the Hardware City takeover is averted and Musselman stock starts climbing again, Quinn will be ready to celebrate. Mark my word, that's when he'll sleep with Andrea Vargas. I guarantee it."

"I hope you're right, Wayland," Kamin said, smiling cagily.

"Would you like to wager on it?" Tate asked, displaying a toothy grin. "Let's say your share of the Musselman take?"

Kamin immediately shook his head, "No thanks."

They both laughed long and loud before lighting up another Havana and ordering more Martinis.

When they finally decided to call it a night, Tate was satisfied that Kamin, while not entirely happy with recent decisions and events, would get over it. What choice did he have? Tate was in control and as usual he would do whatever it took to stay there.

21

Wilson – Cambridge, MA

At four o'clock in the afternoon, Yankee pot roast and stuffed Cornish hen with all the trimmings were spread out on the thirty-foot dining table. His mother and Anita had outdone themselves, Wilson thought. Both of them were great cooks and they loved entertaining. The delicious meal was accompanied by urbane small talk and, of course, a lively discussion about stopping any further investigation and getting on with their lives. It felt like a "B" movie without the canned laughter, but he remained confident that the mock discussion would accomplish its purpose for long enough to fortify their protection. Even if the surveillance crowd didn't believe everything, they would certainly conclude that Wilson, his family, and their friends were sufficiently scared to back off.

After dinner, Carter, Rachel, Emily, and Wilson removed themselves to the belfry library. Everyone else moved to the family room to listen to the string quartet that Wilson had arranged, rehearsing Vivaldi's *Four Seasons* and Bach's Air from Suite No. 3. Once in the library, the four of them sat down at the Queen Anne table while Wilson made sure both nullifiers were turned on. Then, looking at Carter and Rachel, Wilson recounted what he'd found in his father's office at Fielder & Company.

Rachel was as shocked and saddened as he had been when she found out about their great-grandfather's murder. Wilson attempted to console her, but without much success. She remained morose throughout the rest of the meeting.

Carter asked a few questions and then shared his own revelation.

"There are a dozen primary suspects. One or more of them must have orchestrated everything," he began.

Wilson looked at Emily who was studying Carter. "How did you narrow it down?" Wilson asked. *A dozen primary suspects...*

"To tell you the truth, it was quite simple. I merely identified the clients with the most entrenched patterns of questionable practices. There are twelve of them who surpass the others by a substantial margin."

There it was, again, that same elusive enigma and cool resolve that Wilson loved and hated about his father. He glanced at Emily again. How many secrets do Carter and my father share?

"Did you know that my great-grandfather was murdered?" Wilson asked.

"Yes. I think it's what started your father down this path."

Wilson's anger was rising again. "My father told my mother that one of his partners was being wined and dined by descendants of the people who killed my great-grandfather. Have you found anything that ... "

Carter cut him off. "Four of the twelve primary suspects have restructured their corporate debt or acquired new equity funding through a consortium of European and Asian investment banks."

Wilson stared at Carter, reminding himself once again to calm down. Carter would only share what he wanted and only on his terms.

"I'm not surprised," Wilson said.

"From the inception of recorded history," Carter said with a confident professorial air, "Certain malcontents, rebels, zealots, visionaries, and others of similar intent have entered into secret orders with blood oaths to keep their power-mongering and nefarious misdeeds hidden from the rest of the world. Subscribing to the maxim of 'control or be controlled' they formed secret pacts to minimize risk and maximize success. It is the inexorable nature of some men and women to form secret alliances for the purpose of gaining power, wealth, and advantage through whatever means available. As much as I'm loath to admit it, I cannot deny the overwhelming evidence that Charles created such a secret society among clients of Fielder & Company."

Wilson remained silent, keeping his composure, not for the sake of appearance but concentration. He glanced over at Emily while squeezing her hand.

Carter continued, "As I pieced together my own experiences with Charles and the salient elements of Fielder & Company's history, it became clear that his business practices were designed to manipulate stock market prices through sophisticated disinformation and shrewd business changes, thereby creating circumstances advantageous to himself and his clients. Once clients became entrenched in Fielder & Company's methods, which on the surface appeared to be completely legal, they apparently qualified themselves to become members of an exclusive insiders club, where CEOs from the world's largest corporations could amass unimaginable wealth by trading on each other's company secrets. When Davis Zollinger was murdered for what I presume was a desire or threat to leave the club, it must have devastated Charles. He immediately placed a moratorium on corporate restructuring engagements at Fielder & Company and entered into merger talks with KaneWeller. But I suspect he had already lost control of the clandestine partnership and was attempting to regain it when he was shot."

A heavy silence filled the room. Wilson felt a cold numbness spread from the back of his head. Carter's bold conclusions were more emotionally jarring than he'd anticipated. If Carter was right, and Fielder & Company was an elaborate front for some sort of secret network of corrupt CEOs, then the Zollinger sisters were right. They really had uncovered a secret society that was getting away with conspiracy, fraud, and murder.

Carter saw the growing distress on Wilson's face. When he spoke again his tone was quieter and more personal.

"When your father and I were in school together, we vowed to change the world just like the rest of our boomer generation. But Fielder & Company's history suggests an activity level well beyond what I imagined possible from Charles. I'm as astonished and troubled by my findings as you are."

"Who were his closest confidants in the partnership?" Wilson asked, pushing his chair back from the table and feeling suddenly protective and defensive about his father.

"No way to know for certain," Carter answered. "I found nothing that openly revealed the agendas or inner workings of Fielder & Company's secretive meetings with client CEOs. Every year there were dozens of outings with groups of CEOs at exclusive resorts, but no records. The only thing I was able to document was the pattern of manipulation and disinformation among Fielder & Company clients. It's all in the client correspondence, especially emails. Sudden board changes, management reorganizations, carefully timed spin-outs, merger and acquisition rumors, surprise divestitures, frequent IPOs, disarmingly candid press releases, shareholder scare tactics, threatened lawsuits, leaked memos about new products and services, anonymous chat-room revelations, innuendoes about..."

Wilson interrupted. "Daniel claimed everything Fielder & Company recommended to its clients was legally defensible."

"Everything I just mentioned can be made to fit the technical requirements of a legal defense. I suspect it's how the partnership lured its new members," Carter said.

"How did you discover all of this so quickly? I've been through my father's files..."

Now it was Carter's turn to interrupt. "Email logs. As a historian you learn to avoid the most obvious and plentiful information sources in favor of the obscure and hidden ones. They tend to be less manufactured and manipulated. Email logs are easily retrieved, scanned, and queried, if you know how to do it."

"What else, Carter?" Wilson asked, his head full of questions and suspicions about Carter. It was time for confrontation. "You could not have come to these conclusions just from email logs. What else do you know about my father that you haven't told us?"

Carter hesitated a moment. "This is the difficult part. Fielder & Company's more questionable activities were handled through an elaborate shadow network. Charles hinted at it from time to time, but I never understood it until now, thanks to his assistant Anne Cartwright. Either unwittingly or deliberately, she showed me enough pieces to put the puzzle together," he said, pausing to open one of the manila folders lying in front of him. "A network of highly discreet purveyors provided client CEOs with whatever they wanted—competitor espionage, eavesdropping, lobbying schemes, inside tracks on government contracts, political clout, hacking into computer systems, access to restricted databases, off-shore tax shelters, private investment deals available only to insiders, confidential corporate information, mega-stakes gambling, designer drugs, fashion models and actresses, exotic getaways, personalized security, counter surveillance, legal protection, even contract assassins."

The room was deathly silent.

"I think that's why Charles was seeking my help," Carter continued. "He'd created this ultimate insider's club with the intent to one day expose it, showing the world just how easy it is to manipulate stock exchanges, live above the law, and exploit the masses. My guess is he was trying to finish the job his grandfather Harry Wilson Fielder, Congressman Louis T. McFadden, and William Tate Boyles had started decades earlier."

"What about the KaneWeller merger. Won't that expose them?" Rachel asked as she squirmed in her chair, looking terrified.

"By my estimate, less than half of Fielder & Company's client CEOs are members of the partnership; it's safe to assume that they'll distance themselves from the new merger as soon as they can, without raising any eyebrows. Within a year or so, I suspect the partnership will be operating completely on its own through new organizations. The murders have made it impossible for them to dissolve the secret society, which leaves them only one course of action—protect, defend, and expand. The bigger they get, the less vulnerable they become," Carter said, looking at Wilson.

Wilson was deep in thought. The puzzle pieces were finally solidifying into a complete picture. He knew what needed to be done. It was time to act. "We have to stop them," Wilson said resolutely.

"My sentiments, precisely," Carter said. "Otherwise, we'll never be rid of them. They will keep us under surveillance indefinitely, while continuing to exploit and manipulate everything that is near and dear to all of us, right under our noses," Carter said.

"So what are we supposed to do?" Rachel blurted.

"Keep them believing that we are moving on with our lives. Meanwhile, we need to carefully and discreetly turn everything we have over to the FBI. Let our government do what we pay them to do," Carter said, casting a probing look at Wilson. "We have neither the resources nor the expertise to expose them."

Wilson considered Carter for several moments before shaking his head. Carter was baiting him and he knew it.

"I disagree. We're the only ones who can expose them. And thanks to my father, we do have the resources," Wilson was firm; he glanced over at Emily, whose eyebrows were raised in astonishment.

"Carter's right," Rachel pleaded. "We should turn everything over to the authorities. You have to let it go, Wilson."

Emily decided to step in. Taking Wilson's arm, she gently pulled him toward her.

"We need a break," she said.

Wilson didn't put up any resistance, suggesting that everyone take a fifteen-minute. Then he steered Emily toward the guest bedroom.

"You can't be serious," Emily said, as soon as they were alone. "We have no choice but to turn this over to the FBI. Where are you coming from? You can't believe…"

But Wilson cut her off mid-sentence. Although sympathetic toward Emily's stance, he was resolved as to the course of action he needed to take.

"I know it seems like I'm overreacting, but everything we've been talking about just started getting clearer. Much clearer. The CEOs in this partnership are too wealthy, too powerful, and too essential to the American economy for the FBI to expose them. We'd be better off going to *The Wall Street Journal* or *The New York Times*."

"Why do you want to put our lives in further danger?" Emily said, her brow deeply furrowed. "You really think that's what your father wanted?"

"Of course not," Wilson said with a slight edge to his voice.

"Then why won't you accept Carter's advice and leave it to the FBI," Emily retorted, no longer able to keep the edge out of her voice.

"We can't turn this over to the bureaucracy. Not yet."

"Not everyone who works for the government is a puppet or incompetent," Emily insisted.

"Em, it's not a question of competence or expertise or even resources," Wilson replied, his tone softer now.

"What is it then?" Emily demanded, maintaining her ire.

"I don't trust them," Wilson explained. "Exposing this sort of calculated scheming, by hundreds of CEOs from the world's largest corporations, is asking too much of them. The international ramifications and global economic entanglements are too great."

Emily's eyes had grown hard and angry.

But Wilson could see the fear behind the anger. He knew this was what scared her about him. When he became willful and—in her estimation—obstinate and isolated, he was no different than the CEOs he was hired to transform. But he couldn't ignore the sense of rightness he felt about his new resolve.

"Why, all of a sudden, do you feel so committed to this course of action?" Emily asked, her voice growing calmer.

"Let's face it, if Carter is right about this insider's club of CEOs, a full-blown investigation with the intent to expose everything would constitute a threat to national security too great for any government to justify, especially a self-righteous superpower like the United States. We've been preaching market capitalism and the rule of law to the entire world since World War II. There would be immediate global outrage, a wave of international reprisals against the U.S., and then economic chaos throughout the world," Wilson said, seized by a rush of righteous indignation. "If we give this to the FBI now, they'll have no choice but to make some arrests, deliver a few indictments, and then cover it up in the name of national security and global stability. You know that's what would happen."

Emily wrapped her arms around Wilson. "Let's finish this meeting with Carter, then we can talk some more."

When they reconvened in the belfry library, Carter was the first to speak.

"How long have you been thinking this way, Wilson?"

"Less than an hour," he said, glancing at Emily. Then he returned his focus to Carter. "I've been putting the pieces of this puzzle together since my father was shot. Corruption expands until it's exposed. Completely exposed. Even if the FBI, the SEC, the Justice Department, the NSA, or any other government agency actually succeeded in disbanding Fielder & Company's secret network, none of them would ever acknowledge the full extent to which the system of capitalism has broken down. And without full acknowledgement, we will never be able to correct things."

"That's what you want? The possible disintegration of our country, our way of life, every good thing this nation has ever accomplished, just so you can correct Dad's mistakes?" Rachel said, drawing her hair back tightly against her head with both hands.

"Don't you think I've considered the consequences?" Wilson jumped in, before his sister could continue. "There's only one way to protect yourself from evil. You have to expose all of its ugly implications and consequences, so you and your children and their children can have a better life." He stopped when he saw the tears in Emily's eyes.

For a brief moment, he reconsidered his position. *Am I overreacting to my feelings of frustration and powerlessness?*

Can the government do the right thing? Have I become obsessed with my father's and great-grandfather's quest? But his introspection lasted only a few moments before his certainty and commitment returned, stronger than before.

"What else can I say? I honestly believe that our collective future depends on exposing this web of corruption. And I think we're the only ones who can do it. In fact, I believe it's the only way we'll be able to save our own lives."

"Only God can expose evil in all its forms," Rachel said in a final attempt to dissuade Wilson.

Dead silence hung in the air for several moments. Emily and Rachel looked at each other as if awaiting their deaths on the gallows. It was Carter, who broke the silence.

"What did you have in mind, Wilson?"

"I'm open to suggestions."

Carter smiled while Emily and Rachel looked stoic and pale. They all agreed to sleep on it. One by one, they returned to the string quartet's rehearsal in the large family room at the back of the house. Wilson's mother and Elizabeth Emerson were sitting next to each other on the yellow sectional that wrapped around the large glass coffee table. Darrin was lying back on the fully extended moss-green lounge chair with his eyes closed. Aunt Sarah was rocking little Mary to sleep in the Scandinavian rocker. Savoy and his associate Case were standing at the back near the French doors to the verandah. The string quartet was seated in a semi-circle near the stone fireplace. It was a warm and inviting ambiance, if only they could have enjoyed it.

The four of them took seats on the sectional for a few minutes before Carter and his wife had to leave. After a few more minutes of casual conversation with Rachel and Wilson's mother, Emily left for the guestroom on the second floor. She told Wilson she needed some time to herself. He understood her concern, but he wasn't about to change his mind. Tenacity can be a dangerous trait but only when you're wrong. I'm not wrong: their lives depend on my resolve. He returned to the belfry library to begin working on an implementation plan.

22

Quinn – Chicago, IL

Since returning from Banff, David Quinn felt as though he'd died a thousand deaths. Monday's edition of *The Wall Street Journal* carried a front-page article about the J. B. Musselman Company and its decision to fire the prestigious management consulting firm of Kresge & Company for questioning Musselman's future viability and recommending the company's breakup. As a result of the rumor mill generated by the article, Musselman's stock yo-yoed erratically until it plummeted by almost thirty percent in value. Quinn was physically, mentally, and emotionally exhausted from worrying about collateralizing his stock options and agonizing over every quarter point drop in the company's stock. When the stock finally bottomed out at 97/8 a share and Hardware City made its tender offer of 117/8, Quinn was begging for deliverance.

Then, miraculously, another aggressive buyer in the form of Pace Warehouses along with the secret partnership's network of buyers went on a competitive buying spree, eventually bringing the trading of Musselman stock to a near complete halt. All of the shareholders who now owned Musselman's 950 million shares of stock were holding their positions, waiting for someone to sell or offer another premium. That's when the bid price from floor traders began climbing to keep trading alive, just as expected. As the floor price approached thirteen dollars a share, Hardware City announced that it had been blocked in its takeover attempt. The hostile suitor began selling the stock it had purchased to a growing group of anxious investors who now saw Musselman stock as a superb undervalued opportunity. The stock price moved quickly back to fourteen dollars.

Tate and Kamin had delivered on their promise. Quinn felt resurrected, barely able to contain his elation. He kissed Kamin on the cheek three times—once for Kamin, once for Tate, who had already gone to the airport to catch a flight to Rome for another client retreat, and once for the anonymous contingent that had helped to prevent Musselman's takeover by Hardware City.

As the week progressed, things only got better. Thursday's edition of *The Wall Street Journal* carried another front-page article on Musselman, this time heralding the company's upcoming grand opening of America's Warehouse as the reason for David Quinn's courageous stand against Kresge & Company and Hardware City:

> *David Quinn's vision for reinventing the J. B. Musselman Company seems destined for success. His bold strategy to convert thousands of distribution warehouses into bargain basements called America's Warehouse, has already won enormous media attention. According to Musselman's advertising agency Boggs & Saggett, shoppers will find better values and greater varieties than anywhere else.*
>
> *Driven by an unwavering determination to turn Musselman's twenty-five billion dollar roll-up of local and regional warehouses into an industry powerhouse, CEO Quinn has surmounted huge obstacles. He battled a skeptical board of directors, renowned management consultants who recommended dismantling the company, and a hostile takeover bid by Hardware City Stores. Now he claims to have engineered a corporate turnaround epitomized by a marketing campaign the likes of which this industry has never seen.*

After yesterday's dramatic rebound in the company's stock price, some analysts are speculating that Musselman's launch of America's Warehouse next week will revolutionize the industry. This could become the biggest success story in mass merchandising since Amazon.com, but with traditional bricks and mortar, not digital web pages ...

When Quinn read the article, tears came to his eyes. He was beyond elated. Tate and Kamin had come through yet again with flying colors. They'd convinced *The Wall Street Journal's* editor-in-chief, Jeremy Watts, to tell Quinn's side of the story.

Quinn was beaming like a conquering hero when Jules Kamin returned once more to share in the good news.

"I've been born again, thanks to you and Wayland and all your people."

"Your stock is already trading at sixteen dollars," Kamin said, pointing to one of the computer monitors in Quinn's office.

"Now the only thing we need to do is get me out..."

"Don't worry, David," Kamin said quietly, placing his hand on Quinn's shoulder. "Daily trading volume has remained over forty million shares since Monday. We started selling your shares on Tuesday. You'll be out before the end of the day."

Musselman stock moved steadily upward during the rest of the day, seventeen dollars a share by noon, nineteen by mid-afternoon, and twenty-two at closing. It was a phenomenal ride. Thirty minutes before the bell rang, Quinn went ballistic with joy and then started crying again. The last of his ninety-five million shares purchased illegally through the concealed entity had been sold. It had taken four long days and a lot of nail-biting, but he was finally out of the market.

Quinn hugged everyone in sight. First, he hugged Kamin for the fourth time in two days. Then, he hugged two of his senior executives, who had come to congratulate him on the rising stock price, three of his administrative assistants, and all ten of the Musselman and Boggs & Saggett team members, who were hunkered down in a nearby conference room to hammer out the final details of America's Warehouse grand opening. He kissed Andrea Vargas twice.

Turning back to Kamin who'd followed him to the conference room, Quinn said with eyes aglow, "This is the happiest day of my life, Jules. I want to acquire Hardware City before the end of the year."

23

Wilson – Cambridge, MA

A dozen alternative strategies for taking down the secret partnership scrolled through Wilson's mind, as he reflected on a past conversation with his father. He was alone in the belfry library, giving Emily the space she needed. The conversation he couldn't stop thinking about had taken place fifteen years ago, during a Christmas break midway through his junior year at Milton Academy. Wilson had just finished studying America's Gilded Age and written a lengthy report on the Pullman Strike of 1894. He was anxious to discuss what he'd learned with his father and had looked forward to what he hoped would be a lively debate.

The family was eating dinner in the chalet at White
Horse. It was the day after Christmas, following a terrific day
of skiing. His father was talking about a Dutch economist
named Jan Pen, who had equated annual income to physical
height. A person with an annual income of $50,000 would
be six feet tall. Someone with an income of $5 million would
be fifty feet tall. Billions of people would be dwarfs less than
three feet tall, many of them standing less than one foot.
Several million in income would make a person sixty to a
hundred feet tall. And there would be a few hundred giants
on the earth, some towering above our tallest skyscrapers,
others rising more than a hundred miles into the stratosphere
with fifteen mile long footprints. From that point, Wilson
mentally replayed the dialogue in remarkable detail.

His fourteen-year-old sister Rachel had started it all by
saying: "Capitalism sucks." Then she teased, "How tall are
you, Dad?"

His father smiled and raised his eyebrows but said
nothing.

"Until we have a better alternative, I think we should be
grateful for the economic system we have," his mother said,
always trying to temper things.

Anxious to share his thoughts, Wilson said, "I just finished
writing a paper on the Pullman Strike of 1894 and how it
shaped the relationship between capitalists and laborers in
America. It's not a pretty story."

"Remind us of what happened," his mother said, noticeably excited to hear more about what he'd been studying at school.

Wilson jumped at the opportunity, having already committed his synopsis to memory for an oral presentation at school. "George Pullman invented his luxury railroad car in 1867 and then joined forces with Andrew Carnegie to build the Pullman Palace Car Company. In the 1880s Pullman built an entire town on the south side of Chicago for his workers, to shield them from the vices of the day and Chicago's labor unrest. Paved streets, indoor plumbing, gas lighting, sewage system, communal stables, parks, and an arcade were all part of the model town for his company's ten thousand railcar manufacturing workers. But after workers paid Pullman rent for their new houses, they only had a few cents to buy their families the other things they needed. When the stock market crashed in 1893, the economy went into a recession. Pullman cut workers' wages by thirty percent, making their living situation intolerable. Four thousand Pullman workers, who were members of Eugene Deb's American Railway Union, went on strike in 1894. George Pullman refused to even talk to the union or his workers. He locked up his home and left town. That summer, another hundred thousand railroad workers, from across the country, supported the strike by refusing to handle Pullman railcars. When Pullman fired workers who were union members, entire rail lines began to shut down and the U.S. mail stopped moving by rail. Chicago erupted in riots. Federal troops were brought in from Fort Sheridan, a military base on Lake Michigan. It had been donated to the Federal Government by The Commercial Club of Chicago to protect Chicago's capitalist elite—men like George Pullman, Marshall Field, Cyrus McCormick, George Armour, and Frederic Delano—from labor unrest. On July 8, 1894, federal troops opened fire against the strikers. Thirty-four people were killed. Eugene Debs went to jail and the courts stood behind the capitalists. A federal commission later censured George Pullman for charging excessive rent and forcing his employees to bear unnecessary burdens, but the capitalist elite had already emerged victorious over united labor," Wilson finished as he sat back waiting for comments.

"So what was the conclusion of your paper?" his father asked.

"Capitalism sucks," Rachel repeated to loud laughter.

Then everyone turned to Wilson, awaiting his response.

"It's simple. The government helped capital defeat labor," Wilson said wryly.

"Right or wrong?" his father asked.

"Wrong," Wilson said.

"Why?"

"Because the forces of capital and labor should be better balanced, but after the Pullman Strike, thanks to the government, capital gained the clear advantage. It shaped American history, for the worse."

"What would you have done, if you'd been President Cleveland?"

"I wouldn't have sent in federal troops or allowed Eugene Debs to go to jail. But it was the courts that gave capital its advantage. Capitalists were allowed to use the rule of law—and the shrewdest lawyers they could buy—to control rebellious laborers. Laborers never had the same opportunity or resources to control greedy capitalists."

His father nodded without saying anything for several moments. His mother and Rachel remained quiet, finishing their dinners. "So how do we correct things?" his father had finally asked.

"Our system of favoring capital over labor has become entrenched. It's too late," Wilson said, baiting his father. He could still remember the excitement he felt when provoking his father into a heated debate. The fact was he loved arguing with his father, because it allowed him to penetrate his father's enigma. "The capitalists rule. Control or be controlled, isn't that what you tell your clients?"

His father waited a moment before taking the bait. "It's never too late, Wilson. Control or be controlled is an argument used by the powerful to justify their exploitation of the weak. That's exactly why the laws in this country must be changed—to prevent the strong from crushing the weak.

Wage slavery is a reality for most of the population and I hate it as much as you do," his father said firmly.

Wilson remembered smiling to himself, thinking that the polemics were about to commence. "How can you say that you hate it when you continue to make yourself and your rich clients richer, just like every other capitalist? It's capitalism that promotes exclusivity, inequality, unemployment, overwork, and poverty—and in its current form, it will never be compatible with democracy," Wilson said, heightening the drama.

His father stopped eating and placed his elbows on the table. "No form of capitalism, fascism, socialism, communism, libertarianism, communitarianism, or any other "ism" is going to prevent the powerful from exploiting the weak—and you can't force equality when it doesn't exist. If the powerful few were wise, noble, and committed to spreading the wealth, then the powerless many would have little to fear. But every governing hierarchy on earth, public or private, is designed to give a few control over the many. The secret lies in making capitalism more accessible to all."

Perfect, Wilson remembered saying to himself. It's time for a frontal attack. "So, when are you going to begin using your wealth to make the weak more powerful or teach your clients to become less cutthroat and more inclusive? And for what it's worth, I don't think making big donations to Harvard is going to make much of a difference." Wilson cringed as he replayed the dialogue in his head. He'd been such a smartass.

"Wilson. This is not…" his mother began before his father cut her off.

"What makes you think I'm not already doing more than making charitable donations?" his father said defensively.

"What exactly are you doing?" Wilson asked, unwilling to let his father off the hook. "The fact is most capitalists don't want to change things because they need the slaves."

"That's enough, Wilson," his mother said decisively. "It's Christmas. Rachel and I are not interested in sitting here while you and your father have another one of your jousting sessions."

"Your mother's right," his father said. "It's time to lighten the conversation. The snow is falling and our new hot tub is beckoning. However, I will say one more thing in response to your questions. Fielder & Company is in the process of launching a rather novel approach to humanizing capitalism. But you need to give me a decade or so to see if it works. If it does, we may finally overcome the generations of concealed corruption that have created our current version of capitalism. If it doesn't, you may have to pick up the pieces." His father smiled, looking as if he wanted to say more but then decided against it. His intense blue-green eyes suddenly softened. "Who's ready to hit the hot tub?"

"I am," Rachel squealed, as only fourteen-year-old girls can.

That was the end of the now troubling conversation. Wilson had questioned his father about it on numerous occasions after that, but his father only responded in vague terms, usually saying something like 'We're still working on it'. Then he'd typically shift the conversation to why it was difficult, but never impossible, to change deeply entrenched and widely accepted systems. I should have pressed harder, much harder, Wilson thought. But at the time, he was leaving for Princeton and his own fight against the abuse of power.

Wilson returned to considering his options for attacking the secret partnership. He continued to favor an infiltration strategy, assuming he could convince the secret partnership that it would be safer to bring him inside. Regardless of which strategy he ultimately pursued, picking up the pieces of his father's life had become his reality and that meant figuring out how his father planned to use his secret insiders club to humanize capitalism. The lives of his loved ones, his father's reputation, and his and Emily's future depended on it.

Over the next few days, Wilson was so thoroughly absorbed with planning his attack or reassuring Emily that he'd completely missed the two *Wall Street Journal* articles on the J. B. Musselman Company and his old antagonist David Quinn. When a colleague at Kresge & Company emailed him about the articles, he immediately accessed the stories online and read with rapt interest.

David Quinn had managed to pull off another turnaround, but Wilson knew it wouldn't last. Sooner or later, the Musselman roll-up would unravel. He was sure of it. Wayland Tate must have found a way to appease Musselman's Chairman James MacMillan. Wilson had never believed in Tate's strategy of going head-to-head with Costco and Sam's Club, but Tate was extremely persuasive. Wilson had known that for years, ever since they first met at White Horse when Wilson was a boy. He remembered his father's introduction of Tate as the most brilliant advertising executive of his generation. Tate and his father had shared common clients over the years. Was he part of the secret partnership? Wilson made a mental note to ask Carter about him, but right now he had his hands full.

Since Sunday, Emily had continued her attempts to dissuade him from his course of action, so when she entered the belfry library, he prepared himself for another lengthy discussion.

"As much as I hate to admit it, you may be right about the path forward. But it scares me to death. I don't want to lose us," Emily said as her large brown eyes glistened.

Wilson's heart immediately filled with gratitude and empathy. "There's nothing I want more than a life with you, no matter where we live or how crazy our schedules get. I never want to live without you again. Never. But we can't live in constant fear that some paranoid member of a secret society might one day decide to take us out, just because we represent a potential risk. We can't live that way," he said, reaching over and running his fingers through her blonde curls.

"You're right. I just…"

Wilson placed his finger on her lips and then kissed them gently. "I promise not to take any unnecessary risks. If it gets too dicey, we'll go to the authorities. I promise," he said, putting his arms around her.

"Thank you," she said, holding him tightly.

"Trust me. There's no death wish here. Not when I have you. And I have been listening to you. If the KaneWeller merger goes through, we may have no choice but to involve the FBI immediately."

She squeezed him as tight as she could, desiring never to let go of him. "I love you, Wilson," she said as she took Wilson by the hand. "I think it's time for something less stressful."

Later that night as Wilson was lying in bed next to Emily, Bill Heinke called to inform him that KaneWeller had decided to withdraw from the merger with Fielder & Company. "We can challenge it, if you choose," Heinke said with a voice that sounded either reluctant or weary.

"No, that won't be necessary. I'll be taking Fielder & Company off the market for now," Wilson said, looking over at Emily with eyes that said I'm sorry. Emily got up from the bed and went to the bathroom.

"I understand," Heinke said in a low serious voice. "Liquidation of all non-Fielder & Company holdings is now fifty percent complete. We should be able to finish almost everything within two weeks. Some of the real estate holdings will take longer."

UBS had been providing Wilson with daily encrypted updates on proceeds from the ongoing liquidation, which were immediately reinvested through concealed accounts. Daniel had set up the reinvestment structure and strategy, so he wasn't worried, but he did want to find out how involved Bill Heinke had been with Fielder & Company.

"Fine," Wilson said. "Were you able to find the missing files?"

"Not yet," Heinke was curt, offering no explanation.

"In the wrong hands, that information could cause a lot of problems."

"We are acutely aware of Fielder & Company's exposure and have contracted the necessary resources to find the missing files. We remain optimistic. In the event that the missing files are not recovered, however, we are prepared to indemnify Fielder & Company against any and all resulting damages. We've already discussed the issue at length with Atlas Casualty and Surety. They provide our catastrophic insurance coverage. $1.2 billion in potential damages has already been preapproved."

Wilson thanked Heinke and replaced the phone in its cradle. He'd said enough about the missing files to Heinke. If he was a member of the secret partnership, he'd alert his cohorts. If he wasn't a member, then the conversation served to make sure there were no missteps by his firm regarding anything that had to do with the Fielder family. Wilson knew that his first moves against the secret partnership would have to come in the next few days, and they'd have to be the right moves. There would be no second chances.

When Emily returned from the bathroom, they held each other for several minutes without saying a word. Everything in their lives was about to change—more than either one of them could possibly imagine.

24

Tate – Sorrento, Italy

Music from Sorrento's Spring Fest floated across the water as Tate strolled into the posh bedroom of his three-hundred-foot luxury yacht, *Bacchus*. The yacht was anchored in the Bay of Capri, on the south side of the Gulf of Naples, Italy. He answered his phone. "I've been waiting for your call."

"This morning's *Wall Street Journal* was sheer serendipity," Kamin said. "Have you seen it?"

"Diane emailed it to me. Not bad huh?"

"Your complaint about Monday's story must have put the entire editorial board on pins and needles—referees trying to make up for a bad call, just like you said."

"Dispassionate, objective journalism at its finest," Tate chuckled.

"America's Warehouse could not have received a better preview, even if we'd written it ourselves," Kamin exclaimed.

"We *did* write it," Tate quipped.

They both laughed, heartily. All vestiges of the recent strain between them had disappeared. "Tell me about Quinn's reaction," Tate said.

"This is the best part," Kamin exclaimed, more than eager to relate the juicy details to Tate. "The stock price rebounded to fourteen dollars and then moved steadily up to twenty-two at closing. Quinn was ecstatic. But when I told him that we'd finally finished selling his ninety-five million shares a few minutes before closing, he started crying like a baby, hugging everyone he could get his hands on."

"Aahhh, Quinn," Tate sighed. "You beautifully predictable and talented creature."

"When he finally settled down, he pulled me aside and told me this was the happiest day of his life. He wants to acquire Hardware City before the end of the year."

"He's right on track," Tate said.

There was a short silence on the line before Kamin spoke again. "You called this one perfectly, Wayland. The partnership has already banked over five billion dollars in profits on Musselman stock."

Tate seized the opportunity to secure Kamin's loyalty. "What happened today was the result of perfect execution, and that wasn't me. That was you, Jules. Congratulations!"

"Thank you, Wayland."

"Savor the long weekend, Jules. You're entitled. Unless I hear from you first, I'll call you Monday," Tate said.

"Give my regards to Tiberio," Kamin said.

"I already have. We visited Villa Jovis this morning. You know, it was much easier to dispose of undesirables back then. Tiberius just threw them off his thousand-foot cliff into the sea. And to think he controlled the entire Roman Empire from the Island of Capri for over a decade—he would have been a good partner."

They both laughed vigorously before saying goodbye.

As soon as Tate clicked off, he placed a call to Morita in the New York office.

"I just talked to Kamin," Tate said.

"Is he feeling better?" Morita asked.

"All his concerns seem to have vanished for now, but once the Musselman glow wears off over the next few days, his distrust and paranoia could return."

"What do you want to do?"

"Nothing for the moment. Any news from Swatling or Malouf?" Tate asked, wondering about his other partners.

"Malouf hasn't heard anything from KaneWeller or Bill Heinke. Swatling has completed his review of Morgan. He was quite optimistic. He's bringing it with him."

"Good. Did we get Quinn's transaction documented?"

"Yes, I'll have everything tonight—video, audio, and signed documents."

"Where are we keeping everything this time?"

"Safety-deposit box at Chase."

"Perfect," he said before redirecting his attention. None of the Musselman success would have been possible without Morita's behind the scenes support network. "Still planning to join us?"

"Of course. You think I'd miss Capri?"

"You must have been Italian in a former life," Tate said, knowing how much Morita loved Roman archeology and history.

"Queen Zenobia of Palmyra," Morita said, laughing. "The woman who manipulated the Roman Empire and controlled its most important trade routes for years. If I wasn't her in a former life, I wish I had been."

"Isn't she the one who claimed to be a descendant of Cleopatra and some Persian ruler?" Tate asked, chuckling.

Morita laughed. "The very same."

"Are you exhausted?"

"Only when I think about it," she said.

"Why don't you stay here for the week," he said, aware that the recent string of retreats had worn her out.

"I can't. There's too much happening next week."

"Sure you can. The *Bacchus* is now wireless. You'd have online access to your entire staff," Tate said before turning on the charm. "You deserve it, Diane. None of this would be possible without you, I hope you know that."

There was silence from Morita's end, which made Tate smile. At least she was mulling over his suggestion. The intense pressure of recent weeks was getting to everyone, and the last thing he needed was for his most trusted confidant to lose her edge.

Tate continued, "The Villa Jovis Symposium runs through Tuesday. Don't forget, it was the most luxurious villa in Roman history. You could even spend a couple of days at the Quisiana, without a single client to worry about. I know how much you love the narrow streets and hidden alleyways of Capri, not to mention the shopping. What do you say? We all need to spend some time celebrating Musselman."

"Let me think about it," she said. "I'll let you know Sunday morning."

"Thank you, Diane, for everything," he said, smiling again as he ended the call and lay on his bed listening to the Mediterranean lap against the ship's bough. He was certain that Morita would take him up on his offer.

Within seconds a knock came at his door. "It's open," he said.

"Are you ready, my love?" said the taller of two stunningly beautiful models who entered his master suite, locking the door behind them. They moved like silk in a breeze.

"I am. I am," he said, inviting the women to lie down beside him, beneath the carved mahogany canopy adorned with Italian lace. Tate was definitely ready to celebrate.

25

Hap – Boston, MA

Hap Greene was quietly enjoying the subdued atmosphere inside the Bostonian Club's elegantly appointed library, when Wilson found him. His stylishly short gray hair made him look even more distinguished than Wilson remembered. Hap was in his late forties, but his six-foot-three-inch frame looked as fit as that of a thirty-year-old. He was impeccably dressed, as always, this time in an Armani charcoal tweed suit and a starched white shirt with a striking turquoise tie. Wilson was also in uniform—black pin-striped suit with white shirt and red club tie.

They greeted each other as old friends and then sat down for lunch in the main dining room. Wilson discreetly reached into his briefcase and pulled out the mobile nullifier Hap had sent him and placed it on the table behind the large salt and pepper shakers.

Hap smiled before commenting, "I wouldn't place too much confidence in that gadget, Wilson. It was intended to frustrate the casual eavesdropper and maybe a PI or two, but not skilled professionals, at least not indefinitely."

"That's not very comforting," Wilson said as he examined Hap. Precise, decisive, no-nonsense, with a flair for the unexpected—that was the Hap Greene Wilson had come to respect and admire. Wilson looked around the main dining room. His father had been a member here for years, but Wilson didn't recognize anyone. Then he stared at the nullifier, questioning whether the secret partnership had already de-nullified it. He then looked at Hap.

"Don't worry, the building is clean," Hap said. "We swept it this morning."

"You never use these things?" Wilson asked, nodding toward the nullifier.

"Sure we do. But you have to assume that serious surveillance teams will find a way to pierce them."

The waiter arrived with water and menus, rattling off the day's specials. They ordered quickly. When they were alone again, Wilson asked, "So how do we guarantee our privacy?"

"Regular sweeps of your premises with constant monitoring. But before we get into that, maybe you should update me on what's happened since we last talked."

For the next several minutes as they ate lunch, Wilson told Hap everything, including his intent to infiltrate the secret partnership. Just as Wilson was finishing, Hap raised his finger to his lips, giving Wilson the quiet sign. Then, Hap got up from the table without saying a word and walked to the restroom. Three minutes later, he returned.

"We have an eavesdropper, a Mr. Robert J. Swatling. Evidently he's a member here. Do you know him?" Hap asked.

"He's an associate of my father's. Lives in New York City, but has a law practice here as well."

"He and two others have just set up a portable wall-penetrating microphone and recorder in the private dining room on the other side of that wall," Hap said, nodding toward the wall twenty feet away.

"How do you know?"

"It's my business to know," he said cheekily. Then, pointing to his ear, he explained. "I'm online with my people."

Wilson couldn't see anything in his ear. "What do you want to do?"

"Your nullifier and our jamming equipment outside will handle things until they bring in better equipment, and believe me they will, sooner or later. We know Swatling. He used to be a client."

"How did you identify him?"

"The van parked outside has enough equipment to decipher every electronic eavesdropping device inside this building. After conducting a sweep this morning to give us a baseline, we've been monitoring changes. We also placed a few video cams. Swatling was identified as soon as he entered the building. When he turned on the microphone and recorder, we immediately assessed and jammed it. He's using a level-two device capable of piercing most nullifiers, including yours, but only under ideal circumstances. Have you been using it regularly?"

"Yes."

"Why aren't they using better equipment?" Hap asked, but the question wasn't for Wilson. Staring at the Club's large arching windows, Hap listened to input from his colleagues while formulating his own answer. "Swatling knew we'd identify him and his listening device, so what's he up to?"

Wilson waited until Hap had finished listening to his colleagues. "You said Swatling was a former client. Who quit who?" Wilson asked.

"We did. His demands began compromising our ethics. Is he part of this secret partnership?" Hap asked as he took another bite of his salad.

"Until now, I had no reason to think so," Wilson said, feeling vulnerable. "He's a close friend of my father's. They were board members here at the club for several years. I went to prep school with his son, Bobby. Haven't seen him in years. I don't know what to tell you. There's still plenty I don't know about my father."

"I brought an additional team with me. All of you are under twenty-four-hour surveillance, counter-surveillance, and coverage for maximum physical protection."

"You're worried about Swatling, aren't you?" Wilson said, the muscles in his neck and shoulders tightening.

Hap nodded. "Swatling knows we're meeting. He knows we're jamming the conversation. He wants us to know he's here. He'll escalate. Better equipment, better surveillance teams, until he gets what he wants." Hap stopped to study Wilson carefully. "Based on what you've told me and our preliminary assessment, not to mention Swatling's involvement, I suspect this secret partnership will do whatever it takes to neutralize you."

"What's the price tag for your twenty-four-hour services?"

"$200,000 a week plus expenses, payable at the end of each month."

"I'll pay five times that if you'll guarantee no body bags."

Hap leaned forward continuing to examine Wilson like a therapist. "You need to understand something, Wilson. What we do is anticipate and react. We don't control anything. If there are extreme measures, we'll do everything we can to protect you in the short term. After that, we bring in the authorities. If what you want is a guarantee, walk away from this and go to the authorities right now."

"I can't."

"Then your well-being depends on exposing them quickly, before they figure out what you're doing."

"Does your involvement automatically increase their concerns?"

"Not necessarily. Based on the fact that we've worked together before, a contract with my firm would be a logical next step, especially after the death of your attorney and threats to your mother and girlfriend. They already know you're worried about the surveillance. Plus you've just taken over your father's firm. They were expecting this, and they let us know a few minutes ago."

"Any reservations?"

"None. You're already paying double my usual fee."

Wilson scanned Hap's eyes, asking himself again, if he was ready to place the well-being of his family and loved ones in the hands of a man he admired and respected professionally, but with whom he had only a limited personal history. But if not Hap, who? Wilson didn't know where his feelings of assurance came from as he pondered the question, but he grabbed a hold. "Okay, when do we move my father?"

Hap took his last bite of salad before responding. "We don't. We have a better chance of protecting him right where he is. I have three people at the hospital working undercover. He'll have 24/7 protection. You, on the other hand, will have to move. We're arranging for an apartment near the Fielder & Company building. We can do a better job of protecting you and your family if you're separated."

Wilson nodded hesitantly, but decided to trust Hap's judgment. "I'm planning a trip next with Fielder & Company's senior executives to tour the firm's seven offices. After that Emily and I are going to Venice for a week."

"You're not going to make this easy are you?"

Wilson didn't say anything as the waiter cleared their plates.

Hap continued, "I'll need people here to watch Emily and at least two with you on your office tour. And, I'm afraid you won't be going to Venice alone. They'll be discreet, but they'll be there, watching your every move."

Wilson nodded his head in agreement. "What about the others?"

"Looks like you won't be having much contact with them this week or next, which is good. The less contact the better. I'll be conducting deep background checks on all of them, including Emily."

"Why?" Wilson said, caught off guard.

"Trust no one, Wilson. It's safer."

"I trust these people with my life."

"Your father probably felt the same way about his circle of intimates."

Wilson placed his napkin on the table in front of him. "Carter Emerson is the only one who could be a member of the secret partnership, but I'm satisfied that his interests are aligned with mine and my father's. I have to trust that, otherwise we have no chance of exposing the people who shot my father, killed Daniel Redd, and have been fleecing Wall Street."

"I hope you're right, but I can't rely on it. We never take on this level of risk without knowing everything about the principals, and we never accept anyone's assumptions about anything. Isn't that what they taught you at Kresge & Company?"

"You've already started the background checks, haven't you?" Wilson asked, questioning his own fears.

"As soon as you called."

They spent the rest of the afternoon going over Wilson's plans for infiltrating the secret partnership, as well as details about each of the people Hap Greene and his associates would be protecting. Having Hap on board was a relief.

26

Wilson – Boston, MA

Wilson was shocked by the hearty welcome he received when he stepped out of the elevator on the tenth floor of the Fielder Building on Friday. He slowly worked his way through the busy corridors shaking hands and meeting people until arriving at his father's office, with its impressive vista of the Charles River and MIT campus. Even though his perspective had changed dramatically since the last time he'd been in the office, the actual act of officially occupying his father's workspace, with the intent to assume his father's previous mantle of authority, felt weightier than he'd anticipated. Can I pull it off?

Just as he'd requested, Wilson spent the afternoon interviewing each of the firm's six vice presidents. He'd met them all before, but things were different now that he was their boss, and his life literally depended on knowing them. His first meeting was with John Malouf, the most senior of the vice presidents and head of the corporate restructuring practice. He was an extreme version of his father, both in stature and demeanor, less talkative and more prone to glare, which proved unsettling for Wilson. Malouf seemed perfectly content with his arrogance and enigma. They sat down at the stone table.

"Do people ever mistake you for my father?" Wilson said.

"Sometimes," Malouf said, deadpan.

"Are you as good as he is?" Wilson asked, deciding to be equally direct and to the point with this man who was still glaring at him.

"Yes and no," he said without blinking an eyelash.

"Tell me about the no part," Wilson said.

"Like every good student, there are some things you learn to do better than your teacher and other things you don't. I still haven't acquired his social adeptness or consciousness," Malouf said.

They stared at each other for several moments until Wilson asked him to describe the corporate restructuring practice at Fielder & Company, which Malouf did for the next twenty minutes in a rather cryptic, matter-of-fact fashion. When

Malouf was finished, Wilson said, "I look forward to getting to know you, John."

Malouf shook Wilson's hand without another word. As he left the office, Wilson asked him to send in Leigh Tennyson, the firm's newest vice president. She directed the strategic change practice. She reminded him of a former professor—tall, brunette hair pulled back in a French roll, uneven facial features with a piercing look of confidence in her hazel eyes. Reportedly she had the highest IQ of the six vice presidents. Wilson liked her style, and it didn't hurt that she was a Harvard Business School alum.

When she was comfortably seated on one of the French sofas at the less formal end of the office, Wilson asked her if she enjoyed working at the firm.

"I was, until your father's coma. He was the reason I left the Boston Consulting Group," she said. Then she took the next several minutes to tell Wilson what she'd been doing to strengthen the firm's strategic change practice.

When she finished, Wilson asked her what the firm had been like in his father's absence.

"Tense. Confused. Lots of positioning for power, especially from Malouf."

"Do you have a problem with Malouf?"

"Yes I do. Not only is he secretive and arrogant, he doesn't want to be a team player."

"You don't hold anything back, do you?"

"Only when it's productive to do so," she said without changing the serious look that defined her face.

As they stood up and shook hands, Wilson realized that as much as he liked her, she was as enigmatic as Malouf, only less cagey. He followed her out of the office and asked Anne to send in Frank O'Connor. Wilson then stepped into the concealed bathroom and dressing room, thinking about what Tennyson had said about Malouf. When he returned, Frank was sitting on one of the French sofas. He was a Ph.D. psychologist who managed the firm's organizational effectiveness practice. O'Connor instantly made Wilson feel as though he were talking to a personal therapist. There was something about his warm, inviting eyes and bald head that caused Wilson to feel comfortable enough to be open and candid.

"How are you feeling about taking over your father's firm?" O'Connor asked.

"Anxious and apprehensive."

"Perfectly normal for someone in your situation. Are you disappointed that KaneWeller backed out?"

"Part of me is. But the rest of me has accepted it. Sometimes I even feel grateful."

"Good sign. Your father would appreciate that response," he said. "I like it, too. You're going to do just fine here, Wilson."

"I hope so."

Just as Wilson was feeling as though he'd found a confidant among the vice presidents, O'Connor said, "This is no ordinary firm, you know. There are a lot of things going on beneath the surface."

"Such as?"

"Hidden agendas, special services for preferred clients, affiliations with other firms, and lots of turf issues," O'Connor said, raising his eyebrows and causing his forehead to wrinkle up to where his hairline used to be. "Your father pretty much gave us a free hand, and we each did what we wanted with it."

Wilson wanted to probe further, but he couldn't, not until he knew more about O'Connor and the rest of the vice presidents. As he did every day, Wilson reminded himself that his first moves to crack the partnership had to be the right moves. Instead, Wilson asked O'Connor to tell him more about his own practice area, which he did for the next half hour.

When Wilson escorted O'Connor to the door, Corbin Ashford was standing outside talking to Anne.

The firm's VP of finance and administration walked into the office and immediately began extolling the virtues of Wilson's father. Ashford was handsome, smooth, and articulate. He recited the firm's impressive growth record before taking a seat. As he continued telling Wilson everything he must have assumed Wilson wanted to know about the firm and its financial situation, Wilson grew more and more uncomfortable with Ashford's blatant egotism.

"How's the firm's cash flow?" Wilson asked, interrupting him.

"We haven't missed a beat. The firm's cash flow is stronger than ever," Ashford said as he stood up again and walked toward the wall of windows overlooking the Charles River.

"No setbacks?"

"None. And I don't expect any," he said, arrogantly.

"What problems do we face?" Wilson asked.

"To tell you the truth, everything's running smoothly. We're ahead of our profit projections—revenues are up and operating expenses are down."

Wilson wouldn't hear about any problems from Ashford. Never tell the boss bad news. Just what I need from a CFO, Wilson said to himself sarcastically. He wondered how his father had handled Ashford.

Before Ashford left, he returned to extolling the virtues of Wilson's father and his financial genius. "The world actually knows very little about your father's contributions to creating wealth and humanizing capitalism. Thanks to him, billions of people will someday be accessing capital, investing in themselves, building businesses, and spreading the wealth more than ever before."

Wilson was quietly stunned as he listened to Ashford espouse his father's philosophy. He couldn't decide whether

Ashford was trying to impress him or opening a door into the secret partnership. Either way, Wilson wasn't ready to commit himself. He quickly thanked Ashford for the information and said he'd have more questions later. He asked him to send in Joel Spivey, vice president of human resources.

Spivey was a cynical and witty ex-marine sergeant and Stanford MBA who looked like Spike Lee and was by far the most decidedly extroverted of the vice presidents.

"It's great to have you here, Wilson," Spivey said as he walked into the office with an air of cool.

"How are the people handling all this?" Wilson asked.

"Like victims, just as you'd expect," he said, laughing. "But don't get me wrong, they're definitely survivors. We pick our people well and they don't disappoint us when times get tough."

"Anyone planning to leave?"

"Everyone's planning to leave sooner or later, that's the nature of our business. Five to ten years on the Fielder & Company learning curve and they're ready for a cushy senior executive position with a client company."

Wilson smiled, but only slightly. He didn't want to encourage Spivey too much. "Are there any personnel issues I should know about?"

"Nothing pressing," Spivey said.

"What about the vice presidents?"

"You've probably already heard complaints about Malouf and Ashford," he said.

"Malouf, yes, but nothing about Ashford," Wilson said.

"They've been trying to take charge in your father's absence."

"Anything I should be worried about?"

"Only mutiny," he said, grinning.

Wilson forced a smile. He asked Spivey to tell him about the firm's website and how it was used in recruiting staff and marketing services. For the next twenty minutes, Spivey took Wilson through a brief demonstration on the computer, explaining that all the programming and design work had been done by Fielder employees. When he finished, Wilson was convinced that Fielder & Company's website not only represented state-of-the-art interactive programming, but the work of an in-house IT team capable of anything.

As Spivey left, he answered one of Wilson's lingering questions. "The technology nerds report to Ashford, and believe me, you don't want them against you."

Wilson took another bathroom break before meeting with the last of the vice presidents, Bob Throckmorton, who headed the operational redesign practice. He was short, stocky, curly headed, and had eyes that seemed ready to burrow into anything. But as soon as Wilson asked him what he was working on, Throckmorton became oblivious to everything outside his area of responsibility.

"We're re-engineering one of GE's appliance businesses, but Immelt's decision to sell the division has everyone covering their rear ends, which is unusual for GE. They all know fifteen percent of them will get the axe from Immelt, that's normal operating procedure from the Welch era. But now they're expected to cut another fifteen percent, before the sale. It's produced a victim-hunting culture that's not only compromising productivity but also creating more victims. I'm going to the company's management training center at Crotonville to discuss the issue with a group of business heads. It'll be fine in the end, because GE prides itself in firing those managers who make people feel like victims. Anyway, we're trying to minimize the trauma so we can get the re-engineering completed."

"Is GE concerned?"

"Are you kidding? GE couldn't be happier. Immelt's attitude is if GE can't whip a person or a business into shape, then no place can. He's not a screamer like Welch, but he's more determined to make changes than most people realize."

Before Throckmorton could continue, Anne opened the door and stuck her head in to remind Wilson, as he had requested, about his 6:30 p.m. dinner reservation.

"Good to have you on board," Throckmorton said, as he stood up from the black wing chair and extended his hand.

Throckmorton could have gone on for another hour about his project with General Electric, Wilson thought, but his focus had already turned to anticipating an evening with Emily.

27

Quinn – Lake Forest, IL

David Quinn stepped to the front of the cavernous living room overlooking the water at Musselman's secluded mansion on Lake Michigan. More than sixty senior executives, middle managers, staff from corporate headquarters, and advertising executives from Boggs & Saggett were rejoicing euphorically. It was the first Musselman celebration party in almost two years. Quinn raised his glass of champagne above his head.

"This has been a glorious week for the J. B. Musselman Company. Our stock price has finally reached thirty dollars," he said to whoops and hollers and rowdy applause. "And the best is yet to come. Next weekend we roll out America's

Warehouse." The room erupted with more shouts, noise-makers, and applause.

The stately thirty-six room Lake House—traditional English brick and stucco with half timbers, cedar shake shingles, abundant ivy, beautiful heated gardens, antique furniture, and layers of nineteenth-century craftsmanship—was the perfect place for a party. The house was designed by well-known Chicago architect Arthur Heun in 1896 for the son of John V. Farwell, the dry goods magnate who launched Marshal Field's and was a founding member of the controversial Commercial Club of Chicago. It stood on several acres of secluded lakefront property in Lake Forest, Illinois, about forty minutes north of downtown Chicago via Lake Shore Drive and Sheridan Road. The house was maintained by a discreet property management firm that employed the latest security surveillance systems and guaranteed absolute privacy.

Quinn had purchased the Lake House property several years earlier for the purpose of entertaining preferred customers and suppliers. No one gained entrance without his personal authorization, and the property management firm reported only to him. But even with such exclusive control, Quinn had rarely used the Lake House for personal pleasure. Tonight, however, would be an exception, he thought to himself. All week long, while fretting about newspaper articles, takeover bids, and stock positions, he'd secretly fantasized about being with Andrea Vargas. Then, when his ninety-five million shares of Musselman stock were cashed out at half a billion dollars in profit, his fantasies turned into a call for celebration.

As the increasingly raucous crowd quieted down momentarily, Quinn thanked them for their tireless efforts in preparation for next week's grand opening of America's Warehouse and challenged them to keep the momentum building in the weeks ahead. There was another burst of applause and catcalls as Quinn raised his arms to quiet them down.

"I want all of you to know that none of this would be possible without each and every one of you. So enjoy yourselves tonight and stay as long as you like." The crowd noisily expressed its pleasure while Quinn waved gleefully and then removed himself to the soundproof library where he called his wife Margaret. When she answered, Quinn asked, "Did you see where the stock closed?"

"Yes, Jenny and Bob came over. Everyone's been calling," Margaret said enthusiastically, referring to the Quinn's' oldest daughter and son-in-law who also lived in Hinsdale.

"Next week's grand opening will take it even higher. It's all coming together, Maggie."

"No one deserves it more than you, David."

The comment brought pangs of guilt, but only for a moment, as he looked up to see Vargas opening the door to the library. He knew she'd sensed his craving for her. "Hang on a minute Maggie," Quinn said before pushing the hold button.

Vargas sashayed up to him in her tight-fitting black evening dress, placed her hand on his neck, and began kissing his ear. "I'll be in the hot tub in the master suite, if you'd like to join me."

Quinn was melting inside as he watched Vargas' body swaying back and forth before she disappeared through the door. Raw ecstasy, he thought. "Hey, I'm back," Quinn said into the phone. "We still have miles to go before the grand opening, but we're almost there."

"Everyone wants to know when you're coming home to celebrate," Margaret said.

"I know," Quinn said as a pang of conscience returned momentarily. "We've got a long weekend of warehouse visits, making sure everything's ready for the grand opening. I should be back by the middle of next week. Tell the kids we can celebrate then."

"Don't push yourself too hard, dear. You're not the young buck you used to be, but I love you more than ever."

This time the pang lingered. "I love you, too, Maggie. I'll call you over the weekend."

"Travel safely. We'll have everything prepared when you get back."

Quinn put down the phone, feeling guilty. He wouldn't be getting on an airplane tonight or tomorrow or the next day for any warehouse visits, all of that was being covered by his executive staff. He questioned himself one more time about joining Vargas in the master suite. As he left the library, the sound of music and revelry helped him answer the question.

He found Vargas in the mosaic-tiled private spa, soaking in the sunken whirlpool bath and covered in bubbles. She looked so unbelievably alluring. There would be no turning back now. Quinn revealed the red roses from behind his back. Vargas rose slowly from the churning water and sensuously ascended the tiled steps one at a time, her smoky eyes focused on Quinn. "Thank you for the flowers. Come join me," she said seductively as she took the flowers and descended back into the bubbles.

Quinn's entire body quivered with excitement as he dismissed all thoughts of anyone or anything except Andrea Vargas. He began removing his clothes, pleased that he'd lost ten pounds for the occasion—especially when Vargas noticed.

28

Wilson – Boston, MA

After a restless weekend of treading water, Wilson met with Fielder & Company's vice presidents first thing Monday morning to go over a few more basics concerning the firm's business activities. The company was currently working on 476 consulting engagements in 412 client companies with average revenue-per-engagement of approximately $2.4 million. It employed 684 consultants and 243 staff, 927 employees in total, located in six offices—Boston, Chicago, Dallas, San Francisco, London, and Hong Kong. Projected revenues for the year stood at $1.2 billion with anticipated pre-tax profits of $310 million. The firm's share of large multinational corporations as clients was stronger than ever. Almost every client had inquired about Charles Fielder's condition and how it might impact the future of the firm, but according to the vice presidents, only a handful of clients had expressed serious concerns or reservations about continuing to do business with Fielder & Company.

Next, they reviewed the content of an internal memorandum and press release prepared by the firm's PR staff, informing employees and clients that Fielder & Company and KaneWeller would not be merging and that Wilson would be assuming his father's position as Chairman and CEO. When they reached agreement on the content, Wilson made a courtesy call to CEO Marshall Winthorpe of KaneWeller, who suggested a few minor changes to the memo to reflect KaneWeller's reasons for backing out of the deal. Wilson then persuaded Winthorpe to limit his firm's discussions with the press regarding Fielder & Company.

Just before noon, Fielder & Company released, by fax and email, the following statement to 927 consultants and staff, 1852 past and present clients, and 128 business press contacts:

In the interest of fortifying the company's current focus on investment banking and brokerage-related businesses, the Board of Directors of KaneWeller has decided not to proceed with the acquisition of Boston-based management consulting firm Fielder & Company. For the near term, KaneWeller has chosen to defer its entry into the management consulting business.

Fielder & Company's new Chairman and CEO Wilson Fielder, majority shareholder and son of founder Charles Fielder, plans to continue the philosophies and policies set forth by his father during the firm's twenty-two-year history and expects to expand the firm's impressive record of assisting major multinational corporations improve bottom-line results and increase shareholder value.

Prior to assuming leadership of Fielder & Company, Wilson Fielder spent seven years with the management consulting firm of Kresge & Company as an associate consultant, engagement manager, and partner. He co-directed the firm's corporate transformation practice for the past four years. He earned degrees from Princeton University and the Harvard Business School.

No further changes in Fielder & Company's management structure or personnel are currently anticipated. Any requests for additional information should be forwarded to www.fielder.com or 100 Beacon St., Boston, MA 02140, 1-888-303-2121.

With the press release memorandum on its way, Wilson met again with the vice presidents in the afternoon, hammering out the details of a whirlwind office tour. Over the next four days, they would visit Fielder & Company's six offices, personally assuring every Fielder & Company consultant and staff member of the firm's strong financial position, as well as Wilson's commitment to carry on his father's philosophies and policies.

By the time they finished at three o'clock, the vice presidents had their assignments and the rest of the day to prepare. The first stop on the tour was scheduled for tomorrow morning at eight o'clock, in the large, ninth-floor conference room of the Fielder Building. After that, they would fly to Chicago, Dallas, San Francisco, Hong Kong, and London.

Later that night, after packing for his trip and their move from Brattle House, Wilson and Emily went to the hospital to visit his father. Nothing in his father's condition had changed. Once again, they stood by his hospital bed holding his hand and talking, hoping that he might be able to hear them and one day respond.

"What would he have to say about your plan to convince the secret society to bring you inside?" Emily asked, her fear persisting, even though Hap Greene and his people had made her feel much better.

"Control or be controlled," Wilson quoted without hesitation. "That's the world we live in, he'd say. Then he'd remind me how depraved and enslaved our society has become for embracing such a false dogma."

Emily put her arms around Wilson's waist and hugged him tightly. "I do believe that everything he was doing at Fielder & Company was intended to bring about change. Profound change."

"I'm glad you think so," Wilson said before kissing her. "So do I." He gazed into her eyes, their faces inches apart. "If you want to know the truth, I couldn't do this without knowing that you feel the same way. But I couldn't tell you that until you arrived at it on your own."

"You think I didn't know that?" she said, giving him a nudge.

Neither one of them liked the idea of being apart for the next five days, but they agreed that it would be better for Wilson to do this alone. It would also give Emily time to review the publisher's initial round of edits on her manuscript. Fortunately, the anticipation of spending a whole week together in Venice had emboldened them.

When Wilson and Emily left the hospital, they took their things to the fully furnished Back Bay apartment, overlooking the Fielder & Company building. After entering, they stood at the apartment's newly installed one-way, bulletproof windows, watching the lights come on inside the Fielder Building. Hap Greene's people along with building security personnel had just started conducting their nightly sweep. It was a little after midnight.

"When will it end?" Emily asked.

"Soon, I hope," Wilson said, holding her in his arms. "One way or another, we'll get out of this alive, free to pursue our dreams. I promise."

29

Quinn – Lake Forest, IL

Beneath the ample canopy trimmed in an eighteenth-century Chinese coverlet, Quinn lay deliciously drained. The Levitra had worked miraculously during the past three days, just as his doctor promised.

"Your hands are absolutely amazing," Vargas whispered into his ear as he gently stroked her long, slender body. "Has anyone ever told you that before?"

"Actually, no," he said, but he was lying. His wife Margaret had told him the same thing years ago.

"You could hire them out and probably make more money than you do as CEO of the J. B. Musselman Company," she said giggling and running her fingers through his chest hair.

Vargas had grown more carefree and silly during their three days together and so had Quinn. But her innocuous comment about hiring out his hands bothered him. Was it a Freudian slip in a lighthearted moment that had exposed her true self? His old suspicions had gradually started to return. No matter what she says about wanting to be with me, she's still a hired hand, Quinn said to himself.

She shifted her lithe body, lying face down and snuggling her head into a pillow. Quinn gently stroked her neck and back until she was asleep. As he lay awake next to her, waiting to escape once more into sexual bliss, Quinn grew more cynical. He began admitting to himself that his passion for Vargas had been little more than a fabulous fantasy, facilitated by Wayland Tate as part of a larger strategy to manipulate him and the J. B. Musselman Company.

Musselman's stock price had continued to climb on Monday, closing at 393/4. Tate and his partners have *got* to be raking in billions, Quinn thought. *You and I, Jules, and a group of clients committed to helping each other make a lot of money*, Tate's words reverberated in his head. Quinn was finally admitting to himself that Tate might have orchestrated the whole thing. Was Tate really that good? Yes, Quinn told himself, and Vargas was probably getting a nice cut of the action.

His new sarcasm wasn't really the result of anything Vargas had said or done, other than maybe performing too perfectly. Nor was it attributable to Tate's baiting and trapping him. He only had himself to blame for that. In truth, his growing disillusionment derived from the interludes over the past three days when he was physically depleted, emotionally melancholic, and mentally introspective. That's when he first realized that his appetites were feeding on themselves— more control demanded more scheming requiring more appeasement and double-dealing, eventually leading to more indulgence and escape.

Ashamed that his desperation in recent months had so easily impaired his judgment, Quinn began to reconsider his current state of affairs. Had it not been for his principles, the seductive cycle might have continued indefinitely. While he had indeed ignored them in recent weeks, he had never abandoned them. It was time to end the illusion and the manipulation.

Once Vargas was sound asleep, Quinn quietly got out of bed and removed his briefcase from beside the nightstand. He put on a robe and left the master suite.

Downstairs in the library, Quinn sat down at the antique desk and drew the telephone toward him. Wiping away the perspiration on his forehead with the sleeve of his robe, he removed a business card from his briefcase: *Samuel P. Wiseman, Deputy Director, Federal Bureau of Investigation.* Quinn punched in the numbers. He had met Wiseman a year earlier at a Chicago Children's Museum fundraising event, where they instantly struck up a friendship. They'd seen each other twice since then, once at another fundraiser, and a second time when Quinn had invited Sam to join his foursome at a private golf tournament.

The line rang twice before a voice on the other end caused Quinn's heart to skip. "Federal Bureau of Investigation, Chicago bureau, Special Agent Mullrose speaking."

"Agent Mullrose," Quinn said, his voice trembling slightly. "I'd like to speak to Deputy Director Sam Wiseman."

"He's not in, sir. How can I help you?"

"Do you have a number where I can reach him? It's very important. He told me to call him personally if I ever needed his help. I need his help, and I need it now."

There was a brief silence on the line before agent Mullrose said, "Just a minute, sir. I'll connect you. Can I have your name?"

"David Albright Quinn, CEO of the J. B. Musselman Company," he recited, closing his eyes and waiting. The senior security officer of the property management firm that maintained Lake House had assured Quinn that the mansion's counter-surveillance system would intercept and jam any possible electronic eavesdropper, but Quinn's nerves were still frayed.

Five minutes later, Samuel P. Wiseman, Deputy Director of the FBI and acting head of the Chicago bureau was on the line. "How can I help you, David?"

Quinn swallowed hard, his throat and his voice trembling slightly, "I'd prefer not to do this over the phone, but I have no choice, Sam. My people have assured me that the phones are clean. I have detailed information about a web of illegal stock manipulations and I'm fully prepared to tell my story, including testifying in court. But I want immunity for myself and the J. B. Musselman Company."

"You'll have to give me a few more details, David," Wiseman said.

"If I do, what guarantees will I have?"

"There can be no guarantees without more information."

"I have first-hand information about an organization that cleverly blackmails CEOs into manipulating stocks, making illegal stock purchases, and providing insider information to its clients."

"Give me a name," Wiseman said.

"Wayland Tate, CEO of Tate Waterhouse, the advertising firm."

"Who else?"

"I need assurances," Quinn insisted as he wiped the beads of sweat from his forehead once again.

"Who else, David?" Wiseman insisted.

"Jules Kamin, COO of KaneWeller."

"What sort of evidence do you have?"

"Loan documents, stock purchases, and my own eyewitness testimony," Quinn said becoming more nervous. "But only for immunity."

"I'm sorry David, but I can't promise anything without going over the evidence."

Quinn ran through his options, finally recognizing that he had no choice. "I'm under heavy surveillance. Can you at least allow me to determine how, when, and where the information will be delivered?"

"Of course," Wiseman said.

"Come to my company's Lake House mansion at the end of Illinois Road in Lake Forest tomorrow at one o'clock with a female agent that can pass for your wife. Identify yourselves as Dale and Shirley Frederickson from Austin, Texas, owners of the Cap and Tool chain of hardware stores. Bring some luggage to make it look like you're going to stay for the night."

"We'll be there," Wiseman said.

Quinn replaced the receiver and returned to the master suite where Vargas was sleeping. The seductive cycle had been broken. Now it wouldn't be long before he'd have to tell his wife and children, and ask for their forgiveness. Maybe someday he would be able to forgive himself.

For now, however, Quinn's plan depended on continuing his relationship with Vargas. She was the only one who could keep Tate convinced that he hadn't succumbed to feelings of regret or remorse—only bliss. Surprisingly, Quinn felt considerable guilt for having to keep Vargas in a charade to serve his purpose. Part of him still wanted to believe that she really loved him, the other part recognized the lie.

Nevertheless, Quinn resolved to enjoy the remaining moments of his love affair with Andrea Vargas—until he had to face the insufferable consequences that awaited him.

30

Quinn – Lake Forest, IL

At precisely one o'clock in the afternoon as Quinn was preparing to join Vargas in the large whirlpool bath, the phone rang. He picked up the extension in the master suite's spa and bath area. It was the voice of senior security officer Jackson Ebbs informing him that Dale and Shirley Frederickson, a.k.a. Deputy Director Wiseman and companion, had arrived.

"Take them to the library," Quinn said. He knew that meeting with the FBI while Vargas was in the house presented a risk, but it also offered the necessary cover. Tate and his people had to be assuming he was totally involved and preoccupied with Andrea Vargas, which he had been.

In any case, Jackson Ebbs and his security team were well instructed to alert him if anything looked out of the ordinary.

"Who was it," Vargas asked from the whirlpool.

"Just one of our clients and his wife, Dale and Shirley Frederickson from Austin, Texas. I told you about them. They'll be staying at the Lake House tonight, but there's nothing to worry about. We won't have to do a thing. I only need to spend a few minutes making them feel welcome. Stay right where you are until I can join you," he said with a big smile. "Pamper yourself."

"Hurry back," she said as she half-rose out of the water and rested her breasts on the edge of the whirlpool.

He leaned down and kissed her cheek. Saying goodbye to her would be one of the hardest things he'd ever done, Quinn thought. "Believe me, I won't let this take any longer than necessary," he said, wishing for a brief moment that he'd never called the FBI.

When Quinn arrived in the library, Sam Wiseman greeted him and then introduced the woman standing next to him as Kirsten Kohl, head of the Bureau's Corporate Crime Division. Wiseman looked like the prototypical version of a mature, experienced FBI agent, fifty something, perfectly combed brown and gray hair, even features, gray suit, white shirt, conservative blue tie and a trim, six-foot physique. His partner, Kirsten Kohl, was equally predictable, forty something, dark blue business suit, light yellow blouse, short brunette hair, plain features, and a stocky five-foot-eight-inch frame.

The three of them sat at the center of the richly decorated, knotty-pine-paneled library, while David Quinn spent twenty minutes recounting the Musselman saga up to this weekend's celebration with Andrea Vargas. He then gave them his copies of the documents he'd signed. The Nevada corporation documents that showed his stock options as collateral and the Nevis Trust papers that showed the borrowed funds to buy ninety-five million shares of Musselman stock on margin.

As Kohl reviewed the documents, Wiseman's clear green eyes studied Quinn's face. "Are you ready to have your life examined with a fine-tooth comb?"

"If that's what it takes to make things right—yes, I am," Quinn said, feeling certain once more about his decision to bring in the FBI.

Kohl looked up from the documents at Wiseman. "I don't think immunity will be a problem."

"When will you know for sure?" Quinn asked, feeling suddenly apprehensive.

It was Wiseman who answered. "We'll get back to you within twenty-four hours," he said. "Will you still be here?"

Quinn nodded as Wiseman and Kohl rose from their seats. Quinn walked them to the mansion's ten-car garage, where they had parked their gray Ford Expedition.

Wiseman removed his tie and jacket and put on a yellow sweater. Kohl took off her jacket and put on sunglasses. They both assured Quinn that their return to the office would be disguised as a trip to Michigan Avenue for shopping. There were three FBI units in the area. Two would provide cover or intervention, if needed, for Wiseman and Kohl. The third unit would keep the Lake House under discreet surveillance.

As Quinn returned to the master suite, he wondered what an FBI investigation would mean for Andrea Vargas. Suddenly, a craving for her engulfed him. A wicked man's lament, he told himself, grieving over a once fulfilled but now fleeting fantasy.

Lying on two towels spread over the steam room's spacious sitting area, Vargas had been savoring the time to herself. When Quinn returned, she quietly prepped herself. Having a man consumed with her the way Quinn was carried its share of burdens.

Twenty minutes later, after surrendering once more to his ardor, Quinn lamented, "I wish I could stay here with you forever." He was half lying and half telling the truth. "But tomorrow I need to spend some time with my family."

"I'd love to stay too, but I understand," she said, placing her arms around his neck and stroking the back of his head. "Your family needs to celebrate with you too."

Quinn kissed her gently. They both stood under the large shower head in the steam room, feeling relieved as the cool water washed over them. Quinn's relief was spiritual, having reclaimed his integrity by going to the FBI and now preparing to face the inevitable consequences. For Vargas, the relief was mostly physical, since her body was now in pain from their long weekend together. But she was determined to make sure that Quinn never knew. Little did she know he'd already slipped away.

31

Wilson – Boston, MA

Wilson's purpose for conducting the whirlwind tour was twofold, one stated and one unstated. Aside from the much-publicized official purpose, the unstated reason for the excursion was, of course, to climb into the minds and hearts of the six vice presidents, planting seeds of trust and baiting those who were part of the secret partnership.

The kick-off meeting began at precisely eight o'clock in the morning with all 161 consultants and 64 staff from the Boston office seated in the stylish auditorium on the ninth floor of the Fielder Building. After a brief but generous introduction of Wilson and his years at Kresge

& Company by Human Resources VP Joel Spivey, Wilson reviewed Fielder & Company's illustrious twenty-five-year history. He spoke about his father's basic philosophies of rigorous analysis, creative solutions, and exceptional results. Then he presented five initiatives that he promised to begin implementing in his first ninety days as Chairman and CEO of Fielder & Company. Embodied in his five point plan were two initiatives intended to make the secret partnership very uncomfortable. They would serve as Wilson's bait:

> *Create a five-year growth plan, building on the firm's existing philosophy, policies, and culture.*
> *Open the door to global alliances with targeted firms in strategically attractive regions of the world.*
> *Empower vice presidents, office-managing directors, and project leaders with greater autonomy and streamlined management systems.*
> *Launch a marketing and publicity campaign focusing on the firm's innovations, with new emphasis on writing and publishing by the firm's consultants.*
> *Expand the firm's performance-based equity and profit-sharing programs.*

After Wilson finished his hour-long presentation, the six vice presidents each took twenty minutes to review the firm's performance in their areas of responsibility, while elaborating on their own initiatives. The presentations gave Wilson the opportunity to see them in action and assess their loyalty to him and Fielder & Company. Some of their acclamations of allegiance seemed more natural and true than others. Wilson took note of every nuance. Following the three-hour block of presentations, they held an hour-long question-and-answer session. Most of the questions dealt with the initiatives and were easy to answer, but some went deeper.

A stern-looking consultant in her late twenties, who had joined the firm out of business school nine months earlier, asked, "What new information do you have about what happened to your father in Sun Valley?"

"We have no new information," Wilson said, "but I don't believe he was responsible for anyone's death." Wilson had anticipated the question, but decided not to dwell on it. He quickly moved on to the next question.

A senior consultant in his early forties who'd been with the firm for more than ten years asked, "The publicity campaign in your initiatives seems to be a break from your father's policy of letting our clients do the praising of Fielder & Company. Could you comment?"

"Given our current circumstances, I believe it's what my father would recommend. More exposure is vital to our firm's future growth and most of it will come from you, through articles, interviews, and books. My commitment is to make sure that what you write gets placed with the most respected publications and publishers. As you know, I started my career at Kresge & Company, and we all know how publicity-conscious they have become. We can do it better. Leigh, you used to work for BCG; would you like to make any comments?"

VP Leigh Tennyson seemed happy to reply. "I agree one hundred percent with what Wilson has said. The right kind of publicity has to be one of our strategic priorities, especially now with a cloud of uncertainty hanging over the firm. Word-of-mouth praises from our clients have served the company well in the past, but the world has changed and so have we."

Wilson smiled to himself, thinking that she couldn't possibly be part of the partnership, unless she was an exceptional poker player. The last thing the secret partnership needed was unnecessary publicity.

The most difficult question came from a thirty-something consultant who said he'd been with the firm for three years. "What was the reason for the moratorium on corporate restructuring engagements, and where do things currently stand?"

Wilson decided to give the question to John Malouf, VP of the corporate restructuring practice. "John, would you like to handle this one?"

"Supply and demand," he said in his usual arrogant, enigmatic way. "Too few staff for too many clients. We simply had to slow things down. We should be ready to take on new clients by May."

He handled the question skillfully, if not truthfully, Wilson thought. The real reason for limiting corporate restructuring engagements, according to Daniel, had been to stop the growing abuse of Fielder & Company's methods and practices. Although a part of Wilson liked John Malouf—perhaps because he reminded him of his father—it seemed more and more likely that Malouf was a member of the insider's club.

After the Q&A session was over and everyone was mingling around a lavish luncheon buffet, a recent recruit from the Wharton Business School asked Malouf why Fielder & Company had been dubbed the most secretive consulting firm in America. Wilson couldn't help overhearing the conversation and Malouf knew it.

"Secrecy sells," Malouf said.

"What about the new marketing and publicity initiative?" returned the recruit.

"Publicity also sells," Malouf said.

"You don't consider the two of them mutually exclusive?"

"Not if you publicize Fielder & Company's furtiveness the way Kresge publicizes its mystique," Malouf said, more talkative than usual.

"Is that what we're planning to do?"

"That's what I'm planning to do," Malouf said as he glanced over at Wilson.

Wilson held Malouf's eyes for a moment to let him know that he'd heard his response. Then, a man about Wilson's age and height tapped him on the shoulder and informed him that they should be leaving for the airport. It was Hap Greene's man, Mike Anthony, who was also serving as one of their pilots for the whirlwind tour. The game was afoot.

32

Tate – Sorrento, Italy

Bob Swatling fought down his mounting panic as he called Wayland Tate on one of the disposable encrypted phones. It was three o'clock in the morning in New York, nine o'clock on the Bacchus in the Bay of Sorrento.

Tate answered the phone from the upper deck where he was enjoying coffee with his lady friends. "What is it?" he asked, recognizing the emergency ID. He stood up and walked toward the ship's stern.

"We just finished analyzing the telephone and video monitoring feeds after hacking into the Lake House security system. Fourteen hours ago, David Quinn met with Sam

Wiseman, Deputy Director of the FBI, and Kirsten Kohl, head of the FBI's corporate crime division. He spilled the beans on you and Kamin. Vargas was upstairs in the spa. She knows nothing about it."

Tate's body tensed, his mind immediately immersed in contingencies.

"Keep Vargas uninformed. I'll contact Marco. You can advise Kamin. He's in Rome. Tell him to switch identities and get lost for a few days. I'll be doing the same," Tate said decisively. "Double check the Musselman trading entities. Close down anything that won't withstand an SEC inquisition. I'll take care of the other partners. Call me again in two hours."

"Will do," Swatling said before clicking off.

Tate left straightaway for the ship's bridge one deck below. He told the captain to raise anchor, display the yacht's alternate identity, and chart a course for Monaco where he had full diplomatic immunity. Then he went to his private office off the master suite and opened the concealed vault. He withdrew two encrypted cell phones. His first call was to Diane Morita who was staying at the Quisiana on the island of Capri. He told her to begin executing emergency contingency plans and to advise key partners, the clandestine supplier network, and her staff—with the exception of Andrea Vargas. His second call was to Marco, notifying him to begin damage control immediately.

33

Quinn – Lake Forest, IL

Less than twenty-four hours after Deputy Director Wiseman and Senior Agent Kohl had set the wheels of justice in motion, there was a soft knock on the door of the master suite at the Lake House. David Quinn got up from the bed and put on his robe, before entering the suite's foyer to open the door. It was Jackson Ebbs telling him that Mr. Frederickson wanted to talk to him on the secure phone in the library. Quinn told Vargas that he would be right back.

"Quinn here," he said when he got on the line in the library.

"It's Wiseman," The FBI executive said. "Immunity for you and your company has been approved. Arrest warrants for Tate and Kamin have been issued, but they're currently out of the country. We're trying to track them now. Federal Grand Jury subpoenas could come as early as Friday afternoon," Wiseman said.

Quinn was both relieved and stunned. In return for immunity, Quinn had promised the FBI that he would testify, but he never imagined it would happen so quickly. He'd been expecting to have more time to end things with Vargas and prepare his family. Suddenly, that seemed impossible.

Wiseman continued, "We're still uncovering the full range of surveillance on you. To say it's extensive would be an understatement. Security systems at the Lake House seem adequate, but the sooner you leave the better. Go about your business as usual, until we advise you otherwise. Don't do anything that will raise suspicions. I suggest you limit what you tell your family for as long as you can. You and your family will be relocated and placed under twenty-four-hour witness protection, prior to any subpoenas or arrests."

When Wiseman finished, Quinn said, "All I ask is that you make sure surveillance at my home in Hinsdale and in my office at Musselman is jammed or curtailed." Then he said good-bye and hung up. Despite Wiseman's warnings, he'd have to tell his wife and family, before overzealous journalists exposed his sins to the world. When he returned to the master suite, Vargas must have seen the lingering torment on his face, even though he tried to clear his thoughts before opening the door.

"Is everything okay?" she asked, walking up to him and placing her hands on his chest as she looked into his eyes.

"Everything's fine," Quinn said, trying hard to act casual. He couldn't afford to raise any doubts in Vargas' mind, at least not until he and his family were under full protection. He could only imagine what Tate might be capable of doing if he found out too early. "For the first time in my life, I'm actually lamenting going back to work."

Vargas kissed him on the lips. "Not as much as I am," she said, laying her head on his shoulder, her lips caressing his neck.

Quinn turned his head and kissed her on the forehead, but he knew she was lying. He had seen the veiled pain on her face during the last time they'd made love. That would not be the time he'd choose to remember for the rest of his life. "Maybe we can get away again this weekend," he said.

The two of them picked at a platter of fruit and cheese as they got dressed and prepared to leave what had been their love nest for the past several days. After they said their saccharine good-byes, Vargas left for Musselman headquarters to resume her preparations for the grand opening, and Quinn drove home to Hinsdale where his wife was preparing for a celebration.

Later that evening at the Quinn family home in Southeast Hinsdale, David Quinn struggled to feign excitement for the benefit of his wife, his four married children, and close family friends. Musselman stock had closed a few hours earlier at forty-eight dollars a share, making everyone jubilant. Everyone but Quinn. He could only lament that his family and friends, most of whom were Musselman shareholders, would soon know all his ugly secrets. By the time the celebration ended, it had become sheer agony for Quinn, who could no longer stomach keeping his lies to himself. But after thirty-two years of marriage, the least his wife deserved was a private confession.

Quinn held off through a sleepless night, before approaching his wife in the morning. She was in the kitchen cleaning up from the night before. When he asked her to join him in the living room, she immediately dropped what she was doing and followed him to one of the white Bellagio sofas and sat down. She was smiling until he reached down and turned on the central vacuum system to muffle their conversation. He calmly told her that there were people who might be listening. Then he moved closer to her on the couch and took her hand.

"Maggie, I've got something to tell you and it's pretty bad. In fact, it's downright ugly. And I'm horribly ashamed of it."

All animation left Margaret's face and her green eyes filled with fearful premonition as she tightened her grip on her husband's hand.

He wished to God he'd never met Wayland Tate. "I got involved with another woman when I was in Switzerland," he said quickly.

Margaret turned pale, her lips beginning to quiver. But she didn't utter a word.

Cursing his very existence, Quinn would have gladly extinguished himself in that moment if he could have. "Wayland Tate arranged the encounter behind my back. I guess I was so distraught over the company's problems that I didn't see it coming."

Although Margaret continued to hold his hand, she looked away.

"It was a terrible moment of weakness and I accept full responsibility for it. But it's over. And, I promise you, Maggie, I've never done this before and I'll never do it again. My only hope is that you will be able to forgive me."

She sat motionless on their expensive sofa, her eyes glistening but barren. In a low hollow voice, she asked, "Is she who you were with this weekend?"

"Yes, but it's over, Maggie. Believe me. It was all part of a scheme to manipulate Musselman. Tate sucked me into an illegal stock deal, but I've already turned him in to the

FBI. He won't be able to do this to anybody else ever again. There'll be some ugly press in the coming weeks. But it's over. He's been exposed."

"Are you going to tell the children?" Margaret asked, staring absently, obviously still in shock.

"Yes," Quinn said firmly. His confession had been quick and to the point, like telling analysts about lower than expected quarterly earnings. He'd learned the hard way that analysts liked to get bad news early and straight. But this wasn't about quarterly profits or stock analysts; this was about his wife and family. Regrettably, nothing in his experience had prepared him for this.

When the tears finally came, Margaret couldn't stop crying. The more he tried to comfort her, the more she cried, saying, "All I ever cared about was you and the children."

He stayed by her side for the rest of the day and night, trying to console her but with little success. Mostly, she just cried. Repeating the same words over and over again, until they were both emotionally exhausted. They finally fell asleep sometime after midnight.

34

Wilson – Charter Jet G650, Inflight

The Gulfstream G650 took off from Logan International with Fielder & Company's senior executive team, two pilots, and a flight steward, en route to a repeat performance of their presentation in the Chicago office later that afternoon and evening. The sleek new executive jet came standard with twin Rolls-Royce turbofan engines, Mach 1.0 flying speed, a 7,000 mile range, 45,000 foot cruising altitude, and customized interior. The cabin could be configured to seat twenty passengers in comfort or seven to ten executives in plush, fully reclining seats, with stylish work tables, and individual computer monitors. Wilson had chosen the luxury configuration to carry himself and the six Fielder & Company vice presidents on their four-day, six-office dog and pony show.

As Wilson sat back in his soft leather chair, Frank O'Connor leaned across the aisle and said, "You show a maturity well beyond your years, Wilson."

"Thank you," Wilson said. "But don't be too quick to judge. New circumstances and responsibilities have a way of bringing out the best in some people. Give me another assessment in three months."

"In my experience, maturity is not something you can fake, even at the beginning of a new assignment," he said, smiling.

"Thank you, Frank," Wilson said sincerely.

"You're also very good at the human dimension. Better than your father—and he was superb when he wanted to be. You seem to understand—or should I say empathize—with people at a deeper level," O'Connor said.

"Not always," Wilson said.

"None of us do all the time," he said, smiling again. "But, I watched you today. You have a gift for it, and I'm never wrong about this sort of thing."

"I'll try not to disappoint you, Frank," Wilson said, a little sarcastically, with controlled laughter.

"You won't. The five initiatives you outlined already convinced me of that. Can I get you something to drink?"

"No, I'm fine. Thanks," Wilson said as Frank got up and walked to the small bar near the front of the plane.

Hopefully, Wilson thought as he looked out the window at Boston Harbor, his five initiatives would also strike the right chord and send the proper signals to those in the secret partnership. Someone would have to respond soon, because Fielder & Company's days of low-profile secrecy and clandestine operations were about to come to an end. Anne had already sent out a request for proposals from the top advertising and publicity firms.

The rest of the week turned out to be a blitzkrieg for both Wilson and Emily. Emily's editor flew in from New York City and they began working around the clock to finish the copy-editing of her latest manuscript by the end of the week. Wilson's meeting with company employees in Chicago unfolded with few surprises, as did the meetings that followed in Dallas, San Francisco, Hong Kong, and London. Each office had received them with enthusiasm and excitement. Almost everyone seemed genuinely relieved that the KaneWeller deal had fallen through and that Wilson was carrying on his father's leadership of the firm. Concern for his father had been abundant. Most employees seemed to believe his father would eventually be exonerated of any wrongdoing. Their expressions of concern and loyalty had been heartwarming.

Ironically, Wilson's biggest surprise during the four-day excursion came when he finally acknowledged to himself how much he enjoyed the feeling of following in his father's footsteps. His most lasting impression, however, came from the people who worked for Fielder & Company. The overwhelming majority of them were bright, ambitious professionals of the highest caliber, delivering highly valuable services, with seemingly no knowledge of a clandestine insiders club. Wilson vowed to preserve everything that was good and right about Fielder & Company.

On the flight back from London, Wilson reflected on his assessment of the six vice presidents, each of whom had performed brilliantly during the week. His father had picked his lieutenants well. Unfortunately, Wilson still couldn't say for certain who was corrupt and who wasn't, except for John Malouf. Malouf was a purveyor of secrets and even more shrewd and clever than Wilson had initially thought. Corbin Ashford, and his penchant for trying to make everything seem perfect, continued to be a big question mark.

As for the other four vice presidents, Wilson remained hopeful. Joel Spivey was extremely perceptive and caring, once you got past his veneer of cynicism. Leigh Tennyson was not only bright, but she was street savvy and felt as strongly as Wilson did about his initiatives. Bob Throckmorton was a bona fide sage. His attention to detail could only be characterized as operational omniscience. Frank O'Connor continued to make Wilson feel comfortable; in fact, Wilson had come to rely on O'Connor's intuitive insights and friendly vigilance.

After a long, tiring week of dangling himself and his five initiatives as bait in front of the furtive insiders, there was only one thing left to do: sit back and wait. And that's exactly what he was going to do. In Venice with Emily. But first, he had to get one of them—Malouf or Ashford, maybe Spivey—to swallow the bait, which meant conducting one more mid-air meeting before they landed in Boston.

35

Quinn – Hinsdale, IL

At ten o'clock in the morning, family physician Dr. Michael Drury arrived at the family home in Hinsdale at Quinn's request to care for Margaret. She was still in the same emotional and mental state as the night before. Margaret had never wanted anything more than a faithful husband, a loving family, and sweet memories to cherish during her golden years. She loved being a wife and mother and had looked forward to her husband's retirement, so they could spend more time with each other and their grandchildren. Now her memories would be scarred forever. She and David had sacrificed and struggled through the worst and best of times, but they'd never been untrue to each other or their values or their family. Nothing would ever be the same.

After the doctor examined her, he advised Quinn that a strong sedative would put her back to sleep for a several hours. Physically, she was fine. She just needed to calm down and relax. Time would take care of the rest. The doctor gave Margaret an injection of Secobarbital and by eleven o'clock she had fallen into a deep, dreamless sleep.

With Margaret resting soundly, Quinn left for the office. It would be his only chance to take care of a few loose ends before the America's Warehouse grand opening began on Saturday. He managed to avoid Vargas during the four hours it took him to return calls and follow-up on last-minute details. Then, as he was getting ready to return home, she appeared at his office door.

"Are you trying to avoid me?" she said with a provocative smile.

"Just trying to stay focused, my dear. You have a habit of distracting me," Quinn said, considering himself lucky that no one had showed up with news about impending arrests or subpoenas. Running Musselman from a remote location wasn't going to be easy, but he'd mentally prepared himself to do just that for as long as the board would let him.

"Are we going to the Lake House this weekend?" she asked coyly.

"Saturday night we'll have it all to ourselves," Quinn said to appease her.

"Okay, I'll let you off the hook for now," Vargas said, satisfied with his response. "But first I need some attention." She closed and locked the office door before prancing over to Quinn, wrapping her arms around him, and smothering him with kisses. Then she loosened his tie and began unbuttoning his shirt.

Quinn melted to her touch. Just one more time.

36

Quinn – Hinsdale, IL

When Margaret Quinn opened her heavy-laden eyes after several hours of deep sleep, there was a man standing over her. At first she thought it was Dr. Drury, but as her eyes slowly focused she realized he was a stranger. "Who are you?" she asked in an alarmed but groggy voice. Her body felt like cement.

"I work for Dr. Drury," Marco said. He had entered the house at five o'clock in the morning, when the FBI's surveillance expanded from two agents in an unmarked car to a team of surveillance specialists in a delivery van. The switch had provided enough distraction for Marco to momentarily disable the security system and enter the basement, where he spent the next several hours assessing the FBI's surveillance. Once the van of surveillance specialists had set up, the perimeter of the house became virtually impregnable. Sophisticated sound and movement surveillance equipment monitored every inch of space outside the home; however, the FBI was relying on wall penetrating listening devices and outside cameras to monitor activity inside the house. As long as the FBI didn't upgrade their internal surveillance equipment, Marco's handheld jamming device would keep all movements and speech within a radius of twenty feet of the device masked from detection. Getting out of the house, on the other hand, would pose a challenge.

"He was called into emergency surgery," Marco said. "He asked me to come over and check on you."

"Where's my husband?" she asked, feeling more and more nervous about the pleasant-looking young man standing next to her.

"He had to go to the office for a few minutes. Said he'd be back soon."

"I've never seen you in Dr. Drury's office," she said, trying to move away from him but barely able to lift an arm.

"I'm a registered nurse in my third year of medical school. I started working part-time for Dr. Drury about a month ago, when my wife had to quit her job to keep the baby. She's seven months pregnant but started having preterm labor. It's our first. This job is allowing me to stay in medical school. Dr. Drury has been a life saver," Marco said, enthusiastically.

The young man's pleasant manner seemed to make Margaret feel better, until she remembered why she was lying in bed sedated. She began crying all over again, replaying her husband's confession in her mind.

Marco leaned over and gently raised her up to drink from the cup he held in his other hand. "Drink this, Mrs. Quinn, it will taste a little like alcohol but it's only a mild sedative to help you sleep."

It tasted like gin and cough syrup mixed together as she drank it. "Dr. Drury gave me an injection before."

"I know," Marco said. "I'm going to give you another one now, so you can sleep without interruption."

She was already beginning to feel woozy. "Why do I need…" but she was unable to complete her sentence. The last thing she remembered before losing consciousness was the young man removing a needle from her arm.

Marco placed the used needle in his bag and returned to his hiding place in the basement. Thanks to Wayland Tate, his recent string of assignments had made him a lot of money. He liked Tate, not merely because he paid well, but because he saw the world the same way Marco did. Dominate or be dominated.

Quinn felt relieved to find his wife sleeping soundly in their bed when he returned home. But when he spotted the

Sapphire Gin and Tonic on the nightstand, he checked her more closely. She wasn't breathing. Frantically, he grabbed her in his arms, trying to find a pulse. It was barely discernable. He called 911 and then gave her mouth-to-mouth resuscitation. The FBI agents arrived within seconds of his 911 call, followed by the Hinsdale paramedics minutes later. Efforts to revive her en route to Adventist Hospital a few blocks away gave way to frenzied procedures in the emergency room. But it was all in vain. Margaret Emory Quinn was pronounced dead from an overdose of barbiturates and alcohol, at twenty-seven minutes past five in the evening.

When Dr. Drury arrived a few minutes later, he immediately contacted the Quinn children and then attempted to comfort their grieving father. Quinn, however, was already well beyond Dr. Drury's reach.

"Was she alone when she woke up?" Dr. Drury asked.

"I don't know," Quinn said, coldly.

"Was she conscious when you found her?"

"No."

"I'm so sorry, David. I never expected…"

"It's okay, Doctor. You're not to blame for this. I am."

"Is there anything I can get you?"

"Nothing," Quinn said.

Dr. Drury began questioning one of the ER physicians who had attended Margaret, but Quinn had no desire to relive the tragedy. He excused himself to the restroom.

Three undercover FBI agents and a fourth man hired by Bob Swatling watched as Quinn entered the restroom. One of the FBI agents followed him.

"Mr. Quinn," the FBI agent said once inside. "I'm Agent Sylvester, FBI. I'm very sorry about your wife." He paused for a moment. "I don't mean to rush you, but we have received instructions to move you and your children to a secure location, immediately."

"Go to hell," Quinn said defiantly. "Protect my children when they get here. I'll be at the Lake House until I have to testify. Supposedly your people have secured it. Tell Wiseman I'll be expecting his visit." Quinn turned from the urinal and began walking out of the restroom.

Agent Sylvester grabbed his arm, but Quinn jerked it away. "Don't touch me. I'm a protected witness not a fucking criminal," Quinn said without breaking stride. Sylvester spoke into a small microphone attached to his suit sleeve. "He's coming your way. Defiant and going to the Lake House. Stay with him. I'll advise Wiseman and Kohl. Wait until I arrive."

Quinn walked out of the emergency room at Adventist Hospital and got into a taxicab that took him to the end of Illinois Road in Lake Forest. When he entered the Lake House property, he spoke briefly to Jackson Ebbs before going to the library. Once inside, he pushed the power button on the stereo system and inserted a Mozart Exsultate CD, selecting the last number, "Benedictus from Requiem K 626." Five minutes and fourteen seconds long. It wouldn't take longer than that, he said to himself.

Sitting down behind the antique Chippendale desk, he removed a yellow pad of lined paper and a Waterman fountain pen before unlocking the thin center drawer to remove a Springfield Super 38. He placed the pistol on top of the desk and began writing his note.

> *To Jennifer, John, Rebecca, and David,*
> *I don't expect you to forgive me for the tragedy I've caused, but you must know that your mother was not in her right mind when she took her life. We meant everything to her. Sadly, I realized too late what all of you really mean to me. I will miss you, but it's better this way. I will do everything I can to comfort your mother on the other side.*
> *Father*

At twelve minutes past six in the evening, David Albright Quinn placed the five-inch barrel of the Super 38 in his mouth—moments away from blowing his brains out. Everything had become corrupted because he wanted more. I t was a common disease among prosperous men. H e tried to pull the trigger, but couldn't. After removing the gun from his mouth, he began sobbing like a child. He deserved to die for killing his wife, but killing himself wouldn't fix things. It would never bring her back. But there were other things he could fix.

As he opened the drawer and replaced the 38, a man he'd never seen before entered the library and walked toward him with a gun in his hand. He was a Latin-looking man of average height in his early thirties, striking facial features, broad shoulders, extremely fit, and dressed in a jogging suit. His moves were fluid like an athlete's. "Who are you?" Quinn cried in a loud voice, hoping to alert Ebbs, but the Requiem was just beginning its finale, masking his plea.

"Push your chair away from the desk, slowly," Marco said, having arrived at the Lake House only minutes before Quinn. After the paramedics had arrived at the Quinn home in Hinsdale, Marco had gambled on the FBI surveillance specialists leaving the scene with the two ambulance vehicles, which is exactly what they did. As soon as they were gone, he walked three blocks to his car in a nearby church parking lot, and drove to Adventist Hospital where he waited in the parking lot, listening carefully for updates from his contact inside.

When Quinn had announced he was going to the Lake House, Bob Swatling's man quickly conveyed the information to Marco, who made sure he got there first. A day earlier in Lake Forest, using advanced surveillance detection equipment developed in Israel, Marco had found a nearly surveillance-free corridor, giving him access to the Lake House. Twilight had provided cover as he made his way onto the estate. Once outside the house, he found Jackson Ebbs. In a single blow to the temple, he rendered Ebbs unconscious and then administered an injection of concentrated alcohol before pouring Jim Beam down his throat. After disabling the security system, he entered the den.

Quinn pushed his chair backward, "How did you get in here?"

Marco said nothing as he went to the desk and retrieved the Super 38 from the drawer.

Just as Quinn made a lunge at the intruder, Marco jammed the Super 38 into Quinn's mouth and pulled the trigger.

The deafening blast was the last thing Quinn heard.

Marco disappeared the way he'd entered, thirty seconds before FBI Agent Sylvester found David Quinn's body lying on the floor in the den, the back of his head splattered across the wall and credenza.

37

Wilson – Charter Jet G650, Inflight

Midway over the Atlantic, Wilson called an ad-hoc executive staff meeting to evaluate the whirlwind tour and its expected impact on the firm. It was six o'clock in the evening London time, but on board the G650 it was time for someone to swallow the bait he'd been dangling all week. Everyone turned their chairs toward the center of the aircraft, so they could face each other. The six vice presidents seemed anxious to talk, although most of them looked tired from the week's arduous schedule. After a few words of praise and appreciation for their efforts, Wilson opened the meeting to general comments and feedback.

Not surprisingly, Joel Spivey, Mr. Human Resources, started it off.

"I think the response to your leadership has been extremely positive. Headquarters has received numerous calls and emails expressing appreciation for the tour. I think it's laid the perfect foundation for your future here."

"I agree," Frank O'Connor added in his pleasant, therapist-like voice. "Your five initiatives have created a lot of excitement."

"They've also created a lot of high expectations," Leigh Tennyson cautioned, seemingly hard-wired to anticipate change issues. "If we don't show real progress on your initiatives within ninety days, the tour will become an obstacle, not a foundation."

"Absolutely," Wilson said, smiling at her. She was refreshingly candid and non-apologetic. He liked her more every time he listened to her.

"I must say, I have some concerns about the marketing and publicity initiative," John Malouf said.

Silence filled the plane's cabin. The rushing air and hum of the Rolls-Royce engines grew louder. Everyone seemed to sense this criticism was coming.

Malouf continued, "I have no problem supporting our consultants in their writing and publishing activities, but the wrong kind of publicity campaign could backfire."

Here we go, Wilson thought. It was now clear that Malouf's earlier comments about publicizing Fielder & Company's furtiveness belied his opposition. Maybe Tennyson's comment had made him anxious, Wilson thought. More likely, the partnership was forcing his hand. Either way, Wilson decided it was time to freshen the bait. "How's that, John?"

"High visibility has its own risks," Malouf said.

"Such as?" Wilson said.

"Losing clients who don't want more public scrutiny, compromising our credibility as independent and unbiased consultants, exposing the firm's methods and approaches to our competition, diverting our focus from real issues, do you want me to go on?" he concluded with barely suppressed hostility.

Wilson waited a moment to rehearse what he was about to say. Then he leaned forward in his chair and locked eyes with Malouf. "I understand your concerns, John. And we will address them. But in my judgment, the benefits of higher visibility clearly outweigh the risks, especially when it comes to expanding the firm internationally," Wilson said firmly.

"Let's talk about Kresge & Company's mystique," Malouf said condescendingly, his irritation beginning to show, as he sat back in his chair and folded his arms across his chest. "If they're not careful, their increased publicity could destroy the aura of mystery and veneration that has surrounded the institution and its methods for decades."

Wilson could see that anger was loosening Malouf's tongue. "I don't have a problem capitalizing on Fielder & Company's furtiveness, although I think we should find a better word," Wilson said.

A ripple of quiet laughter broke out among the other vice presidents as they took advantage of the break in tension to shift in their seats and cross or uncross their legs.

With obvious effort, Malouf softened slightly. "Sometimes, less is more, Wilson. I'm sure you understand that better than any of us. Kresge's zeal for protecting its privacy and the privacy of its clients is legendary."

This was the first serious challenge to one of Wilson's initiatives and everyone was waiting to see how he would handle it, especially Malouf. Wilson responded matter-of-factly, "I am fully aware of Kresge's position on privacy and publicity, but it's outdated and behind the curve." Wilson paused before continuing, "We live in a new era of public exposure and transparency. It's time to learn how to capitalize on it."

Malouf bit down hard on the freshened bait. "I can assure you, our clients will resent that attitude," he said, no longer attempting to disguise his anger.

Make Malouf take action, Wilson told himself. "Privacy is a dying myth. It doesn't exist, John. Secrecy is not only becoming unfashionable, it's becoming impossible. We owe it to our clients to prepare them for a future when nothing they think, feel, say, plan, or do will escape the scrutiny of their employees, customers, shareholders, suppliers, competitors, the press, and society in general." Wilson said, knowing exactly how arrogant he sounded. *Bring me inside.* "Creating more publicity-savvy consultants will make us more, not less, effective with our clients. Besides, I think it's time we replaced Kresge & Company as the world's premier management consulting firm."

"That's exactly why David Quinn and The J. B. Musselman Company fired Kresge & Company. Because privacy became a myth," Malouf shot back spitefully.

Wilson's blood ran cold as he listened to Malouf's words and saw the cunning smirk on his face. For an instant, his confidence faltered, his mind jumping into hyperdrive to bring it back. *What was Malouf trying to tell me? Was there a connection between David Quinn and the secret partnership? Or, was Malouf merely pointing out that I'd been wrong about Musselman?*

Even though The J. B. Musselman Company had never been discussed during the week, Wilson assumed the vice presidents already knew that he was the Kresge partner who had prophesied Musselman's doom. Then it struck him. *Malouf was still trying to convince someone that Wilson was a loose cannon who needed to be stopped. Ashford?*

Spivey? He couldn't believe it was Tennyson or O'Connor. Certainly not Throckmorton. Or was it intended for someone else, listening from a distance or to a recording when they landed?

The silence and Wilson's runaway train of thought was broken by Leigh Tennyson. She looked at Malouf as she spoke, "I agree with Wilson. We can't keep playing the same old game; it's too risky. A more proactive approach to visibility could give us a big advantage."

Wilson was shocked. The way Tennyson was looking at Malouf, there was no mistaking it. She had to be involved. Wilson was sure of it. Leigh Tennyson, who he'd come to admire and respect, was a card-carrying member of the secret partnership, signaling to Malouf that Wilson needed to be brought into the fold. We can't keep playing the same old game, Wilson repeated in his mind.

"The initiative does represent a major departure from your father's philosophy," Corbin Ashford remarked.

The comment was both innocent and revealing. Ashford was talking to Wilson, not Malouf or Tennyson, and he seemed completely oblivious to any hidden agenda. But Wilson had to be sure. "My father changed his will a few weeks before he was shot," he said slowly, letting the words sink in. "In his new will, he expressed a desire to put Fielder & Company on a high exposure path. He said it was time for the firm to come out of hiding." Another pause. "I have committed the firm to act on his desire, and I invite all of you to do the same."

From opposite sides of the cabin, Malouf and Tennyson exchanged looks of urgency, most likely pondering how much Wilson actually knew about their insiders club. He could see Malouf squirming. Wilson had just become a bigger threat to the secret partnership, but this tour had also made him harder to eliminate.

After that, there were no further questions or comments about initiative number four. The discussion turned to issues of implementation, timing, costs, responsibility, and anticipated obstacles. Malouf and Tennyson became more and more removed, apparently considering a new set of initiatives.

When the meeting ended, the six vice presidents relaxed quietly in the Gulfstream's comfortable surroundings. Four days together, and this final meeting had provided more than enough dialogue, even for the talkative Spivey. And while Wilson still couldn't believe that he'd been so easily deceived by Leigh Tennyson's candid complaints about John Malouf, he'd now done everything he could to force the partnership's hand. He hoped he'd done enough—and not too much. But his misreading of Tennyson continued to worry him. What else would they do to take him by surprise?

For now, all he could do was wait. A week in Venice with Emily would afford him the space and distance he needed to be patient and give the secret partnership enough rope to develop a response. He was looking forward to endless, uninterrupted hours with Emily.

38

Emily – Venice, Italy

Emily and Wilson landed at Marco Polo Airport in Venice a little before ten in the morning. It was a balmy spring day with calm waters reflecting a clear blue sky. The grand architecture—a glorious panoply of Byzantine, Gothic, and Renaissance styles—fit magnificently here, in this city on the sea. As they ascended from their water taxi in front of the Palazzo Ducale and the Torre dell' Orologio on Piazza San Marco, the couple was greeted by three porters. These porters escorted them to Fielder & Company's private apartment overlooking the restoration of the Teatro La Fenice, the oldest opera house in Venice. The first thing they did after the porters placed their luggage in the apartment was to fling themselves onto the king-size bed and sleep for two hours. When they woke, they showered and then sat on their balcony overlooking the Piazza La Fenice, nibbling at a lavish fruit and cheese basket and drinking Prosecco, courtesy of the management at Hotel San Fantin.

Smiling, Emily took hold of the sash around Wilson's robe and led him back into the bedroom. For the next few hours they shared their deepest emotions. At one point, Wilson proclaimed his love from the balcony, causing Emily to clasp her hands over his mouth in sweet delirium. Such sacred intimacy was priceless.

That evening they immersed themselves in the Venetian experience, a long gondola ride through the canals to La Caravella's for dinner and then back along the canals at night serenaded by their gondolier with Italian love songs. They strolled arm in arm past the endless shops and restaurants to their third-floor apartment. *Venezia e Amore.*

While some people like D. H. Lawrence thought of Venice as "an abhorrent, green, slippery city," Emily and Wilson relished its uniqueness, preferring Elizabeth Barrett Browning's reflection, "nothing is like it, nothing is equal to it, not a second Venice in the world." Fawning over the city on water like new lovers, they spent the rest of the week exploring the labyrinth of streets and waterways, touring palaces, museums, and private collections, meditating in

Dante's Chapel, dining in Lord Byron's favorite eatery on the Grand Canal, feeding the pigeons in glorious San Marco Square, enjoying a new cultural venue each evening, and of course, making passionate love most nights and mornings— and not always in their apartment. Through it all, they had been only vaguely aware of Hap's men, Mike Anthony and Pat Savoy, watching over them.

One morning before dawn, they ran to Piazza San Marco to watch it emerge from night's darkness into early morning light, before the pigeons, school children, and tourists filled the space that had been Venice's social, political, and religious gathering place for centuries. The most beautiful drawing room in Europe, according to Napoleon. He was right, Wilson thought.

"I could stay here for a thousand years," Wilson said as they walked along the piazza's arcaded Procuratie Vecchie in the first light of morning.

"Why don't we?" Emily said.

"Maybe we already have," Wilson said, playfully.

Emily stopped to drink him in. "Please go on."

"Last night was worth at least a thousand years."

She laughed loudly and then led him to the center of the square where they smothered themselves in each other until a hundred pigeons had surrounded them.

Wilson looked up and screamed at the top of his lungs, causing the pigeons to take flight, "I love this woman."

Tears came to Emily's eyes and then to Wilson's. "We're so lucky we found each other—again," Emily said with an initial soberness that turned to teasing. That's how it had been for an entire week, every day the same, yet extraordinarily different—San Marco Basilica, Rigoletto, Rialto Bridge, Giovani, the Doge's Palace, Vivaldi, the Grand Canal, Tintoretto, Prosecco wine, Veronese, Venetian Cuisine, Titian, and always the sweet intimacy of melting into each other. Their Venetian getaway had been absolutely idyllic.

On the day before they had to leave, high tides and early morning rains flooded San Marco Square with a few inches of water, transforming the ceremonial courtyard into an *aqua alta* sea of mirrors. The scene transfixed Wilson, leaving its timeless image engraved upon his mind. They walked above the water on wooden planks, but they still got soaked.

After changing their clothes and getting ready to leave the apartment for lunch, the telephone rang for the first time since they'd arrived. It was the Hotel San Fantin located directly across the piazza from their apartment, informing Wilson that he had received a fax. The hotel had a long-term contract to service the apartment and rent it out when Fielder & Company guests were not using it. Wilson told them they would come down to pick it up. But as he hung up the phone, he wondered why someone hadn't just delivered it to the door—or to Anthony or Savoy, who were staying in the apartment on the second floor. Then he remembered that Anthony had taken possession of all duplicate keys when they arrived. The sudden return of paranoia felt like an ugly intrusion. He asked Emily if she was ready to leave.

"I need ten more minutes with my hair," she said from the bathroom.

"Take all the time you need, sweetheart, we're still on vacation," Wilson responded from the small foyer of the apartment.

"Who was on the phone?"

"Hotel reception. They have a fax. I'm going to get it while you're finishing."

"I promise I'll be ready when you get back."

Wilson stepped into the bathroom to watch her. "I've always loved how you take care of yourself. Do you know how beautiful you are?"

"Thank you for bringing me here. This week has been divine."

He leaned over and kissed her on the cheek as she held a curling iron in her hair. "I adore you, Emily Klein. I'll be right back."

On his way down the stairs, he greeted Mike Anthony who stuck his head out the door of his apartment. When Wilson told him about the fax, Mike advised Savoy that Emily was upstairs alone and that he was going with Wilson to the front desk at the hotel. Wilson and Mike entered the lobby through the sliding glass doors and went directly to the reception desk, where they asked the clerk about the fax.

"*Un minuto*," she said and then disappeared through a door behind the desk. Two minutes later, she returned with an envelope and handed it to Wilson. Wilson opened the envelope and unfolded a single piece of paper:

FAX TRANSMISSION

Pages:	1
Date:	April 4
To:	Wilson Fielder, Hotel San Fantin
Fax #:	041-523-1401
From:	The Fenice Partnership
Subject:	Mutual Benefit Insurance
Comments:	*She's gone. The getaway's over. Go home. She'll be safe as long as you don't do anything stupid.*
	We'll be in touch.

Wilson exploded with pain. He ran from the hotel lobby with Mike behind him, across the Piazza, up three flights of stairs, and into the apartment. Emily was nowhere to be found. Mike ran back down to the second-floor apartment where he found Pat Savoy lying in a pool of blood, with a bullet hole in his forehead. They frantically searched the apartments again, including the empty apartment on the first floor. Then they called Hap.

Hap's voice was even and collected, despite his obvious anguish over Emily and Savoy. He urged them not to panic. "They won't keep her in Venice. If they wanted to kill her, she'd already be dead. They'll want her close by to control the situation and make sure they use her to blackmail you into cooperating. They'll expect you to go back to Fielder & Company."

"Can the FBI or CIA stop them from leaving Venice?" Wilson blurted.

Hap immediately warned Wilson not to go to the FBI, the Italian authorities, or the U.S. Consulate. "They can't afford to have word of her kidnapping get out anymore than we can. It would only increase the probability of her death and their exposure. This is about manipulating you, Wilson. They'll want her to talk with you, sooner rather than later, to reassure you that she's fine and will remain fine, as long as you cooperate. When she does talk to you, we'll need to listen for any piece of information that will help us locate her. She'll be thinking the same thing. You need to get back here as soon as possible. We'll prep you when you arrive," Hap said confidently.

Then he instructed them to find the first plane back to Boston. Hap and the rest of his people would be checking all the airports along the Eastern seaboard for private jets arriving from Europe. They arranged to meet at the Back Bay apartment as soon as Wilson and Mike got in. "Leave everything where it is. Don't pack your bags and don't move anything. Lock the apartments and leave. I'll take care of bringing Pat home."

"How can you be so sure of everything?" Wilson asked, trying not to hyperventilate.

"I'm not sure, Wilson. It's just experience and calculated judgment," Hap said firmly.

Wilson remained silent. What Hap said made sense. What good would it do to stay in Venice? The secret partnership would want him back at Fielder & Company, so they could force him to do their bidding. Emily would be kept somewhere near Boston or New York, just in case they needed her to do some extra persuading. But that wouldn't be necessary; he would do their bidding.

By the time Wilson hung up the phone and regained some semblance of control over his anguish, Mike had already booked two first class seats on a Delta flight to JFK, with a connecting flight to Boston. The flight left in two hours. They locked the apartments and exited the building, leaving everything as it was, just as Hap had instructed.

Wilson cursed himself repeatedly for leaving Emily alone in the apartment. His father's godforsaken insider's club was now his eternal enemy, and he would not stop until they were utterly and completely destroyed. But first he had to find Emily. Before they killed her.

39

Tate – JFK Airport, NYC

From behind a pair of slightly tinted sunglasses and an outstretched copy of *The New York Times*, Wayland Tate watched as Wilson Fielder exited customs at JFK and then rechecked his bags onto a connecting flight to Boston. Like a chameleon, Tate was in disguise—mustache, white-blonde hair, and earrings—using a false identity. He'd risked reentering the U.S. for only one reason, and that was to deal with Wilson personally. He knew Wilson would be tormented, but he wanted to judge for himself just how vulnerable or volatile Wilson had been rendered.

For the past twenty-four hours, Tate had been studying Wilson's behavior and mannerisms on digital video, downloaded from one of Tate's many private contractors. Reading another human being by the set of the mouth, look of the eyes, wrinkles on the forehead, speed of facial movements, and any other idiosyncratic gestures, had become integral to the art of manipulation for Wayland Tate. He now recognized Wilson Fielder's most common mental and emotional states—tranquility and contentment, anger and hate, commitment and resolve, uncertainty and fear, and curiosity and discovery.

Unfortunately, what he saw on Wilson's face as he exited security was not a welcome sight. Tate followed him to his connecting gate just to make sure, but there was no mistaking the combination of anger and resolve on Wilson's face. Tate had hoped for uncertainty and fear, or at least a combination of anger and fear, but that was not the case. He returned to the main terminal before calling Morita, who was now in the New York offices of Tate Waterhouse.

"Plans have changed," Tate said. "I'm going to Boston for a few days."

"Are you sure it's safe?" Morita asked, her voice filled with concern.

"I'm still traveling in disguise just to make sure," Tate said. Then he added, "We need to take a different course with Wilson Fielder. If I'm wrong about our ability to influence him, I want to be close enough to adjust things quickly. Can you find me a suite at one of the larger hotels, the Westin or Marriott in Copley Square? I'm traveling under the name of Marsden Welker. You have the account numbers. Tell Swatling to meet me for breakfast tomorrow morning in my room—six o'clock," Tate said, knowing that either one of the hotels near the Copley Place Mall would provide him with sufficient cover.

"I'll take care of it."

"One more thing. Who was handling surveillance in Venice?"

"Sutton and Turley."

"Did they arrive on the same flight as Fielder?"

"Yes."

"Tell them I want to see them tonight. Looks like the shuttle is light; I should be there within two hours. Have them meet me at Bar 10 in the Westin Hotel."

"Anything else?"

"How's the press handling Quinn's death?"

"There was a lengthy obit in the *Chicago Tribune*. Fortunately, the article focuses on Quinn's legacy, which was what he always wanted anyway. It concludes with a few details of the double suicide. None of it is negatively affecting publicity or customer visits, thanks to the twenty million new customers who went to the America's Warehouse grand opening," Morita said.

"Most people seem to delight in stories of the rich and famous failing in their personal relationships—makes them feel less envious and more satisfied with their economic status. Quinn's death may actually increase customer visits," Tate scoffed.

"I think it already has. The President even commented on the marketing campaign during a press conference on the economy. He said America's Warehouse symbolized the American spirit and corporate renewal at their finest. I've ordered a transcript."

"Poor Quinn, if he'd only learned to enjoy the ride. How's his replacement doing?"

"He's become national news as the man who replaced a tragic visionary. Musselman stock closed at eighty-two dollars today."

"It's all so fucking predictable," Tate said, pausing. "How's Vargas handling things?"

"A little harder than we expected. I think she actually liked him, but she's ten million dollars richer as of last week," Morita said, pausing a moment. "She'll be fine, but…"

"She could use a rest. Right?" Tate said to complete Morita's sentence.

"You don't miss anything, do you?"

"I misread Quinn."

Morita didn't say anything.

"Still nothing from the FBI?" Tate asked.

"Nothing. They don't have anything without Quinn," Morita said. "But that won't stop them from keeping us on their radar screen."

"We'll just have to sting them," Tate said with a snort, looking around to see if anyone was watching him as he approached the gate to his flight. "How's the story coming?"

"The press will have it by tonight. Vargas still has a few pieces of evidence to place, just to make sure."

"Perfect," Tate said, smiling to himself. "Deputy Director Wiseman and Special Agent Kohl will be up to their asses in alligators, explaining why they got duped by a deranged, sex-crazed CEO. How's Kamin handling things?"

"He's working from a villa outside of Rome, consumed with the Musselman sell-off and negotiations with Morgan. I think he's actually excited about leaving KaneWeller," she said.

"Let's keep it that way. Don't say anything about me being in Boston for now. I'll talk to him in a couple of days."

"You're worried about him, aren't you?" Morita asked.

"Not worried. Uncertain," Tate said, making a slow search of everything and everyone around him before entering the jetway. He was worried, but he wasn't about to let Morita know that. Too much depended on her cool-headedness. Besides, now that they had Emily Klein, Wilson wouldn't do anything stupid. But he had to make sure.

"How did Wilson look when he got off the plane?" Morita asked.

"Angry and resolved."

"What are you going to do?"

"I don't know yet. If he's eminently dangerous, we'll know in the next day or two," Tate said as he arrived at his seat. "I think it's time to tell him the truth."

40

Emily – Learjet 60, Inflight

Emily slowly regained consciousness only to discover that she was tied to her seat inside a small jet airplane. She spied the label on the seat next to her— Learjet 60. Her eyes darted around the cabin. There was no one else in sight, but she could hear voices talking beyond the drawn curtain, several feet in front of her. The window shades on both sides of the airplane were pulled down. It was still light outside. They were traveling west, she thought, into a setting sun.

Replaying the abduction in her mind, she tried to remember as many terrifying details as possible. After Wilson had left the apartment to get the fax, she had stopped curling her hair and pranced to the open window overlooking Hotel San Fantin. She'd wanted to shout *buon giorno* and *ti amo* to Wilson as he came out of the hotel. That's when she'd heard the hardwood floor creak behind her. She turned around quickly, thinking maybe it was Wilson already back with the fax, but it wasn't him. Two men stood no more than six feet away from her—dark hair, swarthy skin, one with a mustache, and the other with heavy stubble. She'd never forget the terror she felt.

Whipping back around toward the window, she started to scream, but her cry was barely audible as the larger of the two men clamped his huge hand over her nose and mouth and grabbed her around the waist. The last thing she remembered was the smell of ether.

As she sat tied to her seat, she could only imagine what torment Wilson must be going through. She tried to move her arms and legs, but the leather lashings were too secure. Methodically weighing her options, she felt surprisingly calm and lucid, even though she'd been horrified by her captors only hours earlier. Wilson was right. This secret society, insider's club, or whatever the hell it was, could not be allowed to continue in any form whatsoever. She wished she'd never questioned Wilson's resolve to expose them. She'd only done it out of fear. Fear of death. Fear of harm. Fear of difficulty and struggle. Fear of being alone without Wilson.

But now that her worst fears had materialized, she felt her a new resolve burning inside her.

She swore to herself that if she was able to get out of this alive, she would never again allow fear to control her. Never. She repeated the word never again and again until she remembered how her captors had fondled her body before she lost consciousness. She fought back the tears. Everything can be taken from you except your freedom to choose your thoughts and feelings, she said to herself, even in the worst of circumstances.

Wilson would be moving heaven and earth to find her. She knew that. The thought strengthened her. She would find a way to help him find her. Her emotions were on fire. The only way they could stop her would be to kill her.

41

Wilson – Boston, MA

When Wilson and Mike Anthony arrived back in Boston, they took a cab to the Back Bay apartment. Hap Greene and three of his associates were waiting for them. Wilson sat down across from Hap and the others. Driggs was the only one of the associates Wilson had previously met; Hap introduced the others as Jones and Taylor. He then informed Wilson that, since yesterday afternoon, 153 private jets had arrived from Europe at more than three-dozen airports along the northeastern seaboard. Hap studied Wilson before asking, "What are you going to say to her when she's on the phone? You'll only have a few seconds."

Wilson appreciated the directness. He'd already given Hap's question considerable thought. "Nothing. My guess is that after they get me on the phone they'll shove the phone in her face to let her say a few words and then take it away. There won't be any dialogue. Emily is savvy. She'll be thinking the same thing we're thinking. She knows we'll be recording and analyzing every word she says. If she has any idea where she is, she'll find a way to give us a clue without making it obvious."

Hap looked at Wilson with a slight smile. "Good. You're right about the dialogue. I hope you're right about Emily." After a pause and a glance at his associates, he continued. "One other thing. Tell the kidnappers that you want to hear her voice telling you she's okay at least once a day. The more opportunity she has to give us information, the better. Even then, we won't get many words from her. The first time all we'll get is I'm okay. After they see you're cooperating, maybe they'll allow her to complete a sentence, but it won't be a long sentence. And, they'll scrutinize her every word just like we will."

Wilson nodded soberly before expressing a concern that had been plaguing him.

"You said public knowledge of the kidnapping would increase the probability of her death. I don't think we'll be able to keep Emily's kidnapping a secret for more than a week or so."

"Which means we have to find her before that," Hap said with a wildcat fierceness in his eyes.

Wilson had never seen that look in Hap's eyes. It bolstered his confidence, but he also recognized that he was grasping at anything to brighten his hope. "How's my father and family?"

"Everyone's safe and heavily guarded. There's been no change in your father's condition," Hap said. Then he reached under the coffee table and brought out three newspapers— *The Chicago Tribune*, *The New York Times*, and *The Wall Street Journal*. He dropped them on the table in front of Wilson. TRAGIC VISIONARY SHAPES AN INDUSTRY was the headline on the front page of *The Chicago Tribune*. The other papers carried similar headlines. Wilson read the *Tribune's* sub headline "Double Suicide Brings Heartbreaking End to Pinnacle of Success", and then looked up at Hap in horror.

"They killed them?"

Hap nodded slowly, "It's definitely possible."

"But why?" Wilson asked as he read with breakneck speed about David Quinn, his wife Margaret, and the J. B. Musselman Company. Moments later, he said, "The America's Warehouse campaign seemed to be working brilliantly, at least for the moment. Why kill him now?" Without waiting for a response, he read further.

Hap and the others remained silent as Wilson finished scanning the three newspapers. When Wilson looked up again, Hap said, "It's also possible that they killed themselves, just as the articles state."

Wilson shook his head confidently. "No. They broke him, and he couldn't live with it. They killed him to keep him from going to the authorities, just like Zollinger," Wilson said, standing up from the black sofa, glaring at his team of former agents.

"They're going to kill her, aren't they?"

"Not necessarily. They need her to manipulate you," Hap said. "You may be right about Quinn and his wife, but you're a much bigger threat than one of their disgruntled CEOs. You're sitting at the center of this thing, in control of the company that created this beast in the first place. They'll stop at nothing to manipulate you. Only if and when they can't, will they kill her. Then they'll try to kill you. But we're not going to let either one of those things happen," Hap said. Then he added, "Let's review the details one more time to make sure we haven't missed anything."

By the time they finished, Wilson was sure he'd summarized everything he knew about his father, Fielder & Company, and the secret partnership. But it still wasn't enough to expose the secret partnership in the way he'd planned. Emily's kidnapping had made it agonizingly clear that they had no intention of bringing him inside. And David Quinn's death at the so-called pinnacle of success meant only one thing—they would not hesitate to kill him and Emily, just as Hap had said. Did I go too far in baiting Malouf and Tennyson—or not far enough?

Now he had to find another way to first appease and then expose the secret society. "I won't let them kill her, no matter what I have to do at Fielder & Company," Wilson said.

Hap pointed to Driggs, who would be staying with Wilson in the apartment, his eyes boring into Wilson. "Don't go to the bathroom without Driggs. We'll be in the apartment next door. First thing in the morning, we'll talk about next steps at Fielder & Company."

42

Emily – Learjet 60, Inflight

When she heard the cockpit door open and close, Emily quickly lowered her eyelids to almost shut. The aircraft was descending quickly. A woman wearing a Venetian carnival mask walked over to Emily and placed a blindfold over her eyes and earphones over her ears. It was the same woman who'd brought lunch and drinks earlier, but hadn't spoken a word.

A few minutes later, after the small jet had landed, Emily's right arm was injected with something that made her feel groggy and lightheaded. She was untied, lifted out of her seat, and assisted into what seemed like a delivery truck.

She gradually began to lose consciousness, but not before the vehicle carrying her had stopped and she was lifted off the hard bench and taken somewhere else. The only thing she knew for sure was that she wasn't in another vehicle.

When Emily awoke several hours later, she was lying face up on a cot in a cold space. Her eyes were blindfolded, her ears covered with tight-fitting earphones that made a constant humming noise, her mouth taped, her arms and legs strapped down, and she was covered with a heavy blanket up to her neck. She could feel the forced air of a space heater on her face and there was a faint smell of oil or gasoline in the air. While she couldn't be absolutely sure because of the injection she'd received, her sense was that the ride in the vehicle with the hard bench couldn't have taken more than a few minutes, which meant she was probably in a warehouse or hangar near the airport where they'd landed. Now all she had to do was figure out which airport and how to let Wilson know.

Just then, a computerized woman's voice spoke through the tight-fitting earphones telling Emily that she would be talking into a phone to her boyfriend in a few minutes. She was to only say, "Don't worry, I'm fine."

Emily's mind raced frantically to figure out how she was going to tell Wilson that she was at an airport, somewhere several hours away from Venice by jet—probably west. The more she thought about it, the more discouraged she became. She could be anywhere in the western hemisphere.

Blurting out that she was at an airport would only get her moved. Besides, how many airports were there in the western hemisphere? She calmed herself down and focused. Any information would be better than none, if she could deliver it without raising suspicions. And just maybe, there would be more opportunities, not only to find out where she was, but to talk to Wilson. One step at a time. One piece of information at a time. Then it came to her. She knew exactly what she was going to say and how she was going to say it.

When the phone rang in Wilson's apartment rang, Hap and his men were on their feet, out the door of their apartment, and into Wilson's.

"I haven't given this phone number to anyone except Emily," Wilson said as Hap entered the living room. It was now on its fourth ring. Wilson was silently pleading for it to be Emily, while looking nervously at Hap for any last minute guidance.

"Go ahead and answer it. Everything's set to record and trace the call as soon as you pick up," Hap said.

Wilson picked up the phone. A male computerized voice said, "Wilson Fielder."

"Yes."

"We have your girlfriend," the voice said. There was a click and brief pause before Wilson heard Emily's voice.

"Don't worry," she said, her voice breaking as if she was about to cry. Wilson could hear her take a deep breath before she exhaled the words, "I'm j…" then he heard her whimper before she said, "…fine."

There was another click and the computerized voice returned to the line. "If you want to keep her alive, you must completely remove yourself from our business affairs. When you do, she will be returned unharmed."

"I want to hear her voice every day and the next time I want to talk to her," Wilson demanded quickly.

"You're in no position to be making demands, Mr. Fielder."

The next thing Wilson heard was another click and the line went dead. Wilson stood motionless. Hap's voice revived him. "Come listen to the replay." In the kitchen, he and Driggs were hunched over a small digital recording device.

Grappling with what Emily had said and how she'd said it, Wilson walked into the kitchen. "Either they've hurt her or she was trying to tell me that she expects them to," Wilson said, feeling like a pinned wrestler.

"Listen to this first. It might change your mind," Hap said.

Driggs pushed the lever to replay Emily's words at a slower speed. "Dooon't woooorrry . . . (break in voice and deep breath) . . . I'mmm jet . . . (whimper) . . . fiiinne."

"Play it again," Wilson said anxiously, wanting to make sure he'd heard what he thought he had. After hearing it a second time, Wilson voiced what Driggs and Hap were now smiling about. "She said the word *jet*. It's as plain as it could be at the slower speed, but I didn't hear it when she was on the phone with me."

"Emily's more calm and lucid than we expected," Hap said, leaning on the kitchen counter. "She added the crack in her voice and the whimper to hide the word. Even then, I'm not sure it's enough to raise suspicions. Smart girl. She's going to get us one small piece of information at a time."

"She was flown somewhere," Wilson said restlessly, looking at Hap for confirmation.

"Right. It could also mean she's being held near where the jet landed," Hap said, raising his eyebrows and returning Wilson's stare. Then Hap called to Jones in the back bedroom, "Did we get anything on the trace?"

"They called from somewhere on the North American continent, but that's all we got," Taylor replied. "They were bouncing the signal."

"Bingo. I wasn't sure we'd get that much," Hap said, smiling at Wilson. "Now we can get even more serious about pouring over the details on those 153 private jets."

Wilson wasn't sure how, but he believed Emily would find a way to give them more information each time she called. It was just enough hope to help him keep his torment at bay.

43

Wilson – Boston, MA

It was just after seven o'clock in the morning when, from his father's office, Wilson began making a series of pre-scheduled, international calls to acquisition candidates in Asia and Europe. By thirty minutes past eight, he'd talked to twenty-three firms and made arrangements to meet with six of them within the next month.

At nine o'clock, he entered one of the conference rooms on the ninth floor to listen to the first of seven presentations from advertising and publicity firms. When the last presentation concluded at one o'clock, Wilson had boiled it down to two firms: BBDO, the first firm to present and the one with the strongest track record with professional service firms, and Tate Waterhouse, the last firm to present and the one with the best understanding of Fielder & Company's history and current needs.

Wilson wasn't surprised when Wayland Tate himself attended his firm's presentation but immediately sensed that Tate's presence was more than a courtesy call in symbolic deference to his father. When Tate invited him to lunch, he was sure of it. Wayland Tate was there on behalf of the secret partnership.

"I'm going to lunch at the Bostonian Club with two of our vice presidents. You're welcome to join us," Wilson said, kicking himself for not talking to Carter about Tate. But would Carter have told me the truth?

"I know the club well. It was one of your father's favorites. You go ahead with your vice presidents," Tate said graciously, no longer in disguise. "I have a few things I'd like to share with you in private. I'm staying at the Westin for the next couple of days. We can set up another time to meet."

Tate's words made Wilson's blood run cold. There was no way he was going to postpone an opportunity to get Emily back. He immediately said, "Let me see what I can arrange with the vice presidents."

After conferring with Frank O'Connor and Bob Throckmorton, Wilson told Tate he would be available for lunch. He agreed to meet Tate at the Bostonian Club in twenty minutes. Selecting an advertising firm to handle Fielder & Company's new publicity campaign had suddenly become a secondary issue.

Wilson's mind flew to memories about Wayland Tate and his firm. While it was true that Fielder & Company and Tate Waterhouse had long exchanged data and analyses on behalf of shared clients, he didn't know any of the details. He repeated his father's words again: *the most brilliant advertising executive of his generation.*

Then he recalled his own experience at the J. B. Musselman Company, where Tate sat on the board of directors. Wilson was certain that Tate had been the one who convinced David Quinn to launch the America's Warehouse strategy. Tate was an unusually persuasive and driven man, a man his father had always liked. But Wilson could no longer deny the probability that Wayland Tate was part of the secret partnership. If he was being paranoid, he'd find out soon.

Wilson returned to his office with nothing but vengeance on his mind. He immediately called Hap Greene.

"We've been monitoring everything," Hap said. "I have people inside and outside the Bostonian Club. Needless to say, we're ready for your lunch. Are you?"

"I've never been more ready," Wilson said.

"We'll find her, Wilson. Just buy us some time. Like you said, let them think you'll give them whatever they want."

"My thoughts exactly. Here we go," Wilson said before hanging up. He then talked briefly to O'Connor and Throckmorton, who both agreed that BBDO and Tate Waterhouse represented the two best firms of the seven for Fielder & Company's publicity initiative.

Minutes later, Wilson walked into the Bostonian Club and was immediately escorted to a private dining room on the club's exclusive third floor. The room looked like a nineteenth-century den with an impressive collection of classic and modern works, an Italian marble fireplace, glazed leather sofas and chairs, exquisite Persian rugs, and two Marsden Hartley originals. He focused on the décor to calm himself, musing on the irony of a beat generation socialist painter, like Hartley, supplying the backdrop for exclusive luncheon meetings among Boston's elite. But the blue-blooded rich always ignored such contradictions. They bought whatever they wanted whenever they wanted, he thought, remembering detective Zemke's comment about his father.

Wayland Tate stepped into the room and closed the door behind him. Wilson scoffed nervously to himself, knowing that this meeting would be far from private. Who else besides Hap's team would be eavesdropping? It was a twisted spectacle of standard operating procedure in a postmodern corporate world.

"You bear a striking resemblance to your father," Tate said.

Wilson smiled without commenting. How much gamesmanship do we have to go through before Tate gets to the real reason for his lunch invitation? He fought back his rising anger. He needed to remain calm and collected.

"He was a visionary, your father," Tate said, staring at one of the Marsden Hartley paintings. "I have no doubt, whatsoever, that he will go down in history as the man who launched the transformation of capitalism, and I don't mean the revolution Marx and Engels imagined. Thankfully, the rich turned out to be too smart for that. But your father was smarter than all of them. How's he doing?"

Wilson placed his hands in his pockets. Tate's candid comment had caught him off guard. "We hope he'll regain consciousness soon."

"Believe me, we're all hoping for that, Wilson," Tate said. "Shall we sit down?"

Wilson nodded, still surprised by Tate's openness and candor.

"How's your mother?" Tate asked once they were seated.

"She's doing well, staying busy," Wilson said.

"Glad to hear it. Back in our college days, your mother and father were the envy of anyone seeking true romance."

Disarmed again by Tate, Wilson said, "I didn't know you went to college together."

"Columbia University, Class of '69—the last summer of love. We all expected your father to become the next Jack Kerouac. Have you read his poetry?"

Stunned yet again, he'd never read his father's poetry because he didn't know it existed. Wilson felt himself sinking fast. "No," Wilson said, nervously picking at the seams of his napkin.

"He always said he'd buried his literary past at the B-school," Tate said while studying Wilson's expressions. "But, luckily for us, he never lost his passion for changing the world."

"There are things I still don't know about my father," Wilson said, as the waiter entered the room with a bottle of Chardonnay, antipasti, fresh bread, and the day's menu.

After they had ordered and the waiter was gone, Tate picked up his napkin and carefully placed it in his lap. "I'm not surprised. Everything he was doing depended on secrecy."

"What was he doing?" Wilson asked, now becoming annoyed with the way Tate seemed to be toying with him.

"Transforming capitalism."

"How?" Wilson said as he moved his chair closer to the table.

"By documenting widespread abuses in the capital markets," Tate said, pausing to take a sip of the Chardonnay. "Without noticeable failure, democracies rarely create change."

There was no more holding back, Wilson told himself. "You mean he planned all along to expose Fielder & Company's insider's club?" Wilson asked as the tablecloth moved under his tensed elbows, almost spilling the glass of wine in front of him.

"At the right time and in the right way, yes," Tate said slowly, continuing to study Wilson over the rim of his glass of Chardonnay.

"When?" Wilson demanded. He wasn't about to sit there chatting amiably while Emily was still being held hostage.

As Tate put down his glass of wine, his face took on a solemn and serious expression. "Our original plan was to document ten years of stock market abuse and then disclose everything. The idea was to galvanize public opinion against capitalism in its current form. The insiders club, as you described it, was created so CEOs from the world's largest corporations could get anything and everything they wanted by trading on each other's company secrets. But the real purpose behind our web of insider trading was to force fundamental changes in the way capitalism is practiced. Ultimately, we wanted to supplant the big money interests, who manipulate the global financial system and crush whoever gets in their way. They've killed four American presidents and bought the rest. They murdered your great-grandfather Harry Wilson Fielder, after killing two of his closest associates, Congressman Louis T. McFadden from Pennsylvania and William Tate Boyles from New York. They were eliminated to keep them from exposing generations of concealed corruption. William Tate Boyles was my grandfather. Your father and I shared a common vow to avenge their deaths."

Wilson's head was imploding. Was Tate telling him the truth? Had this been his father's ultimate agenda? He couldn't wait any longer. "Where's Emily?"

Tate leaned forward, peering into Wilson's hazel-green eyes for several moments before responding. "I'm aware that she's been kidnapped, but I didn't have anything to do with it, Wilson."

"Who, then?" Wilson said in exasperation, as the waiter entered the private dining room and placed house salads in front of them.

Tate picked up his fork and held it over the top of his salad. "Does the name Davis Zollinger mean anything to you?"

"Of course," Wilson said, put off by the condescension. "My father has been charged with the murder of his two daughters. Zollinger was found dead in his Boston office six months ago."

Tate took a bit of salad before proceeding. "Zollinger was a partner with Damien Hearst, the well-known corporate attorney and dealmaker in Chicago. They were both clients of Fielder & Company and Tate Waterhouse, until they started making deals on their own, most of them illegal. Zollinger got smart and wanted out, but Hearst blackmailed him into staying. When Zollinger threatened to go to the FBI, Hearst had him killed and made it look like suicide," Tate said, taking a sip of his Chardonnay. "Zollinger's daughters began their own investigation, which could have compromised everything we were doing. That's when your father decided it was time to accelerate disclosure." Tate paused again. "He invited Zollinger's daughters to White Horse, so he could convince them of our commitment to avenge their father's death. He succeeded. But we failed to protect him from Hearst."

"Hearst shot my father?" Wilson asked, captivated by this smooth-talking, well-heeled man who claimed to share his father's lofty goals for societal reform.

"A contract killer hired by Hearst killed the Zollinger women—your father was shot to make it look like a murder-suicide. Hearst was invited to White Horse with a group of current and former clients who were ignoring our guidelines. He was one of the partnership's legal resources. We threatened to blow the whistle on all of them, if they didn't conform. You have to understand that each of them was a walking time bomb. They still are. If one of them gets caught, it could still jeopardize everything," Tate said, hesitating a moment. "We don't know how Hearst found out about our ultimate plan, but he did. Ever since then, he's been enticing and coercing members of the partnership to join him. He's taken your father's maxim to a whole new level. His latest victim was David Quinn."

Wilson froze. "Why?"

"You remember how obstinate and pious Quinn could be. He couldn't wait to get rid of you. You challenged his vision of the future. He used me to exploit the uncertainty surrounding your father's shooting and the murder charges to discredit you and Kresge & Company. I never should have allowed him to manipulate me, but I honestly believe in the America's Warehouse strategy. I think you knew that all along.

"What you didn't know was that Quinn had a ruthless, unpredictable side. He was having a wild affair with one of our associates and pocketed a cool half billion while manipulating his company's stock. Don't get me wrong, the partnership has made billions on Musselman's stock in recent weeks, especially the Hearst contingent, but it wasn't enough for Quinn. All of a sudden he got righteous and began mourning his lost soul. I tried everything to convince him to be patient, but he didn't trust me anymore. I'd become one of the evil ones who'd corrupted him. He went to the FBI in return for his and Musselman's immunity. Damien Hearst went ballistic. You know the rest of the story," Tate said, his eyes communicating sadness.

Wilson was dumbfounded. Tate was either the best liar Wilson had ever met or a victim just like his father. He remained silent, waiting for Tate to continue.

"We believe Damien Hearst is the one who kidnapped your girlfriend. He knows you're in charge of the company now, and he's made a pre-emptive strike to manipulate you with Emily's life."

"Do you know where she is?" Wilson asked frantically.

"No," Tate said, pausing. "But, I think we can persuade Hearst to give her back. If we can convince him that he and his clients won't be included in any disclosure."

"You're still planning to disclose the abuses and manipulations?" Wilson asked, hoping for the first time since they'd sat down that Tate was telling him the truth.

"Absolutely. But it can't happen piecemeal. We have a lot of work to do before we'll be ready to disclose everything," Tate said, taking another bite of salad. "Your role is crucial, Wilson. That's why I'm here."

"So your publicity proposal was a ploy?" Wilson asked, debating with himself about what to believe.

"Not at all; we want your business. We understand Fielder & Company better than any of our competitors, but that's not why I'm here," Tate said as he leered at Wilson. "I'm here to ask for your help in modifying our plan."

"Which plan?" Wilson asked, feeling toyed with again.

"Your father's."

"Was it part of my father's plan to have Daniel Redd killed?"

"Of course not," Tate said, looking indignant. "That was Hearst and the partners he'd persuaded to join him. Don't worry, we have all of them under surveillance and we won't back off until Emily's returned."

"If you have them under surveillance, why don't you know where she is?" Wilson demanded.

"We don't know which contractors they're using. The only thing we do know is that she was flown out of Venice on Saturday."

Just then, two waiters entered the room, removed their salad dishes, placed their main dishes in front of them, and poured more wine.

"I'm sorry," Tate continued. "I know this isn't easy for you. Why don't you eat something? I'll start from the beginning."

44

Emily – Eastern Seaboard, North America

Emily immediately stopped breathing when someone touched her and then gently raised her from the cot. Whoever it was had the touch and scent of a woman, probably the same woman who'd worn the Venice carnival mask on the plane, Emily thought.

"Do you need to use the bathroom?" an automated voice said into Emily's earphones.

Unable to speak because of the tape on her mouth, Emily nodded her head.

The woman untied Emily's legs and hands. Another person, a man, joined the woman and the two of them lifted

Emily from the cot and walked her to the bathroom. Once inside the small bathroom, the woman removed Emily's blindfold and the tape from her mouth. It was the same woman from the plane with the same mask. "I'll wait for you outside," the automated voice said into the earphones as the woman's lips moved. "Knock on the door when you're finished."

Alone in the bathroom, Emily relieved herself while frantically searching for something, anything, that would identify her location. Her eyes darted to every nook and cranny in the four-foot square space. Then she saw it. She lurched forward, then stopped. They could be watching her. Please God, let it be something I can use. It was the corner of a moldy, water stained match cover folded into a wedge between the floor and the toilet stand to keep the toilet from moving. She leaned hard to one side of the toilet, and then with her arm behind her, she discreetly removed the match cover, trying desperately not to destroy it. When it was free, she buried her head between her legs as if cramping and unfolded the aged match cover. Thank you, God. The printing was barely legible but she could read it:

Teterboro Jet Services, 24-Hour Maintenance and Support to Business Jets, 141 Charles A. Lindbergh Drive, Teterboro Airport, Teterboro, NJ 07608.

She memorized the information and carefully replaced the moldy wedge. Her heart was soaring as she washed her hands and face in the small sink next to the toilet bowl. Then she knocked on the door.

The masked woman entered the bathroom and replaced the blindfold but not the tape to her mouth. Emily was escorted to a straight-backed chair and told to sit down. Her legs were tied tightly to the chair, and a table was pushed in front of her.

"Here is some soup and crackers," the automated voice said, as the woman guided Emily's hands to the bowl and crackers.

Emily picked up the warm bowl and raised it to her lips. Vegetable soup; it tasted good. She quickly inhaled the soup and was given another bowl. When she finished, she expressed her thanks.

"You're welcome," said the automated voice.

Emily had been silently rehearsing what she was about to say. "My parents expect me to call when I return from Venice. If they don't hear from me, they'll start asking questions. If I could just leave them a voice message, that would be…"

The automated voice cut her off, "Let me see what I can do. Do you have the number?"

Emily told her the number. Then the tape was reapplied to her mouth and her hands were retied to the chair.

A few minutes later, the woman returned. "You can leave a brief voice message for your parents," the automated voice said. The tape was removed from her mouth along with the earphones. A phone was placed next to her ear and mouth. "When you hear the click on the line, you will have thirty seconds. Don't do anything stupid or the recording will be erased before the message is sent," the automated voice said.

Emily knew exactly what she was going to say. When the click came, she spoke quickly and enthusiastically:

"Mom and Dad, it's me. Sorry I missed you. Just wanted you know that we're back. We had a glorious time. When we arrived by sea at the San Marco port and I saw the Campanile d'Oro and the Palazzo Ducale, I started crying because it was so wonderfully beautiful. And, where we stayed was only minutes from San Marco. Never fear, I'll tell you all about it when we visit you next week. I love you."

When Emily was finished, the earphones and tape were reapplied and she was left alone. She'd done it. Now, Wilson and Hap Greene would have to decipher the message.

45

Wilson – Boston, MA

As long as Emily was still missing, Wilson had no choice but to listen to Wayland Tate, who spent the next hour spinning a tale of good and evil in the garden of American capitalism. Including, of course, their plans to replant the garden.

"Once transformed," Tate said, "The new capitalism will give individuals more access to insider information, more options for trading, more avenues for taking even the smallest businesses public, more ability to raise and borrow funds, more freedom to act for themselves, more opportunities to collaborate with others, and more hope for people to become what they want to become. No more wage slavery. The primary role of government will shift from controller to liberator. Continuous education for everyone will finally become the undisputed priority of democracy."

Wilson continued to flirt with the idea of trusting Wayland Tate as he listened to the story of how Fielder & Company and Tate Waterhouse along with their affiliates had declared war against the status quo by orchestrating a byzantine pattern of abuses that would force change. But something felt wrong. He was being manipulated and he knew it.

"What do you want me to do, Wayland?" Wilson said tersely.

Tate eyed him cautiously. "We need you to spin off corporate restructuring from the rest of Fielder & Company. Make it a separate entity. We've already arranged for the financing."

"Why?"

"All our manipulations were accomplished through selected segments of our operations. At Fielder & Company it was the corporate restructuring practice, the rest of the firm is clean. Your father planned it that way," Tate said as he took a bite of his lamb chop and chewed for a few moments. "Once you divest corporate restructuring, completely removing yourself from the partnership, we'll negotiate with Hearst to get Emily back. Then, we'll prepare for disclosure."

"Why not do it as soon as Emily's safe?"

"Daniel's death set us back a few months. There are files and histories that have to be recreated. If the disclosure's incomplete, it won't have enough shock value to galvanize public opinion. We also need time to calm the waters with some of my partners who think you're a loose cannon."

"I assume you're talking about the partners who know about your ultimate objective?"

This time Tate stared hard at Wilson before responding. "Until recently, only the seven original members, and to a limited extent Daniel Redd, knew about our ultimate purpose. Damien Hearst changed all that. Right now, I'm not sure who else knows, but we have to find out before we disclose anything."

"Everyone in the partnership except the original seven joined because of the money?"

"Basically, yes," Tate said, removing his napkin from his lap and placing it on top of his plate. "The abuses had to be real, performed by real CEOs with real motivations to exploit the system's weaknesses for their own personal gain."

"How many members are there in the partnership?"

"About three hundred and fifty."

"And you expected to keep them under control?"

Tate raised his eyebrows but didn't respond.

"Who else was in the original group?"

Tate hesitated with a genuine look of concern in his eyes. "The original group formed many years before the Fenice

Partnership was officially launched after the first Gulf War. Robert Swatling, Jules Kamin, and John Malouf," Tate said, hesitating again.

"And?" Wilson said.

"Carter Emerson," he said slowly.

Wilson was immediately nauseated by the response, not because he'd never considered the possibility, but because Carter had withheld it from him. Tate watched closely as Wilson struggled to keep his nausea down. "That's six."

When Tate didn't respond, Wilson repeated his question. "Who was the seventh?"

"Your mother. Charles was the only one who was married when we first got together. We all loved your mother. We did everything together in those early years. It was natural to include her."

Wilson felt his jaw drop and his head spin as he gazed in disbelief at Wayland Tate. A wave of cold sweat swept over him. He felt as though his body was melting.

"Your mother removed herself from the group many years ago. It was too much of a strain on her, even though she believed deeply in what we were doing. Carter wanted to tell you everything, but we were uncertain about your reaction, until Emily was kidnapped. Then we knew we had to tell you. I'm sure you can appreciate the precariousness of our position."

By the time Wilson's legs got the message to get up from the table and leave the private dining room, he was already freefalling into the abyss. He opened the door to the corridor and ran his fingers along the textured wallpaper until he reached the bathroom where he retched repeatedly. Afterwards, he washed his face, rinsed out his mouth and braced himself before returning to the private dining room. Refusing to sit down, Wilson asked Tate for a written copy of his plan to spin off corporate restructuring.

"I'm sorry I had to be the one to tell you, Wilson. Are you okay?" Tate said as he stood up.

"Get me your plan by tomorrow. Let Damien Hearst know that neither he nor his clients and partners will be exposed," Wilson said as he turned and left the dining room.

Walking back to Fielder & Company by himself, he felt depleted and numb. Why hadn't his mother and Carter told him the truth? Did they actually believe they might never have to?

Tate's story was too compelling and too complete for him to ignore or deny it. One way or another, Wilson had no choice but to cooperate with Wayland Tate. Emily's life depended on it, and right now that was the only thing that made sense or mattered.

46

Tate – Boston, MA

Tate walked down the long wide corridor from where he and Wilson Fielder had just finished their luncheon meeting to a room where Robert Swatling, John Malouf, and Carter Emerson sat silently, nursing drinks and picking at a platter of cheeses, seasonal fruits, and mixed nuts. Jules Kamin joined them by phone, having listened to the luncheon dialogue along with the others.

Rolling back the burgundy leather executive chair at the head of the imposing walnut conference table, Tate sat down while the others watched and waited for him to speak. "What do you think, Carter?" Tate asked.

"He's obviously going to need additional explanation and encouragement. But all things considered, I think we can count on his cooperation," Carter returned.

"You're not at all concerned?" Tate probed.

"Of course I'm concerned. Emily's been kidnapped and you just told him that he can't trust anyone, including his own mother. What choice does he have but to cooperate?" Carter said, sitting back and taking a sip of his drink.

"I don't trust him," Kamin said over the speakerphone.

"Neither do I," Swatling agreed.

"John?" Tate said, leaning over the table and waiting for Malouf's response.

"Time will tell," Malouf said finally.

"Let's give him a few days. If he doesn't cooperate, we'll take further action," Tate concluded.

The meeting was over. As the others left the room, Tate slipped Swatling a folded note:

Cut surveillance for a few days. I want Wilson to believe we trust him, but end his contact with Emily after tomorrow. Let's begin in-depth background checks on every single one of Hap Greene's men, ASAP. Call when you have something interesting.

Swatling read the note and then left the room with Tate. "I'm concerned about Carter," Swatling whispered as they walked down the corridor.

"He's proven his loyalty, Bob. That's why we cancelled the contract on him, remember? I think you'd feel differently if you had been there that night," Tate said, dismissing Swatling's comment as elevated anxiety. He recalled that fateful evening in Sun Valley when Carter had saved his life by taking the gun away from Charles. And if that wasn't enough, Tate mulled, Carter was the one who pulled the trigger. No one would do such a thing for the sake of appearances, no matter what was at stake. Carter had more than proven his loyalty to him and the partnership. If he were going to betray them, he would have already done it. Besides, they all had much more to gain by forgetting about the disclosure and expanding the partnership. If only Charles had come to recognize the utter futility of disclosure.

47

Wilson – Boston, MA

Once back at Fielder & Company, Wilson told Anne that he didn't want to see or talk to anyone except Hap Greene. Then he took the leather wing chair from the head of the gray stone table and pushed it to the wall of windows where he sat down and stared out over the Charles River. Five minutes later, Hap entered the office without knocking. He closed the door behind him and walked to the gray stone table.

Wilson remained adrift in thought, trying to make up his mind about which of Wayland Tate's revelations were true and which were not.

"Swatling, Malouf, and Emerson were in a room down the hall listening to everything. Someone was patched in by phone, probably Kamin," Hap finally said. "They met briefly with Tate afterwards, but not long enough for us to break their nullifiers."

"Surprise, surprise," Wilson said sarcastically as he turned around.

Hap stepped to the wall of windows and stood next to Wilson. "We need some clarity, Wilson. And we need it soon."

Wilson didn't respond, but of course Hap was right.

"For whatever it's worth," Hap said, "No amount of intelligence or data mining would have uncovered this scheme. Nothing is what it seems. Manipulation is a way of life for these people. Every word has multiple meanings, every action points to a range of possible outcomes. And everything could change in an instant."

Wilson held his silence. Manipulation and contingency.

"When are you going to talk to Emerson?" Hap asked.

Wilson didn't respond.

"The sooner the better, Wilson. Whether it's Hearst or Tate or someone else in the partnership who's holding Emily, they won't give you much time to convince them that you're cooperating."

Just then Anne's voice came over the telephone speaker, "Wilson, I know you didn't want to be interrupted, but Emily Klein is on line one."

Wilson moved immediately to the workstation. Before he pushed the button with the blinking red light, he looked back at Hap.

Hap was standing a few feet behind him nodding his head. "We're ready."

Emily sat fretfully in the straight-backed wooden chair listening carefully to the sounds around her while she waited for Wilson to come on the line. She was still blindfolded with her hands and legs strapped to the chair, but the tape over her mouth and the heavy earphones had been removed. The same woman who'd taken her to the bathroom and fed her vegetable soup and crackers a few hours earlier was once again holding a phone to her ear and mouth.

"Emily!" Wilson said as he pushed the button.

She could hear the emotion in his voice. "I only have a few seconds. I'm on a seesaw with my emotions but I'm fine. They let me call my parents to tell…"

There was a click on the line and the phone was taken away from her head. Within seconds, the earphones were replaced. The automated voice said, "Do you want anything to eat or drink?"

"No, thank you," Emily said, shaking her head from side to side, feeling jittery and uncertain. But she'd done everything she could for the moment. With any luck, it would be enough. New tape was placed over her mouth.

"Emily? Emily?" Wilson said into the phone, but he knew she was already gone.

"That's all for now, Mr. Fielder." It was the same computerized voice from before. "Remove yourself from our affairs and you'll have her back."

The line went dead and Wilson hung up the phone, racking his brain to figure out what she meant by "I'm on a seesaw with my emotions."

Hap was already on a cell phone to his people, listening to the replay. "What's she trying to tell us with on a seesaw," Hap asked, looking at Wilson.

"I have no idea," Wilson said, pushing back the strands of black hair that had fallen onto his forehead. "Is it a name? A place? Is she trying to tell us she's by the sea? God, I have no idea."

"We'll track down and analyze the call to her parents. Hopefully, it will give us more to go on. In the meantime, I suggest you meet with Carter Emerson. We'll be monitoring everything."

After Hap left the office, Wilson called Carter.

"I've been waiting for your call, Wilson," Carter said with an emotionless voice after his assistant put Wilson through to his office.

The realist in Wilson had known for some time that Carter was intimately involved, but his innocent wisdom still didn't fully comprehend why Carter hadn't confided in him. Carter had been withholding the whole truth from him for reasons only his father and Carter knew. "How could you do this to me and Emily?"

"I know how you must feel."

"You have no fucking idea how I feel!"

"It's time to talk," Carter said.

"So you can tell me more lies?"

"I'm prepared to explain everything. I will be home in an hour. Elizabeth is in Montreal visiting friends. Your man Hap already knows about it. The house will be ours."

"You sure about that?"

"Hap's people already sterilized the place and I'm sure they'll have a van outside. Bring your nullifiers, if you like. See you in an hour."

Wilson stayed at the office for another thirty minutes, waiting until Hap returned with word on Emily's phone call to her parents. When Hap entered the office, he set the handheld recorder he was carrying in his hand on the gray stone table. "They must have placed calls tying up the line to make sure she only got the answering service," Hap said.

"How did you get this?"

"Don't ask. Emily's parents remain unaware of her kidnapping," Hap said. He pushed the play button on the recorder. Emily's voice seemed enthusiastic and upbeat:

Mom and Dad, it's me. Sorry I missed you. Just wanted you to know that we're back. We had a glorious time. When we arrived by sea at the San Marco port and I saw the Campanile d'Oro and the Palazzo Ducale, I started crying because it was so wonderfully beautiful. And where we stayed was only minutes from San Marco. Never fear, I'll tell you all about it when we visit you next week. I love you.

They listened to it two more times before Wilson said, "That's not the right name. There's the Cap-d' Oro and the Campanile, but no Campanile d' Oro. She's definitely trying to tell us something. It's got to be the *Oro.*" Wilson looked up at Hap, who was standing on the other side of the table.

"The 'sea' and the 'saw' are there again. What about the word 'port'?" Hap said.

"*Seesaw* and *Oro.* It's got to be Teterboro Airport in New Jersey," Wilson exclaimed as he jumped to his feet.

Hap nodded with a glint of realization. "We have a group of decoding experts working on possible interpretations right now. Teterboro will go to the top of their list, but they'll want to know if anything else seems strange or out of character, besides the misnaming?"

"She didn't cry when she saw San Marco Square; she kissed me in front of everybody on the water-taxi and then laughed. And, it's unlike her to overstate things like wonderfully beautiful."

"Good. We'll be working on it while you're at Carter's. Another team will be jamming and recording your conversation from the street. They can be inside within ten seconds if you need them. Make sure Emerson knows that."

Wilson nodded to the one person outside Emily he still trusted, and then he left for Carter's house.

48

Carter – Cambridge, MA

The stately Victorian home, only a few blocks away from Brattle House, was originally built in the late 1880s for one of Harvard's presidents. Wilson struck the front door three times using the brass knocker. Carter opened the imposing walnut door and ushered Wilson into his eclectic den where a fire was flickering beneath an ornate Italian mantle. Wilson chose the old brown leather couch while Carter took one of the tapestry wing chairs. Neither one of them said a word. Wilson had no intention of making this easy for Carter, so he waited.

Carter finally broke the silence, "Where would you like to begin, Wilson? With your father? Your mother? Tate? Or me?"

"You."

"Your father had a penchant for contingency, Wilson."

"I said you, Carter."

Carter shifted his position. Wilson could tell he was uncomfortable. "The week before your father was shot, he made two requests of me in the event that something happened to him. First, secure a full and complete disclosure, no matter what, and second, tell you the entire story, once it was over. I promised him I would do both."

As much as Wilson wanted to, he decided not to express the depth of his disgust or feelings of betrayal, at least not yet. He wanted more answers first. "Did he have reason to believe disclosure was in jeopardy?"

"We both did. Our partners had lost their conviction in our ultimate purpose."

"So what Tate told me at lunch was a lie? Everything the partnership did was illegal?"

"Of course it was illegal. And unethical. And immoral. We merely rendered it legally defensible. There's a considerable difference. That's what the burgeoning complexity of our legal system has allowed. And no, not everything Tate told you was a lie. For the most part, his memory and perceptions are surprisingly consistent with my own. What he kept from you were his motives."

"You were listening, weren't you?"

"Along with Malouf, Swatling, and Kamin."

Wilson worked to keep his frozen exterior from melting, despite Carter's apparent honesty. "What are *their* motives?" Wilson asked.

"They want to expand the partnership internationally."

"No final disclosure?"

"None."

"And, if I try to stop them, they'll kill Emily and then me."

"They will stop at nothing to achieve their ends," Carter said, shifting his position again.

"Exactly where do you stand in all this?" Wilson asked.

"With your father. Always with your father, Wilson," he said with a distant look in his eyes. "Even when I have to defer to the other side."

"What does that mean?" Wilson asked in frustration.

"It means I must finish what your father and I began, without the cooperation or knowledge of our partners."

Wilson hesitated for a moment then asked the only question that really concerned him at the moment. "Is Damien Hearst the one responsible for shooting my father and kidnapping Emily?"

"No. Damien Hearst was a rogue attorney who disappeared to South America a few months ago."

"Who then?"

Carter looked at Wilson, his eyes full of what Wilson assumed was sympathy. "Professionals contracted by Wayland Tate."

"Will I ever see Emily alive again?"

"Yes, if you go along with their plan to spin off corporate restructuring," he said as he stood up and began poking at the fire. "They don't want to kill either one of you, if they can avoid it. I think their feelings of guilt over your father, especially Tate's, are deeper than they expected."

"Do you know where she is?"

"No one knows except Tate. Maybe Swatling," Carter said, turning from the fire to look at Wilson.

Wilson leaned back on the couch and shook his head at Carter. "And you still think we can expose them?"

"Me, not you. Going along with their plan to divest corporate restructuring is your best chance of seeing Emily again."

"But you're not certain?"

"No, Wilson, I'm not," Carter said, turning back toward the fire. "Tate arranged Emily's kidnapping without any of the other partners knowing. To protect our deniability, was how he justified it."

Wilson stayed silent, reliving his earlier lunch with Tate and waiting for the returning nausea to subside. What Hap had told him was true. Emily's life depended on finding her before it was too late. To accomplish that, Wilson needed to know everything Carter knew or was willing to tell him about the secret partnership. "You're not worried that Tate will have you killed?" Wilson asked.

"No," Carter said firmly. "He no longer sees me as a threat."

"Why?"

"Your father's coma was enough for them. If I were going to challenge them, I would have already done so. That's what they think," Carter said with the same distant look in his eyes. "Truth is made true, Wilson. Remember your William James? My partners expect me to make sure you spin off corporate restructuring. As long as I continue to contribute to the game, they will not perceive me as a threat."

Wilson studied Carter who was standing by the fire. "Is that why you invited me here? To convince me?"

"That is entirely up to you, Wilson. No more games."

"It's a little late for that, don't you think?"

"Your father put you at the center of things, despite my efforts to dissuade him. Now we have no choice but to work together."

"Why was my great-grandfather killed?"

"To keep him from publishing his memoirs."

"Where are they?"

Carter shrugged. "Hidden. Stolen. Destroyed. I wish I could tell you, but I can't."

"Can't or won't?"

Carter frowned at him. "I've been trying to keep you alive."

"I heard Tate's version. Tell me yours. What exactly were you and my father trying to prove?"

Carter sat down again, his eyes piercing. "That freedom is a lie. That anyone with less than ten million dollars in liquid uncollateralized assets is an economic slave. That those at the top of the socioeconomic ladder are feeding on the weaknesses of those below them. Capitalistic Darwinism is our reality. Democracy is faltering because freedom and liberty are grossly inequitable. Everyone knows that the wealthy have infinitely more freedom and power to self-realize than the poor or the middle class, and the gap is widening. But no one's addressing the underlying cause. Competition is the weakness, not the strength, of capitalism. What we lose from insufficient collaboration and cooperation dwarfs what we gain from rabid competition."

A sudden burst of energy like a stroke of genius or moment of clarity took Wilson's breath away. Trust him. Carter is not your enemy. For an instant, as if observing the scene from outside his body, he allowed himself to admire his father and Carter again. While the feeling lingered, Wilson asked the one question he knew Carter was waiting for, "What do we do now?"

Carter smiled, "I was uncertain you would ever ask that question of me again." He walked over to a locked cabinet amid the bookshelves and gathered up eight large volumes, four at a time, and placed them in front of Wilson. *A History of Capital Market Abuses in the United States of America*, Volumes I through VIII.

Wilson opened the first volume. It was two inches thick and slightly larger than a letter-sized binder. Inside was a well-organized collection of journal entries, company profiles, executive biographies, manipulation summaries, stock price fluctuations, financial analyses, press clippings, corporate memos, and extracts from annual reports. Thumbing through the other volumes, Wilson found more of the same. "Is this your disclosure?"

"These are the paper summaries of eight years worth of corporate manipulations and financial system abuses. The supporting computer files, audio and video clips, and detailed analyses are backed up by hard drives, thumb drives, and CDs. I'm still working on the final disclosure document. It should be ready for the FBI and the Justice Department within a few days," Carter said, his face becoming dour again. He remained silent for a few moments, staring into the fire before adding, "If for some reason anything goes wrong, and I am no longer in the picture, someone will be in touch with you. Your father and I called him the Watcher. You can trust him. Focus on the money at the highest levels. Generations of concealed corruption have created unimaginable wealth and unparalleled institutional protection. If I didn't think you'd already made up your mind about all of this, I'd tell you to walk away from it. But I guess it's too late for that."

Wilson looked at Carter curiously, wondering if he would ever be able to put all the pieces of the puzzle together. He simply nodded. It's too late to keep me out or expect me to walk away, he thought. For the next few hours, Wilson studied the eight volumes of history, discussed disclosure timing with Carter, and mulled over dozens of contingencies. It must have been a trait he inherited from his father, Wilson thought.

Regardless, he knew that as soon as Wayland Tate placed his plan for divesting corporate restructuring into his hands, Hap and his people would have only a couple of days to find Emily. He prayed they'd made sense of her clues.

When Wilson left Carter's home, he considered stopping at Brattle House to confront his mother, but he wasn't ready for that. Hap had assured him that they were safe and that was enough for now. As he drove to the Back Bay apartment near the Fielder Building, he decided it was time to bring in the authorities, mostly because of what he'd read during the past several hours. His concern for Carter's safety was growing.

49

Hap – Boston, MA

There was dead silence in the twenty-by-fifteen-foot bedroom where Hap Greene and his associates—Driggs, Jones, Potter, Irving, and an independent decoding specialist named Rachwalski—had set up a strategy room in Wilson's Back Bay apartment. Coffee cups, water bottles, and paper plates with the remains of pizza and sushi were strewn over the round table in the center of the room.

Hap sat back in his molded plastic chair staring at the wall covered with hundreds of pieces of paper ranging in size from post-it notes to flip charts. Taped to the top of the wall written in black ink on folded flip charts were Emily's three messages with potential keywords underlined:

Dooon't woooorrry . . .(break in voice and deep breath) . . . I'mmm jet . . . (whimper) . . . fiiinne.

I only have a few seconds. I'm on a seesaw with my emotions but I'm fine. They let me call my parents to tell...

Mom and Dad, it's me. Sorry I missed you. Just wanted you know that we're back. We had a glorious time. When we arrived by sea at the San Marco port and I saw the Campanile d'Oro and the Palazzo Ducale, I started crying because it was so wonderfully beautiful. And where we stayed was only minutes from San Marco. Never fear, I'll tell you all about it when we visit you next week. I love you.

Underneath the three messages were eleven columns of pieces of paper in various shapes and colors. Each column was labeled with a yellow three-by-five-inch index card bearing a keyword written in black ink. Under the "jet" column there were no names because everyone in the room had concluded that the word jet simply referred to jet airplane and airport. Under the "seesaw" column were the names of airports near the sea—i.e., Boston (Logan), Atlantic City (NJ), Baltimore (MD), Nantucket (MA), San Francisco (CA), and Teterboro

(NJ), which wasn't as close to the ocean but had the teeter-totter link with seesaw. The "sea" column listed airports containing those three letters—Seaside (FL), Seattle (WA), Seaboard (AL), and Seaview (MI). Under the "port" column were airports with that word—Portland (ME), Portland (WI), Portsmouth (NH), and Newport News (VA). The d'Oro column identified airports with the words oro or gold—Hillsboro Beach (FL), El Oro (Mexico), El Toro (CA), Goldsboro (SC), Bayboro (NC), Gold Bay (British Columbia), and Teterboro (NJ). And, so on for eleven columns.

Of the 300 airports listed, only 128 of them reported that private jets with international flight plans had landed between Saturday afternoon and Sunday night. Of the 128, there were thirty-two that appeared in more than one of the eleven columns and showed more than one private jet landing during the critical period. Of the thirty-two, only eight were located within two hours by air from Boston, but the landing records provided no additional clues. Emily could have arrived at any one of the eight airports. The eight were listed on a flip chart that hung in the middle of the wall. Cap-d'Oro, Nova Scotia; Portland, Maine; Portsmouth, New Hampshire; Clarksboro, New York; Seaview, Michigan; Teterboro, New Jersey; Newport News, Virginia; and Bayboro, North Carolina.

Hap stood up, walked to the flip chart and marked three of the eight airports with a check. "We have to start somewhere. Mark your top three. We'll send teams to four airports at the same time beginning with the top four vote-getters," he said as he returned to his seat and watched the others take their turns at marking the chart.

When they were finished, Hap stood up again. "Driggs, you're at Teterboro. Potter, you take your team to Cap-d'Oro. Irving, you take Portsmouth. Jones, you've got Bayboro. If we haven't found anything in twenty-four hours, you'll be given the next four airports and another twenty-four hours. If we haven't found her by then, I'm not sure we will, unless she can give us more information. Call me on my cell phone if we need to talk, otherwise, check in with the office every two hours for updates and reports. Concentrate your efforts within a five-mile radius of the airport and start with the executive terminal grounds themselves. We're all on twenty-four-hour duty for the next two days, so get your rest when you can. Good luck."

After the four team-leaders left the apartment, Hap joined two other associates in the living room waiting for a briefing from Wilson on his session with Carter Emerson. When Wilson arrived at the apartment ten minutes later, a little past midnight, he nodded at Hap's men stationed outside the twelfth-floor apartment and walked through the entryway into the living room.

Hap started the discussion by updating Wilson on the targeted airports.

"What if she's not at one of the eight airports?" Wilson asked.

"Assuming we don't get any new information that would cause us to change or expand our target sites and we can't find her within the next forty-eight hours, we'll have to bring in the FBI," he said, pausing to see Wilson's response.

Wilson nodded. His own doubts about whether the government would fully expose the secret partnership had been superseded by his concern for Emily. But after reading Carter's history, he'd conceded that no democratic government would be able to sweep this under the rug. "Will she have a chance, if it comes to that?"

"Of course, but the FBI will have to find her before Tate and her captors figure out what's happening."

"Let's bring them in now," Wilson said bluntly.

"I think that's exactly what we should do. Given the extent of Carter's documentation and Tate's penchant for murder, it makes no sense to wait. I can meet with the head of the FBI's corporate crime division first thing tomorrow morning. Her name is Kirsten Kohl and she's as good as they get. They'll need a day to debrief Carter and develop a plan of attack, but Tate won't do anything rash during the next couple of days, as long as you're spinning out the division he wants. With any luck we'll find Emily while you're buying us time by following Tate's wishes," Hap said with the same confidence he'd displayed earlier in the day.

"Tell me the truth, Hap. What are our chances of finding her in the next two days?"

"Her clues are good, Wilson. They allowed us to narrow it down to eight airports. I think our chances of finding her are very good, as long as they don't move her."

Wilson ignored the last part of Hap's comment for the moment. "What will you do when you find her?"

Hap hesitated.

Wilson already knew what he was going to say before he said it. It was the only thing that made sense under the circumstances, but that didn't make it any easier to swallow.

"We'll have to keep her under close surveillance until the FBI is ready to arrest Wayland Tate and everybody else in the secret partnership," Hap said, his eyes firm yet sympathetic.

Wilson nodded noncommittally.

Hap continued, "If we don't wait, Tate and his partners will disappear. You, Emily, and your family will continue to be at risk."

Wilson turned his attention to the other part of Hap's earlier comment. "What if they move her?"

"Then it will be up to the FBI to convince Tate and his partners to give her up."

Wilson closed his eyes. The thought of losing Emily caused his body to ache, as if twisting until his bones were ready to break. When he opened his eyes, the sweat on his forehead was visible. He pushed back his moist hair. "Make your contact with the FBI," he said. "Carter will have to accelerate his disclosure schedule."

50

Wilson – Boston, MA

Just as expected, Wayland Tate, Robert Swatling, Jules Kamin, John Malouf, and Carter Emerson arrived at Fielder & Company first thing Tuesday morning to personally deliver the partnership's five-page plan for spinning out the corporate restructuring practice. Wilson felt like a robot, having to control his emotions in their presence, but he had no choice.

Most of the day unfolded in his father's office with his father's partners and Leigh Tennyson, going over the details of the plan, the principal points of which were outlined in a brutally succinct document:

$900 million in cash to Fielder & Company;
The transfer of Malouf, Tennyson, and over two hundred
consultants and staff to the new firm;
An intensive two-week transition period for physically
separating corporate restructuring from all Fielder &
Company offices and systems; and
Establishment of Malouf & Company as the new spin-
out entity, a limited liability corporation owned and
operated by the group of people currently sitting around
the gray stone table, with the exception of Wilson Fielder.

On the surface the meeting was conducted very professionally, dutifully focused on the spin-out. Beneath the facade, however, everything felt surreal and creepy, like being abducted by aliens. Nevertheless, Wilson kept his cool, suppressing the urge to blow them all to kingdom come.

Discussion of the final disclosure was limited although well orchestrated. Tate projected it to occur in two year's time. Fucking liar, Wilson thought. During the few hours they spent together, each of the six new owners of Malouf & Company personally promised Wilson that his father's vision would be ultimately realized, no matter what, and that Damien Hearst would be convinced to return Emily unharmed. They all seemed so genuine, it was pathetic. Malouf and Tennyson even apologized for not being able to discuss things earlier. They were human manipulators, who could no longer do anything else.

"It was nothing personal," Malouf said, during a short break.

"I understand," Wilson said, acknowledging that nothing was ever personal with Malouf.

"We both wanted to tell you what was happening on the trip, but everyone else wanted to wait. I think they were afraid of how you'd react," Tennyson said.

"Don't worry about it, Leigh, the important thing now is to make sure this transition goes smoothly," Wilson said, repulsed by her two-facedness.

Swatling and Kamin pretended as if they'd known Wilson for years, patting him on the back and congratulating him. Tate and Carter took turns assuming a fatherly role by giving Wilson counsel on how to proceed. It was all too bizarre and eerie—and almost convincing.

Carter seemed surprisingly adept at playing both sides. After counseling Wilson that all shared clients should be given ample opportunity to work with both firms, Wilson said, "That works both ways."

To which Carter immediately responded, "As long as Fielder & Company avoids the temptation to get into the corporate restructuring business."

"Don't worry," Wilson said, furrowing his brow. "We'll refer all our corporate restructuring leads to Malouf &

Company during the next two years. After that, there's no obligation, right?"

"Right, but make sure that no one jumps the gun. We want to give Malouf & Company ample opportunity to establish itself," Carter said.

"No problem," Wilson returned, looking at Carter with a cynical smirk, but no one seemed to notice. He wanted to yank Carter aside and tell him he was overdoing it, but Carter was playing his own hand. Wilson had no more illusions that Tate or anyone else in the partnership, including Carter, would do anything other than serve their own purposes. What he did trust, however, was Carter's disclosure obsession. He kept reminding himself of that moment of clarity; Carter was not his enemy.

At three o'clock in the afternoon, Fielder & Company issued a press release via fax and email, announcing the spin-out of the corporate restructuring practice as a strategic decision to accelerate the development of both Fielder & Company and the newly created Malouf & Company. A three-page summary of the spin-out was also sent to all past, current, and prospective Fielder & Company clients and affiliated firms, explaining how the corporate restructuring practice had grown autonomous over the years. This spin-out would allow the new firm to expand and enhance its unique approach to providing ad hoc staff support services to CEOs and senior executives, while allowing Fielder & Company to do the same with its remaining practice areas.

Things were moving rapidly, but this time Wilson was ready. He'd played his part perfectly, albeit with a deep resentment in his chest. And even though he hadn't heard from Emily in almost twenty-four hours, he remained hopeful that Hap's men would find her and bring her home unharmed.

Later that evening, when Wilson returned to the Back Bay apartment through a new concealed entrance, Hap was waiting with Philip Johns and Kirsten Kohl. A man in his fifties, Johns was the head of the FBI's Boston bureau; he was medium height with thinning red hair, a weathered face, and a trim physique. Kohl was a woman in her forties, stocky but fit with sympathetic eyes, and head of the FBI's corporate crime division.

Hap had spent the entire day briefing Johns and Kohl by telephone and in person at the Back Bay apartment. Not surprisingly to Wilson, Johns and Kohl had already obtained authorization to launch a full-scale investigation. The only remaining caveat seemed to be a review of national security implications by the U.S. Attorney General, the National Security Advisor, and the President of the United States. But according to Johns and Kohl, FBI Director Bainbridge and Deputy Director Wiseman would have the necessary approvals before tomorrow morning.

As the four of them sat down together in the living room of the apartment, Wilson asked the most pressing question on his mind. "What about Emily?"

"Nothing from the first four airports where the highest number of aircraft landed. We'll move to the second four before dawn," Hap said.

Wilson's heart sank. If they couldn't find Emily by tomorrow night, the FBI would have to negotiate her release. Would the FBI be willing to negotiate with the secret partnership?

"First of all, let me assure you that we concur with Hap's plan to rescue Emily," Agent Kohl said. "We have dispatched backup teams to be used, as necessary, by Hap's leads in the field. If we haven't found her by tomorrow night, we'll bring the hammer down on Tate, Swatling, Kamin, and Malouf."

"Good," Wilson said, staring at Kohl who was staring back. There was something about her that made him feel comfortable—conviction, resolve, savvy. He couldn't put his finger on it, but he liked the feeling. Maybe it was her concern about Emily. The FBI's involvement made him feel both relieved and anxious. He prayed they'd do the right thing.

"Do you think your mother and Carter Emerson will cooperate?" Kohl asked.

"For immunity, yes," Wilson said, just as Carter and he had discussed.

"That can be arranged," Kohl said, without even a hint of hesitation.

It had probably been pre-approved, Wilson thought to himself. It was almost as if she'd been working on the case for months. The surprise on his face must have been apparent.

Kohl continued. "We've known about Tate and Kamin for a couple of weeks. David Quinn blew the whistle on them. Arrest warrants and subpoenas had already been issued when Quinn died, and our case along with him. We're still not sure his death was a suicide. His wife's death is also in question," Kohl said. Then she added, "Wasn't he a client of yours?"

"Yes," Wilson said as he sat back on the sofa, reflecting on David Quinn and his resistance to breaking up the J. B. Musselman Company. "He didn't want to listen to us. He was too sure of himself. I'm not surprised that Tate got to him. Desperation seems to open the door to manipulation."

"His disclosures have allowed us to mobilize resources faster than usual," Kohl returned.

Wilson nodded at the strange irony before turning his attention back to his family. "My mother has been out of the loop for several years and I would like to keep it that way," Wilson said, feeling new empathy for her.

Kohl and Johns exchanged looks to confirm their agreement. Again, it was Kohl who responded, "We will honor that request as long as Mr. Emerson is willing to cooperate fully."

"He will," Wilson said.

"How soon can we see him?" Kohl asked.

"As soon as the immunity guarantees for Carter and my mother are in place," Wilson said.

"We can have the necessary assurances in writing by mid-morning tomorrow," Kohl said.

"You're welcome to call Carter from here if you'd like, the phones at both ends are clean," Wilson said, glancing at Hap to confirm.

Hap nodded, "All signs of surveillance have disappeared. They appear to have backed off completely, at least for the moment. My guess is it's an attempt to make Wilson feel more comfortable."

"We'd like you to arrange it," Kohl said, her blue green eyes drilling Wilson.

"Why?" Wilson asked.

"We also want assurances," Kohl said, hesitating for a moment. "It might be good to advise him of that before we make contact."

"What sort of assurances?" Hap asked, surprised.

Kohl sat back on the black sofa and waited a moment. It was clear that this was her turf. She began calmly. "Full cooperation. Names, files, recorded conversations, testimony, and entrapment, if we request it. And of course, an ongoing commitment."

"Commitment?" Wilson said, eyebrows raised.

"Commitment that he will in no way use his knowledge of manipulating capital markets in this country or elsewhere in the world at anytime in the future."

Wilson eased back into the sofa, debating whether to probe further or simply agree to call Carter. "Are you more concerned about the cooperation or the abstinence?" Wilson asked.

This time Johns responded, "Any individual capable of such abuses could do it again, without anyone knowing."

"The whole point of their ten-year gambit was to make sure this sort of abuse never happened again," Wilson said with an unexpected flare of emotion.

"We only want assurances, Wilson. Sometimes people change when their circumstances change," Kohl responded.

Wilson picked up the phone from the table and called Carter, who picked up on the first ring as if he'd been waiting by the phone. Wilson informed him of the FBI's demands and their plan to deliver immunity guarantees by mid-morning to his office on campus.

"This is a little earlier than expected, but I'll be ready for them," Carter said calmly.

"Any concerns?" Wilson asked, surprised by Carter's calm. Was this exactly what Carter expected me to do? Wilson reminded himself that Carter had been preparing for this moment for years.

"None," Carter said.

"Anything else?" Wilson asked, sensing that Carter had something else he wanted to say.

"So what was it that finally convinced you that the government wouldn't botch this?"

"Reading your eight volumes of history," Wilson said without hesitation.

"For what it's worth, they would have convinced me too, had I been in your shoes," Carter said. "What about Emily?"

"If we don't find her by tomorrow afternoon, the FBI will put the stranglehold on Tate, Swatling, Kamin, and Malouf," Wilson said, glancing at Hap and then at Kohl and Johns. All of them were nodding their agreement.

After Wilson hung up the phone, the FBI bosses stood up and began walking to the door. Kohl reassured Wilson that he'd done the right thing by bringing them in. "The FBI won't disappoint you, Wilson," she said.

Her eyes communicated more than her words, Wilson thought. Apparently Hap had told them about his earlier misgivings. But now he felt relieved the FBI was involved— Kohl seemed to be signaling that rescuing Emily was her first priority. "I believe you," Wilson said.

As Kohl and Johns turned to leave, Hap reiterated his concern about leaks, reminding them of the partnership's track record of surveillance and manipulation.

Kohl assured him that the FBI would be taking every precaution possible. Her next statement had the ring of a declaration of war: "The FBI will not allow this sort of financial tyranny to manipulate the American people ever again." Wilson noted that even Johns seemed surprised by her barely masked passion. Hope does spring eternal, he thought.

51

Emily – Teterboro Airport, NJ

She could smell them before they touched her. Two sweaty men with strong hands and arms quickly removed the bands from Emily's legs and arms, lifting her from the cot. Her blood ran cold. When they began to slowly rub their hands along her body, she recoiled in disgust. Enraged. Now is not the time to fight, she told herself, although it may come to that, especially if they're moving me.

The two men hurriedly escorted Emily into what seemed like the same truck as before. Once again she was forced to lie on the hard bench where she was strapped down.

"Don't be frightened. We're just moving you to another location," the woman's automated voice said into her earphones.

Oh God, Emily said to herself. If I leave Teterboro Airport, Wilson will never find me. She quickly turned her panic to resolve. No more fear. It had been pure luck or providence that she'd found the folded matchbook wedged between the floor and the toilet. She couldn't let it be for naught. As she racked her brain for a way to let Wilson know, she felt the needle enter her arm.

The truck began to move. She didn't have much time before the unconsciousness set it. It's now or never, she said to herself. Emily began to convulse violently. Using every bit of her strength and determination, she twisted and turned her body like a trapped snake. When she started slamming her head up and down against the metal bench with saliva drooling out of her mouth, the truck finally stopped. Within seconds, she could feel the agitated commotion around her. Then came the crushing blow to her face. Pain surged through her head and neck before she lost consciousness.

From the moment the two in-flight service trucks stopped on the tarmac access road, three of Hap's operatives trained their night vision scopes on their every movement. Two men from the cab of the second truck hurried to the back of the lead truck and lifted the roll-up door. Before the door closed,

Hap's men identified the woman struggling on the bench as Emily.

"It's her!" one of the operatives whispered urgently into the microphone.

"Got it," Driggs said calmly as he studied the monitor receiving video feeds from each man's scope. "Tag it. Twice," he said.

Another operative squeezed the trigger of his Barrett M-82A1, firing a tungsten-tipped microchip into the spare tire attached to the truck's undercarriage. He squeezed again, firing another round just as the two men lifted the roll-up door from inside and quickly returned to the second truck.

"Tracking," Driggs said into his headset as the two inflight service trucks sped away.

It was five o'clock in the morning when Driggs called Hap. "We found her, but she's under heavy protection and they're moving her. We're in pursuit."

"They must have pieced the puzzle together just like we did. Or there's been a leak at the FBI. Whatever you do, don't lose her," Hap said.

"We were able to tag the truck when it stopped," Driggs said. "They're traveling in two Rudy's In-flight Cabin Services trucks on runway access roads to the other side of the airfield. We began seeing dozens of in-flight trucks about twenty minutes ago. She must have done something to make them stop the truck. If they hadn't stopped, we wouldn't have identified her."

"Make sure she hasn't been seriously harmed and then maintain visual surveillance until we extract her. If she's in jeopardy, you know what to do," Hap said, worried about why she was being moved. Whatever the reason, it wasn't good.

Hap strode briskly into Wilson's bedroom to report the news. "They found her," Hap said, leaning over Wilson who was half asleep.

"Thank God," Wilson jumped to his feet.

"She's en route at the moment."

"What? They're moving her?"

"We have a tracking device on the truck. The team will use a thermal imaging camera to verify she's unharmed. We'll extract her at the first hint of danger."

"Why are they moving her?" Wilson said as emotions welled up inside him.

"They're clearly taking precautions. The fact that she hasn't called again suggests they may have deciphered her clues. Just like we did."

"How long does the FBI expect us to wait?"

Hap looked at his watch. "Simultaneous arrests are set for forty-eight hours from right now."

"Have you talked to Kohl?"

Hap nodded slowly. "Her position is unchanged. If we extract Emily now, every member of the secret partnership will go into hiding. FBI surveillance will stop some, but not all. But she said it's your decision."

"I'm not sure I can wait that long."

52

Wilson – Boston, MA

Three hours after Hap had awakened him with the news about Emily, Wilson sat in a meeting with Fielder & Company's six vice presidents to launch the two-week transition period for establishing Malouf & Company as an independent firm. The mood among the vice presidents was somber, yet upbeat. They were finally taking action on a problem that had been tolerated for much too long; the remaining vice presidents seemed relieved that Malouf and Tennyson were leaving.

But Wilson barely noticed the nuances, his thoughts and emotions consumed by what was happening to Emily. Ever the consummate professional, he managed to go through the motions until all the major transition issues had been addressed and resolved. They agreed to reconvene again tomorrow.

By noon, Wilson was alone in his father's office, pacing back and forth along the wall of windows. The last time he'd heard from Hap was over two hours ago. Emily had been taken to a warehouse near Princeton, New Jersey. Suddenly Hap marched into the office unannounced. Anne had become accustomed to the routine. "Emily's fine," Hap said in a high-energy voice. "She's got a slightly overheated right cheek, but there's no other indication of trauma."

"Fucking bastards. What did they do to her? If we have the slightest indication that she's being mistreated, I want her out," Wilson said, eyes blazing.

Hap nodded his agreement. "We now have three teams, a total of twelve people, keeping her under surveillance. The number of people guarding her has increased from four to seven—three armed guards outside the warehouse, three inside, and a woman. They're in constant contact with somebody. As of yet, we haven't been able to decode their encrypted communications. But we remain confident that we can free her at any moment. We've also added another team to Brattle House and doubled the protection on your father."

"What's the absolute minimum time we have to wait?"

"After what Carter Emerson told the FBI this morning, I don't think she'll have to remain in custody for more than twenty-four hours."

"Any change in her condition?" Wilson asked, incensed by the thought of her mental and emotional torment, not to mention the blow to her face.

"She's tied down to a cot, blindfolded, and wearing earphones. She's being fed regularly and has the opportunity to walk around every time she uses the bathroom."

Wilson pressed his fingers into his scalp, trying to alleviate his splitting headache.

Hap waited a moment before responding. "My men already have orders to free her the minute they anticipate any mistreatment," he said slowly and deliberately.

"And what about the mistreatment we can't see? Goddamnit, Hap, we're asking too fucking much of her."

Hap waited a moment before responding. "I understand completely," he said slowly. "Give me the word, and I'll have her freed immediately."

Wilson stared at Hap and then walked to the windows overlooking the Charles River. Emily's words "never fear" from the voice message to her parents stuck in his head. Those words were meant for him and he knew it. She'd become more determined to fight than he was. *If only I could talk to her right now, what would she say? Would she want to be freed immediately? Or wait for the FBI to capture its prey?*

It was an impossible dilemma, he thought. Risking another's life, not to mention the life of the woman I love, based on what? Stratagem? Suddenly, it pierced him, as if Emily had spoken it herself. Destroy the bastards. "I want her rescued at the first sign of anything unusual, and I mean anything. And, I don't want her moved again."

Hap nodded, "You got it." He immediately got on his cell phone to Driggs and relayed Wilson's instructions.

When Hap was finished, Wilson asked, "What happened this morning with Carter?"

"At nine o'clock in William James Hall, room 105, after Federal couriers delivered the necessary assurances of immunity, Carter began briefing the FBI, the SEC, the Justice Department, the NSA, the CIA, partners from Ernst & Young and Booz Allen, and a few others no one would identify. The FBI had the place completely sterilized, but there wasn't a hint of surveillance," Hap said admiringly.

"Is this really going to work?" Wilson asked as he sat down in his father's chair at the end of the gray stone table.

"Yesterday I wasn't sure. But what happened this morning convinced me. The FBI performed brilliantly. I thought I had seen everything, but this tops it," Hap said. "Even the guards in the hallways were dressed like grad students."

"How many people?"

"Thirty-eight."

"How did they arrange the meeting so quickly?"

"I asked myself the same question. They must have been scrambling all night."

"Why Ernst & Young and Booz Allen?"

"Beginning tomorrow, those two firms will deploy approximately six hundred auditors and consultants, working around the clock, to verify Carter's records and independently document eight years worth of stock market manipulations."

"Why so many if they're trying to keep things under wraps?"

"Only six seasoned project leaders know the full picture. They were the ones at the briefing. The work will be parceled out in segments to minimize leaks," Hap said, his eyes dancing. "The more people involved, the harder it will be for anyone to see the full picture before the partnership is totally exposed. The FBI has done their homework on this one. They want to make sure an independent verification of Carter's records is underway when they start asking federal judges to issue arrest warrants."

"How did Carter react?"

"Brilliantly. He lectured for an hour and a half and then fielded questions for another two hours. Needless to say, the audience was spellbound. This was definitely the lecture of the millennium. I don't think Carter has any more worries about whether his disclosure will bring a revolution."

"Where is he now?"

"On an airplane."

"What?" Wilson asked, stunned by the words. Carter was still at it.

"Somewhere outside the U.S. It was part of his immunity package. I assumed you knew?"

"Hell no!" Wilson said, feeling stupid for being blindsided yet again. "Things must be worse than we think if the person who most wanted to see this is fleeing the scene."

"Given the FBI's lightning-fast response, he could be anywhere by now."

"That's why Elizabeth wasn't home," Wilson said, trying to think of what else he may have missed. "What's his cover?"

"A history conference at Stanford University. There's an undercover agent disguised as Carter who'll be arriving in San Francisco in a couple of hours."

"Does Tate know about the conference?"

"Carter said he told him about it."

"Did he leave a message for me?" Wilson asked, his anger spiking.

"Not to panic."

"What?"

"He said not to panic. He would be in touch."

"Well, he's done it again, hasn't he?" Wilson said.

"After what he did this morning, he didn't have much choice, Wilson."

"What about us?"

"Unless you want to call it quits, we're scheduled for another debriefing at the apartment tonight with Kohl, Johns, and whoever else they're bringing."

"Who else?" Wilson asked, pissed off about what else he didn't know. He'd been so preoccupied with Emily that he was no longer thinking clearly or acting smart.

"They wouldn't tell me," Hap said, his eyebrows raised.

"Are you absolutely confident that they know what the fuck they're doing?" Wilson asked, admitting to himself that there was nothing he could do about it even if they didn't know what they were doing, except free Emily and leave the country like Carter had.

"They seem to have marshaled an impressive strike force," Hap said, sympathizing with Wilson.

"I hope you're right," Wilson said, still considering the option of fleeing with Emily. "Are you certain that my father and the rest of my family are safe?"

Hap stepped back away from the door, "Each one of them is under heavy surveillance, twenty-four hours a day, four of our people and four FBI agents for every one of them."

"That has to be raising suspicions."

"We still haven't seen any evidence of surveillance or counter-surveillance since your meeting with Tate at the Bostonian Club," Hap said.

"Doesn't that surprise you?"

"Actually, no. They know we're here in full force, so they're pretending to trust you, even when they don't. They're close to being free from Fielder & Company and they're still holding Emily. But sooner or later they'll figure it out. FBI agents throughout the country are already monitoring the movements of every CEO in the secret partnership, ready to pounce at a moment's notice. Kohl wants the arrests to happen simultaneously."

"How many arrests?"

"Over four hundred."

"They'll never pull this off without something going wrong. What's the actual charge?"

"Conspiracy," Hap said.

"Conspiracy?" Wilson said, louder than intended. *Conspirare*, the Latin root of conspire, means to *breathe together*, he thought. Manipulation is as natural as breathing to these guys.

"Conspiracy to defraud the United States," Hap said as he pulled a business card from his jacket pocket. He began reading from the back of the card, "As defined by the Supreme Court, conspiracy to defraud the United States is 'to interfere with, impede, or obstruct a lawful government function by deceit, craft, or trickery, or at least by means that are dishonest.' They're also going to make a case for treason, calling it 'a breach of allegiance to one's government and levying financial war against the American people.'"

"Carter has been planning this for weeks," Wilson said, cynically. "Why did he need me?"

Hap stood up. "Distraction," he said, not without sympathy. "You were his only means of finding cover from the partnership's scrutiny. All he needed was a little time and enough counter-surveillance resources to accomplish what he did this morning. You provided both."

Hap was right again. Wilson had distracted the partnership just long enough for Carter to deliver his final lecture.

53

Wilson – Boston, MA

FBI executives Kohl and Johns entered the Back Bay apartment with Hap Greene, followed by four FBI technicians carrying several cases of computer and video equipment. Wilson arrived a few minutes later. It was almost eight in the evening and there had been no more calls from Emily. Thankfully, regular reports from Driggs continued to convey that she was safe and unharmed. He wouldn't allow her to suffer much longer, even if she was determined to destroy the bastards.

Within minutes, the FBI technicians had set up five laptop computers and a video camera at the dining room table and then proceeded to log in five reporters—Katherine Fischer from *The New York Times*, Peter Jacoby from *The Wall Street Journal*, Bob Woodward from *The Washington Post*, Martha Kinzer from *The Boston Globe*, and Barry Dietz from the *Associated Press*—for an encrypted high-tech video conference. When all the connections had been tested, Kirsten Kohl asked Wilson to join her in the dining room.

"Each of these journalists is on a secure, encrypted connection. They have been thoroughly briefed on our operation. Each of them attended the meeting with Carter Emerson earlier today. Now, they have some questions for you."

Feeling a bit blindsided by Carter and now the FBI, Wilson's growing cynicism flared. "Seems a bit Orwellian or maybe Chinese to have the FBI orchestrating the press."

"We're not orchestrating the press," Kohl said with a distinct coolness. "It was a non-negotiable part of Carter Emerson's demands."

"Nothing surprising about that," Wilson mumbled.

"We're only here for background, Mr. Fielder," said *New York Times* senior reporter Katherine Fischer. "Could you begin by describing your father's relationship with Carter Emerson?"

"Aren't we going to wait for the networks?" Wilson asked sarcastically.

"Broadcast journalists are scheduled for Friday morning after the arrests," Johns said. "Nothing will be printed or broadcast until then."

"And these reporters agreed to that?" Wilson said in disbelief. He didn't like Johns or his self-righteous smugness. And he couldn't believe all of this was going to unfold without any hitches. Carter had told him about wanting the press to be intimately involved, but no one had bothered to tell him about the details or the timetable—and it aggravated him.

"The national security implications of a premature leak on this story have registered with all of them. Plus, we have agents at each of their locations and sworn affidavits that nothing will be discussed or printed until Friday," Kohl said.

"Of course," Wilson said, ready to have Emily extracted immediately.

"What about your father's relationship with Carter Emerson?" Fischer asked again.

Wilson reluctantly spent the next ten minutes explaining what he knew about Carter's relationship with his father. As he summarized the relationship, he softened, admitting to himself how much he loved and respected both of them, despite the fact that he and Emily had been caught in their web of manipulations.

"What do you think motivated your father and Carter Emerson?" asked *Wall Street Journal* reporter Peter Jacoby.

Wilson stared at the small camera attached to the laptop computer at the center of the table and then at the five faces on the computer screens before answering, "My father and Carter Emerson believed that once the American people saw how frighteningly easy it was for those with wealth and power to manipulate our financial system and get away with it, they would revolt."

"Could you explain what your father considered to be the failing of capitalism?" asked *The Post's* Bob Woodward.

"Capitalistic Darwinism—cutthroat hierarchies that allow the strong to take advantage of the weak, the few to reap the financial rewards earned by the many. It's the noble lie. Only philosopher kings or wealthy elite are capable of ruling," Wilson said, paraphrasing Plato's Republic. I've been preparing for this moment my whole life, he thought, just like Carter and my father.

The questions continued for another two hours until Wilson had told them almost everything he knew about his father and the six people who had formed the Fenice Partnership eight years earlier. When the reporters finally logged off from the video-conference, Wilson was exhausted and nervous. There still had been no call from Emily. Hap again assured him that the updates from his people every half hour indicated that she was fine.

Kohl and Johns promised Wilson there would be no more surprises and no further need to talk to the press, unless he agreed to it.

Fat chance of either one of those promises being kept, he said to himself. Suddenly, he felt squeamish about all the other assurances they'd extolled.

"It will all be over by the weekend," Johns said.

"Will we still be alive?" Wilson replied, his temper suddenly flaring. What an anal dickhead. If it weren't for Kohl, I'd have zero confidence in the FBI.

"We've doubled the surveillance on Emily and your family," Johns said.

"Certainly you're not expecting leaks?" Wilson asked sarcastically. His nerves sufficiently fried that he no longer cared who he offended, especially Johns.

"It's only a precaution," Kohl said, warming up for the first time all evening. "We've never encountered a conspiracy with this scope and sophistication."

"What worries you most?" Wilson asked, staring at Kohl.

"The number of people involved," she said slowly.

"Bound to spring a fucking leak somewhere," Wilson said, feeling himself slipping over the edge.

Hap put his hand on Wilson's shoulder.

Kohl hesitated before responding, "We can relocate you and Emily to a safe-house anytime you choose."

"If we disappear, so will every goddamned member of this partnership," Wilson said, his edginess now out of control.

"Every one of them is under twenty-four-hour surveillance," Johns said. "They won't be going anywhere without us."

Hap tightened his grip on Wilson's shoulder, knowing the defiant thirty-one-year-old was about to blow. "If we see the slightest evidence of counter-surveillance or any other questionable activity, we're going to pull Emily out and move them both to a safe location," Hap said, eyeing Kohl and Johns.

"If you're still up to it, we'd like you to keep everyone at Fielder & Company focused on the transition," Johns said in his official, matter-of-fact tone of voice.

"That's what he's been doing—at no small risk to himself and Emily," Hap said, his voice rising. Johns was getting under *his* skin now.

Kohl and Johns gathered their things, reiterating their assurances and appreciation before leaving.

There was nothing else to do except wait for something to go wrong.

54

Tate – Boston, MA

Swatling's call found Tate in suite 2301 at The Westin Copley Place, in the middle of an acupuncture treatment. The acupuncturist, a beautiful Chinese-American woman, had arrived earlier in the evening to relieve Tate's mounting stress. Tate was lying face up on the massage table as he put the phone to his ear.

"It's not Carter," Swatling said chillingly.

"What?" Tate said, sitting up. He grimaced from the nerve pain caused by his sudden muscle movement.

"The person attending the history conference at Stanford. It's not Carter," Swatling said, this time more loudly.

There was silence on the phone as Tate stood up; the towel covering him fell to the floor. He stood naked in the middle of the spacious suite. Acupuncture needles in his face, neck, and shoulders flopped about in every direction. He no longer felt the pain.

"Who is it?" he finally demanded. The acupuncturist attempted to give him a towel to cover himself, but he dismissed her.

"We don't know yet," Swatling said. "He's disguised to look like Carter, but something didn't seem right. Our people found a way to check his fingerprints when they made contact with him. It's not him."

There was more silence while Tate made his decision. "Find out who he is and what he knows about Carter. Then kill him. Our wait is over."

"It may be premature to…"

Tate interrupted, "Not when you consider the context."

"What are you talking about?"

"One of our FBI contacts called earlier to inform us that several CEOs from major corporations in the Boston area are under twenty-four-hour surveillance. Something's scheduled to go down on Friday. That's why I sent you the message to make contact with Carter. Kamin and Malouf are waiting for a conference call, but that won't be necessary now. Carter has made the decision for us."

"What about the other FBI informants?"

"It's time to pull the plug, Bob. You know what to do. I'll see you in seventy-two hours," Tate said, finally looking over at the acupuncturist, who was now staring at him in fear.

Tate placed the phone down slowly. What had she heard? He'd uncharacteristically forgotten all about her. He began gently removing the acupuncture needles until one of them disturbed a nerve, causing him to flinch with pain. He ripped the rest of them out, leaving several bleeding pinholes on his face, neck, and shoulders. When he turned to look at himself in the full-length mirror, it was a reflection that disturbed him greatly.

The startled woman ran to the bathroom for a warm damp towel. As she tried to wipe away the blood on Tate's neck and shoulders, he pushed her away and walked into the bedroom. When he returned, he held a long-barreled pistol in his hand. He fired it once into her head. She's heard too much, and I feel like killing.

As Tate stood above her, watching the lifeblood ooze out of her body, he vowed to himself that he would never be caught. He immediately called Morita to activate their exit strategy. Then he called Kamin and Malouf to let them know about Carter. The partnership was no longer of any use to him. It would soon be exposed. His firm and his clients would have to fend for themselves. The only thing he could do now was to protect himself and his key relationships.

Twenty minutes later, a cleanup crew dressed in business attire arrived at suite 2301. Tate smiled as he watched them go about their work. With money you can buy anything in this world, he said to himself. Two men attended to the lifeless body of the acupuncturist while others cleaned the room. Two women escorted him to the bathroom where they began working on a new disguise—an artificial nose, raised brow with bushy eyebrows, new receding hairline, sandy blonde wig, and an extended chin were carefully put into place, transforming Tate in a matter of minutes into a completely different-looking person. When they were finished, Tate got dressed while going over the documents of his new identity.

Thirty minutes after they arrived, the cleanup crew exited the suite looking like a group of business associates who'd just concluded a late night meeting—some were going out for drinks while others were leaving to catch flights. Three suitcases carried the remains of the acupuncturist.

55

Hap – Boston, MA

Hap Greene was sitting at the dining room table eating a leftover sandwich from a nearby deli when Wilson joined him. It was two in the morning, and Wilson couldn't sleep or bring himself to eat anything. "Anything else from Driggs?"

"No changes. She's safe and sleeping."

"This is taking too long…and I still can't figure Carter," Wilson said as he sat down.

"I think you're right about him. He's still manipulating you, but probably in an effort to protect you. And no, I don't think he's done," Hap said.

"Explain," Wilson said.

"I think he's left the country because he's getting ready for the next round, whatever it is. I don't believe he'd leave you alone in the middle of all this if there wasn't a damn good reason," Hap said. "Unless I'm totally wrong about him, which is certainly a possibility."

"So what's motivating him right now?" Wilson asked.

"His family's safety, your family's safety, the final disclosure, and a complete dissolution of the secret partnership," Hap said. "I think that's why he left. He's made it easier for you to do what you have to do to rescue Emily, protect yourself, your father, and your family. His family left from Canada for somewhere in Europe or Asia. Disclosure is guaranteed. Now, the only remaining question is dissolution of the partnership."

Just then, one of Hap's associates entered the living room. "There's a Detective Zemke from Sun Valley on my cell phone. He wants to talk to Wilson."

"How did he get the number?" Hap asked.

"He must have called the office. Anne Cartwright has the numbers. I told her that Detective Zemke should have access to me if he called," Wilson returned.

Hap shot him a look of concern. "He's outside the loop. Be careful."

Wilson nodded as he stood up and took the phone from Hap's associate. Hap went to the kitchen to listen through the recording equipment. Wilson pressed the connection button. "Detective Zemke, it's been a few weeks since…"

Zemke interrupted, "There's been no movement until now. But something always breaks—we have a tape of what happened that night."

"What?" Wilson said in shock.

"The room was wired. Some kind of remote microphone. The tape showed up this afternoon. Strange circumstances, but seems legit. Looks like the Zollinger women hired a PI from Chicago to eavesdrop. He was killed in an automobile accident in Hailey the next day. We had nothing linking him to the White Horse murders, until the PI's brother started poking around a week ago. Apparently, the PI spent a couple of late nights at Lefty's Bar and struck up a relationship with the bartender, Jake Pitt. He left the tape with Jake and told him that he or his partner would be back to get it. He must have suspected a tail. According to the PI's brother, he never had a partner. Strictly solo. But Jake never heard about the accident, so he kept the tape in the bar's safe until the PI's brother showed up. No one had listened to it until his brother did. That's when he brought it to us. There's an introduction on the tape from the PI, explaining the circumstances and the reason for the wire. The brother already verified the PI's voice. Of course, you'll need to verify your father's voice and the Zollinger family will need to verify the women's…"

"What's on the tape, Detective," Wilson interrupted impatiently. His stomach tightened like a fist.

"Seems the two Zollinger women were murdered by a professional," Zemke said, pausing for a few moments. "We think your father was shot by someone named Carter."

The living room began spinning as Wilson braced himself against the wall. Zemke was still talking, but only bits and pieces were registering. "...prolonged argument...women were convinced...it was too risky...the PI must have tried to negotiate...But Wayland evidently hired...killed the two... Carter and...another long discussion...your father wanted to end...there was more..."

"Wait," Wilson finally managed to blurt out, trying desperately to regain focus. "What did my father want to end?"

Detective Zemke hesitated for a moment. "Seems he wanted to kill all of them, including himself."

Wilson was too numb to speak.

"Your father apparently tried to stop the two Zollinger women from being shot. After the two women were dead, Wayland called off the assassin and took the gun. There was a heated exchange of words, and then a fight. Your father took the gun from Wayland and told the others to back off. That's when your father kept saying this was the best way to end it. But another person—we think it was Carter—wrestled the gun away from your father and then shot him."

Wilson could barely breathe but managed to utter the words running through his head, "Carter shot my father."

"That's our take on it."

"Who else was there besides my father, Wayland, and Carter?"

"Name was uhh ..." Zemke paused a moment before answering, "...Jules and of course the unnamed assassin."

"When can I hear the tape?"

"A copy is already on its way to you. Overnight. Should arrive at your office tomorrow morning. We'll need you to verify as many voices as you can. Thought about doing it by phone, but the tape isn't that good, and we want to make sure it's legit before we turn it over to the FBI."

"The FBI?"

"They said you were working with them," Zemke said, sounding surprised.

"That's right," Wilson said, quickly, "Have they heard the tape?"

"No. I called your office and talked to your assistant Anne. I told her it was vital that I track you down. Then, I called the Zollinger family."

"Why didn't you call the FBI?" Wilson said.

"They were all over us yesterday, six of them, confiscating everything we had on the White Horse case. Put us through the ringer, if you know what I mean. They won't be getting anything else from me until I know exactly what it is."

Wilson remained silent, trying to think.

Hap motioned for Wilson to keep the conversation going.

"Mr. Fielder," Zemke said.

"Yes, I'm here."

"We assume Carter is your father's associate Carter Emerson. Do you know where he is?"

"No," Wilson said, abruptly.

"They're coming back here tomorrow at noon to officially take over the investigation. If I don't hear from you by eleven o'clock my time, I'll call you," Zemke said. "All I need to know is whether the voice on the tape is your father's."

Wilson agreed to listen to the tape and call Zemke in the morning. When he ended the call, Hap tried to console him, but strangely, Wilson was already over it. All of a sudden, everything had become sickeningly predictable.

While initially dumbfounded that Carter had pulled the trigger of the gun that shot his father, the pieces of the puzzle had been there all along—the contingency plan that Carter wished he'd never agreed to, his father's coma convincing the other partners of Carter's loyalty, their relentless quest to finish what they'd started, the repeated attempts to protect Wilson, and that faraway look in Carter's eyes whenever he talked about Wilson's father. What weren't they willing to do for disclosure?

"I still can't believe it," Hap said.

"I can," Wilson said, Zemke's words still ringing in his head: *this is the best way to end it.* "It was all part of their contingency plan," Wilson said. Why had it taken him so long to accept it?

"What?" Hap blurted.

For the next twenty minutes Wilson tied together the bits and pieces for Hap's benefit. Carter had indeed already told Wilson everything—what they had done, what they expected to happen, and what yet remained to be done. When Hap's doubts were addressed and he had no furthers questions, Wilson said, "Call Driggs. I want Emily extracted now. Her parents and sisters are going to need immediate protection."

56

Emily – Princeton, NJ

Feeling her body being gently lifted off the cot, Emily thought she was dreaming. Then, as her consciousness grew, she assumed she was being raped. She immediately arched her back and attempted to kick her legs. Driggs pulled off her earphones and whispered, "We're taking you to Wilson."

Emily stopped breathing. When her blindfold came off, she was staring into the face of a sympathetic-looking black man whose finger was pressed vertically against his lips.

"My name is Driggs. I work for Hap Greene. We need to hurry," he whispered as he removed the tape from her mouth and helped her stand up.

Emily nodded, still trembling as she placed her feet on the ground. After a few steps, they began running along the wall of a dimly lit, nearly empty warehouse. She hung onto Driggs' arm as they ran. She could see the exit door ahead of them. The nightmare was over, she thought.

Suddenly, a volley of gunshots echoed throughout the cavernous space. Four of Hap's men and four FBI agents hit the floor surrounding the makeshift office where three armed men were taking cover. All three guards outside the warehouse had been subdued without a single shot being fired, but not before one of them alerted the others inside. The woman who had been attending to Emily was lying on the restroom floor in a fetal position.

Driggs gripped Emily tightly under the armpit, speeding up their pace as he steered her toward an open door ten yards away.

Quickly positioning himself behind a large filing cabinet, one of the trapped captors spied Emily and Driggs heading for the exit door. "If we're going down, so is she," he said before training his scope on Emily. He would only have one shot—his last.

"Breech!" was the only word spoken in the radio silence amongst FBI agents and Hap's operatives.

Just as he squeezed the trigger of his M110 sniper rifle, the captor and his two cohorts were blown off their feet—

their bodies riddled with chunks of debris from the blast of a fragmentation grenade.

Driggs slung Emily in front of him, toward the open exit door six feet ahead. Tripping on the door's threshold, Emily tumbled onto the asphalt outside the warehouse. She glimpsed a black Range Rover and a man running toward her. Then, Driggs' body slammed down on top of her.

"Nooooo…" Emily screamed, struggling to remove her legs from under Driggs' body, so she could reach his face. The man running toward her was Mike Anthony, who'd been with her and Wilson in Venice.

"Secure," was the second word spoken over the radio silence.

Anthony quickly examined Driggs' body and turned him over. Emily scrambled to her knees. The captor's bullet had struck Driggs squarely between the shoulder blades. Anthony snapped a small plastic vial and placed it under Driggs' nose.

Thanks to the bulletproof vest, Driggs was only unconscious with a painful bruise in the middle of his back. "Let's get her out of here," Driggs said as he opened his eyes and began coughing.

Anthony helped Driggs stand up and then guided him to the open door of the black Range Rover. There was another man dressed in black, just like Driggs and Anthony, sitting in the driver's seat. When everyone was seated, the Range Rover began speeding away from the warehouse along a graveled access road. Anthony immediately got on the phone with Hap.

"Are you okay?" Emily called out, looking over at Driggs.

"Nothing a hot tub won't cure," Driggs said as he leaned back in his seat. "How about you?"

"I'm fine now, thanks to all of you," she said, still feeling overwhelmed. "Where's Wilson? Is he safe?"

"Yes ma'am. We should have you reunited with him in a few hours."

"Where are we?" Emily asked.

"Just outside Princeton, New Jersey."

"How did you find me?" she said, rubbing the skin around her mouth, trying to remove the remaining pieces of adhesive.

"We've had you under surveillance since you left Teterboro Airport."

"The clues worked?" she said, her eyes beginning to glisten with tears. She had almost given up hope that anyone would ever find her alive.

"You're damn right they worked," Driggs said, handing her a bottle of Gatorade from a pouch on the back of the seat in front of him. "Whatever you did to make them stop the truck when they were moving, you allowed us to find you. As soon as they got out of the truck to deal with you, we were all over it. Our night scopes caught you struggling inside.

Otherwise, we would have missed you. They had you in an in-flight service truck that was leaving for the airfield at the same time as forty other identical trucks." Driggs paused. "It was Wilson who decoded your message."

"Oh god...I need to talk to him." Tears were now spilling down Emily's cheeks. Driggs flinched as he put his arm around her. She laid her head on his chest. "Thank you for finding me, but I really need to talk to Wilson," she sobbed.

"Hap is already arranging the call. As soon we have him on the phone, we'll let you know," Anthony injected while glancing at Driggs. Both of them knew what Wilson was currently dealing with.

"We're just glad you're safe and unharmed," Driggs said, attempting to give her as much comfort as he could. "We'll get Wilson on the phone as soon as we can."

Emily sat back in her seat and tried to relax for the first time in what seemed like months, but she couldn't. She desperately needed to hear Wilson's voice. Was it finally over? Were they still in danger? Then she reflected on the words that had saved her life. No more fear. She reminded herself of her vow: she would never let her fear control her again. Ever.

57

Wilson – Boston, MA

Jerked from the exhausted sleep that had engulfed him after talking to Emily a few hours earlier, Wilson could vaguely hear someone calling his name. When he opened his eyes, he saw her above him. She was stroking his hair and kissing him. "Wilson, it's me," Emily said tenderly.

"At last! Thank God, at last," Wilson cried as he leapt from the bed and embraced her.

They held each other tight for several moments, releasing unspoken prayers of gratitude. Just as they relaxed their embrace to stare into each other's tear-filled eyes, Driggs came running into the bedroom yelling the word "compromised."

He shoved a cell phone into Wilson's face. Wilson grabbed the phone and heard Hap's voice on the other end.

"Counter-surveillance is springing up all over the place. We have to move you now. I'll be upstairs in five minutes. Be ready."

"What's been compromised?"

"I'll talk to you when I get there. Bring the escape bags."

"What's been..." Wilson said before the connection ended. Hap was gone. Wilson screamed at Driggs, "What's been compromised?"

"Your safety, Mr. Fielder. Somebody inside. Word on the arrests is out."

Emily clung to Wilson, this new shock coming too soon on heels of her trauma and the relief of reuniting.

"Get dressed; we gotta get outta here," Driggs demanded.

Wilson threw on his clothes and grabbed the pre-packed escape bags that contained food, water, clothes, and various other survival items. Forty seconds had passed. Suddenly, from the corridor outside the apartment came several crashing thuds and a muffled blast. Commands were shouted. Three heavily armed FBI agents burst through the door of the apartment. One of them turned to Driggs and shouted, "Get them out of here, now! Use the escape route."

Driggs ran to the strategy room's walk-in closet with Wilson and Emily behind him. He pushed aside the rack of clothes and opened a concealed door to a narrow hallway before pushing Emily and Wilson in ahead of him. They ran like scared rats through the dimly lit maze of hallways for what seemed like a city block until they reached another door. "Open it," Driggs shouted from behind.

They entered a small stairwell and began running down twelve flights of stairs. At the bottom they entered another long, dark corridor that took them to an underground parking garage. Driggs pushed past them and stepped cautiously into the garage, his eyes scanning in all directions. He motioned toward a black Range Rover and handed Wilson the keys. "Get in and follow me to the street," Driggs said, maintaining his reconnaissance. "If everything's clear, I'll join you there. Otherwise, get as far away from this place as fast as you can. Any questions?"

"No," Wilson said, as he and Emily climbed into the vehicle obviously customized for battle: two shotguns attached to the dash, handheld automatics holstered on each side of the gear box with similar weaponry positioned behind the two front seats.

Driggs reached in across Wilson and pushed a remote control button on the console to open the garage gate. As the iron barrier rolled past the halfway point, five men dressed in black ran into the garage and opened fire on the Range Rover. The sound of the gunfire was muffled, which meant silencers, but the thuds against the doors and windows were deafening. Driggs hit the ground, violently waving his arm and yelling, "Go!"

Wilson jammed the accelerator to the floor. A barrage of bullets pocked the windshield. Driggs took out two of the five before the Range Rover reached the open gate. The three others kept shooting at the Range Rover as Wilson made a hard right onto Beacon Street, almost rolling the vehicle.

They headed north toward Boston Common. In the rear view mirror Wilson saw more men under the streetlights. Flashes of weapon fire brought more earsplitting smacks to the Range Rover's exterior. He saw two more men fall before turning at the first intersection. Once on Storrow Drive, they sped through the Callahan Tunnel to Route 1 and I-95 North, Wilson continued to watch his rearview mirror. There was nothing.

"I don't think anyone's following us," Emily finally said.

Wilson sighed, "What happened to Driggs?"

"God, I hope he survived."

They drove hard and fast toward Maine with its 3,000 miles of coastline and countless coves and peninsulas, agreeing that it was the best place to hide out. While incessantly scanning the cars around them during their two-hour drive through New Hampshire and into Maine, Wilson asked about the kidnapping.

As Emily recounted her ordeal, Wilson thanked God she hadn't been sexually assaulted or physically abused more than the nasty blow to her cheek. But it was obvious from her tearful account that the experience had taken its toll on her emotional and psychological well-being. He gazed at her for as long as he could without driving off the highway. Soulmates forever, he said to himself. After that, he told her what had transpired in her absence, filling in the details that Driggs had been unable to provide.

It was almost sunrise when they reached Mackerel Cove on Bailey Island in Casco Bay, ten miles northeast of Portland as the gull flies, forty miles on narrow roads by car. Wilson backed the Range Rover under the limbs of a large pine tree so it wouldn't attract undue attention. He removed the two handguns and placed them in his bag.

Thankfully, there was a beehive of activity and plenty of chatter on the pier as local lobstermen gassed up their boats, hauled supplies on board, and gulped down their morning coffee. Wilson had worked on Bailey Island as a lobsterman's apprentice for a couple of weeks one summer during college, and had returned on occasion to visit. The familiarity helped. As they walked into the Mackerel Cove Marina Store, Wilson asked for the owner, Mo Bobicki.

Mo was a heavyset blonde-haired woman who ran her marina store and restaurant with tender loving care. She was also a woman who told you exactly what was on her mind.

"Wilson? You're early this year," she said as she stepped around the corner from the restaurant. "We don't usually see you until July or August. What's the occasion?"

"You might call it an early escape from the insanity down south," Wilson said, smiling at Emily. He introduced Emily and then reminisced briefly about the last time he stayed at the Marina.

"You know the loft's not available until after May 1st," Mo said with a wry smile on her face. "The only reason we're open at all is the unusually warm weather this season. Lobstering started early this year."

"Are you willing to make an exception for a loyal customer?" Wilson asked, expecting she'd say yes. Maintaining the friendly chitchat was draining him of what little energy he had left. He could imagine how Emily felt after her ordeal. But he didn't want Mo to see any of the fatigue or turmoil inside them.

"It hasn't been cleaned. We only have a limited staff."

"Don't worry about it. We'll take care of everything," Emily said, apparently sensing Wilson's need for help.

"You remember how to start the wood burning stove?"

Wilson nodded.

"Okay. It's open," she said, noticeably anxious to return to other duties. "I'll have someone come up later with fresh towels and linens."

58

Wilson – Bailey Island, ME

Perched above the marina store and restaurant, the loft's three walls of windows offered a panoramic view of everything from the single highway onto the island, to the lobster boats in the bay and the Atlantic Ocean beyond the cove. We'll be safe here, Wilson thought.

Emily went to the bathroom to take a shower, while Wilson sat down at the small round table overlooking the pier to call Hap Greene. He punched in the numbers on the cell phone he'd taken from the Range Rover. He'd tried Hap's emergency number earlier, but there'd been no answer. This time he was relieved to hear Hap's voice. "It's Wilson."

"Are you okay?" Hap asked.

"We're fine. What about our families?"

"Everyone's safe. Emily's parents and her three sisters are under protective surveillance on Martha's Vineyard. We flew her sisters and their families in last night."

"What happened at the apartment?" Wilson asked.

"Tate and his partners had an informant inside the FBI. An agent named Switzer. He's in custody, but there's bound to be others."

"Is Driggs okay?"

"Superficial wound to the side of his head, but he's fine."

"What about Tate and the others?"

"Kamin blew himself to pieces with plastic explosive in his Manhattan apartment. Malouf and Tennyson are in custody," Hap said, pausing a moment. "Tate and Swatling have disappeared."

"Disappeared?" Wilson said loud enough for Emily to hear him from the bathroom.

"Unfortunately," Hap said quietly.

"Things are under control, right?"

"We weren't in charge there, but we are here."

"Now what?"

"Arrests of the CEOs and their facilitators of vice have begun and will continue throughout the day, as fast as the federal judges can issue warrants. Everything's happening a day earlier than planned. The FBI's trying to keep a lid on the press until tomorrow morning."

Suddenly, Wilson realized that Hap hadn't asked him where he was. Then it dawned on him. "You're tracking us, aren't you?"

"Yes. You're somewhere on the coast, northeast of Portland, Maine. We've been tracking the Range Rover. I have three of my people on their way to you right now. They should be there in an hour."

There was silence on Wilson's end as alternate reactions dashed through his mind. Then he asked, "What makes you think Tate hasn't compromised one of your guys? Or that the men you sent aren't being tracked?"

"They're the best I have," Hap said.

"Not good enough, Hap. We won't be here when they arrive. Just make sure my family's safe. Tell Kohl and Johns the same thing."

"Wilson…"

Wilson pushed the end button before Hap could finish.

"You remember Boothbay Harbor, don't you?" Wilson asked as he entered the bathroom. They'd hung out there over a long weekend during their college days.

"How could I forget?" Emily said, smiling playfully as she stepped out of the shower and wrapped a towel around her.

It was great to see her smiling and with only a towel around her, but they didn't have much time. "Believe me, I wish we could take advantage of this moment, but the FBI's been compromised. And they're tracking the Range Rover."

"Who's tracking it?" Emily asked, her eyes suddenly on fire.

"Hap is, but the FBI knows everything he's doing. He has three men on their way to protect us. But given the circumstances, I don't think it's in our best interest to stay around waiting for them."

"I agree," Emily said.

"I'm going to drive the Range Rover to Boothbay Harbor. The Marina has a lobster boat. Hopefully it's available. If not, I'll pay double a day's catch to one of these guys," Wilson said, pointing to the hubbub on the pier. "Can you take the boat to Boothbay and pick me up at the main pier downtown?"

"Of course. Will the emergency tires get you there?" Emily asked, knowing that the tires were full of bullet holes.

"The vehicle computer says we've got forty miles left. That'll do."

"Why don't we drive together and rent a boat there?" Emily asked as she quickly dressed.

"As much as I hate the idea of being separated from you again, getting a boat in Boothbay could take time we don't have. This way, I'll ditch the Range Rover in town and find cover somewhere near the main pier. You can drop anchor offshore until you see me. Then we can get lost anywhere," Wilson said insistently. He wasn't going to put her in harm's way again.

"I'm not crazy about you driving to Boothbay by yourself," she said with a frown, running her fingers through her wet hair.

"I don't think we have a choice. We'll only be safe once we get rid of the Range Rover," he said, putting his arm around her and walking to the door. "This way, you won't be put in harm's way again, and they won't try to stop me until I've reconnected with you. It's smart and safe."

Downstairs in the marina store Jaclyn, Mo's store manager, told Wilson that their lobster boat was in the dock shop getting an overhaul. The only charter boat available was a sixty-foot sailing yacht, which would be too much for Emily to handle by herself. Wilson tried to stay calm as he asked if she knew of any other boats for rent. She gave him the names of two retired lobstermen who lived at the end of the cove but warned, "No guarantees this time of year."

"Thanks, maybe I'll give them a try," Wilson said casually. No use drawing any undue attention, he thought.

"Wanna boat fur hire?" asked a large red-faced man as Wilson and Emily walked out of the store. "Couldn't help overhearin'."

"Yes," Wilson said cautiously.

"Where you wanna go?"

"The lighthouses at Cape Elizabeth."

"Name's Paddie," he said sticking out his hand, "I can take you."

Shaking his hand, Wilson began slowly, "We sort of wanted to get out on our own. You know, just me and my wife."

"Got experience?"

"She grew up on Martha's Vineyard boating and sailing since she was five. I worked here as a lobsterman's apprentice, and my family has an eighty footer and a twenty footer on Nantucket," Wilson said, probably a little too anxiously.

The man squinted at Wilson and Emily, his eyes nearly lost in his weather-beaten face. "Costs more for goin' alone."

"How much?"

Once again, Paddie looked them up and down.

They both tried to appear as calm and casual as they could.

"$300 for half day."

"Can we go right away?"

"Just gassed her up."

"Great. My wife is going to meet me in the next cove. I have to pick up a few things."

"I need some collateral."

"Uh. Okay. What did you have in mind?"

"Car keys, driver's license, somethin' of value."

Wilson pulled out his driver's license and his father's Mercedes keys. He gave them to Paddie with $360 in cash. "Tip's included," he said.

Paddie examined Wilson's driver's license and gave it back. "I'll keep the keys. Meet you on the boat. She's the yellow and green one at the end of the pier."

Wilson and Emily kissed each other good-bye, with more than a little apprehension, before Wilson left for the Range Rover and Emily walked to the end of the pier.

As Emily was listening to Paddie's instructions, Wilson was already speeding off the island in the bullet-marked Range Rover. Avoiding attention from the State Police was going to be a challenge.

Ten minutes later, Emily cruised north out of Mackerel Cove toward Boothbay Harbor, knowing she'd make it to the harbor well before Wilson. But she wasn't happy that Wilson was taking all the risk, especially in a bullet-marked SUV in broad daylight. Little did she know what was in store for both of them.

59

Emily – Boothbay Harbor, ME

There was no sight of Wilson as Emily approached Boothbay Harbor, but it had been less than twenty minutes since she left Bailey Island. She dropped anchor off the eastern peninsula and began surveying the main pier six hundred yards away through a pair of binoculars she'd found on board.

Ten minutes passed. Then twenty minutes. Still no sign of Wilson. She pulled up anchor and started the engine. She had to do something. After docking at one of the longer piers away from the center of town, she put on a stocking cap, boots, and a full-length yellow slicker from the boat's storage compartment. Thankfully, a light rain was falling from an overcast sky, allowing her to use the slicker's large hood without drawing unwanted attention. She walked briskly up the pier into the community of Boothbay Harbor. For another ten minutes she scanned the quaint New England streets near the harbor, looking at every face she saw. Panic was starting to set in.

Finally, she spotted him standing with a group of twenty or so people in the store front offices of Montsweag's Whale Watching and Sightseeing Excursions. Emily barely recognized him in the baseball cap and red plastic raincoat. She waited for him to see her, but he didn't. Just as she began feeling conspicuous, he saw her. Their eyes locked for an instant. There was no mistaking Wilson's nod of recognition.

Emily walked around the corner and down a narrow alleyway between two buildings toward the water, thinking there must be fishing boats for rent nearby. So much for their plan to avoid wasting time with boat rentals. Sure enough, there they were—three canopied catamarans and half a dozen twelve-foot outboards, all with the Montsweag's name in blue and yellow letters. It was never too early in the season for fishing, thank God.

Emily hurried back up the alleyway and entered Montsweag's through a side door. Wilson saw her. She turned to one of the clerks behind the counter and asked about the group of people. The woman informed her that they were about to embark on a whale-watching excursion and then asked if she cared to join them.

"Actually, I'm more interested in your twelve-footers," Emily said, realizing that the best way to get out of there was to rent another boat and give Wilson the opportunity to leave the excursion group at the last minute. He obviously wouldn't be acting the way he was, she thought, if he wasn't afraid of being seen.

"The small fishing boats?" the attendant asked.

"Yeah. How much is the rental?"

"$75 an hour with bait and tackle, $200 a half day, $350 all day. $500 refundable deposit."

"I'd like to rent one for all day."

"Fill this out, please," she said, handing Emily a clipboard with a renter's agreement. "How will you be paying?"

"Cash," Emily said, grateful for the $3,000 in one hundred dollar bills that Hap had placed in each of the escape bags. She hoped they weren't marked.

"Fine, but I'll need an imprint of your credit card for the deposit."

Emily quickly filled out the necessary paperwork and read the accompanying instructions. She paid the clerk, who took an imprint of her American Express card for the refundable $500 deposit. Thankfully, Wilson had brought her purse from Venice. She watched closely to make sure the clerk didn't process the credit card. They certainly didn't need a transaction to show up on somebody's computer screen. Noticing Emily's watchful eye, the clerk reassured her that her card had not been charged and that she could tear up the imprint when she returned with the boat undamaged. "Take this to Sam on the pier," she said handing Emily the key and a copy of the agreement, "He'll help you."

"Thank you," Emily said, before timing her exit to coincide with the group of whale watchers leaving the office. Emily blended into the crowd, offering thanks for another small blessing. On the pier, she found Sam who led her to one of the twelve-footers. Sam pointed out a few things, and Emily got into the boat. At the last minute Wilson withdrew from the group and joined her in the small fishing boat. At first, Sam looked surprised at Wilson's sudden arrival and was about to say something, until Emily smiled and gave him a thumbs up. Within seconds Emily and Wilson were crossing the bay through a cluster of anchored sailboats and schooners.

Wilson lay on the bottom of the boat telling Emily how two cars began following him outside Bath. "A dark blue Ford Taurus and a red Jeep Cherokee kept trading positions every mile or so. When I stopped at a gas station in Woolwich to put more air in the tires, the Cherokee stopped at a pottery barn across the road, and the Taurus kept going. After that, both vehicles kept their distance, but they continued following me. I stopped again in Wiscasset at an ATM, just to see what they'd do. Both cars passed me, but I saw them again when I turned onto Highway 27. After that they let me think I'd lost them."

"How many men did Hap send?"

"That's what scared me. There were six of them. Four in the Cherokee and two in the Taurus. Hap said he was sending three," Wilson said, his eyes were full of venom as he looked up at Emily from the bottom of the boat. "When I got to Boothbay Harbor I stopped at Brigham's Inn. A few blocks away from the pier. We stayed there once. Remember?"

"Yes, I remember," Emily said, smiling. She swung her eyes back to the helm and the bay in front of them.

"I left the Range Rover in the parking lot next to Brigham's and casually walked to the B&B. As soon as I got inside, I left through the back door into the garden and ran through the woods to a side street where I entered the first clothing shop I could find. That's where I bought my new Red Sox cap and the raincoat."

"How did you wind up with the whale watching group?" Emily asked.

"I knew the men following me wouldn't stay at the B&B for long, which meant meeting you on the main pier was not an option. Unfortunately, the only way to let you know was to not show up. Sorry. I knew you'd figure it out and come looking for me, so I tried to find a natural cover nearby. When the whale watching group started forming a few minutes ago, I bought a ticket."

"Thank God you saw me."

"My sentiments exactly," Wilson said. "Your outfit was brilliant. I saw you standing there in the rain and didn't think twice about it. Then, when you turned, I knew it was you. I'd recognize that graceful turn of your head anywhere, no matter what you were wearing."

Glancing at him sideways, she said, "We're getting better at this, and I'm not sure I like it."

Wilson didn't respond, except to raise his eyebrows, as the boat motored across the harbor to the pier where Emily had left the lobster boat. They quickly got out of the twelve-footer and into Paddie's twenty-four-foot lobster boat. Emily charted a course around the eastern peninsula to Linekin Bay. When they reached Lobster Cove, they began looking for a secluded place to dock so they could survey what was happening back in Boothbay Harbor. No matter who was following them—Hap's men, Tate's men, the FBI—compromised or not, every local cop and state trooper along the coast would soon be looking for them, Wilson thought. Sooner or later, someone was bound to check the boat rentals, and then they'd have the coast guard after them as well.

When they spotted a small pier with no one around, they docked the boat and hiked up a narrow path through heavy brush past two secluded homes and into a small clearing, which was perfect for spying.

They sat sheltered by a large umbrella from the misting rain on one of the outdoor benches and took turns scanning the bay's environs. Wilson was the first to spot the men who had been following him.

"The two cars that were following me just pulled into the parking lot at the main pier," he said, his eyes glued to the binoculars. "Only five men this time. One must be waiting. Hold it. Here come two more vehicles. One of them is the Range Rover. The other one is a Taurus. Beige. Three more men. The two Fords have to be FBI. The Jeep Cherokee must be Hap's."

"What are they doing?" Emily asked.

"Talking. Just talking."

"Now what?"

"Nothing."

Emily squinted, but without binoculars she could barely discern the cars.

"One of them is pointing toward town," Wilson said. "Looks like he's giving instructions. They're splitting up. On foot."

"Whoever they are, it won't take them long to check the rental records. I think it's time to leave," Emily said.

"I think you're right," Wilson said, handing the binoculars to Emily.

She peered through the lenses at the eight men who were now walking two by two into Boothbay Harbor's commercial district. "At least we know they won't be looking for us back on Bailey Island," Emily said.

"Right," Wilson said. "And, if these guys don't already know we're sitting here across the bay, it means that everything they used to track us is still in the Range Rover."

They returned to the lobster boat and headed back toward Mo Bobicki's loft. As they rounded the point into Mackerel Cove, everything seemed normal. They docked the boat at the gas pumps where Paddie was waiting for them. He'd been hanging out in the restaurant's bar when he saw them enter the cove. It was almost two in the afternoon.

Back in the loft, they made up the bed and futon, pulled down the blinds on the windows, and tried to get some rest since neither of them had gotten much sleep in the past few days. Wilson was overjoyed to have Emily lying beside him again. As he closed his eyes to sleep, he wondered if the FBI or Hap's men or the secret partnership would be able to trace a call if he used the pay telephone downstairs to contact Hap. He needed to make sure their families were safe. It was the last thought he remembered before falling asleep.

60

Rachel – Cambridge, MA

It was Rachel who smelled the smoke first, in the middle of hastily preparing to leave for a safe house. She yelled at Darrin, who had just arrived home from a job interview, to call 911. Then she ran upstairs to get her daughter and mother who were reading in the belfry library. "The house is on fire," Rachel shouted running up the spiral staircase.

Her mother and little Mary met her at the top of the stairs with looks of astonishment on their faces. "What's happening?" her mother gasped.

"The house is on fire. We've got to get out," Rachel blurted before coughing uncontrollably. The three of them descended one after another down the spiral staircase into the hallway, toward the main staircase now filled with smoke.

Darrin came running from the kitchen, scooped his daughter into his arms, and grabbed Rachel's hand. Rachel's other hand held onto her mother's. As the four of them ran together down the wide hallway toward the front door, there was an explosion in the east parlor. Flames shot across their exit path, engulfing the front door in fire and smoke. They quickly turned around and ran for the French doors at the back of the house, but before they could reach them, there was another explosion. All four of them were thrown to the ground by the blast.

Disoriented and coughing as she lay on the floor, Rachel could barely discern the sirens and breaking glass before she lost consciousness. When she regained awareness, she had a plastic oxygen mask over her nose and mouth and was being wheeled into the back of an ambulance. She raised herself up from the gurney to see where her family was, but all she could see was Darrin wrestling with one of the paramedics.

"What's wrong?" she screamed, managing to remove the plastic mask from her face.

The paramedic attending her replaced the mask and pushed her back down onto the gurney, telling her that her mother and daughter were fine. Then she heard gunshots and immediately raised herself up again, just in time to see her husband fall to the ground. She ripped the mask from her face and tried to get up, but the paramedic shoved her back down and stuck a gun in her face.

Rachel screamed as she rolled off the gurney onto the floor of the ambulance. There were more gunshots with blood splattering everywhere inside the ambulance. The bodies of two paramedics dropped beside her, one of them pinning her arm to the floor.

Gunfire continued outside the ambulance for several more seconds. When it stopped, Rachel drew her arm out from under the lifeless body and scrambled out of the ambulance to find her husband who was lying unconscious on the ground. He'd been shot in the shoulder and was being lifted onto a gurney by one of Hap Greene's men and another man she'd never seen before.

"We need to get you to a hospital," said the man she'd never seen before. He motioned to another ambulance that was coming up the driveway. "Your husband's got a minor shoulder wound and a nasty bump on his head, but he should be fine. Your mother and daughter are already on their way to the hospital. They're fine. Just suffering from a little smoke inhalation and a few bruises like you."

"Who are you and what happened?" Rachel said as she walked beside her husband's gurney, clinching his hand.

"Sorry, ma'am. Special Agent Frandsen, FBI," he said. "I think you know Johnson here."

Rachel nodded as she acknowledged Hap Greene's man who was keeping pressure on Darrin's shoulder to reduce the bleeding.

"The crew of paramedics that arrived after the fire broke out weren't real paramedics. They tried to kidnap your mother when Hap Greene and your husband intervened."

She felt dizzy, almost losing her balance as they loaded her husband into the ambulance.

"Get this woman a gurney," Special Agent Frandsen shouted as he grabbed Rachel around the waist to keep her from falling.

Rachel began losing consciousness as scenes of an apocalypse ran through her mind. How had things gone so terribly wrong? Where's my daughter? Mother?

As the paramedics loaded her into the ambulance, Rachel began coughing uncontrollably, throwing her body into convulsions.

"Will we ever be safe again?"

61

Wilson – Bailey Island, ME

Wilson woke up bathed in sweat. He immediately looked at his watch. It was fifteen minutes after five o'clock in the evening. They'd slept for more than three hours. Montsweag's would be closing in fifteen minutes. Wilson bolted down the stairs to the pay phone on the wall outside the marina store. It was raining hard.

After punching the numbers into the pay phone, he heard a woman's voice, "Montsweag's Whale Watching and Sightseeing Excursions."

"We rented a boat this morning. It's in my girlfriend's name Emily Klein. We left…"

"Let me get Mr. Montsweag," she interrupted.

As Wilson waited on the line, he wondered what Carter was doing.

A few seconds later, a deep gruff voice came on the line. "Son, the police have been here looking for the two of you."

Wilson's heart sank as he looked around him in the pouring rain, trying to discern if anyone was watching. "What did they want?" Wilson asked, looking at his watch and trying to remember how long it took to trace a call. It had already been twenty seconds or so.

"Some kind of emergency at home. They didn't say anymore than that."

Wilson braced himself against the wall of the marina store to keep his balance and hung up the phone. Then, he called the number, again, "Sorry. I was cut off."

"Where are you?" Montsweag said when he got on the line, again.

"We got stuck in the storm. We're fifty miles north in Stonington."

"Where you stayin?"

"Uh. Don't know yet," Wilson replied, attempting to keep his composure. "Probably at the Inn by the old Opera House."

"Okay. Better call home, son. You can bring the boat back tomorrow."

"Thank you, Mr. Montsweag," Wilson said, panicking inside. He entered the marina store to get more quarters. As he looked around, nothing seemed out of place. Jaclyn was still behind the counter waiting on customers. When she got to Wilson, she asked, "How many nights are you planning to stay?"

"Can I let you know in the morning?" Wilson asked.

"Sure," she said. "I need an imprint of your credit card."

"I'll pay cash. How much?"

"Off season rate is $89. With food and tax, it's $122.41."

Wilson gave her seven twenty-dollar bills and asked for the change in quarters. Luckily she had several rolls of quarters. She grabbed two and cracked them open.

Back at the pay phone, Wilson dialed Hap Greene's emergency number and then deposited two dollars and fifty cents.

A woman's voice answered, "Hello."

"Who's this?" Wilson asked, startled.

"Wilson? Is that you? This is Agent Kohl."

"Where's Hap?"

"We can't talk on this phone. Call me back at 212-555-0004."

Wilson hung up, dialed the new number, and deposited another two dollars and fifty cents.

Kohl's voice came on the line, "Wilson?"

"Are you trying to trace this call?"

"No," Kohl said. "As long as you're safe…"

"Is my family safe?" Wilson said, interrupting her.

"Yes," Kohl said.

Wilson heard the hesitation in her voice. "Where's Hap?"

There was silence on the line.

"Where's Hap?" Wilson repeated.

"He left this cell phone with a message that he'd be back soon. The agent who was with him is dead."

"What happened?"

"There was a fire and explosions at your family's Brattle Street residence earlier this morning. The firemen took care of it quickly. Your family is fine. A team of paramedics tried to kidnap your mother and niece. Hap Greene and the other agents stopped them. Your mother, your sister, and your niece were not harmed, just a little smoke inhalation. Your brother-in-law was wounded in the shoulder, but he's doing fine. All of them are at Mount Auburn Hospital under heavy guard."

"You said they were safe before. Are you sure they're safe now?" Wilson asked, his voice cracking. He felt responsible for everything. And when his family needed him most, he was too far away to help.

"Yes," Kohl said. "Let us bring you in, Wilson. We can protect you."

"We'll take our chances where we are. Just keep my family safe," Wilson said, looking at his watch. Twenty seconds had passed. "Are you sure no one's tracing this call?"

"Absolutely," Kohl said. "This is my personal cell phone and everything on it is scrambled. I purposely don't have caller ID and I've never used it to trace anyone. Trust me."

"What about the compromised agents?" Wilson asked, deciding to believe her.

"We've identified all of them. The first one we found, an agent named Switzer, confessed to everything."

"How many are there?"

"Eleven. Six from the FBI, two from the Justice Department, one CIA, one NSA, and one of Hap's men."

Wilson swallowed hard. "Tell me they're in custody."

"Five of them are still at large. Three FBI agents, the CIA operative, and Hap's man."

There was dead silence on the line as Wilson digested the information. "There are eight men following us," he said.

"How..."

"Don't ask. We saw them last in Boothbay Harbor. They're driving a red Jeep Cherokee, a dark blue Ford Taurus, a beige Taurus, and a black, bullet-pocked Range Rover."

"I'll run a check on the vehicles. Let us protect you, Wilson."

"Look Ms. Kohl," Wilson said, "I'm not suggesting you don't already know this, but let me underscore it for you. These people are ruthless and relentless. They have their own death squads. They believe anyone can be corrupted at any time and they won't stop until they've won. Do you understand me? They want us dead. They want my family dead."

After a long pause, Kohl responded, "More than twenty FBI agents have lost their lives since three o'clock this morning. Some of them were close personal friends. We've made over two hundred arrests and we expect to double that by midnight. Believe me, Mr. Fielder, we understand."

"Have you found Swatling or Tate?"

"No, but the NSA and CIA are on it."

Just then the automated operator came on line, asking for another deposit. Wilson quickly deposited a handful of quarters. "Why the NSA and CIA?"

"We have reason to believe that Tate and Swatling are no longer in the country."

"Do you know where they are?"

"Somewhere in Europe."

"Italy?"

"Possibly."

"Have you heard from Carter?" Wilson asked.

"No," she said, pausing again. "The undercover agents at Stanford who were in contact with Carter in case we needed information to maintain their covers were murdered early this morning. The men who did it are in custody."

Wilson collected his thoughts. "Have you talked to Detective Zemke in Sun Valley?" he asked.

"No. Why?"

"You haven't listened to the tape?"

"What tape?"

"An overnight package from Zemke should have arrived at Fielder & Company this morning. Open it. Listen to the tape and then contact Zemke. I think it will shed some new light on what you're up against."

"What are you saying?"

"It was Carter who shot my father. And, right now, I'm not sure what he's up to. Tate and Swatling have gone to Europe to either persuade him or kill him."

Kohl remained silent, but Wilson could hear her exhaling with a sigh.

"Find Hap. I'll call you tomorrow," Wilson said. He hung up the phone before she could respond. He hated to admit it, but there was nothing more he could do to ensure the safety of his family. They were now in Kirsten Kohl's hands. He could only pray that Hap Greene was still alive. His first impulse was to find another boat and take off for Canada, but that would present other dangers, especially in this weather.

Just to be safe, Wilson made arrangements with Mo Bobicki to sleep on the sixty-foot charter sailboat docked at the marina. He returned to the loft and told Emily about his conversation with Kohl. When it got dark, they pulled the blinds over the windows of the loft and left the television and lights on, and then exited through the inside stairway to the restaurant. They bought a bottle of wine and sandwiches before leaving the restaurant through the back door and slipping into the trees. When they emerged from the trees onto the road between the Marina Restaurant and a row of beachfront homes and condos on the cliffs overlooking the cove, they were unrecognizable. They had borrowed slickers with hoods from the restaurant and were walking as if they'd just left a cocktail party. Wilson carried the bottle of wine in his hand and Emily carried the sandwiches and two wine glasses. Luckily, it was still drizzling outside.

Once inside the well-appointed yacht, they watched television until well past midnight, waiting for a special news report. But there was nothing, except for a sketchy account on a local news channel about the FBI's involvement in an apparent gang-related shooting in Boston's Back Bay region.

"I can't believe they've kept it under wraps," Emily said.

"Why? They've done it before," Wilson said.

"Not with something this widespread," Emily returned.

"Sure they have. We just don't know about it."

They laughed nervously as they turned off the television and got ready for bed. When they finally lay down in the yacht's cozy master bedroom, they were emotionally and physically exhausted, despite the naps they'd taken in the afternoon. Clinging to each other, they quickly fell asleep.

62

Hap – Bailey Island, ME

Through the scope of his 338 Lapua Magnum rifle, Hap Greene watched his man Jones brace himself against the pylon of an abandoned pier, a thousand meters away on the opposite side of Mackerel Cove. Hap lay in a prone position atop the wooded knoll near Mo Bobicki's marina loft. Jones had been an outstanding team leader ever since Hap hired him away from the CIA three years ago. But he'd been compromised. Hap guessed at how much Tate had offered Jones—five million, ten million, maybe more—to turn him.

As soon as it had become apparent that the FBI was compromised and Wilson and Emily were going to fend for themselves, Hap had hired two independent contractors and sent them to Mackerel Cove to protect Wilson and Emily. He'd taken extra precautions to make sure no one in his organization knew about them by keeping all his communications with them outside the FBI's and his company's network.

Then, just minutes before the fire and explosions at Brattle House, Hap had received a call from the two independent contractors, informing him that Jones and two other men had arrived on Bailey Island and were clandestinely surveying the marina loft. Somehow, Hap realized, Jones had discovered the back-up homing device in Wilson's wristwatch, even though Hap had told no one about it.

After the situation at Brattle House had been addressed and everyone was safe, Hap traveled to Bailey Island, where he confirmed what his two independent contractors had told him about Jones. He also discovered that one of the other men with Jones was Jules Kamin, who obviously hadn't died in the explosion at his Manhattan apartment. The third man, he didn't recognize. Hap had hoped for an opportunity to remove Wilson and Emily from the scene, but Jones' surveillance was unyielding. He sent the two contractors back to their respective positions, inside the cabin of a lobster boat docked at the marina and near the docks on the other side of the island. Their assignment was to make sure none of the three men they'd been observing got near the loft or the sailboat. Hap was now taking personal responsibility for eliminating Jones, Kamin, and their accomplice.

Hap watched single-mindedly as Jones seemed to be waiting for a few more lights to go out before he unpacked the case he'd set down on the rocks next to him. Jones was skilled in the use of stingers, tear gas launchers, and other man-portable missile systems. It had been one of Jones' passions since returning from Afghanistan.

Suddenly Jones pulled a cell phone from his pocket, listened for a moment, and spoke a few words. Then he returned the phone to his pocket.

He must be talking to Kamin, Hap thought. Kamin was waiting at the docks in a sixteen-foot fishing trawler on the other side of the island. Earlier in the day, a few minutes after arriving on the island, Hap had identified Kamin with Jones aboard the trawler surveying the loft and the cove. That was several hours ago. Now it was almost two o'clock in the morning. Most of the lights had already gone out along the island's two slender peninsulas that formed Mackerel Cove.

Jones bent down, opened his carrying case, and withdrew a missile launcher. Before inserting the small missile, Jones placed the launcher on his shoulder and looked into the mounted scope.

Hap knew exactly what he was doing. Using the missile launcher's computerized laser technology, he was taking a reading of the number of meters between him and the north facing windows of the marina loft. Jones then punched in a few numbers on the small keypad below the scope to program the missile for detonation once it entered the loft. The missile probably contained some sort of gas—chlorine, saran, VX, or phosgene.

Jones removed the long, slender mini-missile from the case—twenty-seven inches of carbon-fiber tubing less than three inches in diameter, with small fins on one end. It probably carried enough gas to kill a few hundred people, especially in humid weather like tonight. Even if the stinger missile took out the entire window before releasing its gas, everyone within a hundred meters could be dead within minutes, including Wilson and Emily in the sailboat two hundred feet away. The only sounds would be breaking glass and something akin to the whoosh of lighter fluid being ignited. Jones inserted the stinger and raised the rocket launcher once more to his shoulder, this time in preparation for firing.

Hap squeezed his trigger first. Jones' head snapped back sharply, the back of his cranium disintegrating as pieces of red and gray matter splattered onto the mossy green rocks. His body collapsed on the rocks. Hap didn't move, keeping the scope of his Lapua Magnum focused on his fallen comrade and then raising it slowly to view the highway. He remained in position on the wet, grassy knoll for another seven minutes, until the unidentified man with Jones and

Kamin exited his car and crossed the highway, approaching the bluff above the abandoned pier. The man crouched down in the grass of the bluff, looking through his binoculars until he located Jones' near headless body lying on the rocks. He immediately drew his weapon and looked around cautiously. Hap pressed the trigger of his Lapua Magnum again and the man was thrown back in spread-eagle fashion with a hole the size of a grapefruit between his shoulder blades.

Hap jumped up from his prone position and ran toward his car, which he'd hidden beneath a cluster of pines. His third target would not be so easy, but he was determined to finish this himself. Without turning on his headlights, he drove to the highway where he turned right and continued another two hundred yards before stopping. He quickly worked his way through the trees and brush to the eastern side of the peninsula and then along another bluff overlooking the ocean, searching for the fishing boat that had brought Kamin and the other two to the island earlier in the evening.

Suddenly, there was a steep rise in the terrain and a pathway with cobblestone steps that took him into a thick grove of trees. When he emerged from the trees he was in full view of the secluded cove below. He pulled out his binoculars to examine the small pier. But Kamin was a step ahead of him, having already spied Hap through his own binoculars. By the time Hap dropped to the ground in a prone position and flipped the safety on his rifle, Kamin was five hundred yards farther away in the sixteen-foot fishing trawler and about to disappear behind the point of the cove. The independent contractor got out of his camper and prepared to take the shot.

"I've got it," Hap said into his collar microphone. He fired his third round.

Kamin collapsed to the floor of the boat, his right arm and shoulder completely severed from his body. He was struggling to get up when Hap's fourth round caught him in the chest and propelled him overboard. Kamin's lifeless body rode the waves for several seconds before sinking out of sight.

Hap returned to his car and drove back to the knoll near the marina, parking under the same cluster of pines. He waited a few minutes and then walked down the dirt road to the gravel ramp leading to the marina. His two independent contractors emerged from behind the marina store.

"Targets eliminated," Hap said. "Thanks for the good work. If the local police show up before dawn, call my cell phone and talk to Ms. Kohl. Otherwise, I'll let her know what happened here when I get to Boston."

"You leaving now?"

"Yeah," Hap said. "Let them sleep or do whatever they like, but don't let them out of your sight."

"You got it."

63

Wilson – Bailey Island, ME

When the sounds of the lobstermen woke Wilson and Emily before dawn, the first thing they did was turn on the TV. Nothing. They watched patiently. Then, at exactly forty-eight minutes past six o'clock, it finally happened. The event his father had spent the best years of his life trying to accomplish. Disclosure: full and complete disclosure to the American public of an eight-year-long conspiracy to manipulate the price of company stocks traded on the New York and Nasdaq Stock Exchanges. The breadth and depth of the conspiracy's impact was apparent on Anderson Cooper's solemn face as he reported.

"CNN has just learned that a massive stock market manipulation conspiracy involving the nation's largest corporations, over the past eight years, has been uncovered by the FBI. More than three hundred arrests have been made in the past twenty-four hours, with more expected today. CNN's financial expert, Lou Dobbs, is here to help us understand what all of this means," Anderson Cooper said as he looked over to Dobbs. "Lou, how could something like this go on for so long without being detected by the SEC, the Justice Department, boards of directors, company employees or shareholders?"

"That's a question we'll all be wrestling with in the weeks and months to come, Anderson, but one thing we're certain of; the enormity of this crisis makes the recent mortgage credit debacle look like a misdemeanor," Dobbs said, and then faced the camera. "Based on what we now know, the manipulations were orchestrated through what appeared to be normal business practices such as the hiring and firing of senior executives, company reorganizations, mergers and acquisitions, the spin-off of a company division to create a new publicly traded corporation, new product introductions, and the involvement of high-profile management consulting firms, all of them legitimate business activities."

"So why all the arrests?" Cooper asked.

"For two reasons: first, the FBI claims it has obtained sufficient evidence to prove that the CEOs and some senior executives, from more than three hundred of America's largest corporations, secretly organized themselves with the express purpose of systematically causing their own companies' stock prices to rise and fall. Second, these same CEOs and senior executives shared information with their secret partners from other corporations regarding the orchestrated ups and downs of their companies' stock prices. Trading on so-called insider information is not legal. So, as I understand it, they're being arrested on multiple counts of conspiracy to defraud the United States. The charges could carry mandatory life sentences."

"Financial markets in Europe and Asia are already predicting major declines in anticipation of Wall Street's response," Cooper stated. "What are the domestic and international ramifications of this conspiracy?"

"Domestically, the fact that this could happen on such a large, widespread scale, involving the nation's most respected corporations, without government agencies, industry analysts, or the news media knowing about it, simply means that America's stock exchanges, our economic and financial systems, and the nation's practice of capitalism, in general, will have to change. The war against the middle class has now escalated into open warfare. We now have documented proof of what some of us have long known—the privileged class has been widening the gap between rich and poor by manipulating the system while our government turns a blind eye.

"Internationally, the implications are staggering. The United States with its long record of economic success has been the main impetus behind the globalization of free market capitalism and the democratic rule of law. Every country in the world will be thinking if this can happen in the U.S., it can happen anywhere. And worse, it will most certainly erode confidence in our capital markets, giving some countries reason to question the future of global capitalism and others the justification to wage war against it. Much of what happens either domestically or internationally, however, will depend on how our government responds to this crisis, Anderson."

"We'll have more from Lou Dobbs and a panel of Wall Street experts later, but now, let's go to Wolf Blitzer, outside FBI Headquarters in the nation's capital, to see how the government is dealing with this economic crisis. Wolf?"

"Anderson, here at FBI Headquarters everyone is being very tight-lipped about the arrests that are still going on in various parts of the country. We have been told that more than thirty FBI agents have been killed, and several others wounded while making these arrests. Currently, there are more than three hundred corporate CEOs and their accomplices in custody and we've heard numbers ranging from one hundred to five hundred in additional arrests expected before this is all over. FBI Director John Bainbridge has called a press conference for eleven a.m., Eastern Time, at FBI Headquarters in Washington, D.C. We will be here to provide live coverage. Anderson?"

Emily looked at Wilson with eyes like saucers.

"Hard to believe isn't it. Even when we knew it was coming," Wilson said, feeling a mix of relief and anxiety. Part of him hoped that what his father had set in motion eight years earlier would reap positive benefits, but the other part of him kept questioning whether any lasting improvement would come from the disclosure. He and Emily had already been through so much, it was hard to take on a fresh perspective. Had it really been worth it?

"I'm going to the marina store to get the morning papers," Wilson said, getting up from the bed and walking to the cabin door.

Emily got up to join him. As they ascended the steps and climbed off the yacht, she said, "Tell me what you really think."

"I think it's all happening just as my father and Carter planned, but with more bloodshed than either one of them anticipated."

"Will the country survive it?"

"I honestly don't know, Em. I hope so," Wilson said, opening the screen door to the marina store for Emily.

"Good morning. Checking out?" Jaclyn said, still behind the counter and looking as if she'd never left.

"I think we'll be staying another night," Emily said, looking at Wilson questioningly.

He nodded.

"Fine. I'll have someone bring you a change of linens and fresh towels," Jaclyn said.

Wilson looked around the store. Everything seemed normal. The world hadn't come to an end or stopped dead in its tracks. "What newspapers do you carry?" Wilson asked.

She pointed to the stacks on the floor behind him as she turned to another customer. "Take what you want, you can pay me later."

Surprisingly, the stacks included several major newspapers. He quickly unpacked the bundles and brought one from each stack back to the loft. The front-page headlines told the story:

FBI UNCOVERS MASSIVE STOCK MARKET MANIPULATIONS

CONSULTING FIRM FRONTS FOR WEB OF DECEPTION

CORPORATE CONSPIRACY SHOCKS NATION

SCHEME THREATENS FUTURE OF CAPITAL MARKETS

SECRET SOCIETY CORRUPTS AMERICAN INDUSTRY

For the next three hours they read and reread the detailed newspaper accounts while watching updates on CNN, The Today Show, Good Morning America, The Early Show, and Fox Headline News. They were so engrossed in the media frenzy that they didn't notice, and wouldn't learn until later, about the cleanup that was underway on the mossy rocks across the cove.

Carter was frequently quoted in the newspaper accounts and so was Wilson. David Quinn received occasional mention as the first whistleblower, but it was the independent analyses from Ernst & Young and Booz Allen and the ongoing SEC and FBI investigations that captured the harrowing reality. The patterns of corporate manipulation, the sleazy enticement schemes, the murders and attempted murders—it was all there in black and white. And it was a hundred times uglier than Wilson and Emily ever imagined it would be. The *New York Times* article alone ran for three columns on the front page and continued for four full pages inside.

By half past ten in the morning, all four networks and CNN were providing live coverage from FBI Headquarters.

The usual reporters, political commentators, and financial experts were predicting everything from a constitutional meltdown to global calamity, as they waited for the FBI Director's news conference. CNN's red, white, and blue banner for the story read, "American Capitalism on Trial," NBC's was, "Capitalism in Crisis," ABC called it, "The Corruption of Corporate America," CBS simply dubbed it, "The American Illusion," and Fox christened it, "Wall Street Exposed."

When the press conference began at eleven o'clock, Director Bainbridge read a ten-minute statement and distributed excerpts from Carter's eight-volume history with the promise that all eight volumes in their entirety would be available on the Internet by Monday morning, and in book form by Friday. Then he opened it up for questions.

Wilson was actually shocked by how clearly they presented the facts and discussed the implications. Nothing was being whitewashed, sugar-coated, or covered up. Carter's demand to include the five reporters from the Times, the Journal, the Post, the Globe, and the Associated Press in his debriefing of the FBI and other government agencies had worked. The nation's attention was being galvanized on the largest-scale corruption of its financial market system in history, just as his father had planned.

The press conference went on for about two hours, followed by mostly doomsday commentaries and expert interviews throughout the rest of the day. The most intellectually definitive interview was with Eli Dennison, distinguished professor of economics and former dean of MIT's Sloan School of Management. He summarized the situation this way: "The long simmering conflict between the equality promised by democracy and the inequality produced by capitalism has finally boiled over. An era has ended. We now enter a period of profound metamorphosis in which a new form of capitalism must be invented."

Dennison articulated the problem, just as his father and Carter would have. Maybe lasting change was possible.

64

Wilson – Bailey Island, ME

At six o'clock that evening, as Wilson and Emily ate lobster rolls from the marina restaurant, the national and local evening news focused almost exclusively on the nation's reaction to the crisis. The lead story was the reaction on Wall Street. Panic selling had caused stock prices to plummet until the major stock exchanges hit their circuit breakers, the government's safety net to prevent the markets from crashing the way they did in 1929. Trading on all U. S. stock, futures, currency, and commodity exchanges was halted. In London, Paris, Frankfurt, Tokyo, Hong Kong, and Sidney, exchanges experienced similar panic selling before market declines triggered a halt to trading. Exchanges in Mexico, Brazil, and Argentina reached new lows before trading was halted.

Even though the New York Stock Exchange and other U.S. exchanges were expected to continue trading in the days and weeks ahead, until market circuit breakers went off, the term 'virtual crash' was already on the lips of every news reporter from New York to Beijing. Stock analysts and economists from every major country in the world were predicting that the worst was yet to come. During the rest of the evening, all the network stations and many of the cable channels canceled their regular programming in order to air one special news report after another.

If press coverage was any indication of America's sentiments, Wilson thought, his father's coveted transformation of the way capitalism works in this country seemed guaranteed. By all accounts, the entire nation was suffering from shock and disbelief. And the outrage was growing. Just as Carter had hoped, the disclosure was concentrating everyone's attention on the same issue at the same time. The nation's silent majority finally seemed to be demanding action.

After the evening news, Wilson and Emily used the pay phone to call Kohl. "Agent Kohl, it's Wilson."

"Your family is safe. Darrin is recovering nicely," she said immediately. "All of them, including your father and Emily's family, are under the highest level of security we can provide."

"Thank you," Wilson said with a sigh of relief and a whisper to Emily that everyone including her family was safe and sound. "What about Hap?"

"He's back."

"Where was he?"

"I think you better talk to him about that. Have you been watching the news?" Kohl asked.

"Since early this morning."

"Looks like your father got what he wanted," Kohl said. "Every government office in the country has been overwhelmed by a growing public outcry."

"How do you plan to deal with it?" Wilson asked.

"Our immediate concern is preventing a virtual crash of the financial markets around the world. The President plans to address the nation on Sunday."

Wilson said nothing as he contemplated the difficulty of the President's task.

"Are you and Emily okay?"

"We're fine. What about Tate and Swatling?"

"They're in Venice."

"You have them under surveillance?"

"Based on the tape from Detective Zemke, we convinced the CIA to maintain surveillance, until Carter's whereabouts have been determined."

"Tell them not to lose Tate and Swatling," Wilson said, somewhat disdainfully.

"Don't worry. The global implications have registered..."

The automated operator interrupted the conversation demanding another deposit. Wilson dropped in the coins.

"Wilson, are you there?"

"Yes."

"I thought you might like to know that it's safe to come home," Kohl said. "We're still searching for a few missing employees from Tate Waterhouse and Swatling, Dyer, and Reinthrow, but every other member of the partnership that we know about has been arrested, except for the six who committed suicide. All of the compromised agents are either dead or in custody, except one. And, yes, we are confident that we've identified them all."

"Where's the one who's still unaccounted for?"

"He's in Italy with Tate and Swatling."

"Hap's man?"

"No. CIA."

There was silence on the phone.

"When are you coming back?" Kohl asked.

"When you have Tate and Swatling behind bars," Wilson said, pausing, "And when I know where Carter..."

"We'll find him," Kohl said, cutting him off. "Next time, call collect."

As soon as Wilson hung up the phone, Emily asked, "Where's Carter?"

"They don't know," he said, "Tate and Swatling are in Venice. Carter's probably there too."

"You think Carter's planning to meet with them?" she asked.

"Yes, but I'm not certain of his agenda."

"I think he's going to kill them," Emily said.

Wilson nodded, staring at her, until a lobsterman asked if they were still using the phone. Wilson took Emily's arm and returned to the yacht.

As if they hadn't seen enough, they sat glued to the loft's twenty-one-inch television screen until midnight, watching the endless news coverage of a distraught nation facing up to its long-neglected flaws. At the end of one of the news reports, ABC's Charlie Gibson paused to reflect on Thomas Jefferson's greatest fear for our then fledgling nation over two hundred years ago—that capitalism would not be accessible to all. Gibson ended his commentary by saying, "Had we been willing to pursue Jefferson's vision of distributing capitalism to the end of every row and to the bottom of every hierarchy, instead of allowing the bulk of its benefits to enrich the wealthy elite, maybe America would not be facing this crisis."

At first, Wilson thought the Gibson commentary might launch him and Emily into a heated Thomas Jefferson vs. Alexander Hamilton debate, like the ones they used to have at Princeton. Then it struck him. This was no longer a trendy topic for college campus polemics and public intellectuals such as Noam Chomsky, Paul Krugman, or Umberto Eco. The debate was over. American capitalism was about to be transformed, for better or worse.

Moments later, Wilson and Emily seemed to instantly share a mutual craving for escape into the place only they knew. Their lovemaking went on for hours as they savored the refuge and comfort of being lost in each other.

When Wilson finally closed his eyes to sleep, he tried to forget whose son he was. He still hadn't completely decided whether to think of his father as a heroic revolutionary or a misguided fanatic. Only time would tell.

65

Tate – Venice, Italy

Wayland Tate walked past the two men armed with 9mm Glock automatics standing guard in the archway outside the door of the Venetian apartment. Three floors down, a third armed man paced back and forth on the orange and gray stone tiles of the courtyard. Two others sat across the small piazza observing the apartment building's entrance.

For the second time in less than twenty-four hours his hired guns had turned over every single object in all five rooms of the third-floor apartment, looking for some indication of Carter Emerson's whereabouts. Carter's clothes and personal items were still in the bedroom, but there had been no sign of him since yesterday.

Then, a few minutes after twelve noon, an eleven-year-old Venetian boy carrying a bouquet of fresh flowers with an attached note was ushered into Tate's presence. Tate took the note and read:

> *Meet me inside the Teatro La Fenice at 17:30.*
> *The door on the right will be open. Come alone. I will*
> *be watching.*
>
> CE

Tate studied the note before questioning the security guard who in turn questioned the boy. It was painfully clear that Carter Emerson was in total control of the situation. But Tate had no intention of allowing that to continue. During the next few hours, Tate, Swatling, and the compromised CIA agent surveyed everything within view of the reconstruction site, bribing whomever they could, from construction workers to the local *polizia*. They would not be unprepared for their meeting with Carter or the inevitable presence of Europol and the CIA. Regaining control of the situation was the only thing that mattered, and that meant mobilizing enough firepower to eliminate Carter and ensure their escape.

Tate knew that Carter had chosen La Fenice for some twisted, symbolic reason, but it made no difference to him.

The ancient opera house, under restoration for the third or fourth time, would soon become Carter's final resting place—unless he had some earth-shattering explanation for his actions over the past few days.

When the appointed hour of seventeen-thirty arrived, Tate and Swatling entered the specified door on the right, walking into the cavernous dome of the Teatro La Fenice. The partially restored opera house was breathtaking, but that's not why Tate was breathing rapidly. He waited anxiously, standing with Swatling in the center of the theater below the circular opening in the ceiling.

Without warning, the same boy who had delivered the flowers earlier appeared out of nowhere and invited them to a triangle of facing chairs on the stage. They walked slowly past the orchestra pit and climbed the steps to the three wooden folding chairs. Before they sat down, the eleven-year-old boy disappeared behind the stage. Tate's blood was boiling, but he concealed his emotions as always.

Without warning, they heard a loud voice booming into the theater. Tate turned around three times, trying to locate the source. "Welcome, once again, to La Fenice," the voice said. It was Carter Emerson's voice.

Tate continued searching in all directions, but there was no sight of Carter. He glanced at Swatling who gave him a shrug.

"Don't bother looking, you won't find me. I plan to remain hidden until I know it's safe to enter."

"What are you afraid of, Carter?" Tate shouted, his words echoing in the dome. "Have you betrayed your friends?"

"I have only betrayed myself, Wayland."

"It's a little late for conscience, isn't it?" Tate said.

"Depends on your point of view," Carter returned.

Tate stood up and began pacing around the chairs "Let's stop the games, Carter. What do you want?"

"What do you want, Wayland?"

"I want to talk face-to-face."

"Then call off your men."

Tate sat back down but didn't respond. The vast opera house remained silent for almost five minutes before Tate stood up again. "Okay, I'll call them off."

He pulled out a small communication device from inside his jacket and mumbled into it. Within seconds, two armed men, one on the second tier and Marco on the third, stood up and walked toward the exit door through which Tate and Swatling had entered.

"Tell your remaining firepower to disappear," Carter said.

"And what about your firepower?"

"They will remove themselves with yours, and make sure we remain alone."

"And you expect us to believe that?"

"Of course. What else should we expect from partners?" Carter said.

Tate whispered into his communication device once again, and the CIA agent, who had been a member of the partnership for over three years, stood up and shoved his rifle into a soft leather guitar case before leaving the theater.

"I'll be right there," Carter said.

Tate's eyes motioned for Swatling to look at the back of the stage where the young boy had disappeared, but when he heard footsteps from behind, he quickly turned to see Carter walking toward them from the center of the theater. Tate's eyes remained fixed on Carter, who climbed the stairs to the stage and sat down in the empty chair. The three partners exchanged stares for several moments in silence.

Carter spoke first. "I assume both of you have seen the news reports from home?"

"What's your point?" Tate said, disgusted with the charade.

"Reconsideration of how capitalism is practiced in our country no longer seems to be a dream. It's our new reality. We have succeeded, gentlemen."

"Depends on your point of view," Tate said mockingly.

"Touché," Carter said. "Would you mind sharing yours?"

Tate just laughed. "There will never be a new reality. Haven't you figured that out by now?"

"What about you, Bob?" Carter said.

"You violated the partnership agreement when you took things into your own hands," Swatling returned.

"And so did you when you killed Zollinger," Carter said.

"I hardly think you're in a position…"

"Stop the nonsense," Tate shouted, as he stood up and began pacing again. "What is it you want, Carter?"

"An end."

"An end to what? The partnership?" Tate said, fuming inside. "I think you've already accomplished that."

"An end to the manipulation," Carter said.

"And if you eliminate us, will your conscience be clean?" Tate asked without waiting for a response. He now knew he had no choice but to kill Carter Emerson as soon as possible. "Your precious improvements to capitalism won't last five years before things return to normal. The powers that be have already ordained it. Manipulate or be manipulated; that's reality, Carter."

"You have more illusions than I do," Carter said.

"Depends on who'll be around to interpret history," Tate said, arrogantly. "After you shot Charles, I thought there was hope for you." Tate looked over at Swatling and nodded slightly.

"That was the idea," Carter said. "Charles and I knew it was the only way to convince you that I was on your side."

Tate stood up abruptly and started walking off the stage. Swatling followed his lead. As they reached the bottom of the stairs, Tate stopped and turned around, "You and Charles are ideologues. You may have destroyed this partnership, but you'll never get your hands on the big one. They'll crush you like a bug."

"You've forgotten," Carter said as he stood up and stepped to the edge of the stage.

"Forgotten what?" Tate said as he and Swatling walked backwards toward the center of the theater.

"Where we are."

"You're losing it, Carter."

"La Fenice. Eight years ago. The inauguration of our partnership. We came here that night to see *Rigoletto*, remember?"

Tate and Swatling were now standing near the center of the theater. "So what?" Tate scoffed.

Carter extended his arms and began slowly raising them above his head. "You always did struggle with symbolism, Wayland."

Tate held up his left wrist and placed his right hand over the buttons of the Rolex look-a-like that concealed a remote control detonator, set to ignite enough commercial blasting explosives to return La Fenice to rubble once again. There would be a ten-second delay after he pressed the two tiny buttons on opposite sides of the detonator in a one-two, two-one sequence, giving him and Swatling enough time to exit.

"How's this for symbolism. What burned once will burn again." Tate pushed the buttons in sequence, left, right, right, left, and then ran with Swatling for the exit.

Carter brought both of his arms down fast and ran for the archway behind the stage. Within three seconds, the wall of the theater above the exit door exploded, knocking Tate and Swatling to the ground and blocking their escape. Tate frantically clawed at the rubble, ripping his fingernails on the broken chunks of concrete as the ten seconds elapsed. The second explosion, the one Tate had planned for Carter, was heard throughout the city. It was the fourth time La Fenice would go down in flames.

Emerging from the tunnel that connected the opera house with a hidden dressing room on the subterranean floor of the apartment building owned by Fielder & Company, Carter was soaking wet up to his neck. The old tunnel, now almost completely filled with water, had been used by performing artists in the nineteenth century to shuttle back and forth from the stage to their dressing rooms. It had been sealed for more than a hundred years because of the rising water level. Charles had shown him the tunnel years ago. The past two days had been spent preparing it for his escape.

He quickly changed his clothes and then disguised himself with a false beard, sunglasses, and sea captain's hat. Within minutes Carter was exiting into the alleyway behind the building, ready to disappear into the gathering crowd. He was almost finished with what he had to do.

As Carter left the alleyway and merged into the throng of people who'd come to see what caused the terrible explosion, two men grabbed Carter from behind, one on each side. "Aldrich and Warburg, CIA," one of the men said. "We have instructions to escort you to Geneva, Switzerland. Your family is already there, waiting for you."

"Your names tell me everything I need to know," Carter said, studying the two well-built men. Congressman McFadden had accused United States Senator Nelson Aldrich and German-American banker Paul Warburg of being the ringleaders at the secret Jekyll Island conference of 1910, when the groundwork for the Federal Reserve System was first laid.

"That was the idea," one of the agents said. "We have a helicopter standing by at the airport. Our water taxi is just ahead. We should arrive in a couple of hours."

66

Wilson – Bailey Island, ME

While Emily slept peacefully, Wilson stood on the deck of the sailing yacht unable to rest. Watching the lobster boats leave Mackerel Cove, he wondered whether the looming changes in American capitalism, whatever they turned out to be, would have any impact on these lobstermen. Would capitalism really be individualized for them? Would it be easier for them to buy more boats? To have more leisure time? To continue their education? To pursue hobbies? To serve their communities? To travel the world? Wilson hoped so, but he wasn't overly optimistic.

When Emily joined him on deck, her eyes looked weary. He felt guilty for not spending more time attending to her recovery. She'd been through hell for a week, but that didn't seem to stop her from worrying more about him than herself. She was indeed a remarkable woman. "You look troubled. What are you thinking about?" she asked.

"Whether these lobstermen will be better off because of what my father did."

"What about us?" she said. "Will we be better off?"

"I hope so," Wilson said, losing himself in her large brown eyes.

"How long are we planning to stay here?" she asked.

"Until it's safe."

She gazed out at the bay, following the lobster boats on their way out to sea. "Will it ever be safe for us?"

Wilson matched her gaze, putting his arm around her. "I don't know, Em," he finally answered.

"It's never going to end, is it?"

"Depends on what happens to my father's partners," Wilson said, feeling victimized by every one of them. "But don't worry, we have enough money to protect ourselves, assuming the government doesn't confiscate it."

"That's not very encouraging," she said softly.

"I know. Sorry," Wilson said quietly. "We'll be okay, Em. We've got each other. It's the one precious reality I've held on to through all of this. You are the most important thing in my life."

She hugged and kissed him on the neck and cheek. Then a twinkle flashed across her eye as she kissed him on the lips. "I will always love you, Wilson, no matter how difficult or miserable our lives become."

Wilson's smile broadened. He was grateful to see her playfulness back. "And, I will always love you, Em, no matter how resentful or mean-spirited you become."

She dug her fingers into his sides until he grabbed her hands and pulled them around him. They embraced and kissed again.

"What are you going to do when we go back?" she asked.

"I don't know," Wilson said, staring at the open ocean beyond the cove. "Fielder & Company may not have many clients after today."

Emily was quiet. When she spoke again, her tone was sarcastic. "We could always manage one of my parent's B&B's on the Vineyard. You would be a big tourist draw."

"Now look who's encouraging," Wilson said before kissing her. "What about you? When are you going back to work?"

"Not for a few months. It's no longer the most important thing in my life," she said, looking away.

"What are you thinking?"

"About everything your father gave up to change the world."

"Yeah," Wilson said quietly. "I think about that a lot."

"If he had it to do over again, do you think he would?" she asked.

"Yes."

"Why?"

"Because it's what he cared about," Wilson said.

"Does it make you sad?" Emily said, her eyes probing his.

"Not really. I think I understand him better than I ever have," Wilson said, shifting his gaze from Emily to the other side of the cove. "He got his wish. He changed the world."

There was prolonged silence before Emily asked, "What's your wish, Wilson?"

Wilson smiled, "You mean after the one about living with you forever?"

"That sounds wonderful. But yes, after that, what's your wish?"

"I don't have any others at the moment," he said.

She looked into his eyes and they kissed again, slowly and gently.

After lingering on the deck a little longer, they decided to take advantage of the beautiful day. They tracked down Paddie, who was more than anxious to rent his boat to them for a second day. He set them up with all the gear and by eight-thirty they were leaving Mackerel Cove for a spot

Paddie recommended a few miles south of the cove near Cliff Island. Emily took the helm while Wilson prepared the lobster pots. As they approached the west side of Cliff Island the water was unusually calm, so Emily cut the engine and helped Wilson drop their first pot. Wilson checked the second pot to make sure everything was ready. But before Emily returned to the helm to start the engine, he asked, "So, what did you think about Gibson's comment about Jefferson and capitalism being distributed to the end of every row?"

"I think Jefferson was right," Emily said.

"You think the wealthy will ever allow grass roots capitalism?"

"Don't tell me you're still holding out for socialism?" Emily said teasingly.

"Why does everyone assume that the only way to fix capitalism is to adopt socialism or some other form of utopian equalism?" Wilson said, leaning back to capture the sun's rays against his face. Before Emily could respond, he added, "Assuming Jefferson and Madison and Franklin have been watching as their American experiment has unfolded over the past couple of centuries, I think they'd tell us there is no flaw in capitalism—just a flaw in our competitive natures. We require too many losers. Making capitalism workable and robust for everyone, without resorting to socialistic devices— that's our challenge."

With a mischievous look on her face, Emily reached down scooping up handful of bait. "If the rich and powerful can't find a way to push capitalism to the end of every row, then we'll just have to give them some new incentives," she said, throwing the fish pieces out across the water.

They burst into laughter. It felt good. After that their conversation grew lighter. They dropped the rest of the lobster pots over a two-mile stretch off Cliff Island and then retraced their path to pick up the day's catch. Ten lobsters. A quick run by lobsterman standards, but it had provided much-needed therapy for their stressed souls. When they arrived back in Mackerel Cove a little before three, Wilson placed a collect call to Kohl.

"I thought you'd never call," Kohl said. "Have you seen the news lately?"

"No."

"Swatling and Tate were trapped by an explosion inside a Venetian opera house."

"La Fenice?" Wilson asked.

"How did you know?" she asked.

"Fielder & Company owns the apartment building next door. It's where Emily was kidnapped. It was one of my father's favorite places, and evidently the birthplace of the secret partnership."

Kohl didn't respond, so Wilson continued. "Are they dead?" he asked.

"Swatling is dead. Tate's in critical condition and under heavy guard at a Venice hospital. The CIA agent is in custody."

"Any sign of Carter?"

"Not yet. They're still going through the debris at La Fenice."

"But he was there, right?" Wilson asked.

"Yes. We think he was the one who caused the explosion."

"You have to find him," Wilson said urgently.

"Why? Is he dangerous?"

"Only to himself."

"You're not making sense, Wilson," Kohl said.

"Rising from the ashes. La Fenice means the phoenix. The secret partnership created by my father and Carter is dead, and their disclosure is already accomplishing what they intended for this country. The real solution will rise from the ashes of destruction. Carter's going after them," Wilson said.

"Who?"

"The Overseers, the Council, the Governors, or whatever you want to call them. Conspiracy theorists refer to them as the New World Order, the Council on Foreign Relations, the Illuminati, Shadow Government, the Rothschild Dynasty, Freemasons, or the Bilderbergers, but the conspiracy hype only facilitates their concealment. They're a secretly chosen governing council. A half dozen or so people who represent the world's most wealthy families and control much of the world's wealth creation, monetary supply, financial credit, and central banks like the Federal Reserve. They also practice an exclusive trading game that makes my father's insiders club pale in comparison."

"You don't really believe that?" Kohl said in disbelief.

"Ask the CIA. They know about it. I've been denying it for too long. They are the same elite who had my great-grandfather murdered because he was going to publish memoirs that would have exposed them. They assassinated Congressman Louis T. McFadden, William Tate Boyles, Wayland Tate's grandfather, and possibly four American presidents. I'm afraid my family has been obsessed with exposing them for a long time. Trust me. You need to find Carter before he gets himself killed."

67

Carter – Lake Geneva, Switzerland

The helicopter landed on the lawn outside a large French Renaissance chateau on Lake Geneva, Switzerland. Carter was quickly escorted from the helicopter by two Slavic-looking bodyguards, across the expansive lawn into to the chateau, past a row of twenty- foot high tapestries in the entrance hall, through a glass-roofed winter garden filled with exotic plants, and into one of the most beautiful libraries he had ever seen. Carter breathed deeply as he gazed around the cavernous fifteenth-century Italian interior. Frescoes by Diziani adorned the ceiling above a dozen Murano chandeliers, two-story arched windows overlooked Lake Geneva, and exquisite

French and Italian antique furniture graced the full length of the literary chamber. The library's two-tiered, walnut-paneled shelves had to hold more than 30,000 volumes, many of them works of history, Carter thought as he walked by the ornately carved black marble walk-in fireplace.

At the far end of the library, behind an extraordinary Louis XV Ormolu-Mounted writing table, sat Werner Lentz, Executive Secretary to the infamous Board of Governors. It was the most powerful governing body on the face of the earth, but few people knew about it, other than the conspiracy nuts prone to zealous dramatics. Carter had first met Werner Lentz years earlier, while writing an article for *The Journal of American History* about the influence of the Goldsmith and Rothschild families on American banking and finance.

When Carter reached the extravagant writing table, his two bodyguards left him alone as Werner stood to greet him. "How are you doing old friend?" Lentz asked in a slight German accent as he rounded the writing table. They shook hands while Werner affectionately patted Carter on the shoulder. Lentz was about Carter's age. Trim, gray hair, wireless glasses, and dressed like royalty's banker. "Please sit down," Lentz said.

"How am I doing, Werner?" Carter said as he sat down in one of the two carved walnut armchairs in front of the desk.

"The board is quite impressed with how you and Charles managed to bring the American economy to its knees," Lentz said.

"Is that why you brought me and my family here? To help you reform Europe and the rest of the world?" Carter asked mockingly.

Werner Lentz laughed loudly. "I always love your American sarcasm. I think it's what makes you so dangerous," Lentz said before sitting back in his chair and rocking slightly. "The board wants to make sure you're not like Charles, with ambitions beyond the United States."

Carter said nothing as he studied Lentz.

"All we want is for you and your family to live here in Geneva for a few years in very comfortable surroundings," Lentz said, lifting his arms and looking around the library. "This historic De Vita Chateau is yours for as long as you like."

"And if I choose not to accept your generous offer?"

"I'm afraid that's not an option, my friend. Five years of exemplary behavior and maybe the board will reconsider."

"What are my restrictions?"

"Think of them as incentives, Carter—for insuring a healthy posterity. If you agree to our terms, you will be pronounced dead tomorrow. Buried in the La Fenice explosion. All contacts with your former life will be severed, including your contact with Wilson Fielder and President Roberts. You will have to observe from afar what they do to bring about your anticipated reforms. Travel will be confined to the EU."

"Eventually, you will be exposed, Werner."

"Here's the irony, Carter. Your disclosure will do far more than credit debacles, regional wars, or economic depressions to usher in the new world order we've always wanted," Lentz said, leaning across the writing table with a roguish grin that obscured his beady eyes. "In fact, the board has already made plans to encourage your transformation of capitalism. They acknowledge that it's time to bring the blessings of wealth to another tier of participants. You've misjudged them, Carter. They have always striven to be noble and generous."

"So long as they maintain control. Right?" Carter said in defiance.

"Of course. You of all people should know how chaotic and precarious the world can become when no one is in charge. People are too easily distracted, too easily threatened, and too willing to turn on each other," Lentz said dismissively. "Adam Smith's invisible hand of self-interest isn't enough to bring sufficient order to the world. It's just who people are, they will never change. Big fish eat the little fish. So we need more little fish than big fish. Without that, life on this planet would end. It's the natural order of things."

"That's what separates you and me, Werner; you're much too distrustful and heavy handed," Carter said. Then he added, "Your faith in humankind stopped evolving a long time ago, Werner. People need leadership not control, and certainly not indentured servitude."

Lentz's face morphed into stone. "In the end, no matter what sort of reforms your country decides to adopt, the board will adapt as it always does. Most of the governors believe your precious reforms will strengthen both our position and our concealment. As for you, Carter, everyone has a price. If you agree to our terms, you and your family will live long and wealthy lives. If you decide to die for your principles, we will accommodate you. Either way we win, because we are the biggest fish in the sea. The choice is yours."

"Where's my family?" Carter demanded.

"Your wife and daughters are here at the chateau. They're already preparing to leave tomorrow for your funeral in Boston. Come on," Lentz said, pushing himself away from the desk and standing up. "Let me take you to them."

As the two of them walked through the magnificent library and up the massive stone spiral staircase past more tapestries and classical art to the chateau's master suite, Lentz turned to Carter. "You know, Carter. If you'd work with us, you might discover that our ultimate aims are not that divergent from yours."

"You mean as long as I accept the conditions of Satan's rule in Hell?"

Lentz laughed out loud again. "It's going to be a pleasure having you here, Carter, if for nothing more than your humor."

"Tell the governors I'll be happy to entertain them whenever they like."

Lentz laughed wildly, slapping Carter on the back.

Carter smiled broadly. Manipulating Werner might prove easier than he'd thought. Maintaining contact with Wilson, on the other hand, would be more difficult than expected. But he'd already put a contingency plan in motion.

When his wife Elizabeth and their two daughters Sarah and Amy saw Carter enter the room, they ran to him, throwing their arms around him. At least they were still alive, he said to himself. Now he just needed to keep them that way.

68

Wilson – Cambridge, MA

When Wilson saw his mother, who had returned from the hospital to a fortified, yet blackened, Brattle House currently undergoing repairs and reconstruction, he felt an unexpected outpouring of sympathy and love. She was crying. They embraced. Between the sobs, she whispered in his ear, "I'm so sorry, Wilson. I should have told you everything. Can you ever forgive me?"

"Of course, I can. I now understand why you didn't," Wilson said softly. "I'm just glad you're safe. I love you, Mom. Don't ever question that."

Wilson and his mother held each other in the foyer, while Emily embraced Rachel, Darrin, and little Mary. Everyone had returned from the hospital earlier that morning.

Rachel came over to her mother and Wilson. Little Mary tried to wrap her arms around their legs. Wilson picked up Mary and they pressed their faces together, the way they used to when Rachel and Wilson were children. For an instant, Wilson felt outside himself, viewing the gathering from a distance and wishing his father were present. He looked around, almost expecting to see his father's face. But he wasn't there. Still the feeling lingered, in a singular moment of family forgiveness and redemption.

For his mother, Wilson imagined it must have been a sort of final cleansing. He could feel her body quivering in his arms. He gently tightened his embrace around her and Rachel. "It's over. The long ordeal has finally ended," he said, unsure why he lied to them, but he had, as if to shield them from what was sure to come. He no longer condemned his father and Carter for doing the same to him.

For the rest of the afternoon and evening, they stayed together in the family room, which had been relatively untouched by the explosions and fire. They recounted their experiences of the past several days. Emily called her parents and sisters on Martha's Vineyard, putting the call on speakerphone after a few minutes, giving everyone the opportunity to collectively express their feelings of relief and gratitude.

Wilson's feelings combined an odd mix of peaceful calm and nervous foreboding. He was greatly relieved that the imminent danger facing his family had passed, but deep down he feared what might come next. Where was Carter and what was he doing? Had the disclosure been nothing more than a first assault on their ultimate enemies?

When Hap Greene arrived at eight o'clock and told them what else happened at Mackerel Cove the night before last, Emily and Wilson looked at each other in utter astonishment. They could only express their infinite gratitude, humbly acknowledging that none of them would be alive were it not for the vigilance of Hap Greene and his men. When Wilson told him that he and Emily had slept in a sailboat docked at the marina, Hap nodded with a smile.

"It might have saved you had Jones been successful in launching his missile," Hap said.

"Thanks to you we didn't have to find out," Wilson said before announcing that his family wanted to establish a trust fund for the family of Pat Savoy, the man who'd been slain in Venice. Hap was moved by the gesture, but they all knew it wouldn't even come close to filling the void.

Before Hap left to be with his own family, he pulled Wilson aside, "Give me your watch."

"Why?"

"It's how we tracked you," he said, handing Wilson his original IWC in exchange. The watches looked identical.

"How did they…"

"I don't know how Jones found out, but I will," Hap said. "Go back to your family, Wilson. We can talk about it tomorrow."

"You know this isn't over," Wilson said.

Hap nodded. "I know. We're trying to find out everything we can about what the CIA's doing in Italy and the rest of Europe to locate Carter. I'll let you know as soon as we have something."

"We're going to need your services for a while."

"My men are right outside," Hap said as he patted Wilson on the shoulder and then walked to the front door to leave.

"Thank you, Hap. For everything," Wilson said as a flood of emotion hit him hard.

Hap turned back and raised his hand slightly. "Can't think of anyone or any cause I'd rather fight for."

Their eyes locked for a moment, communicating the deep trust and esteem that had formed between them. Then he was gone.

Less than ten minutes later, Agent Kohl dropped by for a brief visit. Her eyes examined Wilson as she informed them that there was still no sign of Carter.

"We've convinced the CIA and NSA to expand their search. Europol and several other European law enforcement agencies have joined the effort."

"Good. The sooner we find him the better," Wilson said, returning Kohl's stare. There was no mention of yesterday's conversation, but he was satisfied that she believed at least part of what he'd said.

Before she left, Kohl warned Wilson that the FBI agents guarding the house might have difficulty keeping the press away after tonight.

As Sunday morning dawned, Kohl's casual warning turned out to be a gross understatement: the local, national, and international press were gathered outside Brattle House, setting up microphones and cameras and inquiring about interviews. At noon, Wilson gave them a brief statement on the motivations of his father and Carter Emerson. He then answered questions for an hour about Carter's disappearance, the explosion involving Tate and Swatling, the threat of other secret societies, his plans for Fielder & Company, the nation's reaction to the crisis, and the President's upcoming speech.

After that, Wilson and Emily spent the rest of the afternoon in another interview going over the events of the past few days with the same five reporters from *The New York Times*, *The Wall Street Journal*, *The Boston Globe*, *The Washington Post*, and The Associated Press who had interviewed Wilson a few days ago. They peppered him with new questions about his father's business practices and motivations. Wilson tried to explain things as best he could without completely destroying Fielder & Company's reputation. Then, they asked Emily to recount the details of her kidnapping.

As the hour for the President's address drew nearer, broadcasting crews from all the major networks and several local television and radio stations huddled around their TV monitors outside Brattle House, awaiting the President's message from the Oval Office. At precisely seven o'clock in the evening, Eastern Daylight Time, the eyes of the nation and much of the world were fixed upon Alexander P. Roberts, President of the United States of America, seated at the famous desk in the Oval Office and looking into the camera with the resolve required to reassure a jittery world.

Wilson's heart sank as President Roberts began by calling the crisis, "a storm passing over the massive ocean of stock market transactions," and "a tragic exception to the remarkable integrity and stability of financial markets in the U.S. and around the world."

"He's whitewashing everything," Wilson groaned, sharing his concern with Emily.

Emily took his hand. "You really didn't expect him not to, did you?"

Wilson smiled glumly as they continued to listen.

"The excesses among corporations whose stock is traded on U.S. exchanges will be dealt with swiftly and completely," the President continued. "The executives involved will be brought to justice. We are a nation of the people, by the people, and for the people and we will not let these excesses go unpunished. However, we cannot allow this crisis to undermine our confidence in the future of our economic system, our legal system, our government, or our way of life. Continuing to invest your money in stocks, bonds, futures, and commodities with confidence is the best thing you can do to help us correct these excesses. The Justice Department, our federal courts, the Securities and Exchange Commission, and the various capital, futures, and commodity exchanges will do the rest. We have always been and will continue to be a nation that learns quickly and responds appropriately."

Although the realist in him should have known better—as Emily clearly did—Wilson couldn't believe it: the President of the United States seemed worried only about damage control and keeping the masses from revolting. Unfortunately, he appeared to have little interest in transforming capitalism. Surely Carter and his father had anticipated this possibility?

The President continued by giving a detailed description of the steps that had already been taken to prevent such abuses in the future. A presidential task force had already been organized to conduct extensive reviews of every major business sector in the U.S. economy; Senate and Congressional Committees would begin a series of public hearings on alternative legislative reforms, the Justice Department and federal courts would bring all perpetrators to trial quickly, and the Supreme Court had agreed to conduct an unprecedented evaluation of the laws and regulations governing the SEC, the FED, the major stock and commodity exchanges, and investment and commercial banks.

The President concluded his speech with a plea for confidence:

"In the past forty-eight hours, I have personally spoken to each of the G20 leaders and assured them that the American people will unite to resolve this crisis. I now ask for your trust and support during the days and weeks ahead, that we might secure the necessary course corrections for America's future. Tomorrow morning the stock exchanges will open for business as usual, so buy and sell as you normally would, knowing that there is no better economic system in the world than the one right here in The United States of America. I remind you of the words spoken by President Franklin D. Roosevelt in 1933 during an earlier financial crisis in our nation's history: 'The only thing we have to fear is fear itself— nameless, unreasoning, unjustified terror which paralyzes needed efforts to convert retreat into advance.' We cannot let fear or lack of confidence in our financial markets hold us—

and our future—hostage. We will make the necessary course corrections to insure that these abuses never happen again, and we will make them quickly. Let us not retreat in panic but move forward with courage, united in our conviction that We the People can and will emerge stronger and wiser from this crisis. May God bless you and all of us in this time of need. Thank you and goodnight."

No sooner had the President finished than the press crowded around the front door and along the verandah at Brattle House, turning on their microphones, cameras, and spotlights, waiting for Wilson to give his reaction. Wilson walked onto the flood-lighted porch to a barrage of questions about his reaction to the President's speech, the state of American capitalism, what his father would think, and once again, the whereabouts of Carter Emerson.

He stepped up to the row of microphones torn between his conflicting desires to protect his loved ones and ensure the reform his father and Carter envisioned. Realizing all too well that it might be impossible to do both, he chose to speak to the latter issue first.

"I think my father and Carter Emerson would be very disappointed by the President's remarks. They believed our system of capitalism had been hijacked by early industrialists and financiers who emphasized competition over cooperation to solidify their own control and build enormous wealth," he commenced boldly. He would have to find another way to protect the people he loved. It's time the world heard my voice, not just my father's or Carter Emerson's.

"A widening gap between rich and poor, concentration of political and corporate power, and a compromised and disabled democracy are evidence of the flaws in our system. Abuses by those with wealth and power in this country, and throughout the world, have written our history for centuries. It's time for change. We can no longer allow our government to be manipulated by people whose sole objective is to enrich themselves while oppressing and appeasing the majority. Apparently, the President believes a flurry of bureaucratic activity followed by a wave of new rules and regulations will bring change. As long as the strong and powerful in this country continue to exploit and manipulate the weak and powerless, America's capitalistic engine will continue to run at a fraction of its capacity. My father and Carter Emerson hoped that We the People of The United States of America would revolt before allowing the abuses they documented to be swept under the rug. They wanted to end wage-slavery for the working majority and end corrupt privilege for the capitalist elite. As for me, I hope the President will strengthen and accelerate his initiatives. This crisis deserves more than what he's offered tonight. Most of all, I hope the American people will decide to stand up and demand reforms—broad, sweeping reforms to our capitalistic system—regardless of what this president or this Congress or this Supreme Court decide to do. My father and Carter Emerson believed it was time to humanize and individualize capitalism. I believe it's time to unite against the hidden tyranny that controls our lives, and I know that We the People can do it."

There was another barrage of questions that lasted for over an hour. Wilson did his best to carry the banner of his father's vision while speaking from his heart. By the time the last reporter left after midnight, the press had interviewed everyone in the house except his mother and little Mary, both of whom he'd managed to shield from their intrusive probing.

A few minutes after one o'clock in the morning, as Emily and Wilson were still trying to unwind after the day's intensity in the belfry library, Rachel climbed the circular staircase to inform them that Agent Kohl was on the phone.

Wilson answered the phone apprehensively.

"Sorry to bother you so late, but I thought you'd want to know as soon as possible."

"What is it, Kristen?"

"Carter Emerson's remains were uncovered at the explosion site in Venice."

Wilson sat down stunned. "Are you sure?" he asked, unwilling to believe that Carter was dead.

"The DNA tests were verified by Italian authorities and the CIA."

Still unconvinced, Wilson asked, "Does his wife know?"

"I talked to her before I called you."

"Where is she?"

"Geneva, Switzerland with her daughters. They'll be here tomorrow for a graveside service at Cambridge Cemetery. The President plans to attend."

Geneva, Switzerland, Wilson repeated to himself. That's where Carter is. "I'll be there."

"For what it's worth, Wilson," Kohl said slowly. "I can't officially condone what your father and Carter Emerson did, but I think positive change will come from it. Good night, Wilson."

69

Wilson – Cambridge, MA

A FedEx letter arrived for Wilson just as the family was preparing to leave for Carter's graveside service at Cambridge Cemetery. His mother, Rachel, Darrin, and their FBI escorts decided to go ahead while Wilson and Emily waited for Driggs and Irving to examine the thin package for explosives and other chemicals. When they were satisfied it was clean, they handed it to Wilson. Inside was a one-page letter from Carter and the key to a safety-deposit box. The letter was hand-written on Hotel San Fantin stationery. Wilson took a deep breath and walked to the den where he sat down before reading the letter. Emily sat next to him. They read the letter together.

Dear Wilson,

I should never have agreed to pull the trigger. We were both dead men walking and we knew it. Our only hope was to come up with a ploy so shocking and yet believable that it would keep one of us alive. With your father and Tate locked in a power struggle, the 'role' of staying alive fell to me, almost by default. Your father and I had to convince Tate of my loyalty and that I had no intention of exposing the partnership. But now, I can no longer live with what I did. My ambition for this life has been exhausted.

Your inclination will be to finish what we started, but it's not worth it. This obsession has destroyed our lives and brought only suffering and misery to the ones we love. Things will never change. I know that now. The enclosed key is to a safety-deposit box at Boston Private Bank & Trust on Boylston Street. Your great-grandfather's memoirs should be inside. They are what started us down this fateful path. Your father decided not to share them with you until after we had accomplished our disclosure. My advice to you is to let them sleep.

I pray your father will eventually emerge from his coma. I can only hope that the position of the bullet gives

him some chance of recovery. Tell him that I miss him.
Enjoy your life with Emily; she's one in a billion. Forgive
us, if you can. Lastly, would you mind watching over my
Elizabeth and the girls? They know about everything,
but I doubt they fully understand. Maybe you can help,
especially with my grandchildren.

> *With Deepest Love and Sympathy,*
> *Carter Emerson*

Wilson sat motionless on the sofa next to Emily, no longer agitated or dumbfounded by the unending twists and turns. But Carter's letter didn't ring true. *Things will never change. I know that now.* Bullshit, Wilson thought. Neither Carter nor his father would ever believe that.

"Do you believe it?" Emily looked at him, giving voice to the question that was in his mind.

"No," he said as he stood up and took Emily by the hand. "Do you?"

"No," she replied without hesitation and wrapped her arms around him.

As they left for the graveside service, Wilson mulled things over. Generations of concealed corruption could only be overcome by generations of open revolution. His generation had no choice but to engage.

70

Wilson – Cambridge, MA

A small but distinguished group of mourners stood around the freshly dug opening beneath the black casket containing Carter Emerson's alleged remains. Cambridge Cemetery. It was near the Fielder family plot where Wilson's paternal great-grandparents and grandparents were buried. Wilson gazed out over the Charles River. Carter Emerson wasn't dead.

Carter's wife Elizabeth and his daughters Sarah and Amy were sobbing as they clung to each other. There had been no wake or viewing or traditional funeral service, just as Carter had requested. A dozen or so secret service and FBI agents stood several yards away near the line up of limousines, watching every movement. Hap's men were there too. Another two-dozen agents and police officers were spread across the cemetery's entrances and exits. The service was closed to the public and the press.

The President of the United States was there in person to deliver a short eulogy. Without condoning what Carter and Charles had done, he praised them for having the fortitude and foresight to expose the harsh reality of one of the nation's deepest flaws: inequity. Then he repeated many of the things he'd said the day before in his speech from the Oval Office. Wilson wasn't surprised. What else could he do? Even though the service had been closed to the press, somebody would find a way to discover what the President said and put it on the web within twenty-four hours.

After the eulogy, the President of Harvard University offered a prayer over the casket, asking for God's understanding and blessing for one of Harvard's most accomplished and brilliant scholars. Wilson watched Carter's wife and daughters hold each other, but they seemed to be shedding tears of fear and apprehension, not sorrow and grief. Then the short service was over.

As everyone delivered their final condolences to Carter's wife and daughters, President Roberts approached Wilson and Emily. His first words were addressed to Emily, praising her for her courage while being held captive. The fact that he seemed to know all the details surrounding Emily's kidnapping took them both by surprise. "Are you experiencing post-traumatic symptoms?" the President asked.

"No, I'm doing fine. Thank you for asking. I appreciate your concern," she said.

"If it hadn't been for Emily's fortitude, I would have thrown in the towel," Wilson added, putting his arm around her.

"You're an amazing couple. Walk with me," he said, guiding them away from the gravesite and into a nearby grove of trees. "I'd like to invite both of you to a working lunch at the White House with Chief Justice Stanley Vandenberg, Senate Majority Leader Kip MacArthur, Speaker of the House Dorothy Brock, and a few cabinet members and advisors."

Wilson and Emily were speechless.

The President stared at Wilson. "The only reason I attempted to minimize the crisis in my speech yesterday was to stabilize our weakening financial strength," the President said, looking intense and sincere. "New York has already lost much of its global dominance to London, where more than fifty percent of the world's equities are now traded. This crisis could bury New York and weaken the American economy for decades to come. London and Europe would benefit from our weakness once again, just as they did after the '29 crash. It would also accelerate a massive capital shift to emerging financial centers in Shanghai, Hong Kong, Singapore,

Mumbai, Dubai, and Sao Paulo. There's no question that we have to address the changes your father and Carter envisioned, but we must do it without abdicating our global leadership. I assure you the White House is behind this one hundred percent. Congress has gotten the message loud and clear, and the court is committed to reform. There will be change. Trust me."

"Did you know this was coming?" Wilson asked.

"Carter advised me before his disclosure meeting at Harvard. We've known each other for many years. I have the utmost respect for him and your father. And while I will never be able to publicly condone their methods, they did the country and the world a big favor. You should be proud of them. Not a day goes by that I don't pray for your father's recovery," he said, pausing briefly. "I sense you not only understand his quest but have one of your own. The country needs your input."

Again, Wilson was moved by the President's heart-felt sincerity and authentic appreciation, but he remained cautious. He waited for Emily to give him a sign of what she was thinking. She looked weary. Just as Wilson was about to tell him they'd think about it, Emily responded firmly, "We'll come to your luncheon meeting, but right now we don't trust anyone."

The President's admiring gaze alternated back and forth between Wilson and Emily. "I don't blame you a bit," he said.

"Let me work on the trust issue. We need you to help us make sure Charles and Carter didn't live their lives in vain."

Wilson studied the President's eyes, searching for a reason not to trust him. When he found none, he looked over at Emily and slowly nodded his head.

"I'll have my chief of staff make the necessary travel arrangements. He'll be in touch with you in the next couple of days," the President said as he placed his hands on their shoulders and squeezed gently. "Your generation will have to finish this job."

The words hit home. Did my father and Carter orchestrate everything? Including the President's cooperation?

After they said good-bye to the President, Wilson and Emily lingered in the grove. He was worried about her. The trauma of the kidnapping and their hiding out in Maine had taken a toll on her physical health. Her doctor had put her on medication for bronchitis and recommended that she get as much rest and quiet as she could over the next few days. "Are you sure the medication you're on isn't affecting your judgment?" he asked with a playful smile.

"My judgment? You really think I don't know what you're planning?" she said, her face coming alive with new energy. "Here we are at Carter's funeral service and neither one of us thinks he's dead. I watched his wife and daughters the entire time. They may be mourning, but not over Carter's death," Emily said.

"I thought the exact same thing," Wilson said.

"We have to find out what happened to him. Witness protection program? Kidnapping? Another one of his contingency plans? Who knows? But there's no way you're going to do this without me. Who else is going to keep you alive long enough to father our children?"

They smiled broadly at each other before embracing tenderly. "So who's going to set the new date for our wedding?" Wilson asked.

Emily looked at him with a teasing grin. "Someone who can make and keep commitments."

They muffled their laughter, mindful of those at the gravesite fifty meters away. Finding joy in each other at every possible opportunity, no matter how strange or twisted their future became, would be their only refuge. That would be Wilson's first wedding vow.

71

Tate – Venice, Italy

Ospedale Civile. Venice, Italy. April 16th. A nurse entered room 369 just before two o'clock in the morning, to administer the specified doses of antibiotics and painkillers. Before she left the room she woke the patient and turned him onto his side to check the bandages on his back.

"I have a message from Morita," she whispered into the patient's ear. Her English was flawless with only the slightest Italian accent.

"Morita?!"

"Shhh," she said quietly to avoid drawing attention from the armed guards standing by the door.

Tate smiled even though it hurt to move his mouth.

"She wants you to know you're in good hands," whispered the nurse.

"I need to get out…"

"Shhh," she said, again. "They'll be transferring you tonight."

Tate closed his eyes and smiled. This time he didn't feel the pain.

"Buona notte," the nurse said as she left the room.

EPILOGUE

Boston, MA

Emily was still sleeping when Wilson left Brattle House for the bank. He couldn't bring himself to wake her, so he left a note promising to be back soon. The ornate lobby of the Boston Private Bank & Trust on Boylston Street was almost empty when he arrived. He went immediately to member services, where he waited for a personal banker to take him to the safety-deposit vault.

He signed the admission form and showed his identification, along with the legal document that allowed him to sign on all his father's accounts. Once the personal banker reviewed the paperwork with his manager, he led

Wilson to the vault. Inside, the banker inserted his key and then Wilson inserted his key to open box 1952. The box was removed and placed on the table in a private room. The banker then excused himself, leaving Wilson alone.

He opened the box, but it was empty. He immediately left the room to find the personal banker. When he inquired about the last time the box had been opened and by whom, the banker told him he could not disclose that information without a court order. Wilson returned to the private room, closed the door and called Agent Kirsten Kohl's private number.

When she answered, he told her about the empty safety-deposit box. She assured him that she would have a federal court order within the hour. "Two FBI agents will meet you at the bank at noon."

"Thank you."

"Wilson? I'm afraid I have some additional bad news for you. Wayland Tate has escaped from the hospital in Venice. Two men were killed, one from Europol, the other one was CIA. We have a full-fledged international search underway."

"Nothing surprises me anymore, Kirsten. And I still don't believe Carter is dead. Do you know where he is?"

"No, but we're following some leads that I can't talk about right now."

"I'll be back here at noon to meet your agents."

"Wilson?"

"Yes?"

"The President has invited me to your meeting at the White House. Hopefully, I can give you more details then. I think we're going to be working this together, for the foreseeable future."

"Good. You're the only reason I have any trust in the FBI," Wilson said. "I think you want to change things as much as I do."

"I do. And I think we have a platform to do it."

"I hope you're right, Kirsten."

"Me too. Right now, finding your great-grandfather's memoirs is an FBI priority."

"Thanks. See you soon."

When the call was finished, Wilson looked down at the empty safety-deposit box. He thought of his father and then repeated the narcissistic maxim *control or be controlled* over and over again in his mind.

Moments later, a distinguished-looking man with thick white hair and a slight tan entered the private room and introduced himself as Felix Zubriggen, chairman of the bank. He was dressed impeccably and had a worldly-wise air about him. "I'm sorry Mr. Fielder, it seems the last person to access this box was Wayland Tate."

"How could…"

Felix interrupted. "Carter Emerson is not dead, Mr. Fielder. His DNA was placed at the scene of the Teatro La

Fenice by the people he was ultimately trying to overthrow. It's part of an agreement allowing Carter and his family to continue living. His captors are capable of orchestrating anything. They plan to use any changes in the American system to their advantage, by accelerating the establishment of a new global financial system. They're keeping Carter around, just in case they need him. The CIA, or some faction of it, is somehow involved, but we don't know to what extent. Carter has been forbidden to set foot in the United States or have contact with you. Violation will result in his death and the death of his family. He's asked me to be his liaison with you. Your father and Carter call me the Watcher."

Wilson's eyes grew wide as he remembered Carter's words: *if for some reason anything goes wrong, and I am no longer in the picture, someone will be in touch with you.* "Where is he?" Wilson asked.

"Europe. It's better that you don't know the details for now. He and his family are safe, but under constant surveillance."

"And the memoirs that were supposed to be here?" Wilson asked, looking down at the empty safety-deposit box.

"Your father thought it would be better if the world believed they were stolen by Wayland Tate," Felix said as he pulled a sealed envelope from his suit pocket and handed it to Wilson. "I'll wait for you outside."

When Felix was gone, Wilson opened the envelope. It was a letter from his father:

My Dearest Son,

I am writing this letter six weeks after the first one you should have received from Daniel Redd. Felix Zubriggen is the bearer of this letter because he's independent of all my other relationships and I trust him. My worst suspicions have now been confirmed. Our partners have contracted for our assassinations, mine and Carter's, so I had no choice but to develop a drastic counter plan. Carter wanted nothing to do with it, but I insisted. Otherwise, we would have both died. My plan was to keep Carter alive to finish what we started. Forgive me son. I know that all of this has brought nothing but tragedy and turmoil to your life.

I am the one who removed the memoirs and placed them in a safe repository after I received a series of anonymous phone calls. The first call informed me that Wayland Tate had contracted for my death and Carter's, with contingency backup contracts. We used our own sources to validate the information. Unfortunately, eliminating Tate would not have solved our problem or removed the contracts.

In the second call, I received a detailed description of our entire disclosure plan and a harrowing explanation

*of how and why it would never bring about the change
we envisioned. The caller's arguments convinced me that
he understood the world's power structure as well or
better than we did. He and his group have known about
us for years. The third call summarized the content of
your great-grandfather's memoirs and informed me
of their location. I have no idea how they obtained
their information. Sadly, I began questioning every
relationship in my life, including my relationships with
Daniel and Carter.*

*That's when I removed the memoirs and began
writing this letter for Felix to deliver if and when you
came to the bank. Felix is a Swiss banker with a long
history of selling privacy. He's been my agent and banker
for years. Carter knows nothing about the contents of
this letter or the anonymous phone calls, and Felix will
not inform Carter of this delivery unless you request it.
Use him as necessary, but only after you've paid for your
privacy.*

*In the fourth and final call, the caller invited me
to join his group, claiming that working together was
the only way to permanently transform capitalism
and launch a new era of economic freedom. He gave
me instructions for making contact. A painting
commissioned by his group is set to be unveiled in London
at the end of summer, as a symbolic representation of the*

struggle between freedom and oppression. I don't know the name of the artist, but the painting is privately referred to as "The Beholders". I was to make contact with the artist, who would give me further information. The last thing the caller told me was that his group had found a way to make capitalism more accessible and actionable, without requiring government action or acquiescence from the wealthy elite and their shadow government. I don't know anything more than what I've told you. However, my instinct and judgment tell me that an affiliation with this anonymous caller and his group could prove advantageous, even redemptive. If a parallel path to reform can be pursued simultaneously with changes emerging from our disclosure, it could help ensure a lasting transformation of capitalism.

Wilson, I know your heart and I trust your inherent goodness, but I also know that you'll never find peace with yourself until you see this through to a final resolution. I am deeply saddened that I won't be attending the art exhibit in London with you. Learn everything you can and then incorporate it into your own plans. I have always known that my obsession would be yours to finish, which is why I kept you from it for as long as I could. I want you to know how very proud of you I am. You are singularly prepared to make this world a better place. Protect yourself and the ones you love with the best people you can find, and then replicate it three times. Trust in yourself. Until we meet again.

Your Loving Father

P.S. The memoirs are located in a floor safe buried in concrete and steel beneath the hearthstone of the river rock fireplace at our White Horse chalet. There is a switch located beneath a single stone at the apex of the gable that enables the hearthstone to slide back revealing the safe. Simply remove the apex stone cradled in cement to turn the switch. The primary alphanumeric combination to the safe is "HWF1952cmwr". The secondary combination is your birth date followed sequentially by the first and last letters of your favorite childhood hero.

Wilson remained in the private room alone with his thoughts for almost an hour. A few minutes before noon, he found Felix in his office. "What does Carter plan to do?" Wilson asked.

"Nothing for now. The powers that be seem satisfied that Carter is sufficiently content with his disclosure. They plan to let the reforms take place, and then turn them to their advantage," Felix said. "But Carter is always working on contingency plans. Has been ever since I've known him. He said you should be patient and enjoy your life with Emily."

Wilson studied the bank chairman. So these are the final pieces to the puzzle, he thought. At least for now. "Tell Carter that Emily and I knew he wasn't dead and that we're no longer surprised by his and my father's incessant contingency planning. But if I don't hear from him, through you, at least once a month, I'll be knocking at your door," Wilson said.

"I'll pass your requests along, Mr. Fielder," Felix said.

"What are you going to tell the FBI when they arrive?"

"The box was last opened by Wayland Tate, the day he met with you at the Bostonian Club. I have documents showing his signature on an admission form from that date and on the safety-deposit lease agreement, along with your father's and Carter Emerson's."

"Okay, Mr. Zubriggen. You can talk to the FBI when they arrive. I'll call Agent Kohl and tell her about Tate," Wilson said, reconciled to the messy aftermath of his father's and Carter's choices. "You know how to contact me. I'm going home to plan a wedding."

"I think that's a good idea, Mr. Fielder. And I will be in touch."

"Call me Wilson, I'll call you Felix. And tell Carter I have some advice for him. The real lie is that hierarchies can be incorruptible. Tell him to relax and enjoy his sanctuary. He always wanted to live in Europe."

"Until we meet again, Wilson," Felix said, nodding his head and extending his hand.

They shook hands vigorously, "Until then, Felix."

Back at Brattle House, sitting next to each other on the sofa at the foot of the guestroom bed, Wilson and Emily read and reread his father's final letter with a mix of sympathy and wonderment.

"What are we going to do?" Emily asked.

"First we're going to get married, before you get cold feet again," he said with a broad grin. "Then I think we should spend some time in Sun Valley and London."

Emily returned the grin. "You're so predictable my dear, but I'm fully committed to helping you expand your horizons."

They wrapped their arms around each other, quickly slipping into shared bliss—for a little while.

ACKNOWLEDGMENTS

For more than a decade, this book has churned inside me like a perpetual motion machine, slowly building momentum on its way to finally becoming a completed work. During its long gestation, many people from various walks of life in this country and around the world have made important contributions, both large and small. These contributions have included insight, motivation, example, philosophy, belief, struggle, research, expertise, feedback, legal advice, editing, joy, misery, cynicism, and laughter. The most notable contributions came from the following people, whose particular and sometimes peculiar inputs will remain unmentioned out of courtesy and appreciation. Larry Wilson, whose early mentoring and friendship inspired the naming of the book's main character, Chris Raia, James Gulbrandsen, Harris Kay, Jeff Henderson, Lee and Nan Conant, Ray Balee, Bing Zhou, Joe Cannon, the entire Sao Paulo South Mission from 1996 to 1999, Michael and Pat Snell, Gina Patterson, Omar Cintron, Sarah Southerland, John Rizzo, David Beckmann, Lauren Woolley, Karen Miller, Tim McManus, and all the others on the BookSurge team, especially Julian, Blair, Emma of DC3 and Jason, Jenny, and Lauren of TDF1, the entire Varner family, Michael Silva, Eric Marchant, Pamela Lewis, Les Forslund, Craig Holyoak, Marcello Hunter, Mark Hoffman, Neil Andersen, Reid Robison, Kelly Purser, Doris Bigio, Dil Kulkarni, Roger Connors and Tom Smith, Kirk Benson, Margaret and Ray Lewis, Hester Kaplan, Don Mangum, Carl Bacon, David Rothschild, Steve Goldsmith, Jim McDonald, Mary Kowalczyk, Jim Brinton, Dick and JoAnn Losee, Peter Quinn, Jeff Gendler, Dixie Clark, Charles Dahlquist, Michael Yoshino, Harry Hansen, Paul Lawrence, Anthony Athos, Phil Matthews, Tom Mullaney, Bob Kidder, Jim Scarborough, Kim Clark, Doug Matsumori, Keith Adams, Karen Hansen, John Mahaney, David Rockefeller, Phil Matthews, Tom Mullaney, Justin Dart, Neal Maxwell, Alan Wilkins, Dallas Archibald, Craig Zwick, Bill Ewing, Marlon Berrett, Joe Allen, Craig Bott, Stephen Covey, Ken Shelton, Ralph and Trish Faison, Forrest and Cindy Dodson, Troy and Lori Clements, Dave and Sue Herron, Bill and Pam White, Harvey and Jill Seybold, Bob and Joan Scatena, my parents Winston and Verla Hickman, my siblings Larry, Deborah, and Mark, my children Jared, Kimberly, and Leigh and their spouses Aimee, Michael, and Jeremy, my grandchildren Leo, Zeke, Sylvi, and Iggy, my step children Samuel and Jacob, and finally to Laura Hickman and Stan Varner, to whom this book is dedicated, for their unending perception, encouragement, and perseverance.

ABOUT THE AUTHOR

CRAIG HICKMAN is the *New York Times* bestselling author of more than a dozen books, among them such international bestsellers as *The Oz Principle, The Strategy Game, Mind of Manager, Soul of a Leader,* and *Creating Excellence.* His first business novel, *An Innovator's Tale* led to a four year turnaround assignment as CEO of Headwaters Technology Innovation (HTI), an international nanotechnology company in Princeton, New Jersey (NYSE: HW). Prior to joining Headwaters, he founded Management Perspectives Group (MPG), whose clients included some of the largest domestic and international companies such as Procter & Gamble, American Express, PepsiCo, Unilever, AT&T, Amoco, Nokia, Honeywell, and the U.S. Government. He earned his

MBA with honors from the Harvard Business School and has consulted for corporations and organizations around the world, lecturing abroad for the U.S. State Department, and serving as a member of the board of directors for several companies. Currently, he heads the Chicago office of Partners In Leadership (PIL), the premier provider of Accountability Training® services around the world. Clients include many of the "most admired companies in the world," almost half of the Dow Jones Industrial Average Companies, and more than half of the *Fortune* 50 largest companies in the United States. Visit his website at www.craighickman.com or www. ozprinciple.com.